The Potion Maker

To Mary,
with Best Wishes,
Kay McKay

The next title in this series:

The Book of Kyndor - available late 2005

The Potion Maker

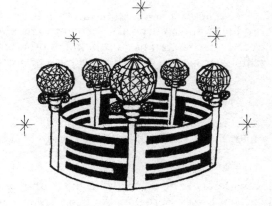

Kay McKay

Parlator Press

For internet orders and to meet the characters visit the website
www.thepotionmaker.com

First published in Great Britain in 2004 by
Parlator Press, 45 Needless Road, Perth PH2 0LE

The right of Kay McKay to be identified as the Author and Illustrator
of the Work has been asserted by her in accordance with the
Copyright, Designs and Patents Act 1988.

A CIP catalogue record of this book is available from
the British Library

ISBN 0-9547845-0-2

Printed and bound in Great Britain by Scotprint, Haddington.
Cover Design and layout by Gordon Low

ACKNOWLEDGEMENTS

The author acknowledges support from the Scottish Arts Council towards the writing and editing of this title.

The author would like to thank Kate Blackadder for her invaluable editorial services, and Stephanie Pickering for providing expert editing services.

Further thanks go to budding artists Rebecca Low, for her help and input into the illustration and design of the book cover, and Katie Smith, for her input into the illustration in the prologue and the illustrations of Zanting Barbelly and Jacobus Mors on the web-site.

This book is dedicated to:

My wonderful son, for his never-ending faith;

My husband, for his never-ending support;
My parents, for their never-ending love;
My step-sons, in memory of their Grandma Fred;
And the real Hannah and Lucy, Katie and Emma.

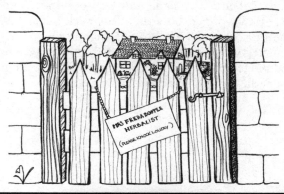

The Prologue

In a place not far away, in a land unseen and unknown to anyone not living there, Dr Herbert Rootvine's day was slowly turning into a disaster. He was peering into a sack on the floor when a look of utter panic suddenly crossed his face. An ear-splitting screech shook dust from the rafters and there was a loud bang as Dr Rootvine's head collided with the shelf above, shaking awake a jar of sleeping pink grubs.

'THELMA!' Dr Rootvine bellowed.

Thelma, Dr Rootvine's assistant, came running dutifully from the back room of the Apothecary, holding onto a fluffy black hat underneath which untidy hair poked out like orange straw. Black stockings hung loosely around her knobbly knees, and skinny legs disappeared into large green shoes.

'Keep that ridiculous raven under control,' said Dr Rootvine, scowling over his half-moon spectacles as a little canary hopped out of a second sack labelled 'Long Thin Things'.

'It's bad enough he looks like a yellow marshmallow without him screeching in my ear.' Dr Rootvine paused from rubbing the lump that was rapidly appearing on his head beneath smooth white hair which hung ruler straight and flicked up before reaching his shoulders. The look of panic returned to his face while the colour slowly drained from his cheeks.

'The nasturtiums,' he said weakly, glancing back at the few, remaining flowers in the sack he had been peering in. 'Thelma, we've run out of nasturtiums.' The wobble in his voice as he said these words was unmistakable. 'Go and get the Chancellor. Quickly, there's no time to lose!' The *Master Potion Maker* badge on Dr Rootvine's lapel began flashing erratically and the pink spotted bow-tie at his neck began twirling madly. Dr Rootvine swayed, then collapsed in a heap at Thelma's feet.

Two Council officials were hastily dispatched, the fate of the whole village resting in their hands, and they found the perfect place – a garden belonging to Mrs Freida Bootle. Only, they hadn't reckoned on her having a cat …

Chapter 1

The Strange Beginning

Hannah, Ben and Lucy were perfectly ordinary children and they did perfectly ordinary things ... well, most of the time. Every year they spent a perfectly ordinary three weeks with their Grandma Freida, although she was, it was true, a little less ordinary than most grandmothers.

Grandma Fred, as they liked to call her, was a plump lady who looked a lot like a raspberry roly-poly on account of her red hair, plaited and coiled on top of her head, and the extra-long ties of her white apron which wrapped twice around her middle. She was well known in Thornyside for her ointments, balms, gels, pastes, potions, lotions, syrups, infusions, concoctions, tinctures and teas. People came from miles around for her herbal medicines. They were famous. The notice on her gate said:

Mrs Freida Bootle
Herbalist
(Please knock loudly)

At the breakfast table in Grandma's cottage by the church that first morning of their holiday there was no sign that anything extraordinary was about to happen. Hannah was sitting quietly eating her cornflakes with a dreamy look in her hazel eyes (which when she'd been born had been different colours – one blue and the other brown) and was twirling a strand of her dark hair, which was neither short nor long, around her middle finger. Ben, at eleven, a year older and eight centimetres taller than Hannah and skinnier than one of Grandma's bean poles, had just slapped two slices of toast together making jam shoot across the table and land in Lucy's long blonde hair. Lucy, once she'd scraped the strawberry splodge onto her plate, sat furrowing her brows in a fearsome scowl behind her round, blue glasses. Grandma Fred didn't look up and continued reading the horse racing section of the *Sporting Times* with her white cat, Gertrude, purring contentedly in her lap.

Even after breakfast, when Grandma Fred, Hannah and Lucy made a big pot of remedy for curing furry tongues and hairy noses (people with one usually have the other) while Ben lay chortling over a comic, and Gertrude patrolled around the house to make sure there were no mice under the beds, all was as it should be.

And there had been no hint last night that today would be very different. Everyone had been tucked up in bed sleeping except Gertrude who had gone for her usual evening stroll with the cat from the church next door; they'd hissed at a barking dog and played their favourite game of weaving in and out of the chimney pots to see who could go the longest without knocking one off. Unfortunately a pot had fallen onto a dustbin lid, making the most awful racket, and woken up the butcher who threw a meat cleaver which took the tips right off Gertrude's whiskers. But you couldn't call that unusual.

Today, though, was going to be different – was going to be as different as it was possible for a day to be.

It was after lunch that it all began …

Hannah began washing up the lunch dishes and was gazing out of the kitchen window onto Grandma's large and peculiar garden when something caught her eye – Gertrude was stalking through the red poppies. She tiptoed past the antiseptic-smelling rosemary, looked beneath the huge hoods of rhubarb she often sheltered under when it rained, trotted past the onions and whiffy garlic – Hannah was sure she was holding her breath – and suddenly swiped the marigolds so violently the flowers flew off in all directions.

'Whatever is that cat up to?' said Hannah, staring intently but seeing nothing unusual. Grandma Fred glanced over Hannah's shoulder and shook her head.

'Mind of its own, that cat,' she said, affectionately.

There was a sudden sharp knock. Grandma Fred smoothed her apron and opened the kitchen door as wide as it would go.

'Good morning Mr Rumfoot,' she said to the old man standing on the step. 'How are you today?'

Mr Rumfoot swore by Grandma Fred's rheumatics remedy. He secretly thought there was some sort of hocus-pocus going on, that she did something more than just boil up a few herbs and dried daisies, but he never said anything. He was just glad it worked. At his feet a grey spaniel sat looking as old and worn out as he did. Neither had any teeth on account of all the peppermints they both ate.

'Same infusion as last time?' asked Grandma with one eye still on Gertrude who had run up the beech tree and was now clamped to it, claws dug in tight, unable to go up or down, and seemed to be hissing at a twig. Before Mr Rumfoot could answer, Grandma's eye fell on the old spaniel's nose. A cut across it looked sore and new.

'Oh dear.'

'You don' 'appen to 'ave anythin' that would 'elp, do yeh?' asked Mr Rumfoot. 'I 'eard 'im barkin' last night … some cat's taken a swipe, I reckon. Ee's a sitting duck, no teeth an' all.'

Grandma Fred smeared some coltsfoot gel on the dog's nose while Hannah washed out one of the jars from the blue plastic bag Mr Rumfoot had given her (one that had had fish paste in it). Grandma filled it, screwed the lid on tightly and gave it to Mr Rumfoot with instructions to apply the gel twice a day – more often if it was licked off between applications. Mr Rumfoot took it gratefully.

'Well, thanks fer that. Much appreciated. I'll be back tomorrow afternoon then, to collect me medicine.'

He turned to go. Out on the path Gertrude sped past, mewing angrily.

'Don't know what's got into that cat today,' said Grandma Fred in Mr Rumfoot's direction. 'She's behaving in a most peculiar manner, chasing around all over the place. It's like she's having hallucinations or something.'

Grandma sniffed the gel on her fingers.

'Hmm,' she said. 'Rubbed some of this coltsfoot on a cut on her ear just before you came but it can't be that.'

Mr Rumfoot's spaniel was thinking *he* regularly had hallucinations about Gertrude being flattened by a steamroller, or her head being chopped off by the butcher's flying meat cleaver. It was his favourite daydream. Gertrude was dangling from an elder tree by one paw when they left.

Grandma Fred closed the door as Gertrude chased past again. She tutted and looked along her crammed bookshelf. Her eyes scanned past *The A to Z of All Ailments* by A. K. Belli, *1000 Edible Moulds* by Dr Marigold Mildew and lingered momentarily on *Potent Potions and Natural Medicines* by Dr Delia Dungwood. *Latin Names of Herbs and Flowers* by Billius Wordsmith lay covered in dust. Grandma Fred had to admit she hardly ever read it because the names were so impossible to pronounce.

She took down a handsome, brown, leather book with *Herbal Remedies* written in fancy white letters on the cover. She read this one all the time. It thumped onto the kitchen table and made her empty teacup bounce in its saucer. In it were recipes to treat everything from *Abdominal cramps* to the *Zoster virus*, which Hannah always thought sounded particularly nasty. There were recipes for everything you could think of – for bruises, gout, rheumatism, influenza, insomnia, fungal infections and flatulence. There were dozens and dozens. There was even a recipe for nervous exhaustion, which Grandma had prescribed with great success to a farmer who needed to treat his cow when it fainted after his truck backfired.

She turned to the back pages and looked up 'Mr Rumfoot'.

Name: Mr Rumfoot

Address: Ingle Cottage, Thornyside

Date:	Complaint:	Recipe:
12th Jan 2002	Upset tummy (bad curry)	Stomach Spasm No.3
3rd Aug 2002	Aches in knees, hips and joints	Rheumatics No.2
	Runny eyes	Dog biscuit (Bob)

'Hmm,' said Grandma Fred again, noting that Mr Rumfoot was now on her No. 2 recipe for rheumatism. She wrote the date and a new entry in the book:

4th Aug 2003	Aches in knees, hips and joints	Rheumatics No.2
	Deep cut on nose	Inflammation No.1 (Bob)

Grandma was just about to look up the possible causes of hallucinations when, outside, there was a sudden, terrified squeal – like someone being strangled and having their toenails pulled out at the same time. Grandma Fred jumped up; Hannah quickly dried her hands; Ben licked the jam from his fingers; and Lucy dashed to open the door, her long fair hair flying out behind her.

'Oh my gracious ...' exclaimed Grandma as she looked across the grass. They all rushed down the pebbly path, Grandma's arms going like pistons and bunches of sage flying from her pockets, towards the large beech tree at the bottom of the garden.

There, hanging from a branch by her tail, although it was not clear how it was attached, swinging backward and forwards as if being pushed by an invisible finger, was Gertrude.

'Whraahrrrr,' Gertrude screeched again.

'Mercy me!' Grandma lunged forward with her arms outstretched trying to catch her.

But it was too late. Gertrude plummeted towards the ground, hitting it the next instant with an almighty wallop.

Grandma Fred, face as white as an uncooked pudding, bent down and prodded the limp body which lay still on the grass. Gertrude didn't move. Even when Grandma picked her up, not a whisker twitched.

Chapter 2

The Disappearing Nasturtiums

In a large copper pot on the cooker, Mr Rumfoot's remedy was almost made. The pot spluttered vigorously, the steam snaked upwards and rolled silently across the ceiling.

'Quick, add it now – it's starting to boil,' ordered Ben. 'The book says to add it when it starts to boil!' He prodded the book sharply.

Lucy pushed her blue glasses further up her nose and peered closely at the recipe beside them.

'Hurry up, Lu-cy.'

'All right, I've got it,' Lucy snapped, tossing her long blonde hair over her shoulder. 'I don't need you to tell me what to do.'

'Stop arguing,' said Hannah.

'It's him,' said Lucy, standing on tiptoes and pouring the powdered gibber root into the boiling liquid. 'Just because I'm the youngest …. You'd think he was the only one who'd ever made a potion.'

Hannah stirred it quickly. The powder dissolved instantly turning the draught bright yellow. It started to thicken.

'Smells all right,' said Hannah, giving a little cough and wafting the strong smelling fumes away from her nostrils. 'And it looks the same as it did last year … I think.'

'But will it work?' said Ben. 'We didn't add the gibber root at the right time. It'll maybe give *him* verbal diarrhoea.'

'It's a *Rheumatics* Remedy,' said Hannah, rolling her eyes and sighing.

'They *all* give you diarrhoea of some sort,' said Ben, brushing his hair out of the way. 'It's a well-known fact.'

'You just made that up,' retorted Lucy.

Hannah kept on stirring.

'Did not!'

'Did so!'

'How are you getting on, dears?' Grandma Fred had strolled into the kitchen and was now squinting over their shoulders at the spluttering draught.

'That's Mr Rumfoot's Rheumatics Remedy made, Grandma,' said Hannah giving the pot one last stir, making sure she followed the instructions precisely.

'Good, good, we'll just let it cool and bottle it later. Now, anyone for some fudge before we start collecting the ingredients for the Vitality Tonic?' Grandma wiped her hands over her apron before taking a piece and chewing enthusiastically. Two hands dived into the bag at once.

'Maybe we should be making an extra-strong Headache Tonic for old flea-bag,' mumbled Ben through a crammed mouthful.

Everyone's eyes fell on Gertrude sitting in her basket in the corner, head wrapped in bandages, looking as if it was painful even to blink.

'She's not a flea-bag, are you Gertie,' said Lucy, bending to stroke her.

'You're both flea-bags if you ask me,' said Ben.

'I've already given her something for the concussion,' said Grandma. 'What she needs now is lots of rest. She'll soon be back to her old self … I hope. Don't know what got into her this afternoon – charging about like a demented gazelle.'

Hannah turned the pages of the *Herbal Remedies* book until she came to the recipe for Vitality Tonic. Below, in spidery handwriting, Grandma had written *Puts the spring back in your step*.

'How much of this do you need, Grandma?' she asked.

'Better make five gallons this year, dear. It always sells out at the Summer Fête. Everybody seems to want some and I always give Mrs Whitehead, next door, two bottles for her roses.'

'Her roses?'

Ben helped himself to another piece of fudge and Lucy tickled Gertrude under the chin.

'She says it brings them on a treat. She won *Best Bloom in Show* last year. You'll find I've got most of the ingredients already dried, Hannah.'

Hannah read the list of ingredients out loud:

Nasturtiums
Shredded napweed
Stewed prunes
Handful of bogbeans
Pinch of fenugreek
St John's wort
A Fisherman's Friend.

'Sounds simple enough,' said Hannah.

'Sounds disgusting,' said Ben between noisy, slobbery chews.

'*You're* disgusting,' said Lucy.

'Shut up, specky.'

'We'll need to shred some napweed, dig up some bogbeans and collect some nasturtiums but everything else is here.' Grandma waved her hand at the multitude of glass jars lining the wall.

Hannah ran her eyes over the strange bottles. In the clear ones she could see bungle weed, catmint, crawley root, glauber salt, wunderwot and dozens and dozens of others. In the dark green jars there were recipes and remedies for dehydration, exfoliation, expectoration, inflammation and infestation – by what, the label didn't say. The fenugreek and St John's Wort sat next to a jar of deadly nightshade. A skull and crossbones showed that it was poisonous, even to touch. Below the thick black letters its Latin name, (*Atropa belladonna),* was neatly typed in brackets. The dark purple powder in the jar looked harmless enough but just a teaspoonful was enough to knock a large gorilla unconscious for an hour or so. Hannah reckoned half a teaspoon might be enough to keep Ben unconscious for a whole afternoon.

'Most of your plants can be eaten can't they, Grandma?' Hannah asked.

'Yes dear, I don't grow any poisonous ones in the garden. Not all the plants taste nice though, I have to say, and some can give you a tummy upset if you eat too much of them and some can have nasty effects if used in the wrong way, but providing you don't swallow a wheelbarrow full you'll come to no lasting harm.'

Hannah noticed the look on Ben's face. It was as if he was already thinking of ways he could get his sisters to swallow a cupful of something iffy – just enough to make them sick.

'Right now, dears, bogbeans and nasturtiums here we come.'

In the warmth of the afternoon they started working. Ben dug up the bogbeans and Lucy shook the unearthed plants into the basket. The beans fell to the bottom like huge yellow peanuts. Grandma Fred and Hannah started collecting the nasturtiums.

'Not many flowers on these. How odd,' said Grandma looking round at a clump of plants with only one small flower left.

Hannah was almost sure she saw a nasturtium disappear from under her nose. She thought she must be imagining it and reached out to pick another. This one was bright orange. She blinked, and when she looked again there was a bare stalk between her fingers. She glanced around her feet to see where the orange flower had fallen. There was nothing there. *That's strange*, thought Hannah. *I must have dropped it but where's it gone*? But before Hannah could look any further she heard Ben calling.

'Hannah! Hannah! Come see! Come see!' Something was trapped in his raised hands; Lucy was trying to peer through the spaces between his fingers.

Hannah ran forward a little then stopped. *It could be a trap*, she heard herself thinking.

'Come see what I've got,' Ben called again. Hannah edged closer. Ben nodded encouragingly.

What has he caught? Hannah took another step forward and, suddenly, she knew. 'Waaaarghhhh!'

A black hairy thing flew through the air towards her but just when she needed them for running away, Hannah's legs turned to cooked spaghetti. Her mind went blank, her tonsils wobbled, and in the distance she heard someone screaming.

'Aaahh! Aaahh! Aaahh!'

A blackbird in a nearby tree squawked in alarm and fell off its branch.

I must get it off! I must get it off! Hannah frantically shook the front of her tee-shirt. A dried-up rosebud with long curling sepals fell to the grass.

Ben and Lucy started roaring with laughter and, next door, Mrs Whitehead's dog was already barking itself into a frenzy.

'That wasn't funny!' Hannah shouted, her heart still pounding in her ears. 'I thought it was a spider.'

'But it *wasn't* a spider,' hee-hawed Ben.

'But I thought it *was*. You *know* I hate spiders and beetles.' Hannah stamped hard on the grass where the rosebud had fallen.

'I think it's dead, Hannah,' said Ben, sniggering.

'It would serve you right if …'

'It would serve you right if…'

Hannah tried desperately to think of something especially nasty to say but she couldn't think of anything. Her mind's eye suddenly fell on one of the bottles on the kitchen wall.

'It would serve you right if I put some deadly nightshade in your drink when you're not looking!'

Grandma Fred's eyes widened.

'You wouldn't want your brother to die now would you, Hannah?'

Hannah looked thoughtful as if considering the matter.

'Would you?'

'I suppose not,' said Hannah eventually, although not very convincingly.

'Well, we'll not be doing anything silly with the deadly nightshade then will we?' said Grandma Fred, patting Hannah's arm.

Gertrude, head still bandaged, watched them from the kitchen window and hissed angrily. Every time the kitchen door opened she tried to escape but only succeeded in getting her nose tweaked trying to dart between someone's heels. Late in the afternoon, once the Vitality Tonic was boiling nicely, her chance came when Grandma left to deliver a dozen jars of hazelnut and redcurrant jam to the village shop and didn't notice the door fail to close properly.

Gertrude crept out into the garden where Lucy was tasting plants.

'This bogbean tastes nice,' said Lucy, handing one to Hannah.

A sweet flavour filled Hannah's mouth. 'Yum, the leaves taste of honey.'

'Bet they don't,' said Ben grabbing three leaves and stuffing them all in his mouth at once.

They all chewed.

'It sort of does. But only if you mix it with enough spit,' said Ben, opening his mouth to show them.

Gertrude darted forward, letting out a particularly nasty snarl at the bushes behind the bogbean.

Ben saw him first but didn't say anything.

Hannah saw him next, blinked both eyes hard, and gasped.

Instead of a bird with a broken wing or maybe a curled up hedgehog, there, wrenching himself free of the thorn bush and muttering angrily, was the oddest person they had ever seen.

'Stupid cat!' the man shouted, briefly examining the rip in his sleeve. 'That's it, I've had enough! Should've sorted that animal properly the first time. Harmony Rules or not – this is an emergency.' The dark-haired man reached into his purple tail coat and pulled out what looked like … *an olive green ruler.* He raised his arm and looked just about to strike.

'STOP!' shouted Hannah, as she dived on Gertrude.

At Hannah's voice the figure zoomed straight up, cracking his head off the branch looming above, and crumpled down into the leaves again, inches from Gertrude's outstretched paws.

'You can s-see me.' He got quickly to his feet and staggered back even more startled than before.

'I know,' said Hannah squeakily, grabbing Gertrude around the middle. Ben stared dumbly ahead.

'You're not supposed to be able to see us,' said the man sharply, now recovered and checking his arms and legs as if to make sure none were broken.

But Hannah could see him quite clearly. Small wings fluttered on his boots, his long dark hair was snagged and snarled and bushy eyebrows hung down over his eyes as he examined another rip in his silk trousers.

'What is *that?*' said Ben.

'Let me see, let me see,' shouted Lucy, throwing the bogbean plant to the ground and forcing her way past Ben.

'Well, I *can* see you and obviously Gertrude can see you too,' said Hannah, ignoring Ben and Lucy, concentrating instead on holding onto Gertrude who was straining to get free. The bandage around her head began to unravel.

'That animal has been after us all afternoon,' said the man crossly.

'You mean there are more of you?' Hannah looked around.

'Just me and Milli Maccabees,' said the man, jabbing the ruler up into the beech tree.

Hannah gazed up. A second figure, lying along a branch with both arms wrapped tightly around it, smiled down. She had a round face, smudged with dirt, and broken twigs amongst curly brown hair. A glossy blue crow feather fell from a tear in her bodice. Wedged in the branch beside her was a bulging sack and out of the top of it Hannah thought she could see, orange petals.

'Holymoley! What are they?' exclaimed Lucy.

'Miaowww!' Gertrude hissed and viciously clawed the air.

'Stand back! Stand back!' the man shouted, waving the ruler about.

'Who are you?' asked Hannah.

'Classified information,' said the man sharply, keeping his eyes on Gertrude.

'Classified? ' said Ben. 'But you must be able to tell us something.'

'You are making this very difficult,' said the man, with a pained expression that made his eyebrows droop even lower.

With a sudden snarling leap, Gertrude sprang from Hannah's grasp and launched herself, claws first, at the stranger.

The man shrieked and bounded into the air, something seemed to explode, and a voice shouted '*FREZKA ICELANDIS!*'

Hannah felt a jolt and for the second time that day, tried to run. But she couldn't move! She tried again but couldn't bend even an arm or lift a foot. Straight in front of her Gertrude was suspended in mid air, like a furry block of ice. Out of the corner of her eyes she could see Lucy to her left and Ben to her right but both were rock still, immobilised and unable to help. Milli Maccabees dropped into view and landed on the ground beside her dazed companion.

Hannah heard her speak. 'Dolfi, why didn't you do something?'

'I was going to! I was going to! That cat is dangerous. Oh, in the name of Zamada, this is not going well!'

'What are we going to do now?'

Hannah could see Dolfi's eyebrows knit together in a serious frown.

We're stuck! You can't just leave us like this, Hannah shouted, but the words stayed trapped in her mouth.

HELP! HELP! GRANDMA! she screamed, but no sound came out.

'We'll just have to take them with us,' said Dolfi.

A cold shiver rattled Hannah's bones.

Chapter 3

The Underground Burroway

Milli pushed Gertrude through the air and across the fence where she was left suspended like a little white cloud over Mrs Whitehead's dog which had barked itself asleep and lay on the grass below in a froth of foam. When Milli returned, Dolfi was examining Hannah, Ben and Lucy.

'They look a bit young for Potion Makers, don't you think?' he said.

Hannah's eyes and ears were the only bits of her that seemed to be working. She wished she could speak.

'Right, now, I know you can hear me,' said Dolfi.

Hannah tried to move her arm. Dolfi saw it twitching.

'No need to bother. You won't be able to move until we let you.'

Hannah felt her stomach tighten as if a fist was in there, grabbing hold.

'Sorry about this,' he continued matter of factly, 'but we need to take you with us.'

Hannah saw him reach into his tail coat and take out a parchment which he unrolled in front of them and started to read.

'By the power invested in me by the Chancellor of Pickletullum, in accordance with exception (b) of Section 2 of the Consecrated Act of Fairy Fair Law and Order …'

'Quickly, Dolfi, before we're seen,' said Milli.

'… 1367 …,' Dolfi's voice trailed away. 'Oh let's just get on with it then.' He stuffed the parchment back into his coat.

Hannah felt herself moving through the air like a stiff piece of cardboard and saw Lucy and Ben alongside her. They shot each other worried glances as they drifted through the gate at the bottom of the garden and along the path by the wood until they eventually stopped by an old chestnut tree. Spiky conkers lay split and strewn in the grass.

Hannah's eyes nervously scanned the area for a hint of what was to come but there was nothing unusual about this place: just the chestnut tree, a laurel bush and a prickly holly.

Milli aimed her ruler at the roots of the chestnut tree.

'*Suo loco.*'

Hannah watched as a large hole about sixty centimetres across and sixty centimetres high opened up.

'This is the entrance to the Underground Burroway,' said Dolfi as if reading their thoughts. 'Now I hope you're going to behave yourselves.' He wiggled his olive green ruler at them. 'This doesn't hurt a bit.'

No, no, yelled Hannah, *What's he going to …?*

'*AD MINIMA!*'

Hannah didn't get a chance to finish her sentence. She felt a shiver and her skin squeeze as if she was being forced into a jumper six sizes too small. She hit the ground with a thump and her arms shot out to break her fall. She could move! She got up quickly, turned around and … Ben's feet looked the size of bath-tubs!

'*AD MINIMA!*' shouted Dolfi again. Ben was suddenly standing beside her.

'How cool was that?'

'Are you mad?' said Hannah, grabbing his arm. 'Get ready to run.'

Lucy towered above them, her long blonde hair swinging wildly about her shoulders like a tangled mass of rope. She smiled down. Her teeth looked huge.

Ben imagined being picked up and having his head bitten off like a jelly baby and was about to promise to be nicer to her when she was standing beside them.

'All right, pea-brain?' he asked, smirking.

'Right then, follow us,' said Dolfi, stepping with ease into the tunnel. 'It's not far to the Portway.'

'Right, now – RUN!' bellowed Hannah, taking off back down the path and sending a sack of nasturtiums flying.

Dolfi turned. 'You have no choice. You must come with us.'

'That's what you think,' Hannah shouted.

'Where are you going, Hannah?' called Ben.

'Back to Grandma's.'

'Like that?'

Hannah stopped dead in her tracks as the realisation dawned. She was less than sixty centimetres tall. She slumped down heavily onto the path.

'Well, I'm not moving until I know where we are going and why, and how we are getting back.'

'I think we'd better tell them,' whispered Milli.

'Oh, all right,' Dolfi swirled the ruler around the sacks, muttered some words and they lined up in a straight row again. 'You want to know where we're going?

Well, I will tell you, but we need to hurry.

'A fearsome fever is spreading through our village.' His voice went quiet. 'Once the fever grips, weakness follows, then death – unless we take the Cleansing Potion in time.'

Milli picked up the story: 'The Cleansing Potion is our only hope but the Potion Maker has run out of nasturtiums. This garden is the only one for miles around that grows them.'

Hannah thought she saw Milli shiver. 'I'm sorry you are getting ill,' she said, not quite knowing what else to say.

'We hope you don't need the nasturtiums yourself. We saw you collecting some today, after midsun.' Milli's ears twitched nervously.

'I don't think Grandma will mind,' said Hannah 'but why do we have to come? Can't you use magic to cure the fever?'

'But potion making *is* a type of magic,' said Milli fluttering several inches off the ground. 'You can't just add baked toad skin to any old stew and hope eating it cures warts. Every ingredient has its powers and each changes the power of every other. You must know that Hannah – we saw you.'

Before Hannah could reply, Milli went on: 'We must hurry now, please, there isn't much time.'

'But you still haven't answered my question,' said Hannah. 'Why do you need us to go with you?'

'Isn't it obvious?' asked Dolfi. 'Our Potion Maker, is ill with the fever. *You* must make the potion.'

Hannah felt her stomach jolt. Ben and Lucy stood open-mouthed.

'*We* can't make a *Cleansing Potion*. We don't know how. And even if we did, we can't go *with* you.'

'But you must,' said Dolfi. 'We need you.'

Milli sneezed again.

'Grandma will be wondering where we are. And besides, I've told you, we don't know how to make a Cleansing Potion.' Hannah was absolutely sure there had been some terrible mistake. She might know how to make a Rheumatics Remedy but that was very different.

'But we saw you gathering the herbs for medicines, today after midsun,' said Milli, taking out a fine silk handkerchief and wiping her nose.

'Yes, but that was something simple,' said Hannah. 'Not like a Cleansing Potion, whatever that is.'

Hannah's words seemed to hang in the air. In the silence that followed, the vigour disappeared from Dolfi's face and Milli's eyes looked sad over the top of her handkerchief.

'You could do it, Hannah. I know you could. We could take Grandma's book,' said Lucy quietly.

'But we don't even know what illness they've got,' protested Hannah.

Nothing more was said for a few moments.

'What are the symptoms of the disease?' asked Lucy.

'Well, it starts with sneezing,' said Dolfi.

'Aitchoo!' Milli sneezed again.

'Oh dear,' Lucy glanced at Hannah.

'Then the shivering starts, as if ice maidens have seized you,' continued Dolfi. 'Then come the aches and pains as if they are jabbing you with their ice forks. Then you get hot, as if a dragon's breath is upon you, and then the sweats come and you dream bad dreams.'

'Not surprised,' mumbled Ben.

'You itch as if thousands of hairy caterpillars are crawling under your skin. Then, if we don't get the medicine in time ….' Dolfi's voice trailed off. He hung his head.

Lucy's horrified eyes, magnified through her glasses, looked as large as two fried eggs.

'… We sleep and sleep, then turn as white as decaying froth fungus as the life energy drains out of us and then … we die.'

Ben looked as if the froth fungus had already got him but he recovered enough to say, 'It sounds like a very bad bout of our 'flu. Millions of people died of a nasty 'flu all over the world yonks ago. I remember Grandma telling us about it.'

'Do you think it could be some sort of 'flu?' said Lucy.

'Could be. What do you think, Hannah?'

'Oh, I don't know,' squirmed Hannah, imagining Ben or Lucy lying ill and in danger of dying.

'Please come,' said Dolfi.

'Please come and try,' said Milli. 'Dr Rootvine has all the powders and fires.'

'Fires!' said Hannah with another jolt of horror. 'What kind of fires?'

'We will help you,' said Dolfi. 'Don't worry about that.'

'Let's go, Hannah. We can help them,' said Lucy.

'What about Grandma? She'll be worried where we are. The Vitality Tonic is only half done; and how will we get back?'

'I can fix all that,' said Dolfi, and in an instant he was gone leaving a flurry of green stars behind him which faded quickly. Before they had time to ask Milli where he was he was back, re-appearing with a little 'pop'.

'Here is your Grandma's book,' he said, handing the book to Hannah. 'She is asleep now in her comfy chair. She'll stay like that until the morning when she will wake up at her normal time.' Dolfi smiled.

'Are you sure she'll be all right? asked Lucy.

'She will have a very good sleep, that's all,' said Dolfi. 'She will think nothing odd has happened except that she has slept so well she has forgotten to go to bed.'

This seemed to reassure Lucy but Hannah was still shuffling her feet.

'What about the tonic?'

'I have left a teaspoon in charge of adding the fenugreek. He will add it at precisely the moment the tonic turns yellow.

'Buttercup-yellow,' said Hannah.

'As you say, buttercup-yellow. He has his binoculars trained upon it.'

'But how do you know we can help you?' Hannah asked, still unconvinced, 'And how will we get back?'

'*Audentes fortuna juvat*,' said Milli, smiling.

'What does that mean?' Hannah asked.

'Fortune favours the bold. It is a good thing to remember,' said Dolfi, raising the ruler again.

Hannah rushed on. 'How do you know we can help you? What if we can't do it?'

'You can only try your best,' said Milli helping Hannah to her feet. 'That's all we ask, that you try your best. We don't ask you to save us, only to give us a chance to live.'

'We will make sure you get home, although you won't remember anything that happens,' said Dolfi. 'But you have my word; I will get you back.'

Reluctantly, Hannah nodded, scarcely realising she had allowed herself to be led inside the tunnel.

Once inside, Dolfi closed the entrance and started off at a brisk march. Hannah, Ben and Lucy struggled to keep up, breaking into a trot every now and then when a sack bumped them onward in the dim light. Firefly, their abdomens aglow, flitted aloft and a faint hum could be heard all around them.

'The Portway is just up ahead here, to the right,' said Dolfi.

The light ahead grew brighter.

'Go-oinggg!!'

Everything seemed to vibrate as the low sound went on and on.

'That's the seventh gong,' said Dolfi. 'We have no time to waste. We'll use the scarabs.'

The next few footsteps brought them into the busy Portway. High above their heads a large green and gold sign fluttered bidding 'HAIL AND FAREWELL'.

They seemed to be standing on some sort of main platform. A tall metal tower was emitting a strange, deep, soothing sort of noise, the same hum, in fact, they had heard in the tunnel only it was a bit louder now they were standing right next to it. It looked like an old fashioned street lamp but wider and it seemed to be some type of machine although it was difficult to tell what it might do. A door on the front looked as if it hadn't been opened in a very long time because it was very dusty. The top was made of glass and in the middle, suspended by no visible means, a hand with one finger was pointing to one of the twelve brightly coloured stones arranged around the edge. There seemed to be moons and stars scattered everywhere in between. Hannah noticed the jewelled stones turning slowly.

'What a strange clock,' said Ben, quite sure it *was* a clock.

'It's not an ordinary clock,' said Dolfi. 'It's a Sound Modulator. It makes sound to cancel out the noise of our beating wings. The noise in the Underground Burroway would be unbearable without it. All that's left is the low, gentle hum you hear now.'

'Was it this that made that "gong" noise we heard earlier?' asked Hannah.

'Yes, that was the Sound Modulator. It keeps time and its echo travels through the Underground Burroway to every village. As you can see, the Portway is a midpoint and a burroway leads straight to each one.'

Five burroways lay before them, the name of a village above each entrance. Sombrono and Puddlelake led to the right, Pickletullum and Gorgonz City to the left and Socratown went off into the brown earth straight ahead. A continuous stair ran over each burroway to join with the next and at each entrance all manner of strange people were coming and going. A man in a dark brown suit hovered before them, took a watch from his pocket, checked it against the Sound Modulator and flew hurriedly off down the Sombrono tunnel. Near the burroway for Puddlelake was a woman whose peach coloured hat hung over her ears and down to the floor. But even odder than the clothes they wore were their wings: some had pearlescent, shimmering wings which were almost transparent; others' wings were small and dark; some only had wings on their ankle boots and some had no wings at all. Around the entrance to Gorgonz City stood four who didn't look so friendly. Squat and warty, dressed in leather and wearing sturdy boots, they huddled and whispered together when they saw Hannah, Ben and Lucy, and their beady eyes followed every move they made.

'Gorgonz City doesn't sound like the kind of place you'd want to go for your holidays, does it?' said Ben, looking in their direction and reading the sign above the burroway.

'Puddlelake does, though,' said Lucy turning in the opposite direction to look at their pretty clothes.

Strangest of all were the giant scarab beetles waiting by the burroways for their passengers to alight. Hannah almost fainted when she saw them. Easily the size of small cars, their huge elytra – the two halves of the hard outer shell on their backs – sat open like canopies flashing iridescent sea-green and purple in the soft light. The passengers sat side by side beneath the great shimmering wings, chattering and pointing nervously in their direction.

'Look at the size of them,' said Lucy, nodding towards the Socratown burroway where there was an enormous dragonfly taking off with a single passenger.

But Hannah didn't respond. She stood transfixed; she hated insects almost as much as she hated spiders and not only were they everywhere but they were all about one hundred times their normal size.

'The scarab is here,' said Milli, pointing towards the Pickletullum burroway.

'Good, we should go now,' said Dolfi striding on, leading the way.

Hannah was breathing heavily. 'I, I can't go on.'

'Of course you can, Hannah,' said Lucy, tugging at her arm to make her follow.

'Oh look, there's a hairy one!' called Ben.

Hannah squealed and jumped towards Dolfi.

'Only joking,' Ben grinned.

'Ben, don't *do* that!'

They made their way towards the burroway, Hannah glancing over her shoulder every few steps, hoping nothing hairy *was* about to come forward.

Beneath the sign for Pickletullum they noticed the inscription *Ab sit in vi dia*, although Hannah was in no mood to know what it meant. Opposite the main platform, below the sign for Socratown, they saw another, *Ae quo animo*, which Milli told them meant 'with a calm and even mind.' All the villages had them, they noticed.

'They are our village creeds,' said Milli.

Ahead, a fat little guard was blowing a whistle and waving a strange five-pointed flag at a scarab. It disappeared down the burroway towards Sombrono. The guard flew from one burroway to the next blowing the whistle and flourishing the flag but it didn't seem to be having much effect; the scarabs seemed to fly off whenever they wanted to.

The scarab for Pickletullum stood munching a root which was poking out from the earth. Its antennae hardly twitched at all when they approached but Hannah was not so keen to make its acquaintance.

'Come on, Hannah, you can't back out now,' said Lucy pulling hard on Hannah's arm as she hung back.

'Pretend you're sitting on a horse,' said Ben, shoving her forward.

'It's all right for you two. I didn't know there would be beetles and … things.'

'But they're nice beetles,' said Lucy, patting the hard shell on the scarab's back.

Hannah felt the creature's leg hair brush against her skin.

'*You* might think so …,' she said, shuddering.

Dolfi and Milli had already boarded. Lucy and Ben shoved Hannah from behind until she landed heavily on a seat.

'Stick your fingers in your ears and hum a tune,' said Ben sitting beside her.

Hannah closed her eyes and started to hum. Anything was better than having to look at a beetle.

'I was only joking,' Ben mouhed across to Lucy.

Just as the scarab started to manoeuvre its way into a flying position the guard fluttered over. He seemed to be very interested in the new arrivals and looked them up and down.

'What have we here then?' he asked, flying around to peer more closely although Hannah, eyes closed, fingers in her ears and humming vigorously, didn't notice him. 'Peeps, if I'm not mistaken. Well, well, well!'

'What's a Peep?' Lucy whispered to Milli.

'You're a Peep,' Milli whispered back behind her hand. 'A human, a person, one of your people.'

'Got the Council's approval have we?' the guard said, nodding towards the children.

'The Council of Alter-Idem are informed,' said Dolfi raising his eyebrows, clearly irritated.

The guard hooked a strand of Lucy's long blonde hair with the end of his flag and held it up in the air. 'Like new spun gold. How fascinating.'

'Leave my hair alone,' said Lucy tossing her head so her hair whipped out of his reach. The guard fluttered backwards.

'Touchy, aren't they?'

'We're in a hurry, Horace,' said Dolfi.

Hannah was still humming with her eyes shut.

'Yes, I've heard things are not good. I've heard that Herbert Rootvine is too unwell to make the Cleansing Potion.' The guard was running the flag through his fingers, watching Dolfi's reaction. The unfriendly looking group at the next burroway seemed interested in what Horace was saying and shuffled closer.

'That's just a silly rumour, Horace, you should know better than to listen to gossip.' Dolfi whistled shrilly through his teeth, sounding just like the guard's reed whistle and without further delay the great wings of the scarab moved out to the side and started rotating in a figure of eight.

'I say, Dolfi …' the guard stuttered, but then the scarab rose, hovered into the tunnel and set off with a whoosh as if the brakes had been released. Once inside the burroway it picked up speed. The huge elytra dropped to shield them from the wind. After a few minutes Hannah stopped humming and slowly opened her eyes.

'See, it's not so bad,' said Lucy, patting her knee.

Ben grinned at Hannah's discomfort. 'Are the villages very different?' he asked, turning to Dolfi.

'Yes,' said Dolfi sighing 'Very different. I suppose you could say we all have our own way of looking at things. There's not much harmony between us all now, I'm afraid.'

'Who were the mean looking group, the ones with no wings?' asked Lucy.

'They're goblins from Gorgonz City,' said Milli, just in time before a sneeze overcame her. 'Aitchoo! And they like to know everything that's going on in the other villages.'

'Elfin and goblin do not have a lot in common, these days,' said Dolfi.

'Is Gorgonz City the capital of your fai …, er … world, then?' asked Ben.

'All villages have an equal place in Aldoris,' replied Dolfi. 'Although it's true the Council meets in Gorgonz City to make the decisions needed to keep our villages running smoothly. But with no Supreme Parlator to guide us the Council is no longer what it was.'

The scarab suddenly rose up sharply and then returned to its normal flight path, making their stomachs heave.

'What was that?' asked Ben.

'Just avoiding a walker,' said Dolfi. 'We don't have to use the transport, you know, but why walk when you can fly? It's quicker by scarab.'

Hannah was still trying to take her mind off the fact she was sitting on a beetle. 'What happened to the Supreme Parlator?' she asked.

'She died,' said Milli, 'of old age.'

'Why can't another Supreme Parlator be appointed?'

'Because the Council can't agree …,' began Milli.

'Indeed, it is rare for them to agree on anything much anymore,' Dolfi interrupted, bristling in his seat. 'The Harmony Rules ensured peace, fairness and harmony between our villages but now, because the Council can't agree, the Harmony Rules are being ignored. Each village lives more and more by its own rules. Look out!'

The scarab suddenly swerved wildly, making everyone slide and grab the seats to hold on. A rabbit, curled up asleep, filled half of the burroway behind them.

'How did he get in here?' asked Ben.

'Happens sometimes,' said Dolfi 'They get lost in their own burrows and start digging and sometimes fall into ours. The guards will get it back home when they find it.'

'You were talking about the Supreme Parlator,' said Hannah.

'Yes, so I was,' said Milli drowsily. 'The Supreme Parlator was learned and respected as having the greatest of all wisdom. Every village lived by the Harmony Rules and the Supreme Parlator's judgement. None were favoured more or less than any other.' Milli yawned. 'It was a happier time then. The old ones often speak of it. But now, as each village discards the old ways, bad things are happening. In Pickletullum we still live by the Harmony Rules. Our own village creed is *Let there be no envy or ill will.*'

Hannah noticed Milli had started to shiver and was sure she had caught the fever too. The fever! Hannah felt the hand in her stomach tighten its grip. She had almost forgotten what they had come to do. Doubts suddenly rushed back into her mind. *What if we can't do it? What if we make a Cleansing Potion that doesn't work?*

Hannah started to feel unwell. Compared to making a Cleansing Potion, sitting on a beetle suddenly didn't seem so bad.

The scarab flew around a sweeping curve. 'Not long now,' said Dolfi. 'The village is just up ahead.'

Chapter 4

The Apothecary

In a rush of sunlight the scarab soared out into bright airy woodland. Ben and Lucy leaned over the side to get a first glimpse of the village but Hannah sat rigidly in her seat staring straight ahead, the drone of the scarab's wings in her ears, wondering what was coming next. The journey hadn't been as bad as she'd expected, it was true, and she had to admit it was fast, but on a bus you didn't see legs dangling out of the back window.

'You needn't worry, Hannah,' said Ben, craning his neck to get a better view. 'There's nothing but trees.'

They weaved through the trees and past a grassy clearing towards a wide swathe of enormously tall ferns. The giant beetle slowed and flew lower, then, swooping and weaving through the stems, they plunged deep into the undergrowth. All at once they were passing dwellings built into the side of the banking: clay houses, rows of shops, and buildings whose windows threw off dazzling spikes of reflected sunshine. The beetle finally came to a smooth stop at the end of a street beside a water barrel. Ben stepped out first, a little unbalanced with Grandma's book in his hands; Lucy followed, then Hannah, relieved to have her feet on the ground again. Milli and Dolfi fluttered gently to their sides. The scarab rested, waiting for return passengers.

They had no sooner dusted themselves down when a man in a billowing coat came running up to them, puffing and blowing and holding onto his hat.

'Dolfi, at last!' he gasped, his eyes jumping from Hannah to Ben to Lucy. 'We are most grateful you could come. Most grateful.'

'Did we have a choice?' muttered Hannah. Dolfi coughed loudly as if to cover up her words and the man bowed deeply with one foot forward and swept his tall black hat out to one side. The red buckled winged shoes matched a folded red silk neck scarf which was held in place by a large pearl.

'On behalf of Pickletullum, may I welcome you. Yes indeed, it is an honour,' he said, holding out his hand and shaking theirs one by one.

Hannah was pleased to see he looked pretty normal – for an elfin. It was a good start.

'May I introduce Chancellor Zanting Barbelly,' said Dolfi, smoothing back his black hair and eyebrows. 'He is our representative on the Council of Alter-Idem and oversees all the business of the village. You could say he is our eyes and ears.'

Zanting Barbelly beamed. 'And some would say, mouth,' he said, laughing at his own joke, waistcoat nearly bursting under the strain.

'We are pleased to meet you,' said Hannah.

'Charming, just charming,' he said hurriedly and with an outstretched arm ushered them to walk with him. 'Shall we proceed? Time, as you know, is of the essence.'

They sped past a carpenter's shop with all the wood-working tools hanging outside. Chancellor Barbelly nodded to the carpenter who was working at a table outside, planing a piece of wood.

'Dolfi will have told you, I'm sure, that Dr Rootvine has also succumbed to the fever. He's not making much sense poor man, keeps going on about nuts or nuggets or something of the sort; went downhill fast. You really are our only hope.'

This news was not helping Hannah feel any better. It now felt as if the fist in her stomach was poking into every corner. In an effort to distract herself Hannah concentrated on the passing shops. The next one seemed to be occupied by coppersmiths who were hammering at an anvil. She could see a huge clay oven and in the middle of it, a red hot flame leaped and roared. She wondered if the shop ever caught fire.

Zanting Barbelly greeted everyone as they passed and everyone in turn stopped to stare and whisper as Hannah, Ben and Lucy walked by. A moving curtain caught Hannah's eye and as she glanced back, Hannah suddenly noticed Milli wasn't with them but was still down the street, leaning against the door of the coppersmiths in an effort to get warm.

'Dolfi!' Hannah pointed at the shivering Milli. 'She looks about to collapse.'

Dolfi reached Milli just as her knees started to buckle and Zanting Barbelly called to two passers-by.

'Take her to Dr Pepper's place. Tell him we'll soon have the medicine. The Peeps are here. We're going to the Apothecary now.'

Milli was carried away on a stretcher and they continued on up the street. The confectioner's and baker's shop both had notices in the window saying 'CLOSED'. The wine maker's was closed too … and the greengrocer's.

'Here we are now,' said Zanting Barbelly, opening the door of an old, dusty shop with very thick glass in the windows. An iron bell clapped once, letting the owner know they were there but Dr Herbert Rootvine, of course, was ill in bed. In his place stood his assistant, Thelma Mex. It was her job to prepare the ingredients and serve the customers. She was tall and very thin.

''Ello, can I 'elp you?' she enquired politely then, seeing it was Zanting Barbelly and Dolfi Greenlees with three oddly dressed strangers, 'Oh, you're 'ere then.'

You'd think she saw Peeps every day, thought Hannah.

A loud cawing filled the shop and in the same instant a yellow streak passed Dolfi's shoulder. Instead of the large black raven they expected to see, a yellow canary, the size of a half-grown sparrow, landed on top of Thelma's fluffy black hat.

'Quiet, Jasper, they're with the Chanc'llor,' said Thelma. The canary started to peck at her untidy carroty hair.

'Still not his old self, then?' chortled the Chancellor.

The canary screeched with its little beak as wide as it could go, obviously not amused by this observation.

'It were a nasty trick to play. Spell'll wear off eventually but if we find out 'oo it was they'll be sorry, won't they, Jasper?' said Thelma and the canary cawed again in agreement.

Dolfi, in no mood for prolonged pleasantries, introduced everyone quickly.

'As you know,' he said, turning to Thelma and tugging on his waistcoat, 'Hannah, Ben and Lucy have, ahem, agreed to help us but we'll all need to work together if we are to have any hope of making up a Cleansing Potion in time.' He paused to take a breath. 'I take it there is no sign?' He didn't sound hopeful.

'None,' said Thelma. 'I've look'd thru all the scripture books, the ref'rence books, the rem'dy books and even in the order books just in case 'e decided to write it down there. But there's nothin.'

'Indeed. Not so good, then,' said Dolfi.

An awful thought sprang into Hannah's mind and the fist in her stomach started making scrambled eggs.

'Am I right in thinking,' she asked 'that Dr Rootvine didn't write down the recipe for the Cleansing Potion?'

'That's right,' said Thelma.

The fist in Hannah's stomach started beating faster.

'But why ever not?' she asked.

''E *did* write down *most* of 'is remedies,' said Thelma with extra emphasis on the word *most*. 'An' all the ancient rem'dies are catalogued an' recorded an' everythin', but 'e kept his most important recipes, 'specially the ones 'e discovered 'imself, in 'is 'ead. Didn't even tell 'em to me.'

'I still don't understand,' said Hannah, feeling faint and shaking her head. 'Why did he do that?' Who in their right mind, she thought, would try to remember every measure of every ingredient of every important recipe he knew? It just didn't make sense.

'Didn't want 'em stolen.' Thelma shrugged.

'But who would want to steal them?' Hannah asked.

'The raiders,' said Thelma. 'They steal things from all the villages. Will steal anythin' that's useful to 'em.'

'Who are *they*?' asked Ben.

'No one knows,' said Dolfi. 'They are invisible, or at least they use an invisible spell to sneak into the villages at night, break in, and take whatever they want.'

Lucy leaned towards Hannah and whispered, 'I bet that's against the Harmony Rules,' but Hannah wasn't listening.

'So, we don't know what the Cleansing Potion is made of?' she said slowly, still hoping there had been some mistake.

'Nope. We only knows the main ingredient's nasturtiums,' said Thelma.

Hannah hadn't expected this. Her heart too now felt as if it was being battered by an out-of-control egg beater. She took a deep breath.

'Ahem, well, I can see that I'll not be much use to you hanging around here. No, indeed. Don't want to be getting under your feet,' said Zanting Barbelly, tiptoeing backwards towards the door. 'Good luck and the spirit of Zamada be with you!'

As the door closed behind the Chancellor there was a very low, deep 'Go-oinggg.' It was the Sound Modulator.

'That's the eighth gong,' said Dolfi, his face turning a pale shade of grey.

'We'd better get started, then,' said Thelma. 'I'll just lock the door so's we're not disturbed.'

Before Thelma had moved out from behind the counter the bell sounded again and the door opened. Two elfin entered the shop then closed the door behind them. One was wearing a hat which seemed to be on backwards; the other had short, brown hair and was wearing an amber necklace.

'We're closed,' said Thelma sharply.

'But your door is open,' said the elfin in the hat. He took a bite of the pie he was holding in his hand and a slurp of his drink, then swallowed.

'We only need some Fly-by powder,' said the elfin in the amber necklace. She held up the deep violet pouch which was hanging around her neck. It looked very like the one Dolfi and Milli had.

'Oh, 'urry up then,' said Thelma irritably, locking the door behind them so no one else could get in. 'How much do you need?'

'About six feckles.'

Thelma reached for a big jar on the shelf, unscrewed the lid and tapped some of the silvery-grey powder into the polished brass scales on the counter, then tapped in a little more.

'That'll be four kippa, please.' Thelma lifted the basin and let the powder slide into a fine cotton sack then pulled the drawstring around the top and sat it down on the counter.

'Thank you,' said the elfin in the hat, picking up the Fly-by powder. Once he'd paid he looked from face to face. 'Sorry to disturb you.'

Even after they left they couldn't take their eyes off Hannah, Ben and Lucy, and lingered outside trying to see through the murky window.

'I'll just get the stove burnin',' said Thelma, hurrying through to the back of the shop with Jasper flying behind her.

In the quiet of the next few moments Hannah, Ben and Lucy gazed around the room. The wall behind the counter was filled from floor to ceiling with wooden drawers, each labelled clearly, and shelf after shelf of bottles. Hannah had never seen so many ingredients before. It made Grandma Fred's collection look tiny. There were herbs and plants she recognised all right but there were all sorts of weird things too, any one of which might go in a Cleansing Potion. There were drawers filled with *Bees Wings, Wasp Stripes, Scabby Woodlice* and *Scratchy Caterpillar Hair*; bottles of *Dandelion Juice, Cactus Paste, Jellied Newts Legs* and *Lizard Livers*; jars of *Flavoursome Flies*, full strength *Snake Spit*, and *Bat Droppings*. Even stranger were three boxes marked *Purple Belly Buttons, Medium Sized Gum Boils* and one marked *Dragon Bladder Warts*. How was she going to choose?

On the counter sat a large jar of what looked like sleeping pink grubs – Hannah thought she could see one with its eyes open – and another of chameleon scales, which were every colour imaginable. Another, labelled *Assorted Claws and Toe Clippings*, was half full. On the counter near the window a small oak cask filled with sycamore seeds sat next to a row of pestles and mortars, each one smaller than the one before. A much larger oak cask sat on the floor beside them. A drip fell from the tap in its side and hit the dust; as it landed a wisp of vapour hissed upwards.

'Did you say that was your Grandma's book?' Dolfi asked.

'Yes,' said Ben, holding it up.

'It's got recipes for all sorts of remedies in it,' said Lucy.

'They might not work on *short* people.' Hannah thought she'd better mention the possibility.

'Well, let's have a look at it, shall we?' said Dolfi, taking the book and laying it on the counter. He turned the first page and read:

THIS BOOK BELONGS TO: Mrs Freida Bootle, The Cottage beside the church, Thornyside.

Dolfi turned over to the next page:

Ailments are listed in alphabetical order at the front and patients treated are at the back.

'What ailments do you think your Grandma would use nasturtiums to treat?' Dolfi asked Hannah.

'Er ….' Hannah was finding it hard to concentrate because the fist in her stomach felt as if it was now pummelling bread dough. Her mind went blank. She tried again. 'Err ….' Thankfully, something clicked into place and she suddenly remembered. 'Germs! They're good for killing germs and fighting infections.'

'That's a good start,' said Dolfi. 'I think we use them for the same thing.'

'But it's the seeds we need, I think.' Hannah was sure she remembered this from somewhere. Thank goodness it was coming back to her. So far so good. But Dolfi suddenly looked serious under his spiky eyebrows. His eyes darted to the back of the shop and fell on the sacks of nasturtiums. Thelma returned with Jasper flying behind her as if he was attached by a piece of string.

'How long do you think it will it take us to de-seed thirty bags of nasturtiums?' Dolfi asked Thelma. Jasper settled down to peck at something white on Thelma's fluffy black hat.

'Eeehh … 'bout four turns of the digit,' said Thelma, holding onto the hat as Jasper pulled.

'Four turns of the digit!' exclaimed Dolfi. 'but we haven't got that long!'

'Then they've got to be dried,' Thelma added.

Hannah bit her lip. Everyone, except Thelma, looked horrified.

'What are we going to do?' wailed Lucy. Ben shrugged. Hannah was keeping very quiet. She was still worrying about what to put in the potion and whether it would work, *if* they managed to de-seed the nasturtiums in time. Her eyes kept flashing across to the ingredients on the wall then back to Grandma's book.

No one said anything for a whole minute.

'We need help,' said Dolfi. 'It's the only way. We'll just have to ask for help. What about the two who were in here a moment ago? And they're bound to have friends.'

'Can't 'ave that,' said Thelma. 'Dr Rootvine wouldn't like so many people in 'is shop, 'specially the young 'uns like them. They'd be breakin' things an' liftin' things an' makin' a right mess. I've got to watch 'em like a hawk when they comes in – whip things off the counter, they do.' She picked up a packet of fish-flavoured throat pastilles as if to indicate the type of thing she meant.

'Thelma, I don't think we have a choice really,' said Dolfi, beginning to pace the floor.

'I don' like it,' said Thelma, folding her arms.

Jasper cawed loudly.

'Is there anyone else who could help?' asked Hannah.

Thelma frowned. 'What about Mrs Chelsea or Gerry Boamm or Rudor Bizar?'

'They're all in the hospital wing with Dr Pepper,' said Dolfi, although he knew that Rudor Bizar had just taken his staff there and hadn't caught the fever himself.

'Well, there's Midas Plank or Yordel Pod.'

'They're all ill, Thelma. Haven't you noticed the bank is closed and the greengrocer's too?'

'I – I haven't left the shop since Dr Rootvine became ill.'

'Before long we'll have no village left. We've got to ask for help before it's too late – it *is* almost too late!' Dolfi's ankle wings flapped excitedly and he lifted off the ground.

'Well, all right. Keep yer 'air on,' Thelma agreed reluctantly.

'What are their names? I'll go after them,' said Ben.

'Landel and Hunnik,' said Thelma. 'But mind tell 'em there'll be no thievin'.'

Ben unlocked the door and sped out of the shop. He didn't need to go far. About a hundred metres further up the street the two elfin were dawdling. He'd nearly reached them when their voices reached him first.

'Did you see their feet!'

'HA, HA, HA, HA, HA!'

'Excuse me!'

'Jumping grasshoppers! Oh my spinning aunt – it's him!' Landel jumped back.

'Sorry to startle you,' said Ben.

The two elfin closed their mouths slowly. 'What do you want?'

'Are you Landel and Hunnik?' Ben asked.

'How do you know our names?' asked Landel.

Ben pointed back down the street towards the Apothecary.

'We, er, didn't mean to be rude about ....' Hunnik blushed and the amber beads at her neck started to glow.

'My feet?'

'Well, yes, but ....' Hunnik stared down at Ben's feet as if she might catch something nasty from them.

Ben looked down too, and stared blankly. 'Oh, I get it,' he said, after a few moments. 'They're trainers.'

'Trainers?' repeated Landel.

'Yes, see, my feet are inside.' Ben pulled his foot out and held it up for inspection.

'Ahh! We thought the foot rot fungus had got you,' laughed Landel.

'The brownies in Sombrono get it sometimes because they don't wear shoes,' explained Hunnik, giggling. 'But not so bad.'

It was hard to tell how old Landel and Hunnik were but Ben guessed around his own age.

'Look, we need help,' he said.

'Just tell us what we need to do,' said Landel.

'Any good at de-seeding nasturtiums?'

'Easier than slicing cucumbers,' said Landel, smiling.

'Know anyone else who can help?'

'They'll all be in Ma Molly's,' said Hunnik. 'Come on.'

Ma Molly's Muffin House was busy with everyone gathering for the evening. Just inside the door four elfin sat together playing a board game with coloured glass balls (it looked a bit like checkers) and were eating the biggest muffins Ben had ever seen.

'The hawthorn ones are better,' Landel told Ben. 'They've got chewy bits in them.' Ben suddenly felt very hungry, but Landel pulled him further inside the Muffin House. At the far end of the room some sort of game seemed to be going on. A piece of chalk was moving against a small blackboard, keeping score on its own, and an elfin in yellow and black striped trousers was throwing a curved winged stick around a pole which itself moved up and down. He shouted 'Oh, for Zamada's sake!' when he misjudged and couldn't get it to turn back at the right time. He stopped playing when he saw them.

'Hiyup, Hornet!' Landel called, beckoning him over.

Ben was very quickly surrounded by a curious crowd, all wanting to be the first to touch him for good luck, all patting him on the head or on the shoulder or almost poking him in the eye.

*

Meanwhile, back in the Apothecary, Dolfi and Hannah were still discussing what should go in a Cleansing Potion. Hannah's head was already reeling. There were just too many ingredients to choose from.

'What do you think of the sound of pigweed?' asked Dolfi, pulling on a drawer which squealed loudly the moment it was open. Hannah's eyes widened. Dolfi shut the drawer again quickly.

'Or what about Terrapin Tonsils?'

Hannah stared at the shrivelled blue-black tonsils in the drawer.

'Ben said the illness sounded like our 'flu,' Lucy reminded them when she noticed the pained look on Hannah's face.

'It did a bit, didn't it?' Hannah agreed rapidly. 'Might be a better place to start.'

'Does your Grandma have a recipe for your, er, 'flu then?' asked Dolfi.

'There's two, I think' replied Hannah, flicking through the pages of Grandma's book, past the 'As, 'Bs and 'Cs until she reached the 'Is.

'Here it is – Influenza (with cough) – Recipe No. 1.' Hannah laid the book open for Dolfi to read:

INFLUENZA (with cough) – Recipe No. 1.
Symptoms:
1. **Sneezing**
2. **Chesty cough**
3. **Fever and sweating**

'Our symptoms do seem to be very similar,' said Dolfi, bending over the recipe, 'except we don't have a cough.'

'I think the other would be better. Hannah turned over the page. As she had remembered, there was a second recipe. It read:

INFLUENZA (no cough) – Recipe No. 2.
Symptoms:
1. **Sneezing**
2. **Runny nose**
3. **Shivering**
4. **Aching in joints and bones**
5. **Fever and sweating**
6. **Tiredness and drowsiness**

'This seems better,' she said, 'although there's still no mention of any itching. Still, I don't suppose we're going to get an exact match.' The recipe followed:

Recipe No. 2.
1. **Dried seeds of nasturtium – 1 measure**
2. **Dried cudweed – chopped to medium grade – 1 measure**
3. **Dried leaves of small-leafed lime tree – powdered – 1 measure**
4. **Mallow milk – 2 measures (do not use plants that have gone rusty)**
5. **Mugwort root – 12 inches – chopped into small pieces**
6. **Salt and pepper to taste**

Method:
Add ingredients slowly to boiling water stirring each six times clockwise and six times anticlockwise. Boil for thirty minutes. Add salt and pepper to taste. Leave to cool, then strain. A half cup should be taken twice a day for two days.

'Well, it's got nasturtiums in it all right,' said Hannah sounding relieved. In her head she saw herself making up the recipe.

'Thelma, what do you think of this?' called Dolfi. 'Tell me if you've ever seen something similar

Thelma peered down at the book and studied the recipe for a few minutes.

'Yeh, well, we 'ave all the ingredients all right, an' we uses small-leafed lime to treat the Chilli Willies in winter, but the las' time Dr Rootvine made a potion usin' cudweed it were fer ol' Witch Magrew's varicose veins.'

'But could it work on the fever?' asked Dolfi.

'It could – I s'pose – but 'oo can tell, an' there's nothin' in it fer the itches is there?'

'The itches, yes, the caterpillar itch,' said Dolfi absently, beginning to scratch his left elbow. 'What would you use for the itching?'

'That depends, donnit? Could try a bit o' the very thin' that drives yer mad an' add some 'air if yeh likes or yer can treat the symptoms an' add somethin' for skin rashes.'

'Well, which one do you suggest?' asked Dolfi, now scratching his right elbow.

'I'm not suggestin' anythin'. I don' makes the potions.' Thelma turned away and busied herself with a feather duster.

'But I'm asking your opinion, Thelma,' said Dolfi sounding exasperated.

'Don' ask me,' she said, flicking the duster at Dolfi.

'But you must have some idea what would be best,' he insisted, but Thelma swept the duster over a string of garlic bulbs hanging behind her and started to whistle.

'We could add them both perhaps,' said Hannah. 'Caterpillar hair to mimic the itching and cactus paste for the skin rash. Grandma used some on me last summer when I fell into a bed of nettles.'

Dolfi stopped scratching. 'And why not,' he said. 'Any reason why not, Thelma?'

'None that I can think of,' she said, rubbing to a shine a stone from a pile marked *Billy Goat Gall Stones.*

'Right, good, is that it settled then? We've got our Cleansing Potion, mark 2? Good thinking Hannah.'

But Hannah hadn't finished thinking yet. It seemed too easy. And what if it didn't work? The thought of all the elfin dying made her bite her bottom lip. Would trying her best be good enough to save them?

The old door bell clapped dully again and the shop immediately began to fill with noise. Ben pushed through Landel and Hunnik and their throng of friends. Jasper started flapping and cawing and jumping from head to head.

'Got plenty of help now,' Ben shouted above the din.

'We'll have the nasturtiums de-seeded in no time,' Dolfi shouted back and turned to smile at Hannah. 'Let's hope nothing goes wrong now.'

Thelma locked the door once more and in the middle of the floor everyone set to, de-seeding the nasturtiums.

'Put the seeds in these,' Thelma ordered, setting down several trays. 'An' put the flower 'eads back in the sacks, we can use 'em later.'

Jasper flew in circles above their heads.

'Now, let's get going,' said Dolfi. Hannah tried to smile. Milli's words kept going round in her head: '*All you can do is try. All you can do is try.*' She knew she could make up the recipe in Grandma's book without too much trouble – it was just a case of weighing everything out carefully, adding everything in the right order, stirring thoroughly and making sure it boiled for the right length of time. It was a simple enough recipe. But would it work?

Chapter 5

The Cleansing Potion

In the back room of the Apothecary a massive stove stretched out along one wall. It had fourteen cooking places on its wrought iron surface, each with a lid that could be lifted by a hook. Two huge ovens sat below, on either side of a fire. Thelma threw in more logs and the flames curled and licked around the open door. It was very hot in the room.

In one corner, at a large pine table several times bigger than Grandma Fred's, three imps sat chopping and grinding up ingredients. Hannah and Lucy stared. The imps were dressed in woolly jumpers and knitted hats and each had an earring hanging from an earlobe. Hannah and Lucy could hardly believe their eyes – it was so hot in here they could hardly breathe.

'They're used to the 'eat,' said Thelma, seeing the expressions on their faces. 'They comes from deep inside the earth.'

'Say "'ello" to Hannah and Lucy.'

Each imp jumped down in turn and bowed so low the tassels on their hats brushed the floor.

'This is Eeni, Meeni and Miney,' said Thelma. A banjo was propped up at an empty place at the table.

'Mo is ill,' Thelma whispered, leaning towards them. "'e's taken the fever 'specially bad. I think 'is resistance is low seein' as 'e's used to it bein' hotter than 'ere.' Hannah got the impression Thelma didn't expect Mo to survive. In a normal voice, Thelma then asked the imps to chop up the cudweed and milk the mallow for the potion.

'They'll do whatever yeh wants so don't be afraid to ask 'em,' she added cheerfully.

Hannah was amazed at how fast they worked. Their arms seemed to move twice as fast as her own.

In what seemed no time at all Hunnik came through with the first tray of seeds. 'First lot of seeds ready,' she said, laying them on the weighing table, taking care not to spill any.

Thelma opened up the double oven doors. 'We'll dry the seeds in 'ere. They'll take half a digit's turn to dry out. Start at the top so we knows which went in first.'

The pots were next. Dolfi raised himself into the air and hovered by a pot pole suspended from the ceiling, the waft from his ankle wings cooling Hannah's face, then lowered to the floor with a pot as big as a pumpkin in each hand. Hannah set them on the stove. Dolfi lowered twelve more and filled them with water.

'Go-oinggg.'

The familiar sound echoed softly through the Apothecary. The ninth gong! Everyone began to work faster. Lucy grabbed a sack of small-leafed lime and dragged it through from the front of the shop, a small heave at a time. Thelma wrestled a heavy basket of mugwort root onto the weighing table nearest the door. The ingredients were piling up.

'More seeds,' said Ben laying two more trays on the table. Jasper swooped, scooped up a beakful, then flew back to his perch, dropping seeds onto Lucy below. Thelma was too busy to notice.

'That bird needs turning into a frog,' muttered Ben.

Hannah pushed the two trays into the oven before Jasper ate any more. Dolfi brought in the cactus paste for the itches, setting the two small tubs down on the table beside the imps.

'That's 'bout it now. The cudweed's chopped, Eeeni's got the mallow milkin' under control, Miney's powderin' up the lime leaves. Just got ter put the fires in place now,' said Thelma, glancing around the room. She lowered her voice: 'Meeni, the basement please.'

Meeni jumped down from the table, went over to a very ordinary looking cupboard and opened it. On the deep shelves, mixing bowls, assorted spoons and measuring jugs, long glass containers and thin rubber tubes lay as if shoved in any old way. Racks of oddly shaped vessels, including several that twisted in spirals, lay on their side. Meeni reached under one of the shelves but Hannah couldn't see what he was doing. The next moment, the shelving rose into the ceiling and a flight of steps leading down into a dark basement appeared.

'Come wi' me, girls,' said Thelma. 'Dolfi, Ben, keep guard – don' let anyone through.'

Hannah and Lucy followed Thelma down the rough steps. There were no windows in the basement. Thelma tapped the wall with the wooden spoon she was carrying and the candles on the wall flickered into life. Hannah and Lucy peered through the floating dust.

Their long shadows cast to the floor and along the shelves of one wall where rows of dark bottles stood upright looking like splintered teeth. Large wooden casks sat covered in cobwebs and everywhere, heaps of books rose in crooked piles. Old robes hung on the wall and in one corner Hannah thought she could make out some funny shaped hats on a box. Thelma led them to the far wall of the basement, towards a door fastened shut with six huge padlocks. She rotated her arm in a large circle and spoke some words in a hushed voice. Yellow stars began to trail from her wooden spoon and form a circle in the air. Leaning forward, she touched the first padlock, muttering '*Actus cantus*', and the thick padlock clicked and opened. She touched the next, mumbling '*Bantus cantus*', and it too fell open. One by one the heavy padlocks sprung apart. As the last padlock unlocked, the door swung open.

Hannah and Lucy gasped. There, in a neat row, were six glass jars filled with blue fire – only the flames seemed frozen solid.

'That can't be fire!' said Hannah.

'Precious Fire,' said Thelma. 'The imps collected it from the Caves of Molten Rock at the centre o' the earth in charmed jars. It 'as great power to 'eal but is very dangerous to collect. They says it can also turn metal ores into gold but I've never seen it done.'

Healing Fire that turns metal into gold! Hannah had never heard of such a thing. Then it struck her.

'We're going to use the fire to make the Cleansing Potion aren't we?' she said.

'Yup, I'm pretty sure Dr Rootvine would 'ave used it.'

'I don't suppose many people know the Precious Fires are here, do they?' said Lucy, on a hunch.

'You're right,' said Thelma 'There's many that would use 'em for their own gain, for wickedness, 'specially in these troubled times. Until another Supreme Parlator is appointed the Precious Fires will stay with Dr Rootvine in Pickletullum.'

Thelma took a jar, closed the door on the remaining five and with a swish that sent a spray of crimson stars shooting forward, all the locks clunked heavily shut at the same time.

'Do you think another Supreme Parlator *will* be appointed?' asked Hannah.

'That depends, donnit? Depends on whether they finds the sixth key.'

'Why's that?

'Don' knows if I'm s'posed ter tell yer all this but I guess you'll be forgettin' it all later anyways.'

Hannah had forgotten that they'd be having their memories wiped later. It seemed a shame to see all these strange and wonderful things and not be allowed to remember them.

Lucy was hanging on every word Thelma said and didn't seem to notice her glasses were steaming up.

'Every Supreme Parlator wears the Crown of Keys,' said Thelma, walking towards the stair. 'The crown is magical, of course. 'Ave to be, wouldn't it, choosin' the Supreme Parlator an' all. As long as the Supreme Parlator's wearin' it their judgement's always sound. Can't never be swayed by a single point o' view.'

'Where does the sixth key come into it?' asked Lucy, which was exactly what Hannah was wondering.

'Oh, right.' Thelma took another step towards the stairs and the girls followed. 'Every village 'as a key and when they' re all put together it becomes the Magical Crown of Keys.'

'Why don't they make up the Magical Crown of Keys and appoint a new Supreme Parlator now then?' asked Lucy

''Cause they needs the sixth key – I've already told yeh that!' said Thelma as if they weren't listening.

'But where is it?' said Hannah, suppressing the urge to shake Thelma.

'That's what I've bin tellin' yeh! Nobody knows, do they. It's lost!'

It was only at the top of the stairs that Hannah realised she could have met any one of a dozen spiders on the way down and up from the basement. She shuddered at the thought, shaking her shoulders just in case one was, at this very moment, crawling slowly up her back, then blanked the thought of spiders from her mind.

Thelma carried the glass jar over to the stove, removed an iron hook from the wall and opened the first flap. She broke a bit off the still blue flame and dropped it into the flap. Immediately, the flame changed from blue to a violent magenta and leaped up from the flap as if trying to escape. A moment later it settled and flickered gently beneath the black pot. Thelma opened the next flap, broke off another piece of the still blue flame, dropped it in and continued until all fourteen flaps had the Precious Fire burning under them. As soon as the Precious Fires touched the huge pots the water in them burst into a rapid boil. The dark red flame was unlike any other Hannah or Lucy had seen before. It flashed like cold steel but burned so deeply it looked liquid at its middle, as if light itself was being melted.

'The first lot of seeds will be ready now,' said Thelma opening the oven door. Hannah removed the first batch of seeds, moved up the two below, placed the new trays that Ben had just brought in at the bottom and closed the doors. Jasper hung upside down from the pot pole looking very disappointed. Ben sniggered.

'Looks like we're ready to begin,' said Hannah, standing with the first tray of dried nasturtium seeds in her hand.

Hannah weighed the seeds in Dr Rootvine's shiny brass scales and laid on and lifted off the little weights until both sides balanced. She read the numbers off the weights.

'Thirty-two feckles. That's enough for two pots. Agreed?'

'Agreed'

Hannah slid half of the nasturtiums seeds into the first pot and half into the second and stirred both six times to the right and six times to the left, the Precious Fires dancing around the base of each.

'Here's the cudweed ... 32 feckles.' Lucy handed Hannah a dish piled high with the yellow and green chopped cudweed.

Once more Hannah divided the dish between the first two pots and stepped back as plumes of steam rose and swirled towards the ceiling. She picked up the wooden spoon to stir the potion again.

'STOP! STOP!' Thelma screeched. 'That's my wand!' Hannah looked closely at the wooden spoon. A glimmer of an angry face was scowling back at her.

'The Precious Fires would destroy the magic in it,' said Thelma, taking the wand and tucking it into her belt. 'Can't 'ave that.'

Hannah stirred the potion with the ordinary wooden spoon. The mallow milk was next and Hannah stirred it carefully, six turns to the right and six turns to the left. The potion turned from watery yellow to bright green and when the powdered lime leaves were added it thickened like castor oil and began to splutter furiously. Long tongues of Precious Fire licked up the sides of the pots and wisps of magenta smoke curled into the air.

'Careful wi' that mugwort root,' said Thelma. 'Don' let it splash.'

Hannah let the pieces slide slowly from the spoon and as they sank from sight, the potion hissed. Once more she stirred it carefully, making sure the root had dissolved, six turns to the right and six turns to the left.

'The cactus paste is last,' said Hannah, stirring it into the steaming potion. The potion suddenly frothed up to the top of the pot then just as it looked about to spill over, it died down. Last of all she added a dash of salt and pepper. The first batch was made.

The fist in Hannah's stomach was still there (doing the dishes now by the feel of it) but something else was troubling her. There wasn't time to think about it now. Thelma removed the next seeds from the oven, making room for the final two trays.

'That's all the seeding done,' said Ben from the doorway.

'Two pots made, twelve pots to go,' said Hannah.

'Thelma and I will do the weighing now we know what to do,' said Dolfi. Lucy and Ben passed the cudweed as Hannah set to work on the next two pots.

'How do you think it's going?' Ben asked quietly.

'Well ... I think ...,' said Hannah 'but I've got a funny feeling something's still not quite right, like we've forgotten something, but I can't think what.' She peered over her shoulder to make sure she wasn't being overheard.

'You worry too much, Hannah,' said Ben, keeping his voice low.

'But what if it doesn't work?' whispered Hannah. 'What if they all die?'

'We've done our best, haven't we?' said Ben.

'I suppose so,' said Hannah.

'We can't do any more than that,' said Ben.

Hannah nodded.

'I need a drink,' said Lucy, wiping her brow and passing the mugwort root.

'Me too,' said Hannah, letting the mugwort root slip gently into the potion. It hissed loudly. 'It's so hot in here.'

'I don't know how the imps stand it in those woolly jumpers,' said Ben. He looked over at Eeni, Meeni and Miney who were still working furiously.

Hannah added the cactus paste, watched the potion froth, added the salt and pepper and took the next two trays of seeds out of the oven. The pots were boiling nicely. The next ten pots were quickly made and Hannah added the last ingredients to the final four pots as the Sound Modulator chimed.

'Go-oinggg.'

'The tenth hour,' said Thelma jumpily. Jasper squawked in alarm.

'How long till the last batch is ready?' asked Dolfi.

'Not long now,' said Hannah. 'It just needs to boil for another half turn of the digit.'

'We need to deliver it as soon as we can,' said Dolfi, fidgeting with his eyebrows. 'Time is running out.'

Hannah and Ben exchanged puzzled glances as something strange started to happen. The shop was becoming fuzzy. Lucy too began blinking furiously as the boiling pots seemed to merge into one.

'You're all fading,' said Hannah, panic rising in her voice. 'The bogbean! It must have been the bogbean leaf. The effect of eating it is wearing off!'

Dolfi appeared at Hannah's side and touched her arm.

'You can't disappear now … I mean, *we* can't disappear now. Oh why didn't I think of this before?'

The imps gathered round; their hats appearing and disappearing as Hannah, Ben and Lucy continued to blink hard.

'We're bound ter 'ave the herb 'ere,' said Thelma confidently. 'Every plant known to witch or fairy, wizard or gnome is in this shop. Describe it.'

'It has yellow beans,' said Hannah, rubbing her eyes.

'We call it a bogbean,' said Lucy, feeling her way along the table.

'And the leaves taste of honey,' said Ben.

'Could be three or four I knows,' said Thelma leading Hannah next door. 'We'll 'ave yer fixed soon as sneezin'.'

Thelma's fuzzy hat had become even fuzzier and Hannah could see two Jaspers sitting on top of it, one at a very odd angle.

Once behind the counter, Thelma looked down a section of drawers, touching each one with her finger.

'Adonis … no, agrimony … hmm, I don't think so but try this anyway … tongue out.'

Hannah obediently opened her mouth. It smelled quite nice but tasted bitter. 'No it doesn't taste right,' she said, swallowing.

'Basil – no ….'

Hannah tried to keep her eyes in focus by reading the labels on the drawers as

Thelma's finger slid from one to the other. It was between 'Bats' Droppings' and 'Coltsfoot' that it hit her.

'That's it,' she yelled. 'That's it.'

'I 'aven't given yer anythin' yet,' said Thelma.

'Not for me, for the Cleansing Potion. I knew we'd missed something but I couldn't think what; we missed out the caterpillar hair.'

'Oh, yeah … the itches,' said Thelma, sniffing a drawer full of mouldy dandelion leaves.

'We could still add it I'm sure, because a tiny trace will do. Cactus paste because it soothes itching and caterpillar hair because it causes itching. A pinch in each pot is all that's needed. Quick, before it cools down,' said Hannah.

Dolfi grabbed the drawer of scratchy caterpillar hair and rushed into the back room. He fluttered above the fourteen black pots dropping a pinch into each one while the imps watched nervously.

Ben and Lucy could hardly see anything at all and sat quietly at the imps' table to stop themselves bumping into things and standing on everyone's toes. The most horrible thing was that now they couldn't hear anyone speak; they could only hear each other talking and, unfortunately, Jasper's cawing.

Thelma carried on opening drawers and sniffing plants looking for the right one to restore their fairy sight.

Hannah felt Thelma push a leaf into her hand and she put it to her lips. It smelled right. She hoped this was the one.

The familiar honey taste filled Hannah's mouth. 'That's it,' she said, putting her hand out for another.

'Thank Zamada!' said Dolfi, when Hannah finally smiled. 'Caterpillar hair added now too. It's all done.'

Relief flooded Hannah but she didn't get time to enjoy it.

'The deliveries are next. Let's get on.'

A cheer rang out when the first of the Cleansing Potion made its way through the door to Landel, Hunnik and the crowd outside waiting to whisk it away to the first of the houses on Dr Pepper's list. Fourteen ladles dipped into the Cleansing Potion and carefully poured themselves into the pint sized bottles Dolfi had conjured up. Bottle after bottle clinked by in a line. Out in the night most elfin were too ill to come to the door, many lying weak in their beds or wracked in spasms; others could hardly talk. Some lay white and close to death. No one could say if they'd reach everyone in time and no one knew if the Cleansing Potion would work. They just kept going.

Chapter 6

The Raiders

The delivery of the Cleansing Potion was well under way and all they could do now was wait. Although Hannah was relieved her part was over, she wasn't feeling any better. Eeni and Meeni helped her tidy up. Keeping busy helped take her mind off it all. She didn't even notice Miney wasn't there anymore. Thelma fluttered about replacing lids and jars and candles that had burned out and Lucy swept the floor, yawning, trying to stay awake.

'Go-oinggg!'

The eleventh gong sounded; the low muffled noise lingering for longer than usual in the night air.

'You'll be goin' back soon,' said Thelma, tapping a candle until it spluttered back into life.

'Once Dolfi and Ben get back I expect,' replied Hannah. She watched one of the large pots hang itself back up on its hook.

'Do you think we'll be allowed to come back?' asked Lucy.

'Don' think that's likely,' said Thelma 'The Council of Alter-Idem don't like 'avin' Peeps around, unless it's fer a reason.'

'That's not very friendly,' said Lucy.

'S'pose not,' agreed Thelma.

'We could always help find the sixth key,' said Lucy, trying desperately to think of a reason why they should be allowed back.

'Don' think that's likely either. The key's bin lost since Zamada died. When the Magical Crown dismantled itself the keys were returned ter the villages but no one knows what 'appened to the sixth key, it was so long ago. It just got lost. But some folks think it was stolen 'cause of the ruby.'

'What ruby?' asked Hannah.

'The biggest ruby in the crown.'

'The crown's got rubies?' asked Hannah.

'It's got all sorts on it, so they say: rubies, sapphires, diamonds, emeralds.'

'What about the sixth key?' said Lucy raising her eyebrows, trying hard to keep Thelma and Hannah on track.

'It's got the largest ruby,' said Thelma.

'So,' said Hannah, trying to imagine the crown. 'The Magical Crown has six keys all with precious stones on the end and the sixth key has the largest – a ruby.'

'That's right,' agreed Thelma 'an'gold.'

'Gold?' asked Hannah.

'The keys are made of gold.'

'No wonder they think it's been stolen,' said Lucy, pushing her glasses up her nose till her eyes seemed twice as big.

'Other folks believe Hironymus Grossus 'as it in Gorgonz City. Nasty sort them goblins – wouldn't put it past 'im to want it fer 'imself.'

'But what good would another key do him?' asked Hannah reasonably.

'Yeh never knows 'ow these goblins' minds work – some say 'e's tryin' to become ruler of the villages 'imself. Might keep the key ter stop the Crown choosin' a new Supreme Parlator.'

'I'd like to see the other villages,' said Lucy, now not feeling in the least bit sleepy.

'Better stayin' out of Gorgonz City, that's for sure – better stayin' here,' said Thelma. 'The others aren't bad, though Sombrono's a bit dull. Socratown's too full o' those 'oo think they're high priestesses if yeh ask me. Puddlelake's quite nice – except fer Quilla Vanepike. Skatin' on the lake's fun when it's frozen, an' their cakes 're scrumptious, but yeh need ter watch yer back wi' that lot too.'

Lucy sighed, wishing they could be allowed back more than anything. There was so much to see and do, they hadn't even seen around Pickletullum properly yet.

The door bell sounded and they knew it must be Dolfi and Ben returning.

Hannah gasped. What time was it? They had lost track talking about the sixth key and the Magical Crown.

'Nearly the twelfth hour,' said Dolfi. 'But we've done it; we've delivered the Cleansing Potion to everyone who's ill. Just need to wait now and see if it works.'

Hannah couldn't help noticing Dolfi was wringing his hands. She crossed her fingers behind her back and tried to cross her toes but that was impossible without falling over. The next few minutes were awkward and tense. No one knew what to say or do. All they could do was wait.

The long minutes trailing by weren't made any shorter by Jasper flying backwards and forwards, from the front of the Apothecary to the back, and squawking at the end of each lap.

Ben looked at his watch. 'We could always play I spy while we're waiting,' he said, looking round at their worried faces. 'I'll start. I spy with my little eye something beginning with … 'S'.'

'I don't think this is the right time, Ben,' said Hannah starchily.

'Bet you can't guess.'

'Be-enn.' Hannah gave him one of her mad-eye looks.

'Spoon,' said Lucy.

'Nope.'

'Don't encourage him, Lucy.'

'Snickleweed,' said Thelma.

'Nope.'

'Snail slime,' said Dolfi.

'Nope and that's two words,' said Ben.

'Sack,' said Lucy.

'Nope.'

There was a sudden movement in the doorway. It was Miney and he wasn't smiling.

'I took Mo some Cleansing Potion as soon as the first lot was ready,' he said.

You couldn't tell from his face what he was going to say next. It was excruciating. Had Mo died? They couldn't bear it.

'He says he's feeling better already but can he have something for the itches.'

'IT WORKED!' Ben erupted, half laughing. Hannah stood, frightened to move or say anything in case she burst into tears.

'I had every confidence in you, Hannah. Well done! Thank you, thank you!' Dolfi had grabbed Hannah by the shoulders and was shaking her hand so fast she was sure it would drop off when he stopped.

Eeni and Meeni threw their hats into the air and started dancing around the room with Thelma, Ben and Miney, grinning widely. Jasper cawed loudly and for a few minutes there was such a din that if a bomb had exploded they wouldn't have heard it.

'See, Hannah, I knew you could do it,' said Lucy hugging her tight.

'We all did it,' she said. 'We made a good team.' No one could disagree. Hannah hoped they would later remember some of the happy feeling they had now.

An hour later elfin were still running in and out of the Apothecary to tell them the good news – that their families and friends were getting better. There was such excitement that many were dancing in the darkness in their night gowns; the whole village seemed awake. But finally, as the night's celebrations wore on, having done what they came to do, their thoughts turned to going home.

'Time to go I suppose,' said Hannah.

A look of disappointment crossed Lucy's face. 'Do we have to?'

'Hannah, we owe you, Ben and Lucy an enormous debt of gratitude,' said Dolfi, draining the last of his cup of celebratory Spice Me Up Tonic. 'I believe the

Chancellor is waiting to thank you himself. Rudor Bizar has opened up the inn for everyone. They want to say thank you in person before you go.'

'You could thank us in Fly-by powder if you liked,' said Ben, but then he caught sight of Hannah's disapproving look. 'Only joking.'

Out in the warm night air Hannah took a last look at the shop as it was locked up and thought how nice it would be to come back. She would have liked to learn more about the remedies they used and to meet Dr Rootvine but that didn't seem possible.

Landel and Hunnik were waiting.

'Will we see you again?' asked Hunnik. She hovered along beside Hannah, carrying a lantern to light their path.

'I don't think so,' said Hannah walking slowly on. 'Thelma said the Council of Alter-Idem aren't likely to agree.'

'You could always ask them,' said Hunnik.

Hannah was rather quiet the rest of the way to the inn. As they approached, music, laughter and light spilled out of the windows into the darkness.

'Here we are,' said Dolfi, pushing open the door, 'Merryberrys.'

The wooden sign above the door said:

MERRYBERRY ALES — FINEST IN THE LAND

Inside, a loud party was going on. Musicians were playing enthusiastically in the middle of the room and many of the villagers were dancing (most still in their night gowns). Wooden goblets were being passed overhead amid much drinking and talking and an odd little man with a balloon taped to his bald head was flying around handing out spinach and frog spawn sandwiches. Hannah felt her foot tapping.

'Come in, come in!' Zanting Barbelly was dressed in his dressing-gown and tall black hat, and was beckoning them from the bar. 'It's a very great pleasure to meet you again,' he said, smiling so heartily that his cheeks creased up into round red moons. There was a loud rapping on the bar.

'Silence everyone, please,' said a gruff voice. Everyone fell silent and the music faded. Then, a whispering broke out as everyone realised they had arrived.

'Thank you, Rudor,' croaked Zanting Barbelly before clearing his throat. 'Thank you everyone,' he began loudly. 'As you know we have a lot to thank these young people for.' He gestured toward Hannah, Ben and Lucy and a cheer went up.

'Without them we would have … well, we all know how serious the situation was and I can hardly bring myself to think of the consequences of this terrible blight on our village if it wasn't for them. We owe them a debt of gratitude.'

'HURRRRAAHHHH!' Some elfin whistled and others banged on the tables. Hannah recognised the coppersmiths in the crowd and saw the carpenter they had seen when they had first arrived, purse his lips and whistle through his teeth.

The Chancellor continued. 'We all know things have not been well in our land for some time, that our village continues to be troubled by disagreements with our neighbours and recently, harmony has been further disrupted by many unexplained happenings. You know too that while our neighbours are abandoning the Harmony Rules, we here in Pickletullum continue to uphold the good work of the late, great Zamada, our last Supreme Parlator, whose wisdom, fairness and justice guided these lands for the good of all.'

A few of the elfin clapped respectfully.

'While I serve you all, I will keep the cause burning by continually pressing the Council to find the sixth key so that we may restore the Magical Crown of Keys and have a new Supreme Parlator among us again one day.'

The crowd cheered and hooted through their hands.

'Why don't you try and find the key yourselves?' Lucy's voice was barely audible above the noise but Zanting Barbelly heard and turned his head towards her.

'What an extraordinary thought, my dear girl,' he said.

'What did she say?' someone called from the front of the crowd.

'Quiet!' called another. The noise subsided. The old man with the balloon taped to his head floated up to get a better view.

'She said why don't we try and find the sixth key ourselves?' The Chancellor sounded as if this was something he had never considered before.

Hannah looked horrified. What was Lucy trying to do? They still had to get back home in one piece, after all.

The whole room was quiet and the Chancellor started to look very uncomfortable as it became clear that everyone was waiting to hear what he would say next.

'Well … now that I come to think of it … I suppose we have always held the view that the Council of Alter-Idem would make any decision to look for the key. It's not that we haven't looked before. Many united searches have been done over the years but none have ever found it. The last search was done about forty moons ago.'

'So it's about time another search was done then?' said Lucy brightly.

Hannah couldn't believe her ears. She started to wonder what they'd do if the scarab refused to take them back through the Underground Burroway. How would they get back home on their own?

'I … I … well … well … I suppose it is,' said Zanting Barbelly at last. The crowd muttered in general agreement.

Hannah sighed with relief. At least Chancellor Barbelly wasn't angry; the sooner they got on that scarab the better.

Dolfi was being passed drinks by Rudor Bizar and he handed one each to Ben, Hannah and Lucy.

Zanting Barbelly raised his glass. 'I'd like to propose a toast,' he said grandly. 'Our heartfelt thanks go to you Hannah, to you Ben, and to you Lucy, for you kindness in agreeing to come to Pickletullum and helping rid us of the scourge which threatened to kill us all. We owe you a debt of gratitude and if we can ever return your favour, we will.'

Everyone raised their glasses and said 'To Hannah, Ben and Lucy!' and the room fell quiet as everyone gulped their drinks.

'We'd like to help you find the sixth key,' Lucy's clear voice rang out.

Hannah spluttered, a spray of dandelion and burdock wine hitting Ben on the back of the head. Ben's own mouthful went down the wrong way.

'We need to go home, Lucy,' said Hannah, wiping her mouth with the back of her hand.

'But we can come back, can't we?' said Lucy, looking up at Zanting Barbelly.

The Chancellor shifted his feet uncomfortably, rose fifteen centimetres into the air and down again. He held tightly onto his lapels and looked at Dolfi. 'I don't think the Council would allow it,' he said in a gentle voice.

'But you've just said you owe us a favour for helping you,' Lucy protested.

'Lucy, we need to go home,' said Hannah again. 'Ben, tell her.' Ben shrugged his shoulders.

'I know we have to go home but I want to come back. Don't you?'

Hannah had to admit that she did.

'Perhaps Chancellor Barbelly could ask the Council,' said Hunnik who was standing nearby.

'We do owe them a very special debt,' Dolfi agreed firmly.

'Ask the Council,' Landel shouted from the crowd. Other voices joined in.

'Let them come back.'

'They helped us, we owe them.'

'We should find the key.'

Zanting Barbelly pulled his eyes away from the clamouring crowd.

'Very well. It is clear you want to return and as Dolfi has rightly said, we owe you a special favour. There is a Council meeting tomorrow. You can come and ask them yourselves. There is no guarantee they will agree, you understand, but I will, of course, tell them what you have done for us and raise again the matter of finding the sixth key. You will not find it easy to convince them – we are not of one mind these days I'm afraid – but yes, we can let you meet them. We owe you that at least.'

Lucy could not have looked more pleased and Hannah and Ben had to admit they were delighted too.

'Be at the horse chestnut tree at the seventh hour tomorrow evening,' said Dolfi, helping them board the scarab a short while later. The scarab set off and the huge elytra dropped to keep them sheltered. Far below Hunnik and Landel were holding their lanterns high and waving.

The Underground Burroway seemed darker than it had before but rows of fireflies lit their path like aeroplane runway lights. The rabbit had gone and there were no walkers to throw them off their path.

The Portway too was quieter but Horace was still buzzing around. He waved his flag, whistled a scarab off to Socratown, then fluttered over to see them.

'Had a good day?'

'Quite satisfactory, Horace,' said Dolfi, doing his best to be brief.

'Got everything sorted then?'

'We've had a nice day, thank you, if that's what you mean,' said Hannah, pulling her shirt over Grandma Fred's book.

'Nothing quite like Ma Molly's muffins, eh?' he said. 'The best in the land, I'd say.'

'Yes, they looked great,' said Ben getting down from the scarab.

'You mean you didn't try one? You'll need to try them the next time you're here.'

'We will,' said Ben, realising too late what Horace was up to.

'We can't stop, Horace. Oh, is that a scarab arriving?' said Dolfi bending his head to look around Horace's ample middle.

While Horace was distracted Dolfi hurried Hannah, Ben and Lucy down the platform towards the path that led to the old chestnut tree.

'Wily old devil – always trying to find out what's going on,' said Dolfi. 'I tell him as little as possible. You never know who he passes his information to.'

'Sorry,' said Ben. 'I didn't realise he was trying to find out if we'd be coming back.'

'Don't worry,' said Dolfi. 'He'll see us back tomorrow night anyway. He probably thinks you'll be returning to Pickletullum so that's OK. It'll be best for you if the Council don't get to hear of your visit tomorrow until you arrive. It will give them less opportunity to think about it.'

'I thought the Council were fair minded,' said Hannah.

'They used to be,' replied Dolfi 'at least, they all strived for a balanced view, but nowadays there is so much suspicion most only think about themselves and their own villages. Some are very stubborn. But you'll see for yourselves tomorrow.'

Dolfi aimed his wand at the solid wall of earth in front of them.

'*Suo loco.*'

The end of the burrow opened up to the wood beyond where the dark shapes of the trees loomed tall and silhouetted against a full moon.

'*Ad maxmima,*' said Dolfi, pointing his wand at Hannah. A strong whoosh of air passed down over her body and she opened her eyes to see the others still small at the burroway's entrance. Dolfi flicked his wand at Ben and Lucy, and Hannah saw them grow bigger and bigger until they were standing beside her.

'Wow, wouldn't it be great to have a wand at school,' said Ben, grinning. 'One flick of my ruler and I could turn Frosty Fotheringham into a mouse, and fling him by the tail into the nettles at the back of the sports hall.'

'And I could turn Janet Bloomer into a chair and get an elephant to sit on it,' said Lucy gleefully. Hannah thought too much blood must have rushed to their heads in the growing process.

Dolfi closed the hole and stayed with them until they reached the gate at the bottom of Grandma Fred's garden.

'See you at the seventh hour tomorrow, then,' he said, hovering by Hannah's shoulder.

Hannah managed to say 'OK' and he was gone, leaving behind the glint of fading green stars.

*

As the children slept soundly in the Cottage beside the church the partying was still going on in Merryberrys. Enough ale had been drunk to put out the fires in the Caves of Molten Rock at the centre of the earth, or so it seemed to those who staggered home and fell into their beds, oblivious to anything the moment their heads touched their soft pillows. As the last revellers left the inn, Rudor Bizar locked up for the night and finally drew his bedroom curtains and snuffed out the candle. The streets around Pickletullum were now quiet and still. Far above the ferns and the trees the stars hung silently in the slate-black sky and nothing seemed to move; even the scarabs were quiet and resting. With the worry of the terrible fever now lifted everyone slept peacefully. Everyone was resting. Except someone. For at the very moment everyone else was falling into their deepest sleep someone was awake and moving. There was a muffled sound of glass breaking but so faint that no one stirred and no one woke to hear the low voices talking.

'Be careful, you oaf. You nearly knocked me over.'

'Watch who you're calling an oaf, you overgrown tadpole.'

'Careful, careful … watch out!'

'Argghhhh – WHUMP!'

A straining, creaking sound filled the room, like a rope swinging from a tree, and moments later a soft footfall landed on a wooden floor.

'Right then, are you sure you know how to get in?'

'Ow! I think me arm's fractured.'

'Never mind that now, Grunt, get on with it.'

If someone had been in the room they would have seen an open skylight with its broken glass lying on the table below, they would have heard a cupboard door opening but they wouldn't have seen the two figures standing by the steps peering into the shadows.

*

'Oh my!' said Grandma Fred at breakfast the next day. 'I don't know what came over me last night. One moment I was sitting reading and the next I was fast asleep in my chair – didn't wake up till this morning. Good sleep too, don't even have a sore neck. Most strange. Sleep well, my dears?'

'Yes, thanks, Grandma,' said Lucy, tucking into her bacon and eggs.

'Yes, thanks,' said Hannah who was still avoiding looking Grandma straight in the eyes.

'Grandma,' said Ben, as he bit into a slice of toast. 'Do you believe in fairy folk?'

'Why ever do you ask, Ben?' said Grandma Fred, not looking up from the horse racing section of the newspaper.

Hannah put a finger up to her lips. It was too dangerous to tell anyone. Ben took another bite of toast, thinking better of his moment of foolishness.

'Just wondered,' he said. Hannah's shoulders relaxed.

'We saw some last night,' said Lucy.

Hannah jerked as if she'd been jabbed by a pin and Ben froze in mid-chew. That had done it now.

'That's nice, dear,' said Grandma. 'Do you want raspberry jam or marmalade on your toast? There is a pot of both on the table.' Grandma Fred could study horse-racing form and talk about jam at the same time but doing three things at once was a bit too much for her. Hannah and Ben stared at each other and started to breathe again; Grandma wasn't really listening, and anyway, no one was going to believe them, were they?

'Gertrude saw them too – didn't you, Gertrude?' Lucy bent down to stroke Gertrude whose headache seemed to be a lot better this morning.

Hannah and Ben waved frantically at Lucy while Grandma, head buried in her paper, drew her cup of tea closer. Lucy had to be stopped before Grandma started paying attention.

'Gertrude can't talk, stupid,' snapped Ben, saying the first thing that came into his head.

'I know she can't but she still saw them and so did you,' shouted Lucy.

'We all know there's - no - such - thing - Lu-cy,' said Hannah, fixing her a look and kicking her under the table.

'Well, where are all the nasturtiums then?'

Hannah and Ben went rigid and waited. Grandma would surely know something fishy was going on now. She had already noticed that some of the plants were bare.

'Oh, that reminds me. Mr Rumfoot will be round for his Rheumatics Remedy soon. Did we bottle it, dear? I can't remember.'

'Yes, Grandma. Its all ready by the door – beside the fudge.'

'Oh, yes, so it is. Thank you, Hannah.' Grandma Fred folded her paper and got up from the table 'I'm just popping over to give Mrs Whitehead some of the Vitality Tonic we made yesterday. I promised I would. If Mr Rumfoot calls give him his remedy will you, dears? I won't be long.'

The kitchen door had no sooner closed than Hannah and Ben turned on Lucy.

'What do you think you're doing? I thought you wanted to go back tonight?' said Hannah.

'I do,' Lucy shouted, 'but how are we going to get out of the house tonight? And Grandma's bound to notice all the nasturtiums are gone. I think it's best to tell her.'

'Grandma will never believe us and even if she did, do you think she'd let us go wandering off into the woods late at night and into an Underground Burroway? I don't think so!' hissed Ben.

Lucy sat back with her arms folded, her blue glasses halfway down her nose.

'Arguing isn't going to solve anything. But she has a point, Ben,' said Hannah 'How *are* we going to get out of the house tonight?'

It was going to be difficult coming up with a good plan. They sat very quietly thinking hard for any excuse that would work.

'I've got it!' said Ben, looking extremely pleased with himself 'We could tell her we're going to sleep over at Gary Edmond's house!'

He was sure this was a brilliant idea and waited for their grateful reaction. But it didn't come.

'But they haven't got a spare bedroom and you always sleep on the floor. We can't *all* sleep on the floor. Besides, he doesn't really know Lucy and me and he wouldn't ask us, would he?' said Hannah.

Ben sunk down on his chair, deflated, knowing Hannah was right. Hannah tried to think of something by twiddling her hair and Lucy wiggled her glasses hoping for inspiration. Minutes passed.

'We could tell Grandma we were going to the cinema,' suggested Lucy.

Hannah concentrated. 'I don't think that will work. The last bus back is half past ten and she would worry if we weren't on it.'

They all studied the table as if a solution might jump up from the table mats. Eyes glazing, Lucy took a bite of cold toast and Ben drank the last of his orange juice.

'What about asking her to take us to the bridge club at the church hall tonight? We could sneak out the back when she was playing,' suggested Ben.

Hannah shook her head and raised her eyes to the ceiling. 'Honestly, that's never going to work.'

'Well, you think of something then!'

'OK, OK, I'm thinking,' said Hannah, but at that moment there was a loud knock. Mr Rumfoot's outline appeared through the kitchen door window.

'Here's your remedy, Mr Rumfoot,' said Hannah, handing him the bottle. 'It's all mixed for you and the instructions are on the label.'

'Thank ye kindly, Hannah. This'll do me a power of good, I can tell you.'

Ben bent to ruffle Bob's ears and give him one of Grandma's chocolate drops from the drawer. He noticed the cut on Bob's nose.

'What's wrong with Bob's nose, Mr Rumfoot?' he asked.

'Well, I told yer Grandma the story: he was in a scrap wi' some cat. Not up to rough stuff these days are yeh, Bob?' Mr Rumfoot paused. 'Was wonderin' if Bob could have more of the yella stuff yer Grandma gave me. Keeps lickin' it off but I think it's doing good. If it's no trouble, that is.'

'It's no trouble at all, Mr Rumfoot. I'll just get a jar.' Hannah rummaged in the cupboard for a small glass container and turned towards the jars on the wall to look for the coltsfoot balm.

Ben read the labels out loud as Hannah tried to find the right one.

'Infections of the kidney and bladder – *nasty*. Bronch-*ch*-itis.' Ben made a disgusting sound in his throat.

'Suppurating wounds – imagine all that yellow pus – *lovely*. Sedative ….'

'Cuts and bruises, that's the one,' said Hannah and she opened the jar, spooned some of the yellow coltsfoot balm into Mr Rumfoot's glass jar and screwed the lid on.

'Cat all right now?' asked Mr Rumfoot, looking round for Gertrude, but she was nowhere to be seen.

'Oh, yes,' said Hannah smiling weakly and catching Lucy's eye across the room in silent warning not to say anything. 'She must have been having an off day.'

'A funny turn more like it,' said Mr Rumfoot. He put the jar into his pocket and gave Bob another peppermint. 'Tell your Grandma "thanks". Bye fer now then and have a grand time on your holiday. I'm sure yeh will.'

Mr Rumfoot slowly made his way down the garden path and Hannah was just about to slide the coltsfoot back in place when Ben yelled.

'I've got it!'

'Got what?'

'I know how we'll get out tonight.'

'How?'

'Look here.'

Hannah and Lucy looked at the jar in Ben's hand. It read 'Sedative'.

'You can't be serious, Ben,' said Hannah.

'What?' said Lucy.

'It's the only way, Hannah. I can't think of anything else, can you?'

'What?' shouted Lucy.

'Well, maybe we shouldn't go back,' said Hannah.

'WILL SOMEONE TELL ME WHAT YOU'RE TALKING ABOUT!'

'Ben thinks we should drug Grandma Fred so she falls asleep again,' explained Hannah, horrified.

Lucy looked wildly at Ben. 'How would we do it?' she asked.

Hannah was aghast. 'Not you too! How can you both consider such a thing.'

'We could put some of the sleeping powder in Grandma's hot chocolate tonight. She'll never know and she'll sleep right through just like she did last night. It would be quite safe,' said Ben.

'You heard her say what a good sleep she had,' added Lucy.

'I can't do it,'said Hannah.

'You won't have to. I'll do it,' said Ben.

'You can't be sure it's safe,' protested Hannah.

'Well, you heard Grandma say there's no poisonous plants in her garden and providing we don't swallow a wheelbarrow full, we'll come to no harm. We'll just make sure we don't give her a wheelbarrow full,' said Ben, grinning.

That afternoon, Hannah felt a dreadful pang of guilt every time she looked at Grandma Fred and tried, as best she could, to stay out of the way. As long as she had nothing to do with making the hot chocolate Hannah reluctantly agreed she'd go back with them.

They still had to work out what they would say to the Council of Alter-Idem. Chancellor Barbelly had said it would be tricky to persuade the Council to let them stay so they needed a plan. In Ben's bedroom they got down to work.

'Well, what do we know about them for sure?' asked Hannah, ready with a pencil and paper to write the points down, trying to blot thoughts of hot chocolate from her mind.

'We know that Hironymus Grossus, the Chancellor of Gorgonz City, is horrible,' said Lucy as a starter.

'And how do we know that? asked Ben sarcastically.

'Because all the goblins are ugly and unfriendly,' said Lucy.

'It doesn't follow that if someone's ugly they're a horrible person,' said Ben. 'That's like saying a good-looking person is a nice person. I mean, look at you. You look OK but you're horrible.'

Lucy stuck out her tongue.

'OK, we know the goblins like to know all about what's going on in the other villages – Milli told us that. Oh, I hope she's all right,' said Hannah.

''Course she'll be all right,' said Ben 'Honestly, Hannah, you worry too much.'

'Hmm … what else do we know?' asked Hannah.

'We know those from Sombrono are a bit moody,' said Ben.

'Do we?' asked Hannah.

'Hunnik said so,' said Ben. 'She said they get foot rot.'

'How do you work out they're moody from that? asked Lucy.

'Well, wouldn't you be moody if you had foot rot?'

'Might be moody,' wrote Hannah.

'You're not writing that down are you? said Lucy sounding disgusted.

'Now, what else?'

'Socratown's full of high priestesses,' said Lucy, sighing.

'Thelma did say something about that, didn't she. I wonder what she meant?' said Hannah.

'All the women have high opinions of themselves?' suggested Ben. 'You two could live there permanently.'

'Very funny,' said Lucy. 'She also said that Puddlelake was nice but you had to watch your back with them too.'

'So, the Chancellor of Puddlelake might be devious then?' Hannah made a note. 'Can you remember anything else?'

'The only other thing I remember, said Lucy 'is that Thelma said some folk think Hironymus Grossus might have stolen the sixth key so no one else finds it.'

'That sounds interesting,' said Ben. 'He'd probably vote against us being allowed to look for it then wouldn't he?'

'Probably,' agreed Hannah.

'I told you he'd be horrible,' said Lucy.

'Well, Zanting Barbelly would likely be on our side so that equals the score there,' said Ben. 'Who else do we think might want the key found?'

'It's hard to say. We hardly know anything about any of them,' said Hannah.

'Where does that leave us then?' asked Ben.

'I think we've got to try and appeal to the Chancellors of Socratown, Puddlelake and Sombrono, and assume Hironymus Grossus, won't agree to anything,' reasoned Hannah.

'Agreed,' said Lucy.

'Agreed,' said Ben.

After tea things got worse. Hannah couldn't look anyone in the eye. Every time she glanced over at the racks of herbal cures, the word SEDATIVE seemed to jump out at her just like the label DEADLY NIGHTSHADE. She started to feel unwell. She couldn't let Ben do it. No, they wouldn't do it, she decided. It was a silly idea anyway. They would just forget all about going back.

'Psst! Hannah, one teaspoon or two?' The teaspoon in Ben's hand hovered over the mug of hot chocolate but before Hannah could tell him to pour it down the sink or knock it out of his hand, Grandma entered the kitchen.

'One sugar for me, dear,' she said.

'Right then, Grandma.' Ben quickly stirred in one sugar with another teaspoon of sedative and handed Grandma Fred the mug. Hannah watched dumbly as Grandma took a sip and went into the other room to watch television.

'Not long now,' said Ben rubbing his hands together.

'Oh, shut up,' snapped Hannah.

After fifteen minutes she could bear it no longer. She crept along the hall and peered into the living room. The back of Grandma Fred's head was visible above the chair beside Lucy who was sitting stroking Gertrude.

'Lucy, psst!'

Lucy swung round.

Hannah pointed noiselessly at Grandma, looking as though she'd found half a worm in her sandwich.

'She's asleep. Don't worry,' said Lucy.

Ben appeared in the doorway. 'Should've practised on Gertrude first,' he said. Gertrude bolted from the room.

'Do you think she'll wake up?' asked Lucy. 'I don't mean, ever, I mean before we get back?'

Ben shrugged.

'Don't know,' said Hannah 'But let's hope she thinks we're in bed.'

'It's ten to seven. We'd better go,' said Ben, looking at his watch.

'Better eat these first,' said Hannah, handing round the bogbean leaves. At one minute to seven they were at the foot of the chestnut tree … waiting.

Chapter 7

The Council of Alter-Idem

Dolfi appeared as he said he would at exactly seven o'clock, his eyebrows flat and shiny. They seemed to be held down by a coating of wax. Hannah didn't mention it. Dolfi brought his wand down smartly, sending yellow and blue sparks hurtling forward, making them smaller again, before Hannah had even finished blinking. Now they knew the shrinking process didn't hurt it was over much too quickly.

The faint hum from the Sound Modulator grew louder as they walked the short distance to the Portway. It was busier than they had seen it before. Villagers huddled around the burroways and angry words rose hissing like steam from every quarter. Everyone seemed to be blaming each other for something although Hannah couldn't quite make out what was being said. Horace was flitting from group to group, straining to hear the gossip, and was too busy to notice them walking over the platform towards Gorgonz City.

Hannah looked at the inscription below the sign. 'What does it mean?' she asked Dolfi quietly.

'*Ad extremum*? It means "to the extreme".'

Given what they'd heard about Hironymus Grossus so far, Hannah thought this very appropriate.

They managed to board the scarab without attracting attention, which wasn't too difficult with the commotion going on, and the beetle moved away from the platform. Just before it spread its wings, they caught a few words:

'Don't know where it came from ....'

'Can't swim in the lake now ... the children are terrified.'

'Wouldn't put it past Grossus to have a hand in this.'

The scarab took off just as Horace noticed them.

'Peeeeeeeeeeeeeeeepp.'

His whistle sounded to make them stop but it was too late and the scarab sailed gracefully into the dark tunnel, away from his searching questions.

'What were the crowd talking about?' asked Hannah.

'I don't rightly know; I haven't heard anything about it yet,' said Dolfi. A piece of wax sprang loose from his left eyebrow. 'They're kelpies from Puddlelake but I don't know what's happened that they can't swim in their lake. Perhaps we'll find out later.'

'How's Milli?' asked Hannah, trying not to stare at the remaining wax.

'She's well on the mend now, thanks to you. What you did yesterday was truly wonderful. We can't thank you enough …. I really feared the worst. I hope you can convince the Council to let you come back. I'm sure you would enjoy seeing around our land. At the very least you'd be welcome in Pickletullum.'

'We've put our thoughts down,' said Ben, waving the paper in his hand.

'Good idea,' said Dolfi. 'You'll need to be well prepared.'

'Are all goblins as mean as Hironymus Grossus?' asked Lucy.

'They are a very single-minded people, Lucy.' Dolfi raised his eyebrows and another piece of wax broke free. 'That doesn't make them mean exactly, but they do tend to think their point of view is the only way to see things when the Harmony Rules tell us points of view other than our own are equally valid. The goblins ignore that wisdom now.'

'That makes them mean then, doesn't it?' she insisted, ignoring the flaking wax.

'Well, it depends on your point of view,' said Dolfi, mischievously. His smile faded. 'I've got something else to tell you.' The scarab buzzed along, the glow from the fireflies zipping past like yellow darts while they waited.

'There was a break-in last night, after you left. This morning when Thelma opened up the Apothecary she noticed glass on the floor and the skylight was broken although everything else looked fine. At first she thought an owl or a land-eagle had crashed into the window. But then she checked the basement. The Precious Fires are gone.'

'Gone? What, all of them?' asked Hannah.

'I'm afraid so. It's very worrying. Very few people knew we had them or what they can do. Thank Zamada they weren't stolen before the Cleansing Potion was made or the weakest wouldn't have survived. The fires increase the effectiveness and strength of any potion so it worked even on those close to death.'

'But this is terrible,' said Hannah. 'Only someone who doesn't want to share their powers would want to steal them.'

'That's what's worrying me,' said Dolfi. 'We regarded ourselves as keepers of the Fires only until another Supreme Parlator is appointed. Then all the villages would be able to use them without fighting about who should keep them or what they should be used for.'

'Have you any idea who stole them?' asked Ben.

'No one saw anything so I guess the invisible raiders.'

Behind them a harsh buzzing had been getting louder and a sudden horn blast made them jump. Another scarab was at their tail honking to make them move over. Two goblins sat aboard.

'Oh, Great Gobstoppers, look at them,' one guffawed, leaning over the side to get a better look as the scarab zigzagged behind. He wasn't even trying to keep his voice down. 'Have you ever seen anything like it in your whole life?' he asked the other, staring straight at Hannah, Ben and Lucy.

Lucy gave them a nasty stare, wrinkling her nose and curling her lip so that even Grandma Fred might think she was not quite at her loveliest.

'What a rude person,' said Hannah loudly.

'Don't point, Kuzu, it's so roo-d,' mocked the second goblin.

The two goblins continued to point and laugh as their scarab swerved and shot off down the wrong side of the burroway.

'He's got a cheek,' said Ben. 'He's the one who looks like a chewed up dog biscuit.'

'That makes you just as bad as him,' said Hannah.

'Whose side are you on?'

Gorgonz City and Pickltullum looked very different. The scarab landed some distance from the burroway beside a landslide of stone boulders which sat against a bleak rock face. Some looked so big and round it was hard to imagine how they had got there. There was nothing much else to see apart from small tufts of grass and straggly heathers which clung to the sheared stone. There were no houses or buildings of any sort. It didn't seem possible for a city to be there.

'Follow me,' said Dolfi, walking towards one of the enormous boulders. He ducked into a narrow crevice. Inside, the rock transformed into a huge stone chamber so highly polished Hannah could see herself reflected in the ceiling and in the walls. Dolfi acknowledged the goblin at the desk.

'Dolfi Greenlees from Pickletullum,' he said. The goblin looked down his list.

'Ah yes, Chancellor Barbelly is expecting you. You know where to go, don't you?'

'Yes, thank you,' said Dolfi.

The goblin pointed the way to his right. All Hannah could see was a smooth, polished, green stone wall.

Dolfi walked towards it; the wall shimmered and ripples appeared on its surface as if a pool of dark water had been disturbed, and a moving escalator appeared from no-where.

'Come on,' said Dolfi, stepping onto it.

They followed on behind him and began to rise. Black candles flickered on the walls which seemed to be covered with smudged lines but, as the escalator rose, Hannah noticed in amazement, the sooty scribbles began to come into focus.

Eventually the haphazard lines formed a perfectly painted face. 'Look at that,' she called.

'That's Hironymus Grossus, Chancellor of Gorgonz City,' said Dolfi watching them staring at the face as it passed.

'Boy, does his face need an iron,' said Ben turning for a longer look.

A dark sorrowful face now appeared. 'That's Jacobus Mors, Chancellor of Sombrono.' They watched the heavy eyes drift past.

'And you know Zanting Barbelly.' Zanting's familiar rosy round face went smiling by. A woman's face began taking shape; a very long nose and pointed chin grew smaller, thin red lines grew shorter and suddenly a haughty face, was looking down at them.

'That's Quilla Vanepike, Chancellor of Puddlelake,' said Dolfi.

Her eyes seemed to look straight at them and eerily held their gaze even when they had passed and begun ascending in the opposite direction.

'And that's Astra Manda, Chancellor of Socratown,' Dolfi said, nodding to the face of a woman whose wispy hair was standing in peaks. Tiny flowers seemed to hang in the air around her ears and spill down onto her shoulders.

'She looks nice,' said Lucy.

'And that, of course,' said Dolfi looking up as the escalator reached the top, 'is the last Supreme Parlator.'

They stepped off the escalator and lifted their eyes to the portrait of the late, great, Zamada above the doorway. She did indeed look like a great queen. She had a hooked nose and held her head very straight and high as if she was looking into the distance a long way and was able to see what was there. She had a calm and steady look on her face, kind but firm at the same time. On her head was the Magical Crown of Keys with the large red ruby of the sixth key at the front. Even in the portrait the Crown seemed to radiate magical essence. It was magnificent. Beneath the large red ruby two diamonds sat side by side. To the right of the ruby a sapphire blazed above two diamonds and to the left, an emerald gleamed. Three other jewelled keys made up the crown, their gold teeth curving and interlocking with the next.

They stepped through the doorway and immediately passed under a huge bronze statue of a tree whose branches spread like an umbrella over a large square hall. Several large red sofas rested along the smooth polished green stone walls.

Outside a large, imposing set of gold doors a goblin was sitting in a glass chair. Scenes from the five villages were intricately carved upon the doors and they could quite clearly make out Puddlelake's lake.

'Can you let the Council know that Dolfi Greenlees is here, please,' said Dolfi. The goblin got up from his chair and disappeared inside.

'This chamber is called the Crystal Room,' said Dolfi quietly 'You'll see why in a minute.'

The goblin reappeared a few moments later. 'You may enter,' he said and held the door open for them to walk through.

'Ah, Dolfi, I was just telling the Council you were late because you were bringing important information for them to consider,' said Zanting Barbelly jovially from the end of the table.

Only one seat, at the head of the table, remained empty and Hannah supposed that was where the Supreme Parlator would sit, if there was one.

The chamber was the most amazing room they had ever been in. The white walls glistened and from the domed ceiling hung a mass of glinting, sparkling, silver crystals. The largest of them looked as if it might fall onto the great table below at any moment and shatter into a million shards. All around gold ornaments and chalices glinted.

Across the table Hannah could see the wispy-haired woman sitting with her hands clasped before her. She looked up and gave them a bemused smile. Next to her Jacobus Mors looked even more sorrowful than his portrait. He looked slightly surprised when they entered but said nothing.

It wasn't long before the regal quiet was broken.

'What is the meaning of this!' someone shrieked. Quilla Vanepike, Chancellor of Puddlelake, jumped to her feet and drew herself to her full height. The pearls around her neck quivered. Towering above her shoulders, her pointed wings looked like spears.

One Chancellor still sat with his back to them, but not for long. Hironymus Grossus, Chancellor of Gorgonz City, turned brusquely when he heard Quilla Vanepike's outburst.

'WHAT ARE YOU UP TO, BARBELLY?' he thundered, in a voice that sounded like a lorry load of gravel being tipped onto a tin roof, when he saw who was with Dolfi,

Lucy shrank back in fright. Hironymus Grossus was covered in warts. One eyebrow, and the bulging eye beneath it, was higher than the other. A tusk-like tooth protruded from his blubbery lips and his breath, which reached them in a wave, could have knocked out a rhinoceros.

'Nothing that won't be explained,' said Chancellor Barbelly cheerfully. 'It's Council business I assure you. It's on the agenda if you care to look.'

Quilla Vanepike stood stiffly with both hands stretched down to the table in front of her, looking as if she was deciding what to do.

'This is most irregular. You've got one minute to explain yourself, Barbelly,' she said defiantly before sitting down.

'Just what I intend to do … it's Council business,' said Chancellor Barbelly, wiggling the tips of his fingers together as if he was playing an invisible instrument.

Hironymus Grossus glowered like a mad bull and blustered. 'Funny smelling business more like, Barbelly!'

Dolfi guided Hannah, Ben and Lucy to sit in glass chairs against the wall then went to sit at Chancellor Barbelly's right hand side. Each Chancellor exchanged words with his or her second in command. One man sat on his own. They didn't like the look of him.

Chancellor Barbelly began to speak.

'Fellow Chancellors and Under-secretary Odo, what I have to tell you is a story that will cause you to give thanks, as do the people of Pickeltullum. Only three short days ago Pickletullum was in the ravages of a fatal disease. A fever was spreading among us at a frightening pace and we knew we had limited time to treat it. When Herbert Rootvine, our respected Potion Maker, fell ill himself I dispatched Dolfi to bring the Peeps, who we knew had knowledge of herbs and the ways of our medicine, to come and help us. Only once before in our land's history have we known such a fever – in the time of Zamada when a similar plague ravaged our lands. History tells us every village was then affected. It could have happened again but the Peeps have saved us. We owe them a great debt.' All eyes fell on Hannah, Ben and Lucy in the quiet that followed.

'However, this fever is not the only bedevilment we have suffered of late.'

Mumbles of agreement issued from around the table.

'Under-secretary Odo, can you remind us of the afflictions so far endured by our villages?'

The Under-secretary rose from his chair and walked to the front of the large glass table. His black hair, parted down the middle, was greased down at each side. Hannah saw a drip of something fall onto the document he was holding; she wasn't sure if it had come from his hair or his nose.

The Under-secretary began. 'Sombrono has had its Vision Ball stolen,' he said importantly.

Some muttering was heard from Jacobus Mors and his second.

'Anything to add, Jacobus?' asked Chancellor Barbelly, his eyes smiling. Jacobus Mors shook his head, looking as dull as Zanting Barbelly looked bright.

'Wonder what they use a Vision Ball for?' whispered Ben.

Vasril Odo forced a cough to signal silence and then continued. 'Socratown has had its Scales of Balance and Judgement stolen.' His deep-set eyes peered in the direction of the Chancellor of Socratown who conferred with her second.

'Anything to add, Astra?' asked Chancellor Barbelly.

'Only that our Scales are a great loss to us all, not just the people of Socratown,' said Astra Manda calmly.

'They are indeed,' agreed Chancellor Barbelly, nodding. There was a brief pause. 'Under-secretary, if you please.'

'I DON'T SEE WHERE THIS IS LEADING US, BARBELLY,' boomed Hironymus Grossus. He wasn't the only one to be impatient.

'Nor do I,' roared Quilla Vanepike 'Not only have *we* had our entire store of air-lilies stolen, which won't bloom again for another thirty moons, we have now been *invaded*!' She thumped the table with her fists. Hannah jumped. 'This is too much. Even if the sixth key *was* found now we wouldn't be able to reach our key without the air-lilies and now this … this … MONSTER!'

This was obviously news to Chancellor Barbelly, who blinked while taking it in.

'What monster?'

'THE TERROSAUR THAT'S IN OUR LAKE,' screamed Quilla Vanepike, her voice shaking with fury. Her clenched fists flew open revealing long nails that looked as if *they* belonged on a monster except that they were pink.

'A water-dragon? In your lake?' spluttered Chancellor Barbelly.

'You heard.'

'You sure you didn't put it there yourself!' said Hironymus Grossus, slapping the table and guffawing. Quilla Vanepike turned to give him the most scornful look Hannah had ever seen.

'Oh my, this is serious. Under-secretary, please make sure this is recorded in the minutes,' said Chancellor Barbelly, flapping his hands as if they were on fire.

'What good is that going to do?' bellowed Quilla Vanepike.

'That brings me to my point,' said Chancellor Barbelly. 'Please bear with me. Just last night the invisible raiders struck Pickletullum too and stole something that was very … er … precious to us.'

'Stole your supply of Black-Hag whisky did they?' Chancellor Grossus belly-laughed so loudly and forcefully that Quilla Vanepike stuck her taloned fingers in her ears but how she didn't do herself an injury was hard to guess. A second later Grossus's putrid breath once again rolled across the table, reminding them strongly of a camel on a dung heap eating rotting sprouts for lunch. Ben went cross-eyed.

'It is no laughing matter, my dear Chancellor,' said Chancellor Barbelly, 'if the raiders are among us and are making themselves invisible to plunder their own people. Not only is it against the Harmony Rules …'

'Harmony Rules … Pahh!' spat Hironymus Grossus contemptuously, a thread of spit swinging from his lip.

But Chancellor Barbelly continued: 'These happenings are lamentable, just deplorable, the closeness and support we have all enjoyed in the past is being destroyed. Instead of working with each other as we did in Zamada's time we are working on our own and become more suspicious of each other with every moon that passes. Not a good state of affairs. I therefore propose that we make another search for the lost sixth key. Once found, the Crown of Keys can be assembled. It will choose a new Supreme Parlator and we will enjoy unity and guidance once more.'

'Pretty words, Barbelly,' Grossus slavered. 'Why will this time be any different? It hasn't been found in the past.'

Nods and murmurs of agreement croaked around the room.

'This time will be different because … *we have help*.' Chancellor Barbelly spoke the words very clearly. 'The Peeps have agreed to help us find it.'

For a second time all eyes in the room fell on Hannah, Ben and Lucy. They wished the glass chairs weren't quite so uncomfortable.

Grunts and garbles passed once more between Chancellor and second as they reacted to this proposal but before the objections could start Zanting Barbelly went on:

'Of course, there should be a vote but before we make up our minds completely we owe these young people the chance to put their case to us. We owe them that at least, for in truth, we can never repay the debt we owe them in saving Pickletullum.'

Dolfi leaned back to whisper to them and as the last piece of wax pinged to the floor the final tuft of eyebrow escaped. 'You will only get one chance, so grab it. Remember: *Audentes fortuna juvat*.' He quickly resumed his position.

'What does that mean again?' Ben whispered to Hannah and Lucy.

'Search me,' said Lucy.

'Fortune favours the bold,' said Hannah without thinking.

'How did you remember that?' asked Ben in surprise.

'I don't know,' said Hannah.

None of the Chancellors spoke to object. It was a good start.

'*THWUMP!*' Under-secretary Odo walloped the table with a red, padded, wooden hammer and stepped forward to address the Council once again. His black wings lay flat against his black jacket and from behind, the points of his tail coat made him look like a tall earwig. Hannah shivered.

'I call upon our invited guests to state their business,' he declared then walked to sit down again. As he passed they sniffed another very strange smell – a cross between toilet cleaner and a tuna sandwich. Unpleasant as it was it was not nearly as revolting as Hironymus Grossus's bad breath which they still occasionally got whiffs of even though they were farthest away.

Ben rose from his glass chair, which had heated up nicely now, and went to stand on Chancellor Barbelly's left hand side.

'Ladies and Gentlemen … er, Chancellors …'

There was a little noise from his left and Ben remembered: '… and Under-secretary Odo. We are not from this land it is true, and we understand that you might not want us here.'

'You've got that right, Peep,' sneered Grossus.

'The boy deserves a chance, Chancellor Grossus,' said Astra Manda mildly.

'Humph.'

'My sisters and I would like to help you find the sixth key. We are not looking for anything from you except to be allowed to visit your villages. Maybe *because* we are different we may think of clues and places to look that you have not thought of so far. We might come up with new ideas. Perhaps a fresh approach is needed. The important thing is to find the lost sixth key. In our world too we often think our own way is best and that we don't need each other but the greatest things have always been achieved by co-operating with a common purpose.' Ben looked around the room. Everyone still seemed to be listening, except Hironymus Grossus who was cleaning out his ear with a grey hanky which he had twisted into a spiral.

'Milli Maccabees asked us to try to make a Cleansing Potion and we made one. I'm asking you to let try to find the lost sixth key. I think we can find it.' Ben sat down.

'Well done,' whispered Hannah and Lucy.

'Well spoken, young Ben,' said Chancellor Barbelly. 'Does anyone have anything they would like to ask our young friends?'

Predictably, Hironymus Grossus spoke first.

'Everyone talks about co-operation. *Sugar fancy* in my opinion and like too much sugar, it causes rot!' Hannah looked at his single yellow tusk and large belly which didn't look like they belonged to someone who lived on rain water and lettuce leaves.

'We need more independence, not less,' he bellowed. 'Co-operation is for the weak and feeble minded! The strong should get their just rewards.'

'No one is suggesting we all behave the same, Chancellor. Our differences can become, in fact, our greatest strength if we work together,' said Astra Manda calmly.

'Sugar fancy!' barked Grossus.

Quilla Vanepike had been whispering with her second for a long time and now looked about to speak.

'Our biggest problem is the raiders … and the Terrosaur in our lake,' she announced, to make sure no one had forgotten, as she got to her feet. 'You're not going to be able to help us with them are you?' Her tone suggested she already knew the answer.

'No, we're not,' Ben agreed reluctantly.

'Any more questions?' Chancellor Barbelly cut in quickly.

'What's the point of more upheaval?' said Jacobus Mors, his voice heavy and sad.

'I would have thought it was obvious, Jacobus,' said Chancellor Barbelly, trying not to sound unkind. 'So we might reach a better place, so we might each benefit in the future. Your own village creed is *Vivimus veritas* – let us live with truth. Isn't it true that finding the sixth key will bring a better life?'

'It is also true that we've tried before and failed,' said Chancellor Mors.

In the moment or two of quiet that followed everyone gathered their thoughts and Vasril Odo scribbled a record of what had been said in his minutes book. Hannah noticed the page turning itself.

'Does anyone else have anything to add before we take a vote?' asked Chancellor Barbelly. Hannah and Lucy exchanged anxious glances.

'It's not looking too good is it?' Hannah whispered. Ben wasn't smiling either. The Chancellors were conferring again and when they finally turned towards the table Hannah, Ben and Lucy all sat tensely, knees together.

'No further views?' said Chancellor Barbelly a final time, 'then the vote please

Under-secretary.'

Vasril Odo stood to address the chamber.

'*THWUMP!*'

'Chancellors all rise,' he called. 'I ask you to declare your vote when your name is called. The vote is: 'Should we allow the Peeps to return to look for the sixth key – Yea or Nay.' Everyone rose from the heavy glass chairs and looked forward into space.

'Oh no, I can't bear to hear,' whispered Lucy, holding her hands over her ears.

'Me neither,' said Hannah, biting her bottom lip.

The time had come. In a few seconds they would know if they would return or not. If they were going to win they wished it was all over and if they were going to lose they wished the moment would last forever.

'Gorgonz City,' called Vasril Odo.

'NAY,' Grossus bellowed.

'No surprises there then,' Ben whispered, shuffling in his seat. The suspense was almost too much.

'Socratown.'

There was a moment of silence.

'Yea,' called Astra Manda in a steady, dignified voice.

'One vote each way,' said Hannah, smiling weakly.

'Pickletullum.'

'Yea.'

'Good old Chancellor Barbelly. That's two to one,' said Ben. All too quickly the next vote was called.

'Sombrono.'

'This is the one we want,' said Ben.

'Please! Please!' Lucy mouthed silently; Hannah crossed her fingers. Every hair on their arms seemed to be prickling their skin. Then they heard it.

'Nay,' said Jacobus Mors.

'Bad luck,' said Dolfi, seeing them look like their hearts were weighed down with sandbags.

'Grumpy old git,' said Ben in a mumble. 'That's two yeas and two nays. Vanepike has the last vote and she isn't going to say yes, is she?'

'Does that mean we can't come back?' Lucy's lip started to wobble.

'Puddlelake.'

'I'm afraid it looks like it,' said Hannah. Lucy looked as if she was about to cry. It wasn't fair. They hadn't been given a fighting chance. It just wasn't fair.

They waited.

'Yea.'

Lucy looked up. 'What does that mean?' she asked.

'She voted for us – I can't believe it!' cried Hannah.

'Yes!' said Ben, punching the air with his fist.

'YES!' they cheered together.

Chancellor Barbelly grinned widely at them and Dolfi turned round to congratulate them.

'Quiet *please*!' demanded Vasril Odo, giving them an unpleasant stare. 'The Yeas have it,' he said finally, and sat down.

Chancellor Barbelly spoke. 'This is a great day for us all. I have a good feeling that times are changing for the better.' He beamed at everyone sitting around the chamber.

'This is a mistake! There'll be nothing but more trouble to come, mark my words!' shouted Hironymus Grossus.

'Due process has been followed, Chancellor. We must all abide by the rules or we'll never get anywhere,' smoothed Chancellor Barbelly.

'Well, they won't get Gorgonz City's key. The raiders have stolen it!'

'My dear Hironymus, you didn't mention this before ….'

'Well, I'm mentioning it now,' Grossus stormed. 'It's gone and there's nothing I can do about it.'

Everyone in the room looked stunned except Vasril Odo who made a note in his book. There was turmoil in the chamber as once again everyone started complaining about what had gone wrong in the villages, all that had been stolen, and Quilla Vanepike ranted again about the Terrosaur in their lake which, she said, was scaring them all witless, had eaten all the ducks and fish and was now eating the cows that stupidly wandered too close. It wouldn't be long before it started eating the villagers. Everyone started shouting to be heard. It was chaos.

Dolfi ushered Hannah, Ben and Lucy outside the chamber where they waited on one of the big red leather sofas until the Council finished dealing with its other business.

'I can't believe we can come back!' said Lucy, bouncing up and down.

'We were so lucky,' said Ben. 'Fancy Vanepike voting for us.'

'I told you Hironymus Grossus was horrible,' said Lucy.

'What about that breath?' said Ben, holding his nose.

'And what was all that about their key being stolen?' said Hannah. 'I don't believe him.'

'Neither do I. I wouldn't trust him further than I could spit.' Ben was just about to show them how far he could spit when he remembered there was a goblin watching.

'Thelma did say the raiders had stolen things from all the villages,' said Lucy.

'Could be a cover though, couldn't it, unless the raiders are not from the villages,' said Ben.

'I wonder what will happen next,' said Lucy, lowering her voice.

'I think that will be largely up to us,' said Ben.

'I agree,' said Hannah. 'If we're going to try and find the key we really ought to think about what we need to do now.'

'I think we should speak to Thelma again,' said Lucy.

'Good idea.'

'And Dolfi's bound to tell us everything he knows,' added Ben.

They had no idea how long the Council business was going to take but they scarcely noticed the time going by as there was so much to talk about.

'Even if we do find the sixth key we won't be able to put the crown together without all the other keys,' said Ben. 'We'll need to collect them all.'

'Sounds like Puddlelake's key is kept at the bottom of the lake and now there's some sort of water-dragon swimming around in it,' said Hannah.

'Bit of bad timing.'

'Sounds suspicious, doesn't it?' continued Hannah.

'I bet Hironymus Grossus put it there,' said Lucy.

'You would,' said Ben.

'And there's something else that's strange,' said Hannah, 'The fever. This is the second time they've had a fever ....'

'But this one only affected Pickletullum,' Ben reminded her.

'Yes, but it could just as easily have spread to the other villages too. Chancellor Barbelly said so.'

'We've got enough to think about now without bothering about that,' said Ben.

They heard a heavy clunk and the Goblin quickly moved from his chair to help open the huge gold doors. The Chancellors and their seconds filed out and walked towards the green wall beneath the bronze tree statue. One by one they stepped through the quivering marble and disappeared. Hannah noticed Hironymus Grossus look up uneasily at the statue as he stepped through.

'Sugar fancy,' they heard as the last pronged tip of his leather girdle disappeared.

Dolfi and Zanting Barbelly appeared at their side.

'A most satisfactory ending to the day,' said Chancellor Barbelly. 'I am most pleased at the outcome.' He smiled. 'I will leave you with Dolfi and look forward to greeting you again soon. If there is anything you need in your search for the key just make the arrangements with Dolfi. I wish you luck and the spirit of Zamada be with you.' He bowed and followed on behind Astra Manda through the rippling wall.

On the way down the escalator with Dolfi they noticed the painted faces had changed; Chancellor Grossus now looked even grumpier, Chancellor Manda looked even calmer and Chancellor Barbelly was positively beaming. No one could tell if Jacobus Mors looked any different but Chancellor Vanepike had a very strange look in her eye. It was as if she was smirking but trying not to let it show on her face.

Just as they stepped off, they noticed the late, great Zamada's portrait smiling down at them.

That night in bed Hannah couldn't stop herself thinking over everything that had happened that evening. Was it a coincidence there was now a water-dragon, a

Terrosaur, in the lake? Who were the raiders and why were they stealing all these things from the villages? Was Chancellor Grossus telling the truth about Gorgonz City's key? And was she imagining it or was there something about the tree statue that Grossus didn't like?

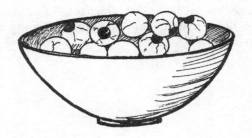

Chapter 8

The Prophecy

'That hot chocolate was delicious,' said Grandma Fred next morning 'You'll have to take charge of making it every night, Ben. And do you know, I fell asleep in the chair again. These warm summer evenings are so relaxing.'

Hannah smiled guiltily while Ben managed to keep a look of perfect innocence on his face and asked if they could go to the cinema that afternoon. Hannah thought he had no conscience at all. Grandma wiped the crumbs from the side of her mouth. 'I don't see why not, you know the way after all and the bus brings you straight back.'

'You don't have to worry about us so much, Grandma,' said Hannah.

'Oh, I know that, dear,' she replied, 'but I wouldn't like you to be stranded somewhere, when I haven't got a car. What's on anyway?'

Ben and Hannah stared at each other; they hadn't thought to check the paper.

'It's *A Bug's Life*,' said Lucy suddenly, saying the first film that came into her head.

'Funny name for a film,' said Grandma. 'When I was younger it was *Lassie Come Home* and *The Lovebug* … but that was a car not a bug … in my day anyway.'

With the matter of the cinema settled they were free to meet Dolfi at one o'clock and Hannah quickly changed the subject.

'What do you need done this morning, Grandma?' she asked.

'Well, there's still all those stems waiting to be hung up on the pulley there.' Grandma pointed to three big baskets full of sage on the floor beside the kitchen table. 'And I'd like all the marigolds picked today if we can.'

'That'll not take us long,' said Ben and he lowered the pulley to make a start.

'I can't wait to go back now,' Hannah whispered when Grandma had left the room.

'Me too,' said Ben.

'Where's Lucy?' asked Hannah.

'Fussing over Gertrude no doubt. Stupid cat just chases mice all day.'

'I seem to remember you saying you'd do something unpleasant to a mouse.'

'That was different. That was Frosty Fotheringham.'

'Rrright,' said Hannah, raising her eyes to the ceiling.

As soon as they had finished hanging up the bundles of sage, Ben and Hannah headed out to the garden to pick the marigolds.

'At least Grandma doesn't suspect we're up to anything unusual and we don't have to put anything in her hot chocolate tonight. If she spent the next fortnight waking up in her chair she'd start to wonder,' said Ben and he beheaded a clump of marigolds with a whack from his stick.

'We'd better take more of these,' said Hannah, picking the leaves off a bogbean plant nearby and putting them in her pocket. 'Just in case we need them.'

At ten to one they headed for the door.

'Got your money,' asked Grandma Fred.

'Yes, Grandma.'

'Just checking,' she said. 'Enjoy your film.'

At one o'clock they stood waiting at the foot of the chestnut tree.

They heard the now familiar *zing* and watched as the hole opened up between the roots of the chestnut tree. Dolfi had arrived and this time Milli was with him.

'I'm so much better, thank you,' Milli replied when they asked how she was. 'Dolfi's told me all about the Council meeting and you coming back to look for the sixth key. Everyone's talking about it in the village.'

'Yes, and Horace is furious he didn't know before anyone else,' added Dolfi.

He certainly was.

When they arrived in the Portway he could barely contain his irritation. He hovered over them, wings humming noisily on the spot, and forced himself to smile.

'Back to start your search then,' he said, still hoping to find out something no one else knew.

'Yes, we're looking forward to it,' said Hannah.

'You'll not find everyone willing to help but you can count on me. Whatever you need to know, I'm the one to ask,' he said tightly.

'We'll keep it in mind, thanks,' said Hannah, hurrying past.

They heard him mutter 'Dribbling dandelions,' as they boarded the scarab and flew off towards Pickletullum.

They had barely walked a couple of yards up the village street when they were surrounded by a hoard of excited people.

'We are so grateful,' said one man, not happy until he had shaken each of their hands in turn and whose wife and children were waiting to shake their hands too.

'We are so pleased to meet you,' they said.

'Midas Plank,' said a man, tucking his hat under his arm and taking Hannah's hand. 'Bank manager in Pickletullum. You saved my life, I believe. Very grateful, very grateful.'

'Roselle,' said a young woman. 'It is so nice to say thank you in person.'

They could hardly move for people wanting to thank them for making the Cleansing Potion and wish them well in their search for the sixth key. Some though, were not quite so enthusiastic.

'Can't see you findin' it,' said an old man with a crooked walking stick, 'but so long as it's you doing the searching and not me. Some of us got no strength left.'

Slowly, they made their way to the Apothecary and prised themselves inside. Jasper, still looking like a yellow canary and still no bigger than an egg cup, immediately started cawing. Outside, people jostled and waved to them through the window.

'Quiet, Jasper,' called Thelma.

'We didn't expect this,' said Hannah, leaning heavily against the door.

'Everyone's so friendly.' Ben noticed a lopsided smile appear on Dolfi's face.

'Anyone like a cup of tea?' asked Thelma.

'That would be very nice, Thelma. I'm sure we could all do with one,' said Dolfi, wiping his brow then trying to smooth his eyebrows flat and loosen his collar at the same time.

Thelma led the way. Through in the back of the shop, Dr Herbert Rootvine, now fully recovered, was watching them over the top of his glasses when they entered. He was a tall man with white hair that flicked up from his shoulders and he was wearing a pink spotted bow tie. Studded to the braces of his blue and green striped trousers was a badge in the shape of a cauldron with the words 'Master Potion Maker' on it.

'This is Dr Herbert Rootvine,' said Dolfi.

'I hear you did some splendid work,' said Dr Rootvine, smiling. 'A marvellous job! May I offer my congratulations. I hear that you are now going to try and find the sixth key!'

He certainly seemed welcoming enough, Hannah thought, almost too welcoming, as if he was trying to sound delighted but wasn't really.

'Let's all have a cuppa and you can tell us about your plans,' he said, gesturing towards the table.

Dr Rootvine flourished his wooden spoon and seven cups and saucers rose from a shelf and floated down smartly, one after the other, clinking to a stop at each place round the table. Thelma filled the teapot, dropped the lid into place and watched it bob across the room. It landed on a mat in the middle of the table beside the milk jug and the sugar bowl, which winked at Hannah. Jasper stayed perched on Thelma's head but made it clear he didn't like anything else flying around except him.

'Now, Lucy, what are your favourite biscuits?' Herbert Rootvine asked. Lucy thought for a minute.

'Coconut mallow.'

'Coconut mallow it shall be,' said Dr Rootvine, twiddling his wooden spoon.

A plate appeared in the air in front of them and a second later flakes of coconut sprinkled out of nowhere, and fell like snow, on top of half a dozen pink mallow biscuits lying on the plate.

'And you, Hannah, what would you like?' he asked.

'Caramel shortcake, please.' No sooner had she spoken than several pieces of caramel shortcake appeared to pile up beside the coconut mallow; a delicious layer of chocolate covered a thick layer of golden toffee with not too much biscuit base.

'What about you, Ben, what would you like?' Ben wondered if he could say a new game for his computer but asked instead for a piece of carrot cake. Instantly, a whole cake appeared with real carrots on the top, the leafy green fronds hanging down all round the sides like pond weed.

Ben hesitated. 'I'd rather have butter frosting on top, if that's not too much trouble.'

'You should have said,' said Dr Rootvine cheerfully, and transformed the carrots into butter frosting. Ben couldn't wait to sink his teeth into it.

'Blueberry tartlet all right for you, Dolfi?' Dr Rootvine enquired.

'Thank you.' Dolfi nodded.

'And what about you, Milli?'

'The same, thanks.'

'Just say what yeh wants in yer tea,' said Thelma, 'it'll pour for yeh.'

Dolfi was obviously used to this because he said 'One sugar with milk' and the sugar bowl and milk jug sprang into life and spooned and poured the correct amount into the cup before him. The teapot followed and poured a perfect cup of tea. Even the spoon jumped up and did the stirring so he didn't have to.

'Well then, this is nice,' said Dr Rootvine sipping his tea with his little finger in the air. 'Do tell me what you intend to do first in your search for the sixth key.'

Hannah looked at Dolfi for any sign that they should keep quiet but there was none.

'We're hoping to speak to you and Thelma first to see if we can get any clues from what you know and then we hope to speak to anyone else who thinks they might be able to help,' said Hannah.

Ben was digging into his carrot cake and Lucy was just about to bite into her second biscuit.

'Don' knows that I can tell yer much more'n I already 'ave,' said Thelma. 'I knows we've searched this place from top to bottom often enough.'

'That's certainly true,' confirmed Dr Rootvine. 'What kind of thing do you want to know exactly?'

Hannah was wondering where the imps had gone as there was no sign of them anywhere but thought it might be rude to ask. Instead, she enquired 'Has there ever been anything you thought was strange or anything you always wondered about but never got an answer to?'

'Can't say that anything strikes me,' said Dr Rootvine through a mouthful of blueberry tartlet, 'except, I've always wondered how the Magical Crown fits every Supreme Parlator that's ever been chosen. Not everyone has the same size of head, wouldn't you agree? Do you think you can only become a Supreme Parlator if you take a certain hat size?'

Dr Rootvine didn't seem to be taking their search for the lost sixth key very seriously.

Thelma shifted in her seat.

'Well, I've always wondered 'ow they cured the last fever, the one that struck in Zamada's time, when they didn't 'ave a Cleansing Potion,' she said.

'But they didn't cure it, did they?' said Dolfi knowledgeably. 'It very nearly wiped out all five villages. We barely survived. It was all documented in the library archives.'

Thelma nodded. 'Didn't know that,' she said.

'Where did the fever come from?' asked Hannah.

'Now there's a question,' said Dr Rootvine taking another little sip of his tea.

'And why did some survive?'

'That's just nature at work, I'd say,' said Dr Rootvine. 'Some things are indeed hard to explain.'

Hannah didn't much like this answer but moved on to something else. 'Is there anyone still alive who knew Zamada?' she asked.

'None in Pickletullum that I knows, is there, Milli?' said Thelma.

'Can't think of anyone offhand,' Milli agreed.

'But there's plenty still around 'ose relations were alive then an' one or two old 'uns 'oo were children in the last years. Witch Magrew is one for a start. 'Er mother and Zamada woz friends – so she always says anyways – and witches do live much longer than fairy folk. Me own grandmother used ter work in the Shop of Sounds in Socratown when she woz a girl and I r'member 'er telling me when I was a young 'un that Zamada used to go in there occasionally fir soothin' sounds at the end of a long week. Yer can't speak to my grandmother though 'cause she passed over a long time since.'

'It might be worth speaking to Witch Magrew then,' said Ben, with his mouth full.

'As good a place as any to start, I s'pose,' said Thelma, feeding Jasper a few crumbs of the carrot cake.

'What about the break-in two nights ago?' said Hannah. She looked up at the skylight which was directly above the table, now repaired, and towards the cupboard leading down into the basement.

'They appear to have got in through the skylight,' said Dr Rootvine, also looking up towards the ceiling. 'Tight squeeze for a goblin,' he added.

'I thought no one saw them?' said Ben.

'They didn't,' agreed Dolfi.

'Well I'm just *assuming* the goblins are behind all these raids. Most people think they are after all.'

'Best not to jump to conclusions until we know more, I think, Dr Rootvine,' said Dolfi.

'Isn't it worrying that whoever it was, *knew* about the Precious Fires to start with, knew how to get into the basement and also knew how to open the padlocks on the door,' said Hannah.

'It certainly is,' said Dr Rootvine, sounding slightly ruffled. 'I do hope you are not suggesting any indiscretion on my part!'

'No, no,' said Hannah. 'I was just thinking they must have had some inside information to be able to find out all that. How did they do it?'

'I can *assure* you I've *no idea*,' said Dr Rootvine stiffly. He seemed to have gone off his blueberry tartlet.

Lucy and Ben scoffed what remained on their plates as fast as possible. They had a funny feeling they wouldn't be staying much longer.

'Perhaps we ought to be getting along,' said Dolfi, sensing their welcome was over.

'No need to rush off,' said Thelma.

Dr Rootvine bristled.

'Best to get started. Lots to do,' said Hannah. 'Thank you for your help, Dr Rootvine.' She took a last gulp of her tea.

'Not at all. Please feel free to come back another time,' said Dr Rootvine standing up, and looking at that moment as if he'd be pleased if he never saw any of them ever again.

'Good day, Dr Rootvine, and thank you for the delicious tea and cakes,' said Dolfi.

'Not at all.'

'Seemed a little tetchy,' said Hannah once they were outside.

'Yes, he did seem rather upset,' said Milli.

'Not surprised."They must have had some inside information." Not too subtle, Hannah,' said Ben.

'I didn't mean … well, how did they do it?'

'Come on, let's go to Merryberrys so we can talk things over,' said Dolfi and he led the way.

Luckily Merryberrys was quiet and Dolfi managed to shepherd them into a corner, away from people still wanting to meet them and wish them luck. Dolfi and Milli spent the next hour telling them all they knew about the previous searches for the lost sixth key. They told them that Pickletullum had ordered a decree four summers before for yet another search of all the houses, shops and buildings in the village. Every basement and cellar had been searched as well as every attic and every bedroom. Old forgotten chests were opened and every trunk unlocked and rummaged through. Dusty hatboxes were looked in and rusty biscuit tins emptied.

Drawers were turned out and beds looked under; the tops of wardrobes were cleared and the bottoms of fire grates cleaned. Everyone was even instructed to look through the odd sock pile at the bottom of their laundry baskets.

'Then the woods were searched,' said Dolfi. 'We got together the owl keeper and the chief woodsman who, with their owls and their boarhounds, searched the woods inch by inch by day and by night. Everyone helped. Everyone wanted the key found then. It was a huge effort, a real linking of arms.'

Dolfi took another swig from his glass of ale. 'So you see, you have a very difficult task ahead. I honestly cannot think of anywhere we haven't already looked.'

'But it must be somewhere,' said Hannah.

'I've no doubt you're right Hannah, but *where* is the question.'

'I see now why everyone has lost the enthusiasm to find it,' said Ben 'They have already tried so hard.'

'Exactly,' said Dolfi. 'You'll find that most will not be keen to look again. They are just tired. If you have any hope of finding it at all you will need to look where no one has looked before.'

'What about the other villages?' asked Hannah. 'Have they been searched as well?'

'They have all been searched,' said Dolfi 'but how well, is another matter.'

They talked over every new bit of information, trying to learn as much as possible about the unfamiliar lands they found themselves in. They had to know everything.

Through the window they watched a game being played on the grass. Landel and Hunnik were among those playing. Their friend Hornet was throwing a curved stick but it flew off course towards a yew tree in the corner of the garden.

'I saw that being played at Ma Molly's,' said Ben.

'Wingtang. It's very popular. Everyone plays it. Even more popular than the Snail Racing Championships these days, but it's more difficult than it looks,' said Milli.

They were sipping their drinks and still watching the game when there was a cry.

'Doomed. Doomed. We're all doomed! Nothing can save us now.' An old woman in the corner was flailing her arms about. 'We're all do-oomed!' she shrieked again.

'Take no notice,' said Ben.

'It's pretty hard not to notice,' said Hannah, glancing in her direction.

'That's Raving Rena,' said Dolfi.

'Landel said she's off her trolley,' said Ben. 'Says she does it all the time. She was asking Zamada to save them when we were in Ma Molly's and we all know she's dead.'

'Yes, well,' said Dolfi quietly 'You get used to it after a while.'

When they looked again Raving Rena was making her way towards them.

'Oh no, she's coming over,' said Ben.

'Shush,' said Hannah, 'she'll hear you.'

She had.

'No one takes any notice of me,' she said, wagging her finger at Ben 'but I know things.'

'Glad to hear it,' Ben muttered, hoping she'd go away.

'I don't think you'd be so glad if you knew what I knew.'

'And what's that then?' asked Lucy.

'I have things to tell if people would only listen.'

They all waited. Was she going to tell them something? Raving Rena looked vacant for a moment then her eyes fell on Hannah's blackcurrant juice.

'Here, have it,' said Hannah holding it up. 'I'm not thirsty anyway.'

Raving Rena gulped the drink down without stopping, and when she'd finished the faraway look returned to her eye.

'What was I saying?' she asked.

'I knew she'd forgotten what she was going to say,' whispered Ben.

'Give her a chance,' said Hannah.

'You said we were all doomed,' said Lucy, prompting her.

'So I did, didn't I.' She raised a crooked, finger to her wrinkled lips.

'Will she ever get to the point?' said Ben.

'I've seen him!' said Raving Rena suddenly.

'Seen who?' asked Hannah.

'Seen him,' she said again, pointing a wavering finger at Dolfi. 'We're doomed, mark my words.' As Reving Rena walked back to her table they stared after her. She sat down again and started to eat what looked, from that distance, like small pickled onions.

'See, she's bonkers,' said Ben.

Dolfi sat shaking his head. He had heard Raving Rena utter prophecies of doom many times before but there was something in the way she spoke this time that made him uneasy. Who had she seen? He ran through all the people he could think of: Zanting Barbelly, Yordel Pod the greengrocer, Midas Plank the bank manager, Rudor Bizar the inn keeper, Pa Molly, Herbert Rootvine, Dr Pepper, Hick Dockwood …. Everyone he could think of in Pickletullum were good people, some less likeable than others but none of whom it could be said were likely to cause *doom*.

'You're not listening to an old bat like that, Dolfi?' asked Ben 'She's probably just seen someone killing weeds in the garden.' Ben strangled an imaginary weed with his bare hands.

'Do you think she could mean Hironymus Grossus?' Hannah asked.

'A possibility, I suppose, but I don't think he's dangerous,' said Dolfi.

'Well, I'm not so sure,' said Hannah 'I mean, well, we don't believe Gorgonz City's key is lost for a start.'

'I do find that hard to believe myself,' admitted Dolfi.

The back door opened and Landel, Hunnik and Hornet, who was holding his Wingtang stick tightly, made their way towards the table. The stick fluttered every few seconds as if it still wanted to play.

'You're back then,' said Hunnik. 'We heard this morning.' The three of them drew up chairs and sat down.

With so much to do Hannah, Ben and Lucy were very glad when they offered their help. It would be useful having someone else who knew their way around when Dolfi was busy with Council business. They discussed where to look and what to do first.

'Until we get to the bottom of all this and find the sixth key I think we should only discuss it among ourselves. We don't want your efforts hampered in any way,' said Dolfi 'Agreed?'

'Agreed!'

'First stop for us, Witch Magrew,' said Hannah as they made their way outside.

'And the library archives might be worth a look,' suggested Dolfi.

As they passed Raving Rena's table, Ben went pale. 'Yeuch! Did you see what she's eating?'

'Newts' eyeballs,' said Hornet. 'Even nicer than hawthorn muffins.'

Once Dolfi and Milli waved goodbye Hannah called after Ben. 'Don't be late. Meet us back here at the fifth gong.'

Hunnik led the way in the opposite direction towards the scarab resting post. 'Witch Magrew lives in the woods,' she said, 'so we'll take the scarab … unless you want to use Fly-by powder?'

'Don't tell me it works on us too?' said Hannah.

'Don't see why not,' said Hunnik. 'You can use some of mine if you like. I don't need it for flying short distances myself, of course.' Hunnik's ankle wings flapped twice.

Hunnik opened up the deep violet pouch around her neck, took a pinch of the silvery grey powder between her fingers and sprinkled the powder over Lucy's head. Lucy instantly rose up like a piece of stiff cardboard.

'Lean forward gently,' Hunnik told her. Lucy lurched forward, and headed straight towards the door of the book binder's shop.

'Lean left! Lean left!' shouted Hunnik.

Lucy swooped left, still looking like a flying ironing board. 'How do I stop?' she wailed.

'Oooh, I hadn't thought about that,' said Hunnik. Just as Lucy was about to crash into the water barrel, Hunnik pulled out her wand.

'*Restum*,' she called, just in time.

Lucy came to a gentle halt, still upright, Hannah was pleased to see.

'Your turn,' said Hunnik. Hannah saw the sparkling glittering grains fall to her feet and felt herself rise into the air like a starched overall.

'Relax and lean forward.' Hannah did as she was told and found herself speeding off in the direction of the woods.

'Come on,' Hunnik called to Lucy as she flapped her ankle wings and soared effortlessly into the air. 'Just jump and lean as if you are in water.'

Lucy jumped and leaned forward and found herself moving gently through the air. It was working.

They had only been flying a short time when Hunnik signalled.

'That's it up ahead.'

They could see a small wooden cottage with a very neat front garden; not what they had expected at all. It looked too nice and tidy to belong to a witch. They came to a halt a little way from the cottage and walked the last few metres.

On the door was a nameplate:

WITCH FROU FROU MAGREW
7 WINTERBOTTOM LANE.

They knocked and waited.

Chapter 9

Frou Frou Magrew

'Just coming,' a jolly voice called out and a minute later they heard a little honk as the door opened. A duck, wearing an apron and tartan slippers with a hairy pom pom on each, hovered before them and quacked as if to ask what they wanted.

'Who is it, Rosa?' the voice from inside inquired.

Hunnik hesitated then called 'Visitors.'

'Oh, we've got visitors, how delightful. All on your best behaviour now,' they heard.

'Come in, come in,' the voice called again.

The duck moved aside and Hunnik, Hannah and Lucy stepped across the doorway.

'Peeps! Oh my,' said Witch Magrew and there was a sudden flurry of wings and much honking and squawking, quacking and tumbling as ducks and geese, all in slippers, fled in all directions.

'We didn't mean to startle you,' said Hannah, blowing a feather out of her mouth.

Through the blizzard of white and yellow feathers they saw a pink armchair floating in the air and sitting in it was – they blinked to get a better view – a little round woman with curly purple hair. On her feet were big comfy slippers, pink, to match the chair.

'Do have a seat,' she said, pointing her wand and sending a spark flying towards the sofa on the ground. The ducks fled, slipping and sliding across the floor. An orange plume of smoke rose from a smouldering hole.

They sat and waited for Witch Magrew to speak first.

'Now, to what do I owe this lovely surprise?' she said, her eyes twinkling and, noticing Hannah and Lucy's astonished faces looking up at her, she added 'It's the old varicose veins you know, I find this chair much more comfortable than a bony broomstick – it's the only way to travel.' She smiled and the chair did a little twirl.

'I know your face from somewhere,' she said pointing at Hunnik, who was trying to shake a goose off her foot.

'Yes, I'm from the village. My name is Hunnik.'

'An elfin, I see.'

Hunnik nodded.

'And you?' she enquired of Hannah and Lucy.

'We're not from here,' said Hannah.

'I can tell that,' Witch Magrew laughed gently.

Hannah blushed a little. 'I'm Hannah and this is Lucy.'

'You're very welcome, I'm sure,' said Witch Magrew who now spotted the trainers on their feet and stared at them intently. 'Are they comfortable?' she asked with great interest.

'Very. You can walk for miles in these,' said Lucy and she held one leg up so Witch Magrew could get a closer look. The witch leaned forward and peered down over the edge of her chair.

'Hmmm,' She stroked her chin. 'I must get myself a pair of those. Now, what can I do for you girls?'

Hannah took a deep breath. 'Well, we're trying to find the lost sixth key for the Magical Crown.'

'Are you, now,' said Witch Magrew nodding.

'We have permission to look for it from the Council of Alter-Idem.'

'Do you, now,' Witch Magrew was still nodding and seemed not to notice when her hair changed from purple to mint green.

'Yes ….' Hannah had never seen anyone sit in a floating armchair before, never mind someone who's hair changed colour when they nodded their head. She only managed to think that Witch Magrew looked like one of those dogs you saw in the back windows of cars whose head bobs up and down as it drives along. She pictured one in a curly green wig.

'And what do you have to say for yourself?' said Witch Magrew, turning to Lucy.

Lucy blinked. 'We think you may be able to help us,' she said, pushing her glasses into place.

'Ah, a girl who speaks her mind,' said Witch Magrew, 'and what makes you think I can help you?' She sounded slightly amused.

'Thelma, in the Apothecary, says your mum and Zamada were friends,' said Lucy.

'They were that,' Witch Magrew agreed. 'That's a photograph of them together there.' She pointed with her wand and from a side table a photo frame rose and brought itself over to the sofa. Hannah looked at it closely. In it, the Supreme Parlator with the Magical Crown of Keys on her head was smiling and beside her, another three ladies were smiling too. Hannah couldn't tell which was Witch Magrew's mother. She handed the photograph to Lucy. Hunnik peered over Lucy's shoulder.

'That was taken on my mother's two hundredth birthday,' said Witch Magrew. 'Mother is the one in the pointed hat with the bows. All four of them were friends: Zamada, mother, Felone Malandra and Ossinda Odessa.'

It was hard to tell who had the most crooked nose from the photo because both Witch Magrew's mother and Zamada both had a corker. Each looked as though it had been broken in at least three places.

'My mother was a great beauty in her day,' Witch Magrew continued, 'and of course, so was Zamada. They had such a lot in common: they had the same sense of humour, the same hairdresser, cats from the same litter, both liked apple dumplings with lumpy custard … but I think that Zamada liked to visit my mother because she had been around for so long and could tell funny stories about all the famous people she had met.'

Hannah thought they might be getting somewhere and leaned forward to listen.

'She lived here in this house, my mother,' said Witch Magrew without pausing. 'They used to have afternoon tea on Thursdays right here in this room.' Hannah found it hard to visualise the late, great Supreme Parlator, Magical Crown sparkling with jewels, sitting among the feathers and ducks.

'Did your mother talk about the Supreme Parlator to you?' asked Hannah.

'Oh, she wasn't the Supreme Parlator to us. She was simply Zamada. That's how we knew her. But yes, mother did speak of her visits to me. Mother would often say how Zamada asked her opinion about something or other. How long to boil an egg to get the middle just a little runny – that sort of thing.'

Hannah's mind started to wander. She looked around the room for anything that might give a clue to the sixth key's whereabouts or to anything else for that matter. On a desk, between two book ends, was a duckling, eyes closed and fast asleep, and several books. The first, entitled *The Discoverie of Witchcraft* by Reginald Scot, had the date 1584 in gold letters along its spine. Another, *Spells and Counter-Spells for Everyday* by Casta Flywun, sat next to *Hexes and Jinxes* by Nasty & Pastey. Also visible was a glass inkwell filled with yellow ink, a quill holder sprouting short quills, long quills and a fancy curly quill with a ribbon on the end, and a lump of red sealing wax; but there was nothing much else on the desk that was unusual. On the wall was a picture of the forest outside. There were a few birds in the trees and a rabbit nibbling some grass but it wasn't very interesting. When Hannah looked back at the picture a few seconds later she noticed a squirrel that she didn't remember seeing the first time and when she glanced back a third time the rabbit had disappeared! Witch Magrew noticed Hannah looking at the painting.

'That's a very special picture, that is,' she said 'Given to me by my mother before she passed away. It's a "Windoless".

'If you are outside it lets you see inside and if you are inside it lets you see outside. Very useful when people you don't like come to visit – you can pretend you're not in. It's the only one in the land as far as I know so it's valuable but I don't usually tell people what it is. When they come they just think it's a dull painting of the forest outside.'

'It's very nice,' said Lucy tactfully.

But Hannah was more interested in the sixth key than a view of the forest outside and turned the conversation back to Zamada.

'Did your mother or Zamada ever mention what would happen to the sixth key when the Magical Crown of Keys was dismantled? she asked.

'You mean did Zamada ever talk about what would happen when she died?' asked Witch Magrew.

'I suppose so,' said Hannah, although she wasn't sure it was what she meant.

'I can't recall mother ever saying anything to me about the Magical Crown of Keys,' she said. 'Everyone expected that it would be reassembled and it would choose a new Parlator but the keys all went back to the villages for some reason, except the sixth key of course. No one knows what happened to that.'

They didn't seem to be any nearer finding out where the sixth key was but Hannah knew there must be a clue somewhere.

'Can you think of anything at all that you can tell us that might have something to do with the disappearance of the key?' she asked. Witch Magrew thought hard.

'I'm sorry,' she said at last, 'but I can't think of anything which would be helpful.'

Hannah was not about to give up. She tried a long shot. Even though it didn't seem likely that the fever had anything to do with the disappearance of the sixth key she couldn't help wondering about it.

'Did Zamada ever mention the fever that swept the villages and nearly killed everyone?' she asked.

'That was such a terrible time, just terrible. You're too young to remember it, Hunnik, but if your grandmother had died you wouldn't be here now. I knew your grandmother you know.'

'I know,' replied Hunnik.

'She used to work in the Shop of Sounds in Socratown with Greta Mex, Thelma's grandmother.'

'I know,' said Hunnik again.

'Zamada used to go there for some soothing sounds on a Friday after a long week, so mother used to say. It's a wonderful shop – you'll have to take them, Hunnik. It has every sound you can think of – all to take away and listen to when you please. I don't go as often as I would like but I treat myself occasionally and usually buy some harp music or the sound of peas popping out of their shells. That always cheers me up.'

Fascinating as all this was they were still no nearer finding out anything useful. Hannah tried one more time. 'What else do you know about the fever, Witch Magrew?'

'Oh, the fever! Yes well, the least said about that the better.'

'But we need to know,' pressed Hannah.

'You are persistent, child!' said Witch Magrew.

Hannah forced herself to smile sweetly.

'There is not a lot to know really. The fever came, a lot died and a few survived.'

'Your mother survived,' said Hannah.

'Yes, of course she did.'

'Did she do anything or know anything that the others didn't?' asked Hannah.

'Not that I know of,' said Witch Magrew, tapping her chin. Her nails were now the same colour of green as her hair.

'I remember,' said Witch Magrew laughing, 'mother making me eat acorns. Acorns for breakfast, acorns for dinner and acorns and nasturtiums for supper. I was small, you see, she was trying to fatten me up like the herdsmen fatten their swine. And it worked!' She roared with laughter and patted her round belly and her feet shot straight out in front, the pink slippers looking like two huge blobs of bubblegum stuck on the end of matchsticks.

Hannah didn't think she was going to find out anything very much now but asked, 'Is there anything else you remember.'

'Now that you ask, I do remember there was *occasionally* whispered talk,' Witch Magrew said, sounding unsure.

'What kind of talk,' asked Hannah.

'Well, nothing very important I'm sure but I do remember one afternoon hearing my mother and Zamada in this very room and I remember it because they were keeping their voices low. You know what children are like,' she chuckled, 'if they think they shouldn't be hearing something they'll press their ear to the door to hear better. I think I heard them say "He'll have to be stopped."'

'Do you have any idea who they were talking about?' asked Lucy.

'I didn't at the time,' said Witch Magrew. 'But now I look back they could have been talking about an old enemy of Zamada's.'

'Who was that?' asked Hannah.

'Don't think I ever found out exactly, although there was talk in the village of an argument between Zamada and a wizard who she'd been having a bit of trouble with. They say that when Zamada was getting the better of him he stumbled and zapped a spell which went off at an angle, hit the Magical Crown of Keys on Zamada's head and rebounded on him. They say he was trapped in a tree in the forest. Of course, it could just have been one of those stories the grown-ups tell you to stop you doing dangerous things. But there were stories for years about a Drooping Elder that would follow you and try to grab you in its branches if you were alone in the woods in the dark. The forest at night is not a safe place for children.'

'Did you ever see the tree?' asked Lucy excitedly.

'No child, I never did, not that I wanted to either. I wouldn't like to be the first to meet an angry old wizard who's been trapped in a tree for six hundred moons. There's been many children lost in these woods and some have never been seen again. One poor boy was found dead with his eyes and mouth wide open in a look of awful terror, and his hair was still standing on end. No one knows what he saw.'

Lucy gasped and clapped a hand over her mouth.

Hannah decided they wouldn't go wandering about the forest on their own – just in case the story was true and there really was a wizard trapped in a tree somewhere.

'Do you think whatever it was that this person had to be stopped from doing had anything to do with the fever – or the missing key?' asked Hannah.

'I wouldn't have thought so,' said Witch Magrew. 'But I can't be sure.' Then, as if she'd had enough, the chair lowered and zoomed around in a little circle. They had to lean back as far as they could go to avoid being knocked out.

'Who would like some refreshment? she asked.

'No, thank you,' said Hannah. 'We've not long had something. Although it's very kind of you to ask.'

'What about a tour of the garden then? You must see the garden.'

Not wanting to disappoint her they followed Witch Magrew in the floating pink chair as it squeezed through the doorway into the kitchen. The arm of the chair knocked a kettle to the floor and it landed with such a bang the duck waddling in front squawked in fright, laid an egg, and skidded under the cooker. The kitchen led to a conservatory at the back of the house. It had one small door leading out into the garden.

Hannah was wondering how Witch Magrew was going to get out when …

'See you outside then.'

The whole glass roof of the conservatory opened up like a lily and Witch Magrew shot straight out of the top, holding onto her hat with one hand.

The garden was beautiful. It was a mini tropical paradise complete with a waterfall and a small, but perfectly formed lagoon. Blue and yellow toucan birds sat in the banana trees and huge red and pink flowers grew on shrubs on all sides. A hammock big enough to take a pink armchair swung between two coconut palms and a table set out with slices of pineapple, pawpaw and other exotic fruit sat on the grass. Bumblebees the size of golf balls, collecting nectar from the flowers, buzzed around to the tune of *The Grand Old Duke of York*.

The ducks and geese made straight for the lagoon and plunged in, splashing and making a din in the sunshine. They didn't seem to mind that their slippers were getting wet.

'Help yourselves to some fruit. It's very good for you, you know, full of vitamins and things.'

Witch Magrew flew around in her big chair, looking at everything. She stopped to sniff the luscious flowers and picked a banana off the tree.

'I love it here,' she said. 'It's sunny all year round if I want it. But then, if it was sunny all year round it wouldn't be as much fun, would it?' She took a bite of her banana.

'I suppose not,' said Lucy, eating a piece of pineapple. Hunnik wandered among the flowers and watched the ducks in the lagoon dipping and throwing water onto their backs.

'So I make thunderstorms too. I'm very good at thunderstorms and the ducks and geese like them – don't you my lovelies?' She watched them splashing about.

'You know, of course, that everything taken to extreme is bad for you.'

Lucy was just thinking she could never eat too much pineapple. 'Even pineapple?' she asked.

'Even pineapple. Imagine what gallons of those enzyme-y things would do to your insides!' Lucy imagined a hissing, yellow bathful and grimaced.

'What about oxygen?' asked Hannah, sure you couldn't have too much oxygen.

'Even things that do you good only do you good up to a point then do you harm – oxygen, sunshine, philosophy, or carrot juice – everything.' Witch Magrew grinned. 'Zamada taught me that.'

Lucy thought that maybe five slices of pineapple was enough and picked up a slice of paw paw instead.

'It is a very beautiful garden,' said Hannah looking round. Witch Magrew beamed.

'My name isn't Magrew for nothing,' she said admiring her nails, each one now a different colour of the rainbow.

Hannah smiled and looked at her watch. It was half past four.

'It's been lovely talking to you, Witch Magrew, but I'm afraid we have to be going now.'

'You will come again, won't you? You are welcome anytime,' said Witch Magrew. She sounded as if she really meant it.

'Thank you,' said Hannah, making her way back towards the conservatory. Witch Magrew finished the last of her banana and the skin disappeared from her hand.

Inside, Rosa was hovering by the window with a feather duster under her wing. It was only when Witch Magrew screeched 'MARMADUKE!!' that Hannah noticed a black cat poised ready to spring. The cat pounced, missed Rosa and landed in the umbrella stand, sending it crashing to the floor.

'You naughty cat! Rosa is your friend,' scolded Witch Magrew.

Rosa was lying flat on her back, slippered feet in the air, looking in need of resuscitation; the feather duster pointed skyward like a tombstone. Marmaduke sped outside and disappeared under the bushes. Witch Magrew took the duster and began fanning Rosa with it.

On the floor lay four umbrellas: an orange one with pink spots (to match Witch

Magrew's chair), a black one with silver stars, a yellow one with wizards in pointed hats falling from the sky and one with red mushrooms all over, and a flute.

'That's where it went,' said Witch Magrew on seeing the flute, and she drew it to her with her wand. Rosa stirred, got to her feet and groggily waddled off.

'Zamada gave me this when I was a child,' said Witch Magrew turning to Hannah. 'It only plays the one tune though.' She blew through the mouthpiece and a melodic tune played. It sounded the sort of song a band might march to – Hannah thought it an odd tune to be a present for a child – and then it missed a bit before carrying on to the end.

'It has always done that, missed out some of the music. I've never been able to sort it. It resists being charmed but it's cute don't you think?'

Hannah didn't really think so, although she wouldn't have said as much, but there must have been something in her smile which made Witch Magrew think she liked it.

'You have it Hannah. It might behave itself for you.'

'Thank you,' said Hannah taking the flute and wondering what on earth she was going to do with it.

The ducks and geese started to come back into the house, slippers squelching, leaving little puddles everywhere.

'If you come back again I'll tell you all about my dancing days. I was a ballerina in the Witchery Youth Dance Troupe, you know. I was a very beautiful Ugly Duckling. That was my first dance part … but … another day. Time for a nap I think. Come along my lovelies, beaks under wings.'

Witch Magrew clapped her hands and there was a great honking and quacking as the room filled with feathers again and the ducks and geese settled down for a sleep.

Outside, Hunnik, Hannah and Lucy said goodbye and waved as they left. It wasn't long before they arrived back at the end of the street and on the way up to Merryberrys they passed the bank. Hannah had already been wondering what they would do for money. They couldn't keep relying on everyone else to buy what they needed.

'We really should have our own money,' said Hannah 'What do we have that we can sell?'

'What about the herbs in Grandma's garden?' suggested Lucy. It did seem the most promising idea.

'Or what about selling your trainers?' suggested Hunnik. 'Everyone here thinks they're great.'

Lucy frowned. 'I've only got this pair,' she said, looking down at the grass stains and the mud. 'Mum wouldn't be pleased if I went home with my good shoes ruined. I think the herbs would be the best idea.'

'Let's call in at Dr Rootvine's then,' said Hannah.

Thelma was in the shop alone, which Hannah was pleased about as she thought

Dr Rootvine might have seen enough of them for one day. She explained they needed some money and asked if there was anything Dr Rootvine might want to buy.

'I'm sorry, Hannah, I can't think of anythin' we needs. We 'ave our regular suppliers an' now the fever's past we're back up ter normal stock levels.'

'There must be something we can get for you?' said Hannah still hopeful.

Thelma turned to look down the labels on the drawers to make sure. Hannah looked too and realised it wouldn't be easy. She didn't fancy finding Dung Worms or collecting Fish Spittle. Hedgehog Dandruff was a possibility but she had only ever seen one once and you would have to shake an awful lot of hedgehogs to collect a cupful of dandruff.

Hannah's eyes fell on something a bit less improbable: a drawer labelled *Hens' Egg Shells*. 'What about those?' she said, pointing.

Thelma opened the drawer. 'We *are* a bit low.' she said peering inside. 'But they're difficult ter come by. It's mainly the brown shells we use, mind. They're good for makin' anti-spells. I must 'ave used more th'n I thought tryin' ter undo the spell on Jasper.' He cawed the same ear-splitting cry as usual and flew over Hannah to land on Thelma.

'Do you think Dr Rootvine would pay us if we brought in hens' egg shells then?'

''Ee should do's if yer sure yeh can get some?' said Thelma sounding doubtful. ''Ens' egg shells are just about as scarce as 'ens' teeth 'round 'ere.'

How easy could you get? They might be scarce around here, thought Hannah, but we have them most mornings for breakfast!

'Does it matter if the shells are broken?' asked Lucy.

'Whole is best but crushed is good. Most are used crushed anyways. Brown mind, and speckled if you can get 'em.'

'We've got to rush, Thelma, but thanks. We'll see you tomorrow,' said Hannah and they left the shop. They had to get back. They didn't want Grandma to worry. Hannah hoped Ben would be on time.

They ran, panting, to the top of the street where Ben, Landel and Hornet were waiting … but they were not alone.

Chapter 10

The Flute

The five figures faced each other like angry snakes. There was something familiar about the strangers. Then Hannah remembered – they were the same two goblins who had laughed at them in the Underground Burroway and one of them was pushing Landel.

'Just leave us alone, Splint!' said Landel as he pushed the goblin back. Before Hannah and Lucy had taken another step things took a turn for the worse; where Landel's hands had touched Splint, long thick hairs were now sprouting rapidly.

'If you want some trouble that's fine by us,' said Hornet, on seeing Landel's hands. Hornet rose into the air, flicked his wand and, instantly, the hair on the goblins' heads began to grow down over their faces and past their shoulders. By the time they pulled it away from their eyes it was down to the ground.

'Whooah!' Ben felt himself turn upside down. He was hanging in mid-air with nothing visible holding him up.

'Anyone move and he gets it,' one of the goblins shouted. Everyone stopped. Even Hannah, Lucy and Hunnik, wand in hand, stopped dead in their tracks.

'Don't be getting big ideas, Peep,' said the loud-mouthed goblin, backing away but keeping eye contact with Ben. 'No one wants the key found except those that are soft in the head.' The two goblins made their way down the street, still looking back, still staring at Ben going red in the face as the blood rushed to his head. 'You wouldn't want something nasty to happen now, would you?'

Hannah heard Hunnik quietly muttering something under her breath and a large pillow suddenly appeared on the ground beneath Ben. A second later the goblins ran, the spell broke and Ben crumpled heavily to the ground on top of the pillow.

'What was all that about? You all right?' asked Hannah, running to help him up. Ben struggled to his feet.

'Best ignore them,' said Landel, looking down at his hairy palms. 'Grossus and Splint are always making trouble.'

'Grossus?' said Hannah and Lucy together.

'Not related to Hironymus Grossus?' said Hannah.

''Fraid so,' said Hornet. 'There could only be one Kuzu Grossus. Trouble maker and no mistake, big league trouble, trouble with a capital 'T'.'

'Can't say I like him much,' said Ben, straightening his clothes and making sure his neck wasn't broken.

'You're not the only one,' said Hunnik. 'He's horrible. He frightens the children by making smoke come out of their ears so they think their hair's on fire. Thinks he can do anything he likes just 'cause he's Grossus's son.'

'Best to stay out of their way,' said Landel, holding out his hands while Hornet chanted something and tapped his palms with his wand. The hair disappeared but Landel's hands were now covered in feathers.

'Oops! sorry,' said Hornet.

Ben noticed the flute Hannah was carrying. 'What's that you've got?' he asked while Hornet tried another spell.

'A flute, but I'll tell you all about it later. We'd better get home.'

They left Landel yelling in pain as Hornet tried to remove the feathers, which had now turned lilac, by plucking them out one by one. Hunnik accompanied them back through the Underground Burroway. In the Portway, while Horace was busy trying to rouse a brownie who had fallen asleep across three seats, they managed to disembark unnoticed. Before Hunnik left them at the foot of the chestnut tree in the woods, she made the arrangements for the next day.

'Landel will meet you at the same time tomorrow and don't forget the egg shells.'

'Egg shells?' Ben asked as they opened the gate at the bottom of Grandma Fred's garden.

'Well, we might need to buy things while we're here so I'm going to sell Dr Rootvine some brown egg shells tomorrow,' said Hannah.

'They didn't need any herbs or plants,' said Lucy, 'and I wasn't selling my trainers.'

'Who'd want them?' said Ben, holding his nose.

After tea, Grandma Fred asked them all about the film they hadn't seen and asked how Mrs Robertson, the ticket lady, was. They said it must have been her day off. Lucy sat with Gertrude on her knee and stroked her gently while Grandma told them all about the arrangements she was involved in making as a member of the Summer Fête Committee. When she later sat down to watch television, Hannah and Lucy told Ben all about Witch Magrew, her floating pink chair, the ducks and geese in slippers and the tropical garden. He could hardly believe it when they told him they'd flown there using Fly-by powder. Hannah had to admit they hadn't found out much more about where the sixth key might be or even much about Zamada, although she did mention that Witch Magrew had overheard Zamada tell her mother "He'll have to be stopped."

'That was yonks ago so they couldn't have meant Hironymus Grossus,' said Ben keeping his voice low 'and I can't see it having anything to do with the lost sixth key. Can you?'

'No, not really. '

Ben told them that he hadn't had much luck either. He, Landel and Hornet had searched the vaults under the Town Hall in Pickletullum and had looked through an old corn warehouse on the edge of the town which was now infested with mice. Neither had been searched properly before.

'Didn't find anything in the vaults except a forgotten case of Black Hag whisky, but Chancellor Barbelly was really pleased; and we found a rat skeleton in the warehouse; oh, and an old biscuit tin with some mouldy biscuits.'

'You didn't eat them, did you?' said Hannah wincing.

''Course not, Hannah. I didn't eat the mouldy ones.'

Then Ben told them about the library which had been a bit more promising.

'Well, the library is really old and everything … there's a librarian in there who looks quite like Vasril Odo but doesn't smell as strange and the reading tables turn the pages for you if you put a coin in the inkwell … Landel showed me.'

'But what did you find out?'

'Give me a chance, I'm coming to that bit ….'

'Well?'

'I found out that the Council of Alter-Idem used to sing an anthem before every meeting.'

'Is that it?' asked Hannah.

'Don't you think that's interesting?' asked Ben.

'No,' said Hannah grumpily.

'We'll never find the key at this rate,' said Lucy wearily.

Ben ignored them and continued.

'I also found out that when a Supreme Parlator dies their spirit is released in the form of a White Ptarmigan which looks over the villages until the next Supreme Parlator is appointed, so long as the Harmony Rules are kept, that is. If they're not kept the White Ptarmigan leaves.'

'What's a White Ptarmigan?' asked Lucy.

'I didn't know either,' said Ben, 'but it's a bird, like a grouse but much larger, and it's completely covered in white feathers, even its feet, and it has strange green eyes.'

'We're not doing awfully well are we?' Hannah sighed. 'This is going to be more difficult than I thought. Perhaps we'll not find the sixth key after all.'

'It's only our first real day looking, Hannah. Be realistic,' said Ben.

'But we haven't got much time, have we?'

'A lot can happen in a fortnight. Look how much has happened in the last few days. And I found out something else. There was a fire in the chambers in Gorgonz City not long after the last Supreme Parlator died.'

His news exhausted, Ben turned his attention to the flute lying on the bed. He picked it up and blew into it. It started to play on its own, then stopped as if it was missing a string of notes in the middle, then just as suddenly, started again.

'It only plays one tune and Witch Magrew says it always does that,' said Lucy.

Ben looked down its length to see if anything was stuck, shook it and blew it again. The same tune played and it missed the same notes in the same place. He banged the flute hard on the floor and blew into it once more but still it didn't play all the way through.

'We could get it fixed,' said Ben. 'It might play more tunes if it was fixed.'

'We'll have to get some money first,' Hannah reminded him.

'We'll be able to buy hawthorn muffins too,' he said. 'Great!'

'As long as Raving Rena's not there,' said Lucy 'She gives me the creeps!'

'Me too,' said Hannah.

'She's just a batty old lady. Dolfi told me she was a herb strewer, whatever that is. I told you she was ranting in Ma Mollys when I was there the day we made the Cleansing Potion for the fever,' said Ben. This started Hannah thinking about the fever again.

'Don't you think it's strange,' she said, 'that there have been two, almost identical fevers? The first one affected all the villages and nearly killed everyone and the second, although a long time later, would have spread to the other villages too if we hadn't made a Cleansing Potion in time.'

'Hadn't given it any thought,' said Ben.

'Herb strewer – someone who scatters herbs and flowers in front of a procession,' said Lucy reading from one of Grandma's books on her lap.

'How can a fever have anything to do with the lost sixth key?' asked Ben, still shaking the flute.

'I don't know,' said Hannah, 'I don't know.'

*

The next morning Grandma was up and busy very early. The Summer Fête which took place at the end of August every year was only two weeks away and in between organising stands, checking entries and selling tickets she still had chutneys and pickles to make and some herbs to dry. Her sage and onion and cranberry stuffing always sold out and she had decided to make an extra large batch this year.

Hannah and Lucy collected armfuls of sage and Ben volunteered to peel the onions, chop them up and dry them in the oven. His eyes watered terribly and he had to keep going out into the garden for fresh air and long drinks of water. Gertrude hated the smell so much she went off to find the church warden's cat and sit on a tombstone in the sunshine.

'Do you need anything from the shops, Grandma?' Hannah asked, swallowing her last mouthful of lunch.

'Get a dozen eggs for me, dear. You three certainly eat a lot of them,' said Grandma Fred, handing her the money.

Hannah had kept the shells from the eggs they'd had for breakfast and she'd managed to fish out from the waste bin those that had been thrown away the day before. All they needed was a wash to get rid of the tea leaves and bits of turnip.

'Will you be all right on your own this afternoon while I'm up at the community hall?' Grandma Fred asked. 'Remember, Mrs Whitehead's next door if you need her.' Hannah, Ben and Lucy nodded furiously. 'If you're sure … I'll see you later then.' And Grandma Fred was gone.

When Hannah returned from the shops with half a dozen eggs to take to Dr Rootvine, they swallowed their bogbean leaves with a glass of water.

'It's ten to one; we'd better go,' said Ben, jamming the flute in his belt and pulling his tee-shirt over it.

Landel met them as arranged, all traces of lilac feathers gone from his hands although there still seemed to be one or two poking from behind his ears. In the Portway, there was no avoiding Horace this time. He flew over as soon as he'd whistled two single beetles off into the Socratown tunnel.

'Good day,' he said smarmily. 'Back again, are we?'

'Good day, Horace,' said Landel. 'How is the Portway today?'

'Fine, fine. A bit busier than usual. Lots of foot traffic today – ants on the march; rallying in Sombrono for their summer holidays. Same complaints every year about the traffic but nothing I can't handle.' He tapped his flag impatiently in the palm of his hand.

'Pleased to hear it, Horace,' said Landel quickening his step towards the scarab for Pickletullum.

'Er … any progress?' Horace flew jerkily to keep up.

'Not yet,' said Hannah scurrying along beside Landel.

'Thinking of making some anti-spells are we?' he said, looking at the brown paper bag Hannah was clutching.

'None that you need worry about, Horace,' said Landel, helping Hannah and Lucy up onto the scarab. Ben boarded quickly and they set off down the tunnel leaving Horace grumbling to himself once again.

'How did he know I had egg shells in the bag?' said Hannah, astonished.

'He could smell them,' said Landel. All fairies have a keen sense of smell but a brownie can smell a rat a mile away. Well, you know what I mean. There's a Shop of Smells in Sombrono in the same way that Socratown has a Shop of Sounds.'

'A Shop of Smells? What use is a Shop of Smells?' asked Lucy, twitching her nose.

'Smells are very important,' said Landel. 'For animals with poor sight it is the way they recognise other animals. For us it is one of the ways we decide if something is good to eat or not isn't it? And smells give us signals about other things too. We often decide whether we like someone or not because of the way they smell.'

Ben and Lucy were still arguing about who had the smelliest feet when the scarab flew out of the tunnel into the sunshine and came to a halt by the mushroom stop.

When they arrived at the Apothecary, Thelma was in the window hanging up several animal skins by their tails. They still had the feet attached.

'Got to be careful with these Vipners,' she said, accidentally squeezing the foot of one. Razor sharp claws, longer that the foot itself, shot out.

'Wouldn't like to get into a fight with one of them,' said Ben.

Thelma placed a large jar of what looked like pickled walnuts right in the middle of the window in full view of passers by. Hannah noticed the label on the jar: *Troll Brains*.

'Good morning to you,' said Dr Rootvine from behind the counter, closing the book he was looking in. Hannah could read the title upside down – *Alchemy Through The Ages* by Aloyishus Golddigger.

'What can I do for you today?' he said tensely, looking up from the thick volume and absent-mindedly patting its cover.

Ben wondered if there was any chance of being offered more carrot cake but before he could ask, Hannah began the negotiations.

'Dr Rootvine, as you know, everyone has been kind in helping us get what we need so far but we could really do with having some money of our own. We were wondering … would you? … could you? … do you have any need for? … we have some egg shells to sell if you're interested.' Hannah put her paper bag down on the counter.

'Well,' he said more softly, giving the matter some thought. He opened the drawer marked *Hen's Egg Shells* and Thelma quickly turned and busied herself in the window rearranging a stack of brightly coloured birds' nests.

'We *are* short of hens' egg shells I see,' he said, looking at Thelma over the top of his half moon spectacles and closing one eye. Jasper turned himself around on Thelma's hat to look at something terribly interesting out in the street.

'May I?' he enquired, picking up the paper bag. 'Speckled, brown eggs too,' he said peering into the bag with mounting interest.

'I think we can do business,' he said after a few moments, wearing a tight sort of smile.

'Good,' said Hannah, 'I believe hens' eggs are quite hard to come by.'

Dr Rootvine's smile disappeared.

'As rare as hen's teeth,' said Lucy, grinning.

'If one knows where to look most things can be procured,' he said dryly.

Ben wondered how many of Ma Molly's hawthorn muffins they'd be able to buy and was already imagining using Fly-by powder.

'I'll give you three cala for them,' offered Dr Rootvine.

Thelma gave a little cough.

Hannah had no idea how much three cala was or how much that would buy but reckoned that they would be worth more if he was offering three.

'Four,' countered Hannah. Landel whispered in Ben's ear.

'And some Fly-by powder,' Ben added hurredly.

Were they asking too much? Would he change his mind altogether? They saw Thelma smile.

'Oh, all right then,' he agreed. 'Four cala and three feckles of Fly-by powder.'

'How much is four cala?' Hannah asked Thelma when Dr Rootvine was in the back shop looking for the cotton sacks to put the Fly-by powder in.

'Quite a lot. There's five pecs to a kippa and ten kippa to a cala so you've got forty kippa. You could buy a full set of the best copper cauldrons for that and still have change.'

Dr Rootvine handed over the money and a little pouch of Fly-by powder which Ben grabbed and put in his pocket.

'Thank you, Dr Rootvine,' Hannah said and glanced sideways into the back shop.

'Any news about the Precious Fires, or the raiders?' she asked.

'None,' he said. 'Let's hope you have some luck in finding out something soon. The Council of Alter-Idem don't seem to be doing anything about these raids. Useless bunch of bureaucrats,' he said irritably.

'And how is Mo?' asked Hannah. 'I hope he hasn't still got the itches?'

'No, no, they're gone,' said Dr Rootvine. 'In fact,' he said wearily 'they've all gone.'

'What do you mean?' asked Lucy, looking into the back shop where all she could see was the empty table.

'The imps have gone. We haven't seen them for days now.'

'Where are they?' asked Hannah.

'We don't know. It's possible they've gone back ter their 'omeland but they didn't tell us they was goin'.'

'Didn't take their banjo neither,' said Thelma. 'Never goes anywhere without it.'

'I expect they'll come back once they've had their little trip,' said Dr Rootvine. Thelma didn't seem quite as sure because she was shaking her head and pursing her lips.

'They will probably just turn up again,' agreed Ben, anxious to get away to try out the Fly-by powder.

'I hope you are right,' said Dr Rootvine.

'Wouldn't want anythin' to 'appen to 'em,' said Thelma.

Outside the Apothecary, Ben mentioned the book Dr Rootvine had been reading.

'*Alchemy Through The Ages*? I thought Dr Rootvine was interested in the Precious

Fires because they could heal, not because they could make gold out of metal,' he said.

'But the Precious Fires are gone now so it doesn't matter does it?' said Landel.

'Probably not,' said Hannah. 'He wouldn't steal them from himself, would he? I'm more concerned about the imps. Where have they gone?'

'Seems strange to just disappear without saying anything, doesn't it?' said Lucy as they walked on towards the Town Hall.

'We need to try out this Fly-by powder,' Ben's mind was on more important things.

'Not now,' said Hannah. 'There will be plenty of time to try it later.'

'Spoilsport.'

'I thought we were going to Sombrono today,' said Lucy.

'We could fly there ourselves!' said Ben hopefully.

'We don't know how to get there without going through the Underground Burroway do we?' said Hannah. 'Come on, we need to speak to Dolfi.'

Landel led the way up the steps to the Town Hall. Inside, staring from large glass doors was the etched crest of a large bird with two heads. Fanned wings arched above its head and clasped between four feathered feet was a roll of parchment bearing the name Aldoris.

'I bet that's a White Ptarmigan,' said Lucy, sounding full of awe.

'It didn't say anything in the library about it having two heads and four feet,' said Ben.

'That's just poetic licence,' said Hannah.

'Poetic what?' asked Ben.

'It's a design,' said Hannah looking at his puzzled face ' – suggesting the ptarmigan is all-seeing and has a firm grip on things.' Ben still looked blank. 'Oh, never mind,' she said pushing open the door.

'He's away on business,' the elfin behind the desk told them when they asked to see Dolfi. 'I can take a message if you like.'

'Oh, well, nothing for it but to go to Sombrono ourselves then. We'll speak to him later I suppose,' said Hannah.

They left the Town Hall and boarded a waiting scarab. On the way they asked Landel what Sombrono was like.

'It doesn't have a lot of colour,' he said. 'Even the clothes they wear are dull browns and greys.' Landel pulled at his multi-coloured silk tunic as if to indicate the contrast. 'And at first they seem a bit slow-witted but they're not. They just don't see a lot in the world to get excited about.'

'Sound a miserable bunch,' said Ben.

'As long as they let us search the village and give us their key,' said Hannah.

'I wonder if they have hawthorn muffins?' Ben perked up and settled back for the rest of the journey.

Chapter 11

Sombrono

The traffic in the burroway was slow as Horace had said, and the scarab rose up and over trails of walking ants so often that by the time they reached Sombrono they were all feeling quite queasy and glad to get off. Even Landel who was used to such erratic flying was looking quite seasick.

They emerged from the burroway into a vast underground clearing and Sombrono spread before them like a dark carpet. In the middle was a market square and in the middle of that was a stone fountain. Old folk and youngsters sat dangling their very large feet in the water. Everyone else seemed to be going about their business, moving like shadows from doorway to doorway in the subdued light.

In the roof space an enormous plug about three metres across looked to be filling a hole and hanging down from it was a large bell. A rope was attached to the clapper. All around the roof space many smaller plugs surrounded the first, looking like a circle of circles in the compacted earth.

They couldn't have picked a worse day to come. Swarming over the entire square were thousands and thousands of ants, two and three deep in some places, antennae wiggling, heads moving from side to side, all climbing one on top of the other as if trying to reach the bell.

Next to spiders Hannah most hated ants. She tried to scream but no sound came out and there was nowhere to run. She could only stare at the sight before her.

At the far end of the clearing, beyond the market square, there was a sudden shaft of light. Two large doors were opening. Three figures appeared and began to make their way forward. Hannah recognised one of the party. It was Jacobus Mors. All three wore brown moleskin cloaks with stiff collars standing high around their ears. Dark wings carried them the short distance to the bell where they hovered in mid-air above the swarming ants.

'Greetings to you all,' said the Chancellor slowly and loudly, his voice carrying over to where Hannah, Landel, Ben and Lucy were standing.

'The holiday season is upon us and we welcome our fellow creatures as they take rest and water before their annual flight.'

The ants seemed to be getting excited; a few took to the air. Hannah's lip began to quiver.

'Without further ado I declare the summer route open and wish all travellers a safe and pleasant journey.' He pulled solidly on the bell clapper. A single loud 'DONG' rang out and the enormous plug fell from the roof. It looked as if it would crush everything below but jerked to a halt at the last moment and swung upside down, one metre from the ground. Immediately the ants rose up in great clouds and swarmed towards the light streaming in through the hole. Hannah closed her eyes and screamed. She crouched as low as she could as all around the ants' black bodies clashed and the noise of buzzing wings, grating legs and thudding abdomens filled the air. Long seconds passed in a drone of noise and moving air but when she looked again the ants had gone. Bright sunlight was flooding the square. Relieved and dazzled, she held her hand in front of her eyes.

'The light is so bright,' said Lucy squinting. Ben was also shielding his eyes but Landel didn't seem to be minding it too much.

'Your eyes will adjust in a few minutes and they'll close the hole once all the lumas are charged up,' he promised.

At their feet and in every window box they now noticed hundreds of thin, grey flowers starting to move. Petals were becoming plumper and whiter and leaves seemed to swell as the flowers soaked up the sunlight. Finally, the blooms glowed bright white even in the gloomiest corners.

'They light up even the darkest night,' Landel told them. 'When it's winter and the light is weak they open the other wormholes too.'

'Wormholes? Made by real worms?' Ben asked, imagining worms as fat as the fattest sea lions and as long as the longest telegraph poles.

'No,' said Landel, chuckling, 'we just call them that. At night the brownies like to sit out and talk. Only if it's not raining of course. Not even brownies like getting wet.'

Jacobus Mors was talking to a shopkeeper.

'He's seen us,' said Hannah, recovered now the ants had gone. 'We'd better go over.'

'Come to search for the lost key, I expect,' said Jacobus Mors when they approached. 'You'd better follow me.' Jacobus Mors ambled ahead in silence and they followed on past the curious, barefooted villagers as they went. Hannah noticed Sombrono had its own Apothecary but instead of the carved pestle and mortar that hung above Dr Rootvine's doorway, a huge wooden foot hung above this one. A sign in the window was advertising *Fillip Funnigan's Foot Ointment* at two pecs a cup.

Closer now, they could see the glinting doors were made entirely from silver. Jacobus Mors bowed to the glow-worm sentries standing at either side. The head of each was encased in an amber light-shade and was radiating a soft orange light.

'Nice hat,' said Ben.

Through the doors, they found themselves in a large reception hall. Two massive staircases rose opposite each other. Stone troughs sat on either side of the staircases filled to brimming with the bright, white lumas.

'Another strange place,' said Lucy quietly to Hannah. Jacobus Mors still hadn't spoken but they followed him past the staircases, down a long corridor and around a corner where they waited with him beside the first door they came to. Jacobus Mors pressed the palm of his hand against a square in the wall. The door opened and they piled into a little room which hiccoughed; the door closed.

'Going up,' said Jacobus Mors and a few seconds later, after their stomachs had bounced off the floor and risen again, the door opened. They followed the Chancellor down yet another corridor and were just about to ask where they were going when he stopped abruptly in front of a green door.

'After you,' he said, pushing the door open.

Inside they stood facing a window and through it they were astonished to see grassy hills and leafy woodland and far off, in the distance, a stretch of water shimmering in the sunshine. Looking down, quite far below, they could see a clearing and …

'Look!' called Lucy.

'Take a seat please,' said Jacobus Mors.

Hannah glance around the room and noticed Sombrono's key in a casket on the wall.

'You can just make out Puddlelake there … straight ahead,' he said, pointing. 'I can see for miles up here. Could see anyone coming before they could see us. Good strategic point. Get a clear view of the woods – that's very important – and the jackdaws keep me informed if they see anything suspicious.' A bird was sitting on a branch outside the window, moving its head from side to side, scanning the countryside below, as if on guard.

'Er … Chancellor Mors,' said Hannah, 'we don't want to take up too much of your time if you're busy ….'

'Not busy,' he said abruptly.

On the walls several portraits looked down at them. They didn't look a cheery lot; none were smiling, except perhaps one but it was more a grimace than a smile: an old lady stood looking as though her toes were being pinched.

'Great Uncle Harold,' said the Chancellor, noticing their eyes wandering over the paintings and starting with the first. 'My father's eldest brother. Only had one eye – lost the other in a fight with Humbert the Hoary defending this very land.

'Felone Melandra,' he went on, 'my great grandmother.' He pointed to the old woman with the tight shoes; a brown lace scarf lay delicately over her hair. 'Wonderful fighting spirit. Took a bite out of Fectus Core's leg once when he attacked our last Supreme Parlator in the woods there.' He pointed out the window to the woods in the distance.

'Really?' said Lucy.

Hannah remembered the conversation with Witch Magrew.

'Was Fectus Core a wizard by any chance?' she asked. Suddenly these paintings looked *very* interesting.

'He was,' said Jacobus Mors, still not smiling. 'A foul and vicious one too I understand. Cared for nothing and no one but himself, certainly not the Harmony Rules, but Zamada put paid to his vile plans I believe. He thought he could become ruler of these lands. Rule Aldoris?' He looked disgusted. 'Ridiculous notion.'

Was it possible, thought Hannah, that this Fectus Core could be same person Witch Magrew had mentioned – the one who'd had the fight with Zamada? If it was, then it must be true that he was still trapped in a Drooping Elder in the woods somewhere. Hannah opened her mouth as if she was going to speak.

Chancellor Mors raised his eyebrows and waited but Hannah kept her thoughts to herself. Instead, she asked 'Why don't you want the sixth key found, Chancellor? Wouldn't life be better with a new Supreme Parlator?'

Jacobus Mors sat back in his chair. For a few moments his grey face was so still it looked like stone.

'I voted against you because I don't believe the lost key will be found, not because I like the way life had become more difficult in our time.' He stared at Hannah. It was hard to tell what he was thinking. 'We have all looked for the key for years. The villages have been turned upside down time and time again. There is nowhere else to look. I don't believe we will ever find it and we will just have to learn to live without the wisdom and guidance of a Supreme Parlator.'

'So you don't believe the sixth key is here?' said Hannah.

'Like I say, we have looked everywhere in Sombrono. I had always hoped that our Vision Ball would tell us something but now that too, is gone. The Vision Ball told us many things but we never saw where the sixth key was. That is why I don't believe it is here in Sombrono.'

Ben thought a Vision Ball would be very useful at school and wondered if they could buy one.

'What kind of things did it tell you?' Hannah asked.

'We consulted it often. It showed us a lot more than merely what was going on in unseen parts of the village. People frequently say we take too dim a view of life but our Vision Ball confirmed to us we see life as it really is and that the reality of life is harsher than most of us can take. It is others who need to see life as a jolly holiday because they can bear no other truth. We do not hide away our sick and dying, those who have been savaged by badgers or clawed by kestrels in the night, and pretend these horrors do not happen, nor do we hide from the lies we all tell ourselves.'

Hannah had imagined he had used the Vision Ball to find out where he'd left his favourite book or what the cook was making for dinner.

He went on: 'How many times have you told a lie and pretended it was for the good of the other person or told yourself you are doing something for one reason when deep down you are doing it for another?'

Hannah blushed and Ben squirmed in his seat; Lucy examined the mud on her shoes and Landel gave an embarrassed cough.

'You are not alone,' he continued 'It is something fairy folk and Peeps have in common – the capacity to deceive ourselves. But self-knowing is a good thing; never shun its work; for it *is* work.'

There was a knock at the door.

'Come in,' called Chancellor Mors. 'Ah, Grinnard.'

They recognised the brownie who entered as Chancellor Mors's second. He smiled even less than Jacobus Mors.

'We've had some information, Chancellor,' he said but he seemed reluctant to say any more.

'Speak man, never mind the Peeps!'

'There's been a tip-off – the jackdaws have seen something. They say there's been some unusual comings and goings in Gorgonz City.'

'There's always unusual comings and goings in Gorgonz City. Something more unusual than normal?' The Chancellor clasped his hands together as if he was going to enjoy hearing what Grinnard was about to say.

'They saw a large scarab arriving at the entrance to the Council courts two nights ago with only Vasril Odo on board. But then, when he got down he didn't go inside straight away. He waited for a while, looked all around and when he was sure no one was watching, the scarab lurched several times as if others were getting off but there was no one to be seen.'

'Is that all, Grinnard?' Jacobus Mors sounded disappointed.

'No, Chancellor,' Grinnard's black wings rubbed together as if they were scratching an itch.

'They say that they saw footprints form in the dust and walk to the back entrance.'

Hannah couldn't contain herself. 'Who were they?' she asked eagerly.

'We don't know, Miss Hannah. It seems they were invisible.'

'Isn't it against the Harmony Rules to be invisible?' asked Lucy.

'Only to commit a crime,' said Chancellor Mors 'But anyway, Gorgonz City don't abide by the Harmony Rules anymore. They pretend they do but they don't and everyone knows they don't but pretends they do.' He turned back to Grinnard 'How many?'

'Difficult to say exactly but they think maybe five. They can't be sure.'

'Thank you, Grinnard.'

'Oh, and there's something else,' he said. 'They found this in the empty scarab.' Grinnard handed Jacobus Mors a sealed parchment and bowed out of the room.

'What do you make of that then?' asked the Chancellor, smiling faintly for the first time.

'They're up to something – we're sure of that,' said Hannah, 'but what exactly, we don't know.'

'We don't believe their key is lost,' said Ben smugly.

'Nor do I,' said Chancellor Mors, fanning himself with the parchment Grinnard had brought in. 'But as you saw, everyone in the Council chose to keep silent. We allowed Grossus to think we believed his lie.'

'Why didn't you speak up if you didn't believe him?' asked Lucy.

'Because sometimes it is wise not to let someone know what you're thinking,' he said slyly. 'At other times of course, it's very *unwise* not to let them know what you're thinking.'

They all nodded as if they understood.

'Chancellor Barbelly seemed to have believed him,' said Hannah.

'Yes, well, that's his way.' Chancellor Mors began opening the parchment. 'Chancellor Barbelly is a fair and honest man and sees only the good in everyone.'

'But Hironymus Grossus told a lie,' said Lucy protesting.

'Yes, it's likely he did, but he is forced to face the fact he lied.'

'He won't care about that, as long as he gets his own way,' said Ben.

Jacobus Mors looked patiently at their puzzled faces. 'That's a choice we all have to make, isn't it?' he said. 'We choose whether we lie to get what we want or we choose not to lie and deceive.'

'It's very difficult all this lies business, isn't it?' said Hannah, looking as if she had a headache.

'Very,' agreed Chancellor Mors. 'Now then, let's have a look at this.'

On the table before them Chancellor Mors laid out the opened parchment. It seemed to be some sort of map, but not an ordinary map; it seemed to be a map of the heavens, and there was some writing:

IF THE KEY IS WHAT YOU'RE AFTER
THEN LOOK INTO THE STARS
FIND THEM WHERE THEY COME AND GO
CHOOSE ONE THAT GLOWS LIKE MARS.

'The key! It mentions the key,' exclaimed Hannah, nearly jumping out of her seat.

'It mention *a* key, Miss Hannah, not specifically the lost sixth key from the Magical Crown. It is very unlikely that Vasril Odo or any of his invisible guests would just happen to have such information in their pockets, don't you think?'

'Maybe it's a decoy,' said Landel.

'Maybe it's been dropped on purpose to send us off on the wrong track,' said Ben, picking up on Landel's train of thought.

'A possibility,' said the Chancellor 'but why a map of the heavens? – if that's what it is – you can hardly be expected to search the skies now, can you?'

That might be true but Hannah wanted the map none the less.

'May we have this?' she asked, leaning forward.

'Certainly. Although it seems of little use.'

Jacobus Mors, it appeared, was not about to get excited over the strange map, but Hannah took it quickly, folded it and tucked it into the backpack.

'Do you still want to search Sombrono?' the Chancellor asked, glancing out of the window in the direction of Gorgonz City.

'Can you think of *anywhere* that's not been searched?' asked Hannah.

'Not a square centimetre. I can assure you, the sixth key is not here,' he said emphatically. 'You are welcome to look if you'd like to but I really think you'd be wasting your time. Like I say, we would have seen it in the Vision Ball.'

Hannah wondered if Jacobus Mors could be trusted. Was he trying to put them off searching because the key *was* in Sombrono or was he as sure as he sounded and knew it wasn't? Time was short and they had to spend it wisely.

'Well, what about your village key?' said Hannah testing him 'Can we take it back to Pickletullum? If someone is stealing the keys they'll not think yours is in Pickletullum and if we do find the sixth key it will make it easier to assemble the Magical Crown if they're all together.'

To Hannah's surprise the Chancellor agreed.

'You may take it, certainly, but I would like it returned if the sixth key is not found.'

Hannah nodded.

Chancellor Mors got up from his chair and went over to the casket on the wall. He pointed his wand at the lock and when the little door swung creakily open he laid the key on the table.

The gold shaft and long, curved teeth gleamed in the light and the blue sapphire dazzled as if all the bluest whirlpools in the world had been concentrated into this one stone, the size of a plum. Hannah carefully picked it up and put it in her backpack with the parchment.

'Do stay as long as you want,' said the Chancellor, 'I think you'll find our village more interesting than you'd thought.' He had the uncanny knack, Hannah observed, of saying what she was already thinking. Sombrono and its Chancellor were indeed more interesting than she'd first thought.

'You don't happen to have a musical repair shop do you?' asked Ben, feeling the flute under his tee-shirt.

'We don't have one here but there's one in Pickletullum – you must have missed it – and the Shop of Sounds in Socratown do repairs. My father was a music lover you know.'

He pointed to his portrait on the wall.

'Mostly dirges and funeral marches; he was particularly fond of the dramatic. He couldn't come out of the Shop of Sounds without bringing back a popsicle of monsoon. "Nothing like the sound of an unrelenting downpour to make you realise how trifling a little shower is," he always said.'

Back down on the street the village somehow looked brighter and more airy that it had been when they had first arrived. Children were playing happily and the muted colours of their baggy clothes somehow seemed a little lovelier. Lucy spied the Shop of Smells. Scratchy writing above the door read *Olfactory Factory* and hanging above the entrance was a rather long nose with cavernous nostrils, which were wide enough to suck you up.

'Can we go in?' Lucy asked.

'So you've heard of our wonderful Shop of Smells,' said Chancellor Mors. 'It's certainly worth a visit.' He spread his cloak around their shoulders and swept them inside. They were alone in the shop; all was quiet except for a large round copper vessel in the corner which went 'blub, blub' every few seconds. Three tubes protruded from its side and a cork stopper plugged the end of each. Steam rose from a thin curved tube on the top of the vessel and a drip quivered at its end then fell with a heavy plop into a shallow basin on the floor.

'Are you there, Mr Dewberry?' Jacobus Mors called out.

They heard a scuffling and the sound of a cardboard box falling to the ground from the back room and immediately a man appeared with a scrunched up handkerchief in one hand.

'Good aftermidsun, Chancellor,' he said dabbing his nose, 'Sorry to keep you waiting.'

'Mr Dewberry, this is Hannah, Ben, Lucy and Landel.'

Mr Dewberry nodded as he heard each of their names and his wavy hair, which twisted into the air like a mini tornado, wobbled back and forth. Hannah thought that if he nodded too hard he might do a somersault.

'These young people are very interested in your shop and I wondered if you might show them some of its wonders,' said Chancellor Mors.

'Be glad to,' said Mr Dewberry, beckoning them towards the hundreds of little glass bottles lining the walls; thin wispy smoke curled and uncurled inside them.

'Well, as you can see, we stock just about anything you could ever want here; run-of- the-mill smells, strong perfumes, pungent pongs, delicate fragrances, slight whiffs, homely odours, unpleasant stenches – whatever takes your fancy! What would you like to try?'

Jacobus Mors sat down on a chair, pulled his moleskin cloak around him and looked on.

'I've always wanted to know what a rain-forest smells like,' said Ben, going first and leaning over the counter.

Mr Dewberry raised his eyebrows and his eyes moved to the glass bottles behind him. He lifted his wand and pointed to a bottle that was out of reach. It juddered as it moved from its place then floated smoothly down to land on the counter.

'Try this,' he said removing the stopper and circling the bottle under Ben's nose. 'What do you smell?'

Ben breathed in deeply and let the vapour travel down into his lungs. 'Green. It smells green like newly cut grass … fresh raindrops … and hot baked melon tart and there's a smell … like wood, wet feathers and, and antiseptic.'

'Good, very good,' said Mr Dewberry, wiping another drip from the end of his nose and replacing the stopper.

'It really smelled like wet feathers,' said Ben.

'Wonderful, isn't it? the images that scents evoke. Smell is the most powerful of the senses. Did you know that? Nothing can make you recall forgotten memories like a smell. Glad you enjoyed it. Now, what about you, young lady?' he said to Lucy.

'I'd like to smell a baby elephant,' she said, giving Mr Dewberry a wide grin.

'You can't ask for that,' said Ben scoffing.

'Why not?'

'A baby elephant will just pong, and anyway it's a stupid thing to ask for,' said Ben.

'We have it right here,' said Mr Dewberry, turning his back to them. From the highest shelf a bottle wobbled and made its way down. A grey vapour swirled inside the bottle. Mr Dewberry released the stopper.

Lucy sniffed a little sniff and waited for the smell to creep up her nostrils.

'It smells like … boot polish,' she said excitedly before taking a deep breath. 'And soft suede and it's like … a big bristle brush dipped into Grandma's freshly dug potato patch.'

'Excellent, that's exactly what a baby elephant smells like,' said Mr Dewberry.

'Humph,' said Ben.

'Can I try?' asked Landel, 'I've never seen a baby elephant.' He sniffed deeply, taking in a huge lungful and closed his eyes. 'It's a large, wrinkly sort of smell … its tickling the inside of my nose ….'

'Yes, wonderful isn't it,' said Mr Dewberry happily.

'And it does pong a bit,' he whispered to Lucy. Lucy giggled.

Mr Dewberry turned to Hannah for her turn.

'I won't bother, thank you,' said Hannah meekly. 'I can't think of anything I'd like to try.'

'Shall I choose something for you?' he asked.

Hannah nodded.

Mr Dewberry chose a bottle from close by, removed the stopper and held it out. Hannah breathed in.

'Urgh,' she said immediately, 'That's awful.'

She had expected something nice but she didn't like this smell much at all. It smelled just like Vasril Odo.

Mr Dewberry looked amused. 'It's the smell of a particular hair lotion we use,' he said. 'It's very popular here in Sombrono. It makes the hair lie flat and shiny – considered very attractive by many.'

'But not by Miss Hannah obviously,' said Jacobus Mors, a faint smile reappearing on his lips.

Hannah snorted to get the smell out of her nose.

'That's but a tiny sample of the smells we have here. Making up smells to order is our speciality so if you want something we haven't got you just need to ask. Or,' continued Mr Dewberry enthusiastically, 'if you ever want a smell identified, this is the place to come. This nose of mine can identify over one hundred thousand different smells.' Hannah believed it could as she had never seen one as big.

They thanked Mr Dewberry and waved through the window when they left.

As they waited for the scarab to take them home Hannah assured Chancellor Mors that the village key would be kept safe in Pickletullum.

'Keep me informed of your progress,' he said, 'and good luck with your search.'

They boarded the scarab and with a last look back at Sombrono, Hannah, Ben, Lucy and Landel disappeared down the dark tunnel.

Chapter 12

Gorgonz City

Grandma Fred had been very busy on the village Summer Fête Committee. Farmer Digwell couldn't lend them his marquee this year because the week before his bull had ripped two very long gashes all along one side of it when it had charged at the Mayoress who, perhaps, shouldn't have worn her red dress and hat to the opening of the Agricultural and Livestock Show. Grandma Fred was not having much luck in organising a replacement and Hannah, Ben and Lucy had easily managed to get away in the afternoons.

Now that Sombrono's key was safely deposited alongside Pickletullum's key in the vault under the Town Hall, Hannah felt much happier. Having two of the six keys was a good start but there was still a lot to do. They had decided to believe Jacobus Mors when he said he would have seen the sixth key in the Vision Ball if it had been there and left Sombrono unsearched but they had now ventured into Pickletullum's strangest and dustiest places; the places where almost no one ever went anymore; exactly the sorts of places someone might hide a lost sixth key; but there was still no sign. The map hadn't helped; they couldn't work out what it meant. Even upside down it didn't look like any place they'd seen so far.

Their search for clues took Hannah, Ben and Lucy back to the library in Pickletullum and there, deep in the musty Chronicles Crypt, they researched the last years of Zamada's reign. Mr Booker, the librarian, looking as pale as a ghost

(Ben thought it must be the lack of daylight), unlocked the iron gate to let them down the last stairs, lit the torches on the wall then closed the gate behind him with a heavy clang. Huge metal-edged books lined the walls in date order; there were at least a couple of thousand. In the yellowed pages of the most recent volumes, they found details of the fever and how it had ravaged Aldoris, and of the fire that had swept through the Council Chambers at Gorgonz City a few days after Zamada's death, destroying important records of Council business and Zamada's personal papers. But once again there was no mention of the sixth key or where it might be and there was no mention of Fectus Core.

'The fire seems to have wiped out mention of everything that might have given us a clue,' mourned Hannah. 'And there's no mention of anyone called Fectus Core.'

'But even if it was him and he was trapped in a tree like Witch Magrew said, he'd have died of starvation or boredom a long time ago,' said Ben, holding a candle aloft. 'So why are we looking for mention of him?'

'But what if he's still out there?' said Hannah, her face looking yellow in the candlelight.

'Alive!' said Lucy.

'We'll just have to keep away from drooping elders then, won't we,' said Ben, more bravely than he felt.

They still hadn't spoken to Dolfi. He had been away, Milli told them, on Council business, at a meeting of the Scarabs' Transport Association in a nearby town and there was to be a national meeting in Mauldeath the next week which was a sign of how serious the situation was. Outlander beetles, armour-plated and dangerous, were threatening the underground transport systems all over the country. They were attacking the scarabs as they flew with their passengers. On their way home the evening before, they had nearly been thrown to the ground when they were rammed by one. Ben had jabbed it between the eyes with the end of the flute and it had veered off course and crashed into the burroway wall.

When they left the library and called into the music shop to see if they could get the flute working properly it was looking slightly more battered than it had when Witch Magrew had first given it to Hannah. A sticking plaster stretched over the small split that had appeared after Ben had given the Outlander its black eye.

'Doesn't look like it's been played much in its time,' said Mr Hornpiper. 'Been bashed about a bit though.'

He closed one eye and looked down its length.

'Can't see any obstruction – you say it's not playing properly?'

'It only plays one tune and it misses a section in the middle,' explained Hannah.

'Only plays one tune? Queer flute that only plays one tune,' he said, scratching behind his ear. 'Unless it's enchanted.'

'I think it is,' said Hannah. 'You just need to blow and it plays the tune for you.'

'A Unitune, eh. Tricky things. You never know if it means to miss the notes or not. I can give it a good clean for you but that's about all I can do. You can't un-charm a Unitune.' As Mr Hornpiper set to cleaning the flute Hannah wondered if it was worth spending any of their money on it. It was no real use to them after all.

Mr Hornpiper took a large breath and blew into the flute. Once again the march sounded then faltered in the middle. From under the counter he pulled out a long carrying case which contained soft, woolly cleaning rods of all sizes and thicknesses. He poked a short, thin one down the first hole. Dust and cake crumbs came out with the rod. He tapped the flute on the counter – more crumbs fell into a neat pile – then he blew again. The tune was more harmonious but was still silent for a few beats in the middle.

Mr Hornpiper chose another hole and briskly slid the cleaning rod back and forth. A little feather shot into the air, wafted lazily from side to side, and slowly fell to the floor. The sound from the flute was becoming clearer but the tune still didn't play right through.

'May as well do every one,' he said, choosing the next sized cleaning rod and trying the next hole. Bits of fluff and dust billowed forth. The next hole was not quite as easy. Mr Hornpiper pushed harder.

'Seems to be something stuck in there,' he said, ramming the rod forward but nothing budged. 'Dear,dear,dear.'

He lifted it to the light and squinted through it again. 'I'll try the other side'.

Mr Hornpiper leaned forward and pushed as hard as he could, went a bit red in the face and when the rod still didn't move he walloped it on the end with his hand.

A small, pea-sized object shot out, hit the shop counter, pinged off the strings of an instrument, boinged off a drum and slid across the entire length of a huge harp standing in the corner, filling the shop with a tuneful crescendo.

'What is it?' cried Lucy, peering after the object as it skittered across the floor.

Ben picked it up. It was about the shape and size of the tiniest, tiniest sausage roll.

Mr Hornpiper opened a drawer in his counter, took out a magnifying glass and looked at the object in the palm of Ben's hand.

'It's a scroll,' he said, raising and lowering the glass. 'Looks like a piece of parchment's been rolled up. It'll need to be enlarged before you'll be able to read it though.'

They all stared down at the minute scroll.

'Thank you, Mr Hornpiper,' said Hannah.

'That's why it's not been playing properly I suspect,' he said blowing it again. For the first time the flute played the march all the way through.

'It'll only ever play that one tune though. I'll just finish cleaning it for you.'

When he had, they paid him and hurried down to the Town Hall to find Dolfi. Dolfi was in his office shuffling papers across his desk.

'How is your search going?' he asked.

'No sign of the key yet,' said Hannah 'but we've found out a few things.'

'I told you it would be difficult.'

Hannah sat down and filled Dolfi in on what they had found out so far, about the imps still being missing and about the jackdaws in Sombrono reporting mysterious footprints appearing outside Gorgonz City, and about the strange map. She laid the map before him as he listened carefully. He took a minute to study it but it didn't seem to mean much to Dolfi either.

'And look what was in the flute Witch Magrew gave me,' said Hannah. Ben opened his palm so Dolfi could see.

'It's a scroll that's been made really, really small,' said Ben.

'Do you think it could have been put there on purpose?' asked Hannah.

'We'll soon find out,' said Dolfi. 'Lay it on that chair, Ben.'

They watched as Dolfi took out his wand and aimed carefully.

'*Ad maxima!*'

The scroll got bigger and bigger until it was sitting across the chair in full view of everyone, a blue ribbon tied around its middle.

Hannah got to it first, untied it and unrolled it. 'It's a poem.' She started to read it aloud:

IF NO WHITE PTARMIGAN FLIES
IN THE SKY ABOVE OUR LAND
AND NO SUPREME PARLATOR
SITS AT YOUR COMMAND

IF DAYS ARE GETTING DARKER
AND NO MORE YOU SHARE AND CARE
AND WICKEDNESS AILS YOU
IN THE GUISE OF RIGHT, BEWARE.

BEWARE THE POTION MAKER
AND WHAT HE TRULY SEEKS.
BY SLOWLY BREWING FEVER
HE'LL BRING DEATH IN DAYS NOT WEEKS.

GOLD IS WHAT HE'S AFTER
POWER AND GLORY HIS HEART'S DESIRE
WHEN ALL ELSE FAILS BE CAREFUL
GUARD THE PRECIOUS FIRE.

There was no signature.

'Well,' said Dolfi wide-eyed, 'What should we make of that?'

'Wow!' said Lucy, taking it from Hannah and reading it again.

'Worth the money getting the flute cleaned, wasn't it? I knew there was something funny about Dr Rootvine,' said Ben.

'I think we can assume the poem is *not* about Dr Rootvine,' said Dolfi, smoothing his eyebrows as he spoke. 'This scroll looks very old and Dr Rootvine is not the only Potion Maker that's ever lived.'

'But how did it get in the flute?' asked Hannah.

'You say Witch Magrew gave you this flute?' said Dolfi, turning it over and looking at the split.

'Yes. She said Zamada gave it to her,' said Hannah.

But had Zamada put the poem inside?

Now they had two things to think about – the scroll and the map. What was each telling them? Were they connected? How could they be when they seemed to be about two different things?

'The scroll is warning of a Potion Maker who wants the Precious Fires, but if Zamada wrote it, anyone she knew would have died a long time ago,' said Ben.

'I thought no one knew about the Precious Fires before the imps brought them here,' said Hannah.

'They have always been known in myth, Hannah, but we didn't know they existed for sure until the imps brought them.'

'And the map … look into the stars … choose one that glows like Mars. What can that mean?' said Hannah.

'Could be a clue,' said Lucy.

'If it means anything at all it will take time to work it out,' said Dolfi calmly. 'The disappearance of the sixth key has puzzled us all for years and I don't expect it will decide to turn up now we've found a scroll and a map.'

But even if Dolfi wasn't jumping up and down, Hannah was.

'We must find out what these things mean. Is there anyone in the village who knows about the stars and things like that?' she asked. 'We should start with the map.'

'Well, there *is* a Star Map Maker in Gorgonz City, if you think it's worth speaking to him,' said Dolfi. 'I'm going to Gorgonz City today as a matter of fact. You can come with me if you like.' Hannah and Lucy nodded. 'Meet me at Ma Molly's in one digit's turn,' said Dolfi. 'I've got some work to do here first.'

'Any lead is worth following,' said Hannah, as they made their way up the street.

'Especially if it leads to Ma Molly's,' said Ben rubbing his stomach.

Hannah and Lucy felt sure this was their first real breakthrough to the whereabouts of the sixth key although Ben kept telling them they were on the wrong track and twittered on about Herbert Rootvine's crooked nose and shifty eyes.

As they walked Hannah repeated the rhymes on the map and the scroll over and over, trying to fathom out what they meant. Lucy patiently reopened and closed the backpack several times when Hannah kept forgetting the words. Ben started playing the flute; it was quite catchy although a bit repetitive. By the time they reached Ma Molly's Hannah had memorised the poem and the map and could hum the tune all the way through.

Inside it was busy and, thankfully, people no longer stared at them so much. The people of Aldoris seemed to be getting used to having them around. Through the window they waved to Landel, Hornet and Hunnik who were playing Wingtang.

'Can I get you something?' Ma Molly asked, wiping her hands on her apron.

'Four blackberry juices and four hawthorn muffins, with extra chewy bits please,' said Ben.

Ma Molly took their order and busied herself with a ladle in the wooden barrel of blackberry juice.

Hannah noticed Ben staring at something and turned to see Kuzu Grossus and Splint in the doorway.

'Let's just ignore them,' she said quietly.

Ma Molly set their order down on the table; Hannah paid her one kippa and three pecs and Ben sank his teeth into his hawthorn muffin.

Kuzu Grossus sloped towards them, Splint by his side – with one tooth less than the last time they'd seen him, Ben was sure.

'I don't want any trouble in here boys,' called Ma Molly sternly.

It was as if she hadn't spoken.

'Not still looking for that key, I hope,' Kuzu Grossus immediately sneered.

'Can't see that it's any of your business,' replied Ben through a mouthful of muffin.

'I'm making it my business,' said Grossus flexing the muscles on his arm. Splint moved menacingly beside him.

'Leave us alone,' Lucy shouted, standing up but only just coming level with Grossus's chest.

'You couldn't squash an orange even if you jumped on it.'

Grossus pulled his hand from his pocket and in the next instant Ben felt his eyes fill with dust and a heavy blow to his chest. He sped backwards off his stool and through the air. His goblet flew from his hand and his hawthorn muffin sailed over the head of someone standing nearby. Ben felt himself wallop into a wall amid thunderous crashing and splattering and muffins and dumplings rained down on him as he crumpled to the floor. Suddenly, there were feet everywhere. ben strugled to his feet and felt a thud in the face. He swung wildly at a towering shape and felt pain surge through his hand. He hoped it hurt Grossus more than it hurt him. More fists and arms whipped by in a blur.

'Get him, Ben!' Hannah was yelling, and he could hear Lucy screech, 'Behind you, Landel!'

There were grunts, crashes and yells all around; it seemed like half the place had joined in the fight although it was hard to see who was fighting who. Several wallops and an elbow in the ribs later, Ben felt someone pulling on his belt.

'THAT'S ENOUGH! OUT! Get out – all of you! And don't come back!' Pa Molly had arrived and began throwing them, one by one, out into the street.

Hannah tried to tell him Kuzu Grossus had started it and it wasn't Ben's fault he'd gone flying into a tray of Ma Molly's apple dumplings and they'd splattered all over the wall. But it was no use. It cost them another three kippa, and worse, the dumplings were too gritty and squished to eat.

'I didn't even get to finish my hawthorn muffin,' said Ben, sniffing and wiping away the blood trickling from his nose.

'We can get another tomorrow when they've forgotten all about it.' Landel rubbed his arm which felt as though it had been put through a mangle.

'We would have licked them for sure if Pa Molly hadn't stopped us so soon,' said Hornet, still jabbing the air at an imaginary Splint.

By the time Dolfi arrived Hannah had shown Landel, Hornet and Hunnik the scroll and the map, Lucy had the backpack fastened ready to leave and Ben's nose had stopped bleeding. They thought it best not to mention the fight.

In the Portway, Horace was too flustered dealing with complaints about the Outlanders hijacking the scarabs to notice who was coming and going. One woman was complaining loudly that her shopping had fallen out into the burroway and her husband was complaining he had been looking forward to a parsnip stew and mumbled something uncomplimentary about her nettle soup. Horace whistled the scarabs off quickly just to get rid of them and one narrowly missed another coming in the opposite direction.

On the way to Gorgonz City, Hannah asked Dolfi what he thought had happened to the imps.

'It's possible, I suppose, that they've returned to the Caves of Molten Rock for more of the Precious Fire.'

Hannah didn't think so. 'But what if they haven't? Something could have happened to them and what if the fever comes back? Without the Precious Fires you would all die.'

'We'll find out where the imps and the Precious Fires are soon enough,' said Dolfi. 'Most things work themselves out.' Hannah didn't feel reassured.

Beyond the Council Chambers, Gorgonz City looked like the rocky remains of a landslide from the mountain behind. Only when they found their way inside the craggy rock faces did everything change. Towers of stone and sheer walls turned into busy streets and from every window and doorway, it seemed, suspicious eyes followed them.

'Move along there,' a voice behind them said when they dawdled by a shop selling *Quills and Quivers*. A goblin guard in a metal helmet with what looked like a brush on top waved a thorny stick to encourage them onwards.

'They are with me,' said Dolfi firmly and the guard left them alone and lumbered on.

'Funny place to keep a lavatory brush,' said Ben once the guard was out of earshot.

'Not much further now,' said Dolfi, quickening the pace.

Two shops later they stopped in front of an entrance which said simply:

STAR MAP MAKER

Underneath, in small print, it said:

TENTH GENERATION

'Got the map?' asked Dolfi. Lucy patted the backpack.

'Right then. Let's see if Cosmick Smallpiece can help us.'

Inside, enormously high walls stretched as far as the eye could see and, suspended high in the vast curved ceiling, the planets of the solar system were revolving slowly.

In the centre of the floor was an exceedingly tall man. His legs seemed to go on forever and from where they stood it looked like he was wearing a red hat.

As the door closed a firework whizzed up into the air and four separate fireballs burst out of it, one after the other; each exploded in turn sending out yellow, blue, green and red flares. The giant saw these and looked down.

'Ah, Mr Greenlees,' he boomed, sounding surprised and looking down curiously at his guests.'Lost your way?'

There seemed to be a balloon above his head, getting bigger and bigger.

'Mr Smallpiece,' said Dolfi. 'How nice to see you again. We've not lost our way but we've got a bit of a puzzle we hope you can help us with.'

Maps the giant had made, detailing vast star clusters, were on every wall. Splendid coloured drawings of gas clouds and asteroids were everywhere. A rock was hanging in mid-air next to Dolfi's elbow by a sign flashing Haley Comet Junior. To the right a chart of the heavens gave the distances of how far all the planets were away from Gorgonz City and Hannah noted that the nearest star was marked as being four and a half light years, two weeks and six days away.

'My young friends here have come across what appears to be a strange astrological map. We're hoping you might be able to make some sense of it.'

'Well, I'll try,' said the giant, lowering his book, *The Revolutions of the Celestial Spheres* by Nicolaus Copernicus. 'There's so much to know about the universe that I doubt anyone could ever know it all, but I'll do my best. You can count on that.'

There was a dazzling explosion of light way above their heads.

Hannah and Lucy screamed and Dolfi instinctively ducked. Ben held both his arms over his head. In the very strange ceiling, a dark shape was rumbling.

'What was that?' exclaimed Ben.

'That,' said the giant 'was a Supernova.' His face was stretched into an ecstatic smile. 'I've been waiting for that to happen for ages. I've been watching it since I

116

was just four feet tall. How marvellously splendiferous! How astronomically, gargantuanly marvellous! You will excuse me, won't you,' he said, fanning his flushed cheeks with his great hand. 'Oh, you must see this. Only happens once in a lifetime.'

The giant bent down and laid the palm of his hand on the floor – they could now see he had very short carroty hair – and they climbed aboard his hand and sat cross-legged. It was like sitting on the softest, most comfortable bed imaginable with the electric blanket on full blast. The giant raised his hand to his chest and started to climb up a stepladder which was leaning against one wall. Soon, they were so far off the ground that their backpack on the floor looked no bigger than a full stop.

'Isn't that wonderful?' said the giant, raising his hand even higher. They were suspended in the heavens looking out into a never ending universe of billions of stars.

'Look! There it is, a black hole. Created when an old star comes to the end of its life and explodes.' A black spiral shape was turning and it seemed the very light about them was being sucked into its centre. Thankfully, it looked very, very far away.

In front of them, the planets of the solar system rotated slowly about the gigantic fiery sun.

Hannah stared. 'Look at the size of the sun. I can't believe it's that big.'

'It would take a million earths to fill the sun if it were an empty bladderball,' said the giant.

'This is awesome!' said Ben.

'Are they real stars?' asked Lucy leaning forward, wanting to touch one.

The giant chuckled. 'They are indeed. Each one is a sun like our own and they might even have their own solar systems like ours. Did you know that there are more stars in the universe than there are grains of sand on all the beaches of the entire world?'

Before they could answer, the giant pointed out Venus and Mercury to their left and Jupiter and Saturn, with their dusty rings, to the right.

'Both Jupiter and Saturn have sixteen moons,' said the giant, pointing while Lucy counted. 'And furthest from the sun, there are Uranus, Neptune and Pluto. They get little of its heat and light. You'd need to take a very large hot water bottle with you if you went there.'

'Look! Look at that,' Hannah had noticed something.

'That's Mars,' said the giant.

'It's red,' she said.

'Of course it is. It's made of rock that's gone rusty.'

'Really?' said Lucy.

'Really!' said the giant.

'The map mentions Mars,' said Hannah once she'd caught her breath. 'It says

"Choose one that glows like Mars".'

'It does, does it? We'd better have a look then,' said the giant.

He carefully lowered his hands and returned them to the floor. Lucy handed the giant the map.

He fumbled in a drawer, took out his glasses and, once he'd hooked the wire legs around his large ears, he held the map delicately to his nose. He looked completely cross-eyed.

'IF THE KEY IS WHAT YOU'RE AFTER
THEN LOOK INTO THE STARS
FIND THEM WHERE THEY COME AND GO
CHOOSE ONE THAT GLOWS LIKE MARS.'

'Well, it mentions Mars all right.'

Hannah nodded vigorously.

'Stars can be blue, white, yellow, orange or red depending on how old and hot they are. If it's like Mars, I guess you'll be looking for a red star but where you would look for one I don't know.' They were listening intently. 'It can't mean you have to go into space now, can it?'

'I suppose not,' Hannah agreed.

'This ceiling's the closest even *I* get to space. You can't just take some sandwiches with you and go there on a scarab.' The giant looked at the map and read the lines once more.

'Stars come and go in the skies all the time but it takes hundreds of millions of years from birth to death so I don't think it means that kind of coming and going,' He thought for a few seconds longer.

'I can't say I recognise this constellation,' he said turning the map on its side. 'Bit of a mystery all right. Sorry.'

'Oh,' said Hannah, feeling like Haley Comet Junior hitting the ground with a heavy thud. The giant gently handed the map back to Lucy.

Thanking the giant they followed Dolfi along the street back towards the Council Chambers.

'I was sure he was going to tell us something that would help us find the lost sixth key,' said Hannah.

'Don't be too disappointed,' said Dolfi, quickly retracing their steps. 'It was worth a try.'

The ride up the escalator in the Council Courts was just as weird as it had been before. They watched as one by one the Chancellors' painted faces came into focus and looked again at the portrait of Zamada before they passed into the square hall outside the Crystal Room. There was no goblin sitting in the glass chair outside the gold doors.

'It's not a long meeting. You can wait here,' said Dolfi then he let himself inside.

Hannah sat feeling gloomy while Lucy fidgeted and Ben lay back against the red leather sofa.

'I wonder what's in all these other rooms?' Lucy got up and peered down the hallway. There was no one about.

'They must be used for something, I suppose,' said Ben, idly slapping the flute in his hand.

Something occurred to Hannah. 'There must be a records office here somewhere.' It said some records of council business were destroyed in a fire here after Zamada died, in the library, remember. If we could have a look around we might find something useful.'

'You're not going anywhere Hannah,' said Ben sensing she was about to do something silly.

'I wonder who those footprints in the dust belonged to?' said Lucy, daydreaming.

Hannah sprang from her seat. 'I'll not be long,' she said, and before Ben or Lucy realised what she was doing Hannah was creeping along the corridor.

'Hannah!' Ben croaked. 'Come back.'

Ben held onto Lucy or she would have gone too and he wasn't going to sit there alone.

Hannah tiptoed along the corridor and listened at the first door she came to. It was large and heavy and she heard nothing when she pressed her ear against it. She tried the door but it was locked.

The next door was smaller and when Hannah tried the handle, it was open. Any hopes of finding something interesting faded though when, peering through the dim light, all she saw were candles – hundreds and hundreds of them, all stacked up; enough to keep all five villages alight for a year. Hannah looked back to see Ben beckoning her. She moved on quickly, but up ahead she heard a click – someone was coming out of one of the rooms. She looked around. Too far to go back now. She lunged for the next door handle and wrenched it round. It didn't open. The voices were getting louder – someone was about to appear in the hall. Hannah's eyes fell on one of the red sofas stretched along the wall and she dived behind it.

'They've got the flute but we shall have it from them. I take it you understand me?'

It was Vasril Odo's voice. How did he know about the flute?

'An' hows we gonna get it then?'

'There'll be a way Grunt, just find it.'

'But they're with Dolfi most times.'

'Don't argue, just get it or Chancellor Grossus won't be pleased,' snapped Vasril Odo.

It was dusty behind the sofa. Hannah felt a tickle … a sneeze was creeping up on her. She rubbed her nose to make it go away but it just got worse. She tried her best to stifle it but it squeezed out like a strangled hiccough –

119

'Hinnew!'

'What was that?'

'Dunno.'

'There's someone lurking around here. Find them!'

Hannah huddled down making herself as small as possible. She could feel their eyes searching the gloom and hear someone opening and closing doors. From beneath the sofa she watched the feet come closer. But Hannah was not alone. A mouse was sitting on a cellar hatch under the sofa preening its whiskers.

'Who's there?' demanded Vasril Odo. Hannah's heart slammed into her ribcage as they stepped nearer.

'Show yourself!'

Hannah stared at the mouse, panic rising.

'There's someone behind that sofa!'

'Aarghh! What was that?'

The mouse ran off down the hall.

'Pahh, a mouse!' Vasril Odo collapsed on the sofa. Hannah didn't let even her eyelashes flutter.

'Remember you've got a job to do,' said Vasril Odo getting up from the sofa.

Hannah ran back to join Ben and Lucy outside the Crystal Room.

'That was close.' She quickly told them what she had overheard. Ben immediately put the flute back in the backpack.

'How did Vasril Odo know we've got the flute?' asked Lucy.

'From the Vision Ball?' asked Hannah.

'So it looks like Hiromymus Grossus is behind the raids after all,' said Ben.

'There's only one way to prove it,' said Hannah 'We'll have to find the Vision Ball and the other things that have been stolen.'

'And how are we going to do that? You can't mean break in and sneak around?'

'Shuush!'

The heavy handle clunked and the great gold doors to the Crystal Room started to slowly open. The Council meeting was over.

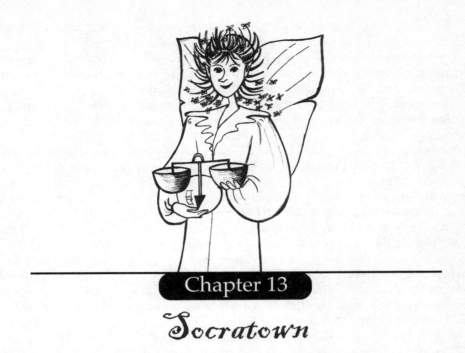

Chapter 13

Socratown

'So, right now, what are you planning to do next?' Dolfi asked next day in his office.

They didn't tell him about overhearing Vasril Odo giving an order to steal the flute and no one mentioned that Hannah was thinking of sneaking into Gorgonz City to search for the Vision Ball, the Scales of Balance and Judgement and the other missing things. Ben and Lucy had agreed this wasn't one of Hannah's better ideas. It would be dangerous. If they got caught they would be thrown out, never to return, and almost certainly have their memories wiped. But there was no knowing what would happen if Hironymus Grossus caught them. They might rot in a dungeon somewhere. Grandma Fred would be frantic and they might never eat Mum's rhubarb crumble and custard again. It didn't bear thinking about. Hannah was insane to consider it. But they wouldn't tell her that just yet.

'We're going to Socratown today,' Hannah told Dolfi.

'Socratown's a funny name,' said Lucy, imagining a town full of socks.

Dolfi smiled from the other side of the table.

'Sprites are great storytellers and their ancient stories contain much wisdom and philosophy. One of the greatest was a philosopher called Socratony who studied in Greece under the Ancient Master of Philosophy, Socrates. Socratony lived there for many years but at the end of his life he came back and brought much of what he'd learned with him. When he died the village was named after him.'

Ben searched his memory. 'Wasn't Socrates the man who drank rat poison?'

'It wasn't rat poison as I recall, Ben, it was Hemlock, none the less poisonous but made from the Hemlock plant. There's no earthly antidote, even today.'

Milli joined them on their visit to Socratown and on the journey they showed her the scroll they had found. Hannah almost told her about overhearing Vasril Odo giving the order to steal the flute but decided against it.

'The White Ptarmigan used to fly over Pickletullum a lot,' said Milli, after reading the scroll 'but we haven't seen it since the invisible raiders began stealing things from the villages.'

Again Hannah nearly confided in Milli that they suspected Hironymus Grossus and Vasril Odo were behind the raids but decided to say nothing until they had some proof. Today, though, they were headed for Socratown. The scarab was soon out of the burroway and dipping and swooping through tall grass. It flew overland for a distance, weaving around thick gorse bushes and tangled broom, and eventually came to a halt halfway up a gigantic oak tree, settling on a broad flat branch where they got out. Milli led the way, only inside, it wasn't like a tree at all. Hannah touched the side of the transparent elevator – it felt like a glass bubble – and when it slowed and came to a halt with a little bump Milli opened a curved door in the trunk and they stepped through. A pebbly lane stretched before them and up ahead they could see the village where just a few seconds before there had been nothing but woodland and grass.

'How? Where?' Ben started as he looked around, but Milli interrupted.

'You should know by now that everything is not always as it seems at first glance. To anyone else but fairy folk this still looks like an ordinary woodland.'

A little further on Milli pointed to Socratony's School of Philosophy and Magic on a hill in the distance. A cloud of dark smoke was billowing from one of the windows. A second later there was a small explosion and a shower of apples rained down into the field below.

'Oh well, we've all got to start somewhere,' said Milli smiling and leading them through a busy market place.

'Get your vegetables here! Get your vegetables here!' a stallholder was shouting as they passed. A large notice announcing Intelligent Vegetables For Sale leaned against a stack of wobbling crates; the limp leaves hanging from between the slats were twitching.

'Carrots,' said Milli, steering them clear in case one of the crates fell. 'They jump out of the ground and run away when they hear rabbits approaching; and those …' she pointed to a table covered with large bunches of bright red and white radishes, 'they're rotting radishes. If they're about to be eaten they turn black. No one wants to eat black radishes; not even rats.'

A little man was giving out pieces of fruit to some children.

'Have a strawberry,' he said to Lucy as she passed . 'Here you are, try one.' The sprite pushed a green strawberry into each of their hands.

'They're camouflage strawberries,' Milli laughed when she saw their faces. 'So the birds don't peck them.'

They were still eating their camouflage strawberries when they arrived at the Major Hall. Inside it was even busier than the vegetable market but the low buzz of conversation told them there would be no one shouting 'Hairy potatoes, three pecs a shovel,' in here. Those who weren't floating cross-legged on turquoise cushions were walking around as if inside some vast church, concentrating deeply or looking up and peering at the carved marble statues of great philosophers, all long dead, standing rigidly beneath the arched ceilings and the thick ribbed columns. But it wasn't quiet like a church. Everyone here seemed to have something to say although, Hannah noticed, the sprites were very good at listening, too, and didn't interrupt each other.

'They're very polite,' she said softly.

'Just like us,' said Ben, smiling angelically.

'There she is,' said Milli, pointing to the top of the Major Hall where Astra Manda, Chancellor of Socratown, and Clarendon Sisco, her second, floated gently on their cushions, a short distance off the ground. The Chancellor smiled kindly and gave them a graceful wave when she saw them.

'This is where all the major debating goes on,' Milli informed them.

It certainly sounded as if a lot of views were being exchanged: they listened to a group nearby.

'Wouldn't you agree that the scarabs should run on time?' a sprite in a bow-tie was saying.

'Then we wouldn't miss our appointments,' someone in a mauve cloak agreed.

'But waiting a few minutes allows the young and old to board,' said another.

'Quite right, of course,' the sprite in the bow-tie was now saying.

'Perhaps we shouldn't have appointments?'

'Or perhaps all appointments should run five minutes late?'

It seemed that every point of view was thought as good as every other and everyone kept changing their minds. In fact, no one seemed to have a fixed point of view on anything at all.

'Any citizen of Socratown can come here and have their say on how things should be run,' said Milli 'Everyone's point of view is equally valued.'

'Then how do they reach decisions?' asked Ben, who secretly thought his own point of view was always the best.

'With difficulty,' said Milli. 'That's why they needed the Scales of Balance and Judgement. 'It would come to a decision for them.' She lowered her voice. 'I think they are rather lost without it.'

A few metres later they came to a stop.

'How nice to see you again.' Chancellor Astra Manda greeted them warmly, looking serene and composed. 'Come to look round and collect our key, I expect?'

'Yes. We hope we're not intruding,' said Hannah.

'You're most welcome for as long as you need to be here,' said the Chancellor.

'We have already conducted another search for the sixth key for you but, unfortunately, yet again we have had no luck in finding it.'

Hannah, Ben and Lucy didn't know whether to be pleased or not. They had been looking forward to being let loose in Socratown.

'There was much debate about whether the possibility of finding the sixth key was great enough to balance the efforts required to do another search,' said Clarendon Sisco breezily.

'I bet there was,' said Ben only half under his breath.

'The balance seemed right when we hit on the idea to search only those places that hadn't been searched before. It didn't take long. But sadly, nothing was found.'

'Well, thank you for trying,' said Hannah.

'Our pleasure,' said Clarendon Sisco, grinning vacantly.

'I hear you want to visit our Shop of Sounds,' said Chancellor Manda brightly. 'You may as well make a day of it now you're here.'

'Everyone has been telling us about it,' said Hannah. 'We've wanted to visit it ever since we first heard of it.' Hannah was hoping they'd find out more about the flute and the Shop of Sounds seemed just the right place. They followed the Chancellor back down the Major Hall and out through the sunny streets to a beautiful, walled garden. On the way Clarendon Sisco stopped to talk to so many people he fell behind and raced at the last minute to catch up.

'This is the Whispering Garden,' said Chancellor Manda, pushing open a pretty latticework gate. Clarendon Sisco charged towards them, robes flapping, gasping for breath.

'And that's the Whispering Wall,' she said. Behind her they could hear Clarendon Sisco's heaving rasps but all he could do was nod towards the stone wall covered with ivy at the other end of the garden. They could hear hissing coming from it.

'S-s-s-stay a while and r-r-res-s-t.'

'A-a-a joyful hear-r-t is-s-s a thing-g of beau-tee.'

'Kindness-s-s spent will be re-pa-aid.'

'This is a wonderful place to sit and think,' said the Chancellor. 'You can add a whisper of your own if you like – although the wall will only repeat it if it thinks it will help someone else. You just buy a whispering candle from the chandlery over there, light it, and when you've whispered what you want to say into the flame, blow the smoke into the wall. Many's the time I have been inspired by the wise words I've heard here.'

As they left the garden and crossed the road Clarendon Sisco seemed to have got both his breath and his tongue back. 'Our Shop of Sounds *is* rather famous. I'm not surprised you've heard of it. Everyone who is anyone comes here: witches, wizards, fairy folk, gnomes and ogres, kings and queens. They all come.'

'It is open to everyone who wishes to make use of it,' added the Chancellor.

'Quite. We had a visit from the giants of Wetherby only a few weeks ago – they were doing a tour of all their heritage sites – ' Hannah, Ben and Lucy must have looked blank because Clarendon Sisco elaborated. 'You know, places where their ancestors have made a name for themselves; the giants of Felixtown, the Campbelltown ogres, the Nottingham Forest giants. Anyway, they were in the area and wanted to see if Mr Sonorus had any historical data.'

'Did he have any?' asked Lucy.

'Just a few grunts and roars although even those were a bit crackly. But they went away delighted.'

You couldn't miss the Shop of Sounds on account of all the noise coming out of it. Mr Sonorus was standing with his arm plunged into a vat, wearing yellow rubber gloves that reached up to his armpits. A long strand of hair (usually combed over his bald head) was hanging free and almost touching his shoulder.

'Trying to catch tunes,' he explained when they entered. 'I won't be a minute. Slippery little devils!'

Mr Sonorus always liked visitors he could explain things to. 'All new tunes must be fermented for forty days and forty nights 'til they become coated with time slime and then they're ready for baking in the Rama-Dama-Ding-Dong oven. Once they're done, they are ground to powder.'

The Grinding Mill was open and gaping wide. Inside, were thousands and thousands of teeth fixed into row upon row of mechanical jaws.

'They look like human teeth!' Ben exclaimed, peering inside.

'They are,' said Mr Sonorus. 'This is where all the teeth that fall out and are put under pillows come. Didn't you know?'

'No,' said Ben.

'I thought they were used to make castles,' said Lucy.

Mr Sonorus and Clarendon Sisco laughed loudly. Chancellor Manda smiled.

'There's only one castle around here and it isn't made of teeth. Plenty of teeth in it though,' said Mr Sonorus, scratching his ear with his dry hand. 'No, this is where they're mainly used.' He scooped out one last tune and plopped it into a bucket at his feet. He peeled off his yellow gloves and a blob of time slime thwacked forward and landed on Lucy's nose.

'Now what can I do for you?' he said, replacing the dangling strand of hair carefully across his head.

'Well, actually, there *is* something you can do for us,' said Hannah pulling out the flute. 'We were wondering if you could identify the song in this Unitune.'

'A Unitune, eh? haven't seen one of those for a while. Let's hear it then.'

Ben took the flute and blew – he thought he was best at it – and the tune they had come to know so well filled the shop.

'Don't know it offhand,' said Mr Sonorus 'but if you play it again into the Melodee-ano-popalus it will give us its name.'

'The what?' asked Lucy.

'The Melodee-ano-popalus, of course,' said Mr Sonorus, walking over to a very strange machine. A funnel like a gigantic hearing horn sat pointing at them atop coils and coils of copper piping, which twisted and curled and looped the loop in every direction before disappearing into a big wooden box adorned with levers and buttons and an oblong aperture where something either went in … or came out.

'Come along …' he beckoned with his finger '… just blow into here. It won't bite!' Clarendon Sisco chuckled.

'This wonderful machine can identify any tune, song, bong, cry, creak, smash, crash, bang, clang, squish, squawk or screech. Any sound at all – soft or loud, man or beast, plant or other worldly thing. It will tell you who or what made it, the date it was first and last heard and even whether it will wilt a cabbage. Some do, you know.'

Ben blew the flute again with his head as far inside the Melodee-ano-popalus as possible. There was a clanking and tooting, churning and popping, a whole series of mini explosions and finally a long, low trumpeting noise which sounded very rude. After a short silence there was a couple of chugs and a sound like a bird sneezing and out of the oblong slot shot a piece of parchment which wafted to the floor. Mr Sonorus picked it up.

'Bless my glass eye,' he said. 'No wonder I didn't recognise it. Would you believe it? This tune hasn't been played around here for over six hundred moons. It's the Council of Alter-Idem's anthem. It says here it was last played on 2nd August 1954 – the day of the last Council meeting before Zamada, the last Supreme Parlator, died.'

Hannah and Lucy immediately realised the significance of this information but when they looked to catch Ben's eye he was staring at a croaking parrot on a perch.

'Thank you, Mr Sonorus,' said Hannah. 'You'll know we are trying to find the lost sixth key and this may help us. By the way, what's the song called?'

Mr Sonorus looked again at the parchment. 'An Upright Life,' he said 'Composed by Brahmbel Crumplehorn in 1476.'

'A funny name for a song,' said Ben, only half listening, as his eyes fell on a row of wooden casks which had puffed out until they could expand no more. The bungs on top shot up in the air, letting out big 'Ooohmm pahs,' and fell back, blocking the holes once again.

'Perhaps you would like a look round?' offered Mr Sonorus handing the parchment to Hannah to keep.

'Yes, please,' said Hannah. Lucy's attention was also elsewhere. She was staring at a handsome orange quill that was writing music on a table behind them. A mouse was running backwards and forwards trying to catch the ink drips with a duster before they landed on the manuscript.

'They do get a bit conceited, these gifted quills,' whispered Mr Sonorus, noticing where Lucy's attention was focused. 'Some have a wonderful talent but are very bad at tidying up after themselves and we cannot have our customers receiving compositions with ink blots all over them.' The quill dipped itself into the black ink once again, tossed its long fronds out of its eyes and continued with its work, the little mouse running behind it.

'Benitto there is composing a piece for the double Fipple flute, the Melanesian nose flute and the hecklephone. We mustn't disturb him – great composers are often sensitive creatures as I'm sure you will appreciate.'

In the next room Mr Sonorus showed them his workshop. 'This is the repair room and hospital wing,' he said, gesturing around the room. They certainly didn't expect a hospital wing in the Shop of Sounds and looked eagerly to see what kind of patients, if any, were there.

Tucked up in the first bed was a rusty saw which was wobbling energetically and sobbing.

'Always wanted to be a musical instrument,' Mr Sonorus whispered, inclining his head towards the poor saw which was doing its best to make some sort of melodious sound and ripping the sheets to pieces in the process. On the cabinet beside the bed stood a can of oil. 'We're oiling him three times a day to get rid of the rust, then we'll be sharpening him and trying to persuade him that a life making sawdust can be just as much fun as a life making music … well, maybe not *exactly* as much fun but almost.'

In the next bed a thick piece of wood was making a loud, ticking noise and Mr Sonorus approached it cautiously. 'He's convinced he's a metronome.' He tutted sadly. 'Alas, he has a very bad case of death watch beetle. All we can do is keep him comfortable.' Mr Sonorus stood shaking his head from side to side for a few moments then moved on to bed three where a cricket bat was sitting, turban dishevelled and unwrapping, tangled up in barbed wire.

'This is the fourth time Henry has been in here. He wants so badly to be a guitar you see, but he's the wrong shape, isn't big enough and is too dense – ISN'T THAT RIGHT HENRY?' Henry's eyes popped open. 'YOU WANT TO BE A GUITAR.' Henry nodded vigorously.

'He's deaf too so he hasn't a hope really – you can't have a musical instrument that's deaf – but we'll do what we can. We'll maybe bore him out, thread a few strings and fit a self-strumming plectrum. He won't sound anything like a guitar of course, but as he's deaf he'll probably not notice.'

There was one more bed. At first it didn't look like there was anybody or anything in it because the covers were flat but they were trembling. Whoever was underneath was shaking like they'd spent the night in a refrigerator. Mr Sonorus gently picked up the corner of the sheet and peeked below it.

'How are you today, Winston?' he asked.

'N-n-n-not a-any b-better I'm a-afraid,' said a timid little voice. They could just see that Mr Sonorus was talking to a *conductor's baton*.

'I just can't get th-that loud b-boom out of my mind. It re-reminds me of the d-day they ch-chopped down my Gr-great Aunt Agatha. It was t-terrible – just terrible.

The ch-chop, chop chop into her gr-great boughs for hours while she pleaded with th-them to stop and finally her c-crashing to the g-ground. It sh-shook the whole forest t-to its r-roots. It was Horr-i-bile! Whooohhh!' Huge tears leapt from the baton as if it had sprung a leak and Mr Sonorus patted his head and laid the cover down again.

'He took stage fright at his last concert when the cymbals, trombones, horns and drums all crashed together in a deafening finale. It brought on some sort of flashback. He'll recover. It'll just take time.'

They left Winston shaking and turned to see Clarendon Sisco, still in the front room of the shop, poking his finger at the rear end of a floating figure with very large ears, as if to check it was real. He looked a bit uncomfortable when he realised he was being watched.

'Such a charming fellow,' said Clarendon Sisco, wiping his finger on his robe. 'I was just making his acquaintance.' Chancellor Manda had been looking at some Water Sounds on the shelf to the right and had obviously not noticed the visitor appear.

'Hello, Hector,' Mr Sonorus called to the floating apparition. 'Lovely day, isn't it?'

'Every day is lovely but the nights are even lovelier,' the visitor chortled, his grey misty body changing shape slightly.

'Ladies, gentlemen, this is Hector Wailing, leader of the Spectral Choral Society.'

'Pleased to meet you,' everyone said together although Ben's 'meet you' came a few seconds after everyone else's.

'Your order's ready,' said Mr Sonorus, bending down behind the counter. He placed a large box on the table.

The ghost put his hand through the box, pulled but couldn't get it out again.

'Silly me, I keep forgetting,' he said, opening the box in the normal way, reaching inside and pulling out a large wax ear. Removing one of his, which upon closer inspection seemed to have melted at the lower end, he replaced it with the new one. Everyone stared at the melted ear on the counter.

'Got a little too close to a church candle, hee hee,' he said sheepishly.

Once the new ear was in place he patted the pair and asked 'How do I look?'

'Quite splendid,' said Mr Sonorus, holding up a mirror. The ghost looked eagerly into the mirror and beamed.

'I do, don't I?' he said.

Lucy managed to twist her neck around to get a squint in a corner of the mirror but all she could see was a large pair of floating ears with nothing in between them.

'You're a ghost, aren't you?' she said.

'I am, little lady, and you are a Peep, I see. Haven't seen one of you for a while.'

'Haven't you?' she replied.

'Well, no. We don't get many live Peeps in graveyard audiences at three in the morning – mostly just dead ones. We've been performing our Ghouls' Lullabies up and down the country for months now – been to all the top graveyards. We've been a sell-out everywhere we've gone – had great reviews. We're becoming quite famous. We've even had our photo in the *Haunted Post*. They said, and I'll quote, "The Spectral Choral Society's Ghouls' Lullaby concert, led by renounced spook Hector Wailing, was the most fiendishly gruesome performance I have heard in a month of Halloweens. Their vibratos and crescendos were spine-chillingly awful and set even the leaves on the trees trembling.'

'Praise indeed,' agreed Clarendon Sisco. Hector's smile became wider.

'Thanks for the ears,' said Hector, picking up the box and patting it. 'It's the secret of our success ...' he confided, winking, '... being able to hear each other so we can screech in harmony.' The parrot on the perch croaked loudly and a loud sob was heard from the saw next door as he floated out through the closed window.

'Care to hear any of our interesting sounds while you're here?' asked Mr Sonorus, sweeping his arm up to indicate the array of bottles sitting on the shelves behind him. While they were still considering the wall-to-wall selection the Chancellor put in an order.

'Before I forget, Mr Sonorus, I would like a capful of shaking willow catkins,' she said politely.

'One of our best-sellers in this range,' said Mr Sonorus, taking down the large bottle from the section marked Soothing Sounds. The bottle was full of bubbles. Removing the stopper he tipped some into a very funny pair of scales. Instead of a flat basin to hold the ingredients the bubbles floated up into what looked like a shower cap which inflated as more bubbles went into it. When the right amount had been poured Mr Sonorus tapped the cap with his wand and the end drew tight.

'Your shaking willow catkins, Chancellor,' he said, handing the cap to her.

'I'll enjoy these very much.' She handed over the money and depositing the cap deep inside her voluminous sleeve.

'Now what would you like to hear?' he asked Hannah. There was so much choice. She looked first at the section headed Assorted Bangs and Clatter then to the next, Grumbles and Mumbles. Further along she saw Exclamations and Whistles and to the right bottles and bottles were arranged under Windy Noises. It was so hard to choose. A bottle under Wibbles and Worbles caught Hannah's eye.

'Can I hear a 'Wobbling Wilbur'?' she asked.

Mr Sonorus took down the bottle but this time it contained not bubbles but a powder like that in the bottles under Tunes, Melodies, Songs and Sonnets, only this powder was pea-green.

Mr Sonorus poured a drop of liquid into a vessel on the counter and pinched a sprinkle of the powder.

'Not all sounds come in ready-made bubbles, as you can see,' he said. 'Some, like these and the tunes you saw earlier, come in powder form after they have been in the Grinding Mill. To hear the sound all you have to do is sprinkle a few specks into bindy juice like this …'

A few bubbles rose from the vessel and when they burst the sound that filled the shop sounded like a cross between a thin sheet of flexing metal and a swordfish gulping down a roast beef dinner.

'What is it?' asked Hannah.

'Its a Wobbling Wilbur of course,' said Mr Sonorus. 'A medieval spinning device they used to drop children into when they wouldn't behave themselves. They would go round and round until they were feeling sick and dizzy. When they were let out they were usually better behaved … once they'd stopped staggering about in all directions, that is.'

Ben chose to hear a Fizzing Fozzlefig and this time Mr Sonorus sprinkled a few grains into lemon juice. The bubbles rose and popped to release a sound like a lighted firework fuse crackling and spluttering. The expected explosion never came.

'That one must have drunk too much munzlepop,' said Mr Sonorus, and he swept it into the bin.

'And what would you like to hear?' he asked Lucy. Lucy had already made her choice and chose from those under the heading of 'Healing Sounds.' The label on the bottle simply read 'Triple Warmer'. Mr Sonorus let three bubbles escape from the jar. The first popped and released a hearty 'Heeeeeeeeeeeeeeeeee.'

'Imagine if you will, a giant rolling pin flattening your entire body, squashing out all the air, right down to the last squeaks in your toes.

'Come along now , don't be shy. To get the full benefit of these sounds you have to say the sounds too. This one is best said when you are lying down.' The next bubble burst, releasing another long 'Heeeeeeeeeeeeeeeeeee.' By the time the third one had burst, Lucy and Hannah were lying on the floor saying 'Heeeeeeeeeeeeeeeeeee' along with it.

'Silly nonsense,' scoffed Ben as he looked at some hissing viper sounds instead.

'No wonder it's so famous,' said Lucy on their way back to the Major Hall.

'Pity there was no sign of the sixth key,' said Hannah, looking under a bush as they passed, just in case. They headed towards the vestibule of the Major Hall, where Socratown's key was kept.

'I'm kinda glad we didn't have to do the searching,' said Ben. 'If only they were all going to be this easy.'

In the vestibule of the Major Hall a great oak table sat surrounded by ten tall, carved chairs.

'Please take a seat,' said Chancellor Manda while she walked to the far wall. There, in a glass case, glowing in the light, was Socratown's key. A ruby sat like a huge red cherry above the curved gold teeth, pulling all eyes to it. The Chancellor opened the case then laid the key before them on the table.

'Good luck with your search,' she said, pushing the key towards Hannah.

'You'll need it,' said Clarendon Sisco cheerily.

On the scarab back to Pickletullum, Ben complained, 'If you were bailing out a sinking boat, Sisco's the sort of person who'd tell you he'd got a sticking plaster for the hole but he'd left it at home.'

'He's right, though,' said Hannah. 'We'll need all the luck we can get. I can't say I'm looking forward to visiting Puddlelake.'

'Me neither,' said Lucy, shaking her shoulders at the thought of meeting Quilla Vanepike again.

'Well, three keys down and three to go,' said Ben.

'How are we going to collect Puddlelake's key if it's at the bottom of the lake? And what if the Terrosaur's still in there?' said Hannah.

'Let's hope it's sitting in a casket on the wall like the rest have been,' said Lucy.

'No worries,' said Ben. 'All you need to do is think soothing sounds, like … CRUNCH, GRIND, CRUNCH.' He continued making sounds like bones being crushed all the way back while Hannah and Lucy sat covering their ears.

Chapter 14

Puddlelake

Milli met them at the entrance to the Underground Burroway the next day as the Sound Modulator boinged one past midsun and they started their journey to Puddlelake.

Hannah thought about the last time they had seen Quilla Vanepike at the Council meeting in the Crystal Room and Ben reminded them that she had been in such a temper she was almost spitting nails.

'If it wasn't against the Harmony Rules she'd probably have people beheaded,' Ben added, whisking a finger across his throat.

'There's certainly not much harmony in Puddlelake these days. Chancellor Vanepike does tend to do things her own way,' said Milli, and they realised Puddlelake's Chancellor might not be willing to hand over the village key or co-operate in their search for the lost sixth key even though she had voted for them at the Council meeting.

Then there was the water-dragon to think about. They had heard that it had eaten all the fish and ducks in the lake and the occasional cow that had stupidly wandered too close, and was now so hungry it roared day and night, great gobs of saliva hanging from its jaws, looking for anything remotely edible.

Puddlelake was the village furthest from Pickletullum and although they sat uncomfortably during the long flight they weren't wishing it go by any quicker. The longer it took to meet Quilla Vanepike the better and they hoped they wouldn't have to meet the Terrosaur at all.

Too soon the scarab flew out of the Underground Burroway into the afternoon light and the surrounding hills. This was it – the dreaded moment had come. They could see the lake before them and prepared themselves for a terrifying sight.

But it was calm. There was no great heaving of water as the Terrosaur thrashed about; no deafening roars. There was not a ripple in sight except for those around a black swan which swam cautiously at one end with its long neck arched high. At the water's edge a bleached skull, picked clean of every morsel of meat, lay beside a pile of bones, but there was no sign of the Terrosaur.

'Where is it?' said Hannah, not really expecting anyone to answer.

'Perhaps it's gone for lunch,' said Ben.

Lucy sniggered nervously.

'Where has it got to?' Hannah asked again. Milli shook her head.

There was no crashing through the undergrowth or panicking screams, no footprints anywhere, no sign of blood.

'Or perhaps it's died?' said Ben, hanging his tongue out of the side of his mouth.

Hannah looked around the lake one last time just in case it lay snoozing somewhere in the reeds and they hadn't spotted it. The black swan seemed to be watching their every move.

'Let's go and see Chancellor Vanepike,' said Milli. 'She'll know where it is.'

'Do we have to?' asked Lucy, quickly going off the idea of being in Puddlelake at all.

''Course we do,' said Hannah, in the mood for business. 'At the very least we've got to get Puddlelake's key, and there's always a chance she'll know what the reference to the stars in the map means.'

The scarab hovered a little longer at the edge of the lake then made for the water cascading down the hill.

Hannah, Ben and Lucy followed Milli up to the thundering waterfall and stopped behind her. The water roared and crashed onto two large stones before plunging in great plumes into a small pool, about three metres across.

'Where does all the water go?' asked Lucy, staring at her reflection in the water.

'Be careful, Lucy,' said Milli. 'You wouldn't want to fall in there. It's miles deep. It leads to an underground river but no one knows where it goes to or where it comes out.' Lucy stepped back but Hannah and Ben continued to peer into the churning depths.

'Who goes there?' an angry voice called.

'Milli Maccabees and the Peeps,' replied Milli, quite unperturbed.

The water hammered down and even though the sun was shining they shivered as chilly air whirled around them and cold spray hit their faces.

'Enter!' As the voice commanded the waterfall stopped and hung like a carved ice curtain, half hoisted and utterly still.

'Hurry,' called Milli, stepping onto the stone and ducking under the motionless canopy of water. A flick of water caught Lucy's heel as she made her last step inside and the water roared down behind them. Milli led the way up some steep stone steps, holding onto the railing as she went.

'Who were you talking to?' asked Lucy, taking two steps at a time behind Milli.

'The water sprite,' said Milli, 'he controls the waterfall. If he's in a foul mood he won't let you pass and you have to come back another day. It's too dangerous to try and get in otherwise. The force of the water would knock you into the pool and you'd be sucked under and lost forever.'

At the top of the stairs a door was opened by a henchman holding a curved axe which he pointed towards them. A three-cornered felt hat made his head look as if it was on back to front.

'We've come to see Chancellor Vanepike, please,' said Milli, and the man drew back the axe and led the way up more stairs, then along a dark corridor and up what felt like a spiralling tower. The next door led them into a grand hall with an equally grand marble staircase.

'Wait here,' the henchman grunted, and he moved to take up a position at the bottom of the stair opposite another who was dressed in exactly the same way in a three-cornered hat and a flapping dress-like garment over leather trousers and stout boots. The curved axes towered above their heads.

A fanfare sounded and Quilla Vanepike, Chancellor of Puddlelake, appeared at the top of the stairs. Her hair was tightly wrapped in pearls and more of them hung in long sweeping ropes around a full length emerald-green dress. A gold-edged purple cloak trailed behind her and, as she stepped down the pearls quivering around her neck, sent specks of creamy light up onto her cheeks. Her wings were so long they touched the step. Behind, her second stood like a shadow in the dark; a close fitting cowl covered half her face. Several paces behind, two servants waited.

The Chancellor made her way down the vast staircase looking straight ahead as if she had not yet seen anyone. She did not smile. It was then they noticed the creature on the leash beside her. It walked like an ape although it's face was as broad as a bulldog's and it's yellow teeth looked cruelly sharp. Between large, pointed ears two small, bony horns protruded. Obediently, it moved forward when she jerked the leash.

'I've been expecting you,' she said when she came to stand opposite them. 'But I do hope you are not going to be tiresome.' She looked down her thin nose at her pet. 'We don't like tiresome people, do we, Sweetpea?' The animal let a rumbling snarl escape its jaws.

Hannah, Ben and Lucy bunched closer together and looked at Milli who had a fixed sort of smile on her face.

'Come through,' commanded Chancellor Vanepike, beckoning with a pink nail long enough to fillet a fish with. They obediently followed her along a corridor and the servants trailed along behind. She stopped abruptly before two large doors with her hand on the gold doorknob of one.

'This is the parlour – where we entertain our guests,' she said, opening the door with a flourish. Long drapes hung from the windows and several wide blue velvet sofas adorned the room. The two servants and the trumpet boy stood by the blue velvet chairs by the door. The axemen stayed outside.

Quilla Vanepike strode up the middle of the room, still holding onto the animal's leash.

'Sit,'

Everyone sat down at once. No one spoke.

Hannah began timidly. 'Excuse me, Chancellor, but are you are in favour of the sixth key being found?' She wanted to be sure they were welcome before they risked life and limb.

Quilla Vanepike turned towards them, whipping the hem of her cloak off the floor.

'But of course! I have nothing to fear from the Magical Crown. In fact, the next Supreme Parlator could be the greatest yet; could bring our little village to the attention of the world. Some of us have a gift you know … for bringing out the best in people.'

She lifted her nose as if to sniff the air.

'I mean, if you succeed in finding the sixth key, and I'm sure you *will* succeed …'

The animal growled menacingly.

'… then a new Supreme Parlator *will* be appointed and without doubt it will choose the best person for the job; someone who is upright and honest and free from wickedness … someone *like myself*.' She flashed a beguiling smile in their direction.

Talking about the Magical Crown seemed to put the Chancellor in a good mood and Hannah seized the opportunity to ask about Puddlelake's key.

'Ahem, … what about Puddlelake's key, Chancellor?'

'What about it exactly?'

'Am I right in thinking it's in the lake?' said Hannah.

'You are.'

'But how will it be retrieved if the Terrosaur's in there too?'

Quilla Vanepike's eyes flashed impatiently. 'I should have thought you would have worked that out by now,' she said, flicking her cloak again. 'If you want the key you'll have to get it yourselves.'

'Get it ourselves?'

They hadn't seriously considered having to get it themselves, not *seriously*. Visions of flesh being torn from bones and eyeballs pinging from crushed sockets popped into Hannah's head.

'No need to worry though,' said Chancellor Vanepike, as if she'd just read their thoughts. 'There's been no sign of the Terrosaur for two days. I checked just before you arrived.'

Now that Hannah was nearer the Chancellor she noticed that her hair was damp and there seemed to be a bit of pond weed caught around a pearl.

'How can you be sure it's gone?' Ben asked, keeping his eye on the gardope. (He had decided to call it a gardope because it reminded him of a gargoyle, a bulldog and an ape all at the same time.)

'We can't,' she replied, 'but it's eaten everything it can reach around here. We think it got hungry and left.'

'But if it's gone, where did it go?' asked Hannah.

'It *could* have died,' said Lucy. 'Maybe it's lying dead at the bottom of the lake.'

'Whatever,' said the Chancellor, waving her hand dismissively. 'It's not here now – that's the main thing, so I suggest you work quickly. We have boats you can use and nets. Gilbert will bring the lamp fish although he'll have to feed them first.'

The trumpet boy by the doors nodded at the mention of his name.

'Lamp fish?' queried Ben and shot Hannah and Lucy a puzzled look.

'Yes, yes,' she said impatiently 'They have a useful little bulb thing dangling from their foreheads which provide light in the murky depths but they are meat eaters with rather sharp teeth. We wouldn't want you to lose a leg now, would we?'

'N-no,' gulped Ben.

'But how will we swim underwater?' Hannah's voice quavered. She wished she hadn't missed so many swimming lessons.

'We have a few air-lilies left. You will be able to breathe underwater after eating those.'

'I thought you said at the Council meeting your entire stock of air-lilies had been stolen?' said Ben.

'Ah, yes, so I did.' The Chancellor smiled coyly. 'I find, however, that it sometimes pays not to tell the whole truth, don't you? And we only have one urn left so it was more an economy with the truth than a complete lie, wouldn't you agree?'

They should be grateful really, thought Hannah. They'd be unable to look under the lake without the air-lilies.

She suddenly remembered the map and the scroll.

'Er, Chancellor Vanepike …' Quilla Vanepike was looking out of the window and turned when Hannah spoke. 'We've found these – there's a map and, we think, a clue to where the sixth key might be. We wondered if you might have any ideas about where it's telling us to look?' She handed over the map and the scroll. Quilla Vanepike dropped the leash holding the gardope and took the parchments as if she might catch something nasty from them. She blinked dramatically as she drew them closer.

'Well, there's certainly no White Ptarmigan in these skies anymore,' she said after reading the first verse of the scroll. A couple of seconds later she gave a dismissive snort and Hannah suspected she had just read the lines about wickedness in the guise of right.

'Never trust a Potion Maker,' she continued, 'especially one whose nose is too long like Herbert Rootvine's. And there's no such thing as Precious Fires. That's just a myth. You're wasting your time with this old rubbish.' She flung the scroll to the floor and turned her attention to the map.

'Strange looking map. *If the key is what you're after, Then look into the stars, Find them where they come and go, Choose one that glows like Mars.*" Interesting.' Quilla Vanepike mumbled the words to herself once more.

'We know that Mars is red,' said Lucy, in case the Chancellor didn't know this. 'Cosmick Smallpiece, the giant, told us.'

'I wonder,' she said, her eyes lighting up. 'I wonder if the sixth key could be hidden in our lake?'

'Has it never been searched?' asked Hannah.

'No,' said the Chancellor flatly. 'I was never very keen on all that searching malarkey. Didn't see what good it would do.'

'But now you've changed your mind,' said Ben. Quilla Vanepike didn't seem to notice his impertinence.

'Well, yes. You could say I've seen the light, I've seen the higher cause. I see the wisdom in having the Magical Crown of Keys restored. It could change everything. Yes! This could be it,' she cried. 'The starfish! Puddlelake's key is kept in a casket in a small cave under the lake. The cave is full of starfish! They are all colours; yellows, blues, greens, oranges, reds. Some even glow! The poem could mean the sixth key is hidden in a red starfish! This is wonderful, just wonderful. We could find both keys today. Isn't that good news, Sweetpea?' She kicked the gardope on the shin and it growled.

'I think this calls for a celebration.' She clapped her hands together. A sound began like heavy raindrops hitting the ground.

'Vida!'

Chancellor Vanepike's second aimed her wand at the wall behind them and a heavy glass pane moved to one side. Thousands of butterflies streamed out into the room, jiggling and dancing in front of their eyes, wings brushing their faces and tickling the backs of their necks. They were beautiful and suffocating at the same time. Chancellor Vanepike strode across to the window and opened it. The butterflies swarmed out into the fresh air.

'Aren't they a marvellous sight?' She conjured up an enormous bottle of champagne and a single glass. 'To the Magical Crown of Keys and me,' she said, raising the glass and talking a gulp. She turned to watch the shimmering cloud of butterflies move through the air like a shoal of colourful fish, dipping and diving, soaring and turning. They swooped down to the lake and flew low over the sparkling water then rose straight up before twisting round in a curve and heading for the trees on the hill.

'I'll just let them play a little longer,' she said gleefully, drinking more champagne.

Lucy was watching Quilla Vanepike with a look of growing disgust. She shuddered and whispered to Hannah. 'She's keeping butterflies as pets. Can't we leave?'

Chancellor Vanepike turned on her heel. 'Not until you find the key!' she said fiercely and the gardope growled and bared its teeth.

'Chancellor Vanepike, may I remind you that it against the Harmony Rules to force a citizen to do something against his or her will,' said Milli, speaking for the first time.

'Whatever gave you the impression I intended to force anyone to do something they didn't want to do?' The gardope strained at its leash, saliva frothing at the corners of its mouth. 'That couldn't be further from my mind,' said Chancellor Vanepike innocently. 'These dear people have come here today to collect Puddlelake's key and far from trying to stop them I am offering every assistance to allow them to do just that. I wouldn't like there to be any misunderstanding.' She went back to the window and clapped her hands three times. Seconds later the swathe of butterflies entered the room and flew back into their glass cage. 'We must all work together if we are to achieve our aims, mustn't we?' Her voice was silky.

Milli sat down.

'Now, if there are no more questions, Petina will take you to the lake, Cordus will get the boats and Gilbert will get the lamp fish.'

Cordus and Gilbert left immediately, leaving the last servant, Petina, still sitting.

'Take Sweetpea with you,' said Chancellor Vanepike, handing the lead to Petina. 'He needs the exercise. Vida! … the air-lilies.'

Vida Vilenewt glided slowly towards a candle sconce on the wall and pulled it downwards. A panel slid open to reveal an engraved urn sitting in a recess. She lifted the urn and carried it over to Hannah, Ben, Lucy and Milli.

'You will need to take the powder with some drinking water,' said the Chancellor. 'Petina will take you to the kitchens.' Petina led the way, holding the urn in one hand and the gardope's leash in the other, the long ties of her peach coloured bonnet swaying as she walked.

Down by the lake it looked calm and peaceful. No one would have guessed there had been such mayhem just a few days before had it not been for the white skull looking up at them from the grass with most of its teeth knocked out. Cordus, who reminded Hannah of a country gamekeeper, appeared with two others, removed his tweed jacket, folded back his cuffs and rolled the boat towards the lake; Gilbert, who had changed his velvet trumpeting outfit for a flat cap and braces, followed behind carrying a large bucket.

'You don't have to do this if you don't want to.' Milli clambered into the boat and held on as it rocked.

'We did say we'd try and find the sixth key,' said Hannah, settling herself on the seat.

'Yes, but you can stop now if you want to,' pressed Milli.

'We said we'd try, so we will. If we can't reach Puddlelake's key, we might have to give up then.'

'Don't know why they don't get it themselves,' grumbled Ben. 'Especially as they have some air-lilies left.'

'They probably don't want Hironymus Grossus to know,' said Lucy.

'To know what?' asked Ben impatiently.

'To know the Terrosaur's gone,' said Lucy. 'He probably put it in the lake in the first place.'

'Well, let's hope it doesn't come back unexpectedly,' said Ben, climbing into the boat. 'Let's just get this over with as quickly as possible.'

Once everyone was in the boat they set off, Cordus and Petina at the oars and Gilbert gripping the bucket. Every so often a flip of fin flung a spray of water into the air.

'Lively little chaps, aren't they?' said Ben, nervously eyeing the bucket. 'I hope you gave them plenty to eat.' Gilbert just smiled.

Hannah could still taste the air-lilies and would have liked another drink of water but it was too late now. She swallowed, hoping the air-lilies would work. The boat glided slowly away from the side of the lake, the oars splishing into the still water as they moved quietly onwards.

'Whereabouts exactly is the starfish cave?' asked Hannah.

'Towards the other end of the lake, miss, and round a little to the right, about one after midsun,' explained Petina, pointing.

'And how far down is it?' asked Ben, casting his eyes over the side of the boat.

'About ten metres down from the top and ten metres up from the bottom. Ain't hard to find,' said Cordus.

Ben and Hannah exchanged worried glances.

'You can rest in the cave before the journey up,' said Petina.

The oars juddered in their metal housing and fell into the water again. The gardope could be seen prowling along the edge of the lake following them from the bank. At least it wasn't in the boat which felt pretty crowded already. The boat ploughed a blue furrow through the water and all the time Ben and Hannah sat feeling very uneasy, thinking about how deep the lake was, about breathing underwater, about finding the cave and about the possibility that the Terrosaur might still be down there. Lucy seemed away in a dream.

'Nearly there,' said Cordus, pulling on the oar. The boat drifted to a stop.

'The swan's gone,' said Lucy unexpectedly. 'I've been looking for it all the way along the bank but it's not here.'

'I've a feeling it'll still be watching us,' said Hannah, looking up at a dark outline in a castle window far above the lake.

'Take your shoes off,' suggested Milli. 'They'll weigh you down.' They piled their trainers into the middle of the boat.

Hannah turned to Lucy. 'I think you should stay with Milli. We might need someone up here to keep watch.'

'Keep watch for what? I want to go too,' protested Lucy.

'But you can't swim very well, and you can't see much without your glasses,' said Hannah.

'If there's any trouble up here, make as much noise as possible,' said Ben. 'Hopefully we'll hear it.'

'What kind of trouble?' Neither Hannah nor Ben replied.

Gilbert pulled on some armadillo skin gloves and plunged his hand into the bucket. He pulled out one of the lamp fish and after a struggle managed to strap it into a very odd- looking harness and throw it over the side.

'Keep a hold of that,' he said to Ben and handed him the end. Gilbert bent over the bucket for a second time and held up a fish with a bite out of its tail. Again, he wrestled it into a harness. 'This one's for you, Hannah.' Hannah held on to the harness as the fish pulled under the water.

'Strap up the last one,' called Cordus, 'I'll go with them.'

'You better hook this onto your belt.' Cordus handed Ben a waterproof bag. 'It's an unbreakable net. It'll swell up to ten times its size when it gets wet so don't take it out till we start collecting the starfish.' Ben hooked the bag over his belt.

Cordus stood up in the boat and started to utter some words. He drew his hand down rapidly over his head and chest and called out '*Amphibiantus*.' Suddenly Cordus's face started to change. It started to widen and flatten. His nose seemed to be getting smaller too.

Hannah stepped back. 'What's happening to him?'

'They're kelpies,' said Milli. 'Most can still change into other forms. Living by the water they're especially good at water creatures.'

By the time Milli had explained this, Cordus had changed into a frogman with webbed hands and feet. His clothes were gone except for his hat, which he threw onto the pile of shoes.

'Follow me,' he said, jumping into the water.

The splash rocked the boat. Gilbert handed Cordus the last lamp fish; it strained at the harness and they could see the bulb on its head shining like a torch under the water.

Hannah and Ben sat on the side of the boat and dangled their feet in the lake.

'Keep your mouth closed and breathe the water in through your nose and out through your ears,' said Petina. 'It's easy.' They hoped it was.

'After three,' said Hannah … 'One, two… three.' Taking deep breaths they plunged in. The cold water pulled at their clothes. They kicked their feet and swam lower. A short way off they could see Cordus in the lamp fish's watery glow. Hannah's lungs were bursting; she had not yet taken a breath. Her head felt like it might explode at any second. It was now or never. Water rushed in through her nose, she felt the tightness in her chest ease and the water bubble out of her ears. Ben was waving and giving the thumbs up sign.

Thank goodness it works, thought Hannah, returning the sign.

Cordus was diving deeper and they followed through the cloudy water. Tiny wiggling larvae floated in front of their eyes and little fish, too small for the Terrosaur to have noticed, darted from left to right to escape the snapping jaws of the lamp fish. Still deeper they swam, very glad Cordus was with them. Even with the lamp fish it was hard to tell where they were going. It was impossible to tell how far from the bank they were now. Cordus's green legs kicked out before them, his webbed feet pushing the water into a swirl. Hannah and Ben kept up as best they could and followed him down.

Up on the boat, Milli and Lucy were keeping a look-out. Everything was calm. The sun was pleasantly warm, making them feel relaxed.

'What's that?' Lucy asked. Large bubbles appearing on the surface of the water in the middle of the lake had caught her eye. 'It's probably just gas from the underground stream,' said Petina.

'What do you mean, probably?' asked Milli.

'Well, it often happens – gas builds up, escapes through the rock and bubbles up to the surface of the lake.'

More bubbles appeared, nearer than the last ones.

'It's moving,' said Lucy.

'But the surface is calm,' said Petina.

'What else could it be?'

Petina opened her mouth to speak but no words came out. From the shore the gardope let out a braying howl.

'But it couldn't be. It's been gone for two days,' said Milli.

'Not the Terrosaur! It can't be the Terrosaur!' yelled Lucy.

The gardope's terrible howl again rent the air. They leaned over the side, eyes bulging, and scanned the water's surface.

Far below the boat, Hannah and Ben kept close to Cordus. Several times shadowy shapes had loomed before them, scaring them, before weeds and plant life floated past.

The water was getting cloudier with every moment. Cordus turned and motioned them forward with his hand; the dark shape of the cave was just a short way off. Soon they would have Puddlelake's key. They might even find the sixth key in a starfish. Every stroke drew the cave nearer.

Hannah's harness began cutting into her wrist and was suddenly pulled away. The lamp fish darted off, straight towards the cave. All around, the water started heaving and churning angrily. What was happening? Then Hannah saw it – a tail as thick as an oak thrashing wildly, the lamp fish hanging from it, teeth dug in deep.

The Terrosaur.

From far above came a metallic bang, bang, banging – a warning from the boat.

They turned around and thrashed through the water, trying to swim as fast as they could in the opposite direction. Cordus streaked away, his webbed feet powering behind him, but Hannah and Ben couldn't keep up. The Terrosaur's monstrous head bent round and ripped the lamp fish from its tail. Its fearsome mouth opened in a silent roar and bubbles rushed out over its dagger-like teeth. Ben's heart almost stopped; his eyes bulged in horror. Hannah stopped breathing with shock. All they could think of was swimming for their lives, lashing at the water as fast as their arms and legs could go, kicking feverishly, hearts racing. The Terrosaur lunged forwards. The banging above continued. Any second now the terrible jaws would seize them. A great wave of water flung them upside down, the Terrosaur's scales ripped into their clothes and across their legs while water churned violently around them. Rushing skyward they broke through the surface of the lake and were tossed through the air to fall slapping and crashing into the depths once more.

'The Net! The Net!' Cordus screeched from the side of the boat. He banged the metal bucket trying to attract the monster's attention. It worked. The Terrosaur exploded to the surface making the boat pitch violently. Lucy, Milli and Petina screamed. The water-dragon's neck towered above them and its cold eyes blinked shut as a petrifying roar ripped from its throat, then down it went again after Hannah and Ben.

Hannah saw its head plunge back under the water and saw its terrible claws, sharpened like iron railings, slicing through the water towards them. One strike and they would be ripped to shreds. A powerful thrust from its tail sent it speeding forward, its mouth open wide, teeth like spears, ready to gorge on its first meal for days. Ben fumbled with the waterproof bag. He tugged at the net but it wouldn't come out. Hannah closed her eyes tight. She felt a heaving blow to her stomach and her arm being wrenched as though it was being pulled from its socket.

'QUICK! QUICK!' shouted Cordus. 'Get into the boat! Hurry! Hurry!' Gilbert and Lucy grabbed hold of Ben who had Hannah by the arm. Cordus was hoisting himself up when the waters parted again. The Terrosaur tossed its head from side to side, trying to remove the net which was clamped to its face. With the boat filling with water from the lashing tail, they rowed for the bank. The gardope howled again from the lakeside. The Terrosaur roared at the gardope just long enough for the boat to hit the water's edge.

'RUN FOR IT!' yelled Cordus. The net was ripped free and the Terrosaur heaved itself out of the water. The ground shook as it started after them. Dust beat up from their feet but the monster from the lake was closing fast.

'Do you think … we'll … make it?' wheezed Ben.

'We will … if the … water sprite's … not … asleep,' Cordus stuttered.

Fifty yards from the waterfall Cordus shouted, 'The Terrosaur – let us in!'

'THE TERROSAUR! – LET US IN! ' he shouted with twenty five yards to go.

'Who goes there?' said a sleepy voice.

'It's us! yelled Lucy. 'THE TERROSAUR'S COMING!' She dived at the waterfall.

The waterfall stopped in mid-air. Milli, Hannah and Petina burst through after Lucy but Cordus stopped and turned round. The Terrosaur lowered its head and opened its jaws to snatch them from the edge. 'GO ON!' Cordus shouted at Ben and Gilbert, pushing them under the waterfall.

Shaking on the ground where they had fallen, they looked around. Hannah and Ben were bleeding but at least they were alive.

'Where's Cordus?' said Milli.

They waited but he didn't appear.

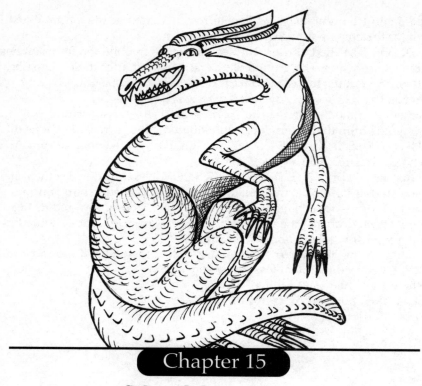

Chapter 15

The Terrosaur

'So … you didn't get the keys ….' Chancellor Vanepike's eyes flashed. 'Well, you'll just have to try again!'

'Chancellor Vanepike, I think that's out of the question.' Milli, jumped to her feet. 'It's far too dangerous. We could all have been killed.' Milli looked at Ben, Hannah and Lucy, all still in wet clothes, shivering on the sofas, and felt she shouldn't have let this happen. Hannah's and Ben's jeans were ripped and ragged, and blood was still trickling down into their socks. 'They've had a terrible ordeal and need some rest.'

'Yes, yes …' said Chancellor Vanepike, looking them up and down as they dripped onto her plush velvet, 'they are making a mess … I mean, they *do look* a mess. Get them patched up, Petina, and give them some food, and we'll see how they're feeling after that.'

Hannah and Ben hobbled after Lucy, Milli and Petina. Their legs had really started to hurt but the kitchen was welcoming and warming; cooking on the stove was a savoury smelling stew.

'Better get you out of those wet things,' said Petina, handing them three large towels. She hung their clothes to dry around the fire and set three bowls down on the table.

'Would you like somthing to eat?' she asked Milli.

'No thanks, there's something I must do. Don't worry, I'll be back.'

When Milli had left, Petina ladled up the steaming stew. 'It's nice to have some company around here. Haven't had many visitors since the Terrosaur came.'

Hannah hung her head, thinking of their narrow escape and Cordus holding back to make sure they all got through.

'Poor Cordus … do you think there's any chance he might have escaped?'

Petina smiled at Hannah's worried face.

'Don't you worry about him, now. He'll be right as rain. You wait and see. Now get that stew into you. It'll warm you quicker than blasted firebreath.'

Petina seemed to be awfully sure Cordus had escaped. Maybe she was just saying that so they wouldn't dwell on the thought of him being the Terrosaur's lunch while they ate theirs.

Ben was looking unusually thoughtful, Harriet noticed, and she wondered if he was thinking the same as she was: How would they board the scarab and get back to Pickletullum?

Petina brought a bowl of warm water and bandages to the table and tended to the cuts on their legs.

'Can't say I envy you trying to find the sixth key,' she said. 'The last time a search was ordered it took me, Cordus and Gilbert a whole week to search this old castle. Looked everywhere we did – up the chimneys, in the coal cellar and under everything that didn't move. Cordus even looked under every flagstone in the courtyard. It's nowhere that I knows of. The lake's the only place that's not been searched and after today I expect you'll not be wanting to go back for another look.'

'You can say that again,' said Ben, wincing as Petina smeared something slimy, green and smelly onto his leg.

'But we have to go back,' said Hannah.

'What do you mean we *have* to?' Ben burst out. Lucy, too, stared at Hannah as if she was delirious.

'We are so close. We could get both the keys at once.'

'Get real, Hannah. We nearly ended up as mincemeat today!' said Ben. 'We should be thinking of giving up not thinking of trying again. I'm not going back anywhere near that lake.'

'I've got an idea,' said Hannah. Ben and Lucy didn't want to hear it. Ben held his leg up and said he'd be lucky if gangrene didn't set in and Lucy talked about wanting to live long enough to go to Grandma's Summer Fête – although she hadn't shown the slightest interest in going before.

'Will you just listen,' pleaded Hannah, so they kept quiet long enough to let her talk.

'We could feed it a sleeping potion,' she said, but Ben wasn't impressed.

'You've flipped, Hannah – must've been that wallop on the head – you *can't* be serious. What do you expect it to do? Drink a mug of hot chocolate?'

'Not exactly,' said Hannah.

'Then what?'

'We'll fill a carcass with sleeping powder and leave it at the edge of the lake. It's hungry, isn't it, so it'll grab the carcass and probably eat it whole. Then we wait until it's asleep and go down to the cave and get the keys. Simple.'

'Simple! And how will we get the carcass to the side of the lake without being eaten ourselves?

Hannah stared at their empty bowls.

'I haven't worked that bit out yet.'

It *was* a plan, though not one Ben or Lucy agreed to try. Nothing Hannah said would persuade them it would work and nothing more was said while they waited for their clothes to dry. The talk changed to other things and Petina tried to cheer them up by telling them about the time Sweetpea tried to eat a porcupine and got spines stuck up his nose. She told them about how kelpies had always lived beside water and how, centuries ago, they had a fearsome reputation for surprising travellers who stopped by the waters for a rest and a drink, then robbing them, or worse. They would wait, in their animal form, until some poor unsuspecting person came by, then, Wham! Nowadays they used their skills more usefully, she was glad to say.

'You can mostly tell what creature kelpies are best at turning into by their last name. My family are good at mudflappers. Petina Mudflapper – see. Some folks have the gift to transform into any creature they want but then again, sometimes the gift's been lost completely. You don't need to change much these days if you're a shop keeper or a cook.'

They heard footsteps on the stone hall outside the kitchen and heard Milli's voice. The door opened and she walked in with her arms full of trainers. Cordus was beside her, holding onto the gardope's leash.

'Cordus Puddock! I knew you'd not be far,' said Petina, obviously pleased to see him.

'Jumped into the pool and waited in the reeds until it went back to the lake,' said Cordus, transformed into his old self, with no sign of his webbed hands and feet. He tugged the gardope. 'Found him in the bushes.' The gardope growled and bared his yellow teeth; the excitement of the afternoon had not seemed to make him any friendlier. Milli handed them their shoes.

'Couldn't leave without these.' She gave them a smile which faded as two dark shadows appeared in the arched doorway at the bottom of the stairs.

'Thinking of leaving us so soon?' drawled Chancellor Vanepike, stepping into the light of the kitchen. Vida Vilenewt stayed in the darkness behind her.

'I trust you are rested and feeling better?'

She surveyed them as though working out to the last gram what each one weighed. 'Clothes not dry yet, I see. Ah well, you'll just have to stay a while longer, won't you? Cordus, let me know when our guests are fit. No one must leave without an escort – it's too dangerous.'

With a sweep of her gown, Quilla Vanepike turned and left the kitchens.

'I can't get out of here quick enough,' said Ben, and Lucy agreed.

There was nothing they could do but wait. Quilla Vanepike hadn't exactly said she'd let them leave and she had left the gardope sitting in the corner guarding them, looking like he was chewing a mouthful of wasps. The little horns on the top of his head looked longer and sharper than before.

Hannah caught Milli's eye.

'We were so close Milli, if it hadn't been for the Terrosaur we'd have both keys now.'

'If it wasn't for Cordus's net we'd all be dead now. Hannah, we're going,' said Ben.

Hannah told Milli and Cordus about her plan to drug the Terrosaur.

'What do you think?' she asked.

'If you gave up now we would be no worse off than we were before you came, so it's up to you. Your plan might work but it is very dangerous,' said Cordus.

'You couldn't do this on your own, Hannah,' said Milli. 'You would all have to agree.'

Half an hour later their clothes were dry enough to wear (Petina had repaired them with a spell) and they were on their way to the parlour to say goodbye to the Chancellor. Only it wasn't that easy.

'Oh, I don't know that you'll be able to leave today,' said the Chancellor. 'The Terrosaur is still on the rampage and the scarabs have left their station and flown up the hillside out of its way.'

'But we *have* to get back,' wailed Lucy. 'Our Grandma will be worried about us if we're not home by teatime.'

'I would help if I could but as you can see there's not a lot I can do,' said Chancellor Vanepike. She gazed, almost fondly, Hannah thought, out at the Terrosaur below. They could see its head gliding through the water and from its gaping jaws heard a chilling quake of anger.

'Can't have eaten anything for three days now. It must be *very* hungry. I wouldn't be surprised if it was *demented* with hunger. You might be stuck here for days. *Very* tiresome, but there you are.'

The thought of them being stuck there for even a moment longer was almost too much to bear. Quite apart from having had enough of Chancellor Vanepike's hospitality and the gardope guarding them a bit too closely, Grandma Fred would be thinking they'd been run over by a bus. If only the truth was that pleasant. It was a choice between risking the wrath of the Terrosaur or risking the wrath of Chancellor Vanepike.

'We have a plan,' Hannah announced. 'But we need to get back to Pickletullum.'

The Chancellor looked round brightly as if she'd been expecting them to come up with something. 'What kind of plan?'

'We intend to drug the Terrosaur and try again,' said Hannah. 'But we'll need to get back to the Apothecary in Pickletullum and make up a Sleeping Powder.'

Ben made a funny spluttering noise by Hannah's side.

'Splendid idea! What an inventive girl you are,' simpered the Chancellor. 'That's exactly the kind of spirit I so admire in you Peeps. We can learn so much from you about getting around our little obstacles.' A long, talon-like nail circled an imaginary obstacle in the air. 'Don't you think so, Vida?'

Vida Vilenewt smiled a thin sort of smile beneath sucked-in nostrils.

'But … but …' Ben stuttered, desperately trying to object but at the same time not wanting to spoil their chances of getting out of there. Hannah dug him in the ribs with her elbow.

'Well, if that's settled I'll get the henchmen to fly you to the scarab,' announced Chancellor Vanepike. 'When will you be back?'

'Tomorrow at the earliest, I think,' said Hannah.

'Good. The henchmen will stay with you so you get back safely and return with you tomorrow.' Chancellor Vanepike smiled triumphantly.

Ben's hopes of getting away and never returning faded as they followed Cordus down through the castle to the mouth of the waterfall.

Milli sprinkled Fly-by powder along the line and Cordus called to the water sprite.

'Stop the waterfall please. Six to exit.'

'Remember, jump and lean,' said Milli.

The first henchman aimed his pointed axe at the still water and flew under its hanging, lacy form.

'Hold onto me. After three. One, two, three …' Milli bent her knees and sprang in slow motion, up into the air, with the three of them holding on. The second henchman followed, last in line.

Out into the afternoon they flew, keeping close to the hillside, moving slowly but making their way higher. Any sudden movement might draw the Terrosaur's attention and they were not out of its range yet. At the top of the hill they looked down onto the Terrosaur below snapping at insects and chewing grass.

On the largest scarab they sat three a side, the henchmen's axes either side of Milli and poking out beyond the scarab's tail. Opposite, Lucy was pinned to her seat.

'We'll need loads of Sleeping Powder,' said Hannah. 'I hope Dr Rootvine agrees to help.' Ben folded his arms and stayed silent, unable to say what he was really thinking. Chancellor Vanepike was clever all right; she *knew* they wouldn't come back if the henchmen weren't with them.

Long stares and worried glances followed them up the street towards the

Apothecary and whispers hissed around them. Hannah thought she heard a mutter about Dr Rootvine but couldn't make it out.

Thelma appeared with Jasper, still a yellow fluff ball, screeching on her shoulder.

'Hello, Thelma,' said Hannah wearily.

'What's up?' said Thelma. 'You look awful – as shrieked an' windy as an ol' witch's broom.'

'That's just about how we feel,' said Lucy.

'Worse, if that's possible,' added Ben.

Thelma cast a dark look over the two henchmen standing by the door with their axes crossed, barring any entry … or escape.

''Oo're those two?' she asked.

'They're from Puddlelake. They're here to, ahem, *help us get back safely.*'

Hannah raised her eyes at Thelma, who immediately understood that they couldn't talk openly. 'We've had the most awful time Thelma …'

'We were almost eaten by the Terrosaur,' Ben interrupted.

'Daft idea ter go there in the firs' place, if yeh ask me,' said Thelma. Milli looked away and guiltily lowered her eyes.

'But you haven't heard the best bit yet, Thelma,' said Ben.

'An' what's that, then?'

'We're going back to do it all again,' said Ben, glowering at Hannah. 'Isn't that a good idea?'

Hannah glowered back. 'It was the only way we were going to get out of there in a hurry,' she said.

Lucy was so hungry she helped herself to a walnut from the dish of seeds and nuts Thelma had left for Jasper on the counter.

'You're goin' back?' Thelma repeated, just to make sure she'd heard properly.

'That's why we're here, Thelma. We're going to drug the Terrosaur. You know, put it to sleep so we can go back and collect Puddlelake's key. It's under the lake. We think the sixth key is there too,' said Hannah.

'Oh my!' said Thelma. She slapped the side of her pale face with one hand. 'Only one thing for it. Better make a cup o' tea.'

In the back shop she set to boiling the water and making the tea. She held a plate and tapped it with her wand.

''ope everyone likes these jammy dodgers. It's the only recipe I can remember right now. Too much is 'appenin'.' She set them down and let the teapot do the pouring.

Everyone sat round the table ravenously devouring the jammy dodgers which kept appearing on the plate. The henchmen stayed by the door.

'Any sign of the imps?' asked Hannah.

'Nope, I've almost given up 'ope of ever seein' 'em again. It was most queer of 'em to just disappear like that but I guess Dr. Rootvine mus' be right. They must 'ave decided ter go home.'

'And how is Dr Rootvine?' asked Hannah.

'OK, I think. Only, 'e wasn't in yesterday an' 'e hasn't come in today either. It's not like 'im. I just 'ope 'e's not ill again.' Thelma swallowed her mouthful of jammy dodger and took another. 'I expect you wants the Sleepin' Powder made up as soon as possible?' she mumbled.

'As much as you've got and as strong as it can be,' said Hannah.

'And add some cyanide if you've got it – it would be nice if it didn't wake up,' suggested Ben.

Milli gasped. 'Oh Ben, we can't do that.'

'I know, I know. It's against the Harmony Rules.'

Thelma looked around to see how much of the sleeping herb she had in stock. There was a small sackful which needed drying out properly before it could be ground to a powder.

'If I puts it in the oven now an' start powderin' it tonight I can 'ave it finished by one after midsun tomorrow, is that all right?'

'Just perfect, Thelma,' said Hannah.

On the journey back to the Portway the henchmen sat with their axes pointing out over the scarab's tail between Harriet and Lucy and the other between Lucy and Ben. The fireflies lit their path and the Sound Modulator hummed in the background. The exhaustion of the day was beginning to tell and the beating of the scarab's wings was making them feel drowsy. Just asHannah started to nod off a sudden thud jolted her awake. Another great whack from the side sent the scarab crashing into the burroway wall. The teetering scarab turned to face an armoured beetle, covered in spikes; it was heading straight for them. At the last minute the scarab shot upwards and the intruder rammed into the hard earth.

'Its an Outlander,' Milli shouted. The thing free itself and took off after them. It flew quickly, with no passengers to hold it back. Its dark shape drew nearer.

'Get away,' screeched Lucy, rummaging in the backpack for something to throw.

The scarab swerved and dipped trying to lose it but the Outlander held fast. It was gaining. Its high-pitched whine was getting louder. One of the henchmen raised his axe, lunged forward and brought it down with a heavy crack on the Outlander's shoulder. The creature shrieked in pain, careered off, hit the wall and fell to earth like a black stone.

'That's him sorted,' said Ben, gleefully shaking a fist at the twitchingOutlander.

'That was close,' sighed Hannah.

'I must report this to Dolfi; they're getting out of hand,' said Milli.

In the Portway several more Outlanders were trying to pick up passengers. Horace was trying to move them on, making sure he kept a safe distance, by prodding them with a knobbly stick.

At the chestnut tree Milli performed the growing spell. 'See you tomorrow then at one after midsun.' The entrance closed behind her.

Hannah tried to get rid of the henchmen one last time.

'I hope you like cats.'

'Ours doesn't like things that fly,' addedLucy.

'And she's got huge fangs,' said Ben, wiggling two fingers by his teeth. But the henchmen were not moved.

'Lead on,' was all they said.

Grandma's kitchen door was open.

'Is that you, dears?'

Grandma Fred looked so normal compared to everyone else they'd seen that day that they couldn't help but hug her. The henchmen hovered at their sides but Grandma, of course, could not see them.

'There must be some flies in here,' she said. 'I can hear buzzing. You're just in time for tea. I hope you're hungry?'

'I could eat a horse, Grandma,' said Lucy.

'You and the Terrosaur,' said Ben quietly.

The smell of home-cooked food filled the kitchen when Grandma opened the oven door. During supper, the henchmen flew around the kitchen.

'Anyone for another potato?' said Grandma, wandering over to get the dish.

'Yes, please,' said Ben.

Grandma hesitated with the dish in her hand.

'Could have sworn there were two left,' she said, tipping the last potato onto Ben's plate.

'There's a little bit of broccoli left if anybody wants ...' Grandma picked up the pot. 'That's funny, I was sure there was some.'

Up in the pulley the henchman finished their potato and broccoli supper and gazed below.

'If that cat gives us any trouble, you get it between the eyes and I'll get its tail,' said one, and he swished his sharp axe through the air and lodged it in the wood. A beheaded white flower fell and landed in the butter. Hannah looked up and saw them take off their hats and settle down for the night.

*

At the Apothecary the next morning, Thelma looked flustered and worried. She had called round at Dr Rootvine's house the night before, she told them, to check if he was unwell, and found he was not at home. The door had been unlocked and when she'd gone in, there had been no sign he'd slept there. She'd checked again this morning and he was still nowhere to be found. Ma Molly had been the last person to see him when he'd popped into the Muffin House for a curried root pie.

'Where can 'e be?' Thelma wailed. 'And there's another thing – 'is book on *Alchemy through the Ages* is gone. First the imps an' now Dr Rootvine. Evil things is happenin', I'm sure of it.'

'Thelma, don't upset yourself. There could be a reasonable explanation,' said Milli, although no one could think of one.

Milli tried her best to console Thelma but by afternoon everyone would know

Dr Rootvine had disappeared. Thelma wouldn't be able to stop herself telling everyone who came into the shop.

'I'm sorry we can't stay, Thelma, but we'll be back tonight. Let's hope there's some sign of him then,' said Hannah.

'Yes, first we've got a little matter to attend to – about ten metres long,' said Ben, sighing.

'It's only about five,' corrected Hannah.

'*Only* five!' Ben repeated. 'That's just its teeth!'

'Sorry,' said Thelma, 'I wasn't thinkin'. 'Ere's yer Sleepin' Powder.' She thumped a package about the size of a bag of sugar onto the counter. 'It's 'eavy for its size, mind. An' don' breathe it in either. There's 'nough there ter knock outa family o' trolls, so there should be 'nough in that ter knock out the Terrosaur all day if it's a big 'un.'

Ben carried the package to the scarab and they set off, once again, for Puddlelake.

The Terrosaur's head was resting on the bank nearest them. Its eyes were closed and it wasn't moving, but they kept to the top of the hills until the last moment before descending. At the mouth of the waterfall one of the henchmen called.

'Water sprite, admit six.'

They waited but nothing happened.

'Water sprite, admit six.'

Still the water tumbled down the rock face.

The henchman jabbed his axe fiercely backwards and forwards into the cascading water.

'Wake up you slimy, good for nothing ...'

In the next blink the waterfall turned to ice; the henchman's axe was held frozen in a solid wall of water, and there was no way in. There was a sudden roar. They turned to see the Terrosaur's mouth open in a wide yawn.

'There's enough room between its teeth for the whole Arsenal squad,' said Ben goggle-eyed.

'Aaarghhh! Let us in! Let us in!' The henchmen began picking up stones and throwing them at the frozen waterfall. Still nothing happened.

'Mr Water Sprite, this is Milli Maccabees,' said Milli. 'I am standing out here with our three guests and two of Chancellor Vanepike's henchmen. We are here on her business and I'm sure the Chancellor would *not* be pleased if she heard that our lives were being put in danger.'

The Terrosaur yawned again.

'Now, PLEASE, let us in!'

They heard a low grumble. The waters flowed again and the axe was swept away in the downpour, swirling and spiralling into the depths of the pool at their feet. The sheet of water halted and they entered before the water sprite changed its mind.

Up in the parlour Quilla Vanepike was jubilant.

'You've got the Sleeping Powder? Excellent, excellent. You wonderful girl. What a day this will be. The sixth key will finally be found after all these years and the Magical Crown will shortly be reassembled. I will fulfil my destiny at last.'

'Haven't you forgotten something,' asked Lucy bravely.

'Forgotten what, child?'

'We've still to collect Gorgonz City's key. Hironymus Grossus says theirs has been stolen by the raiders and we might not find it.'

'He would say that, wouldn't he?' said Chancellor Vanepike dismissively. 'We can deal with him later. Vida! ...' The Chancellor clapped her hands. 'Vida! The air-lilies, please.'

'Not – so – fast,' said Ben.

If it had been up to Ben he'd have fed the powder to Sweetpea and sent *him* to say hello to the Terrosaur.

'We still need to agree some details.'

'And what details are those?' said the Chancellor forcing a smile as her patience thinned.

'We need a carcass and we need to get it to the edge of the lake,' said Ben.

'A carcass? You mean a dead animal?' she asked.

'Yes,' said Hannah and Ben together.

'Will a butterfly do?' She looked towards her glass cage where the skittish creatures were resting.

'No,' said Hannah 'it has to be a large animal.'

Sweetpea growled as all eyes fell on him.

'Perhaps not. Oh, well then, what about a vipner? Cordus catches them in his traps all the time. Cause awful damage. Dreadful beasts.'

'It needs to be bigger,' said Hannah, remembering the skins Thelma had hanging up in the Apothecary.

'There's a vellypig we could use,' said Gilbert. 'It fell off the cliff into the back courtyard this morning and broke its neck. Nearly fell on me when I was watering the strangleweeds. I took it to the kitchens – thought it might feed Sweepea for a few days.'

The gardope started to drool.

'Good idea. That's that settled then,' said Chancellor Vanepike, dodging the gob of saliva that hurled across the room as the gardope's head swivelled in her direction. A look of disappointment settled around its mouth as the realisation dawned it wouldn't be having vellypig for dinner after all.

'I thought,' began Hannah, 'that I could fly down to the side of the lake carrying the carcass, drop it and fly back. As long as the Terrosaur's asleep, that is.'

'Superb! Didn't I tell you she was a smart girl, Vida?' said Quilla Vanepike, seemingly quite willing to let anyone risk their life so long as she got what she wanted. *Especially* if she got what she wanted.

'What are we waiting for then? Let's not waste any more time. We don't want the Terrosaur to wake up now, do we?' She smiled benevolently around the room while impatiently opening and closing the talons on her right hand. 'I'll be watching from the window.'

In the kitchen, Petina stuffed the vellypig with the Sleeping Powder and made sure the package was sewn in tightly. Gilbert went to feed the lamp fish and Cordus went to get the boat ready.

'How long will it take to work?' asked Petina.

'About ten minutes, I think,' said Hannah, whose tummy rumblings had started again. Her old friend, the fist, it seemed had decided to toss some pancakes.

'You're mad, Hannah,' was all Ben managed to say, half aghast she could be so stupid as to take such a risk and half amazed at her courage. He knew he couldn't stop her, short of sitting on her. Once Hannah made up her mind to do something she did it … or at the very least tried as best she could. If it was up to him, he thought, they'd be home now in front of the television eating Grandma's home-made ice cream with fudge sauce.

'As long as it stays asleep, I'll be all right.' Hannah gulped and rushed to the bathroom returning a short while later, pale but composed.

'Just make sure the waterfall is stopped and I can get back in quickly,' Hannah was saying as Milli sprinkled the Fly-by powder over her head.

'I will. Now, be careful. Whatever you do, don't land. OK? You will be very vulnerable if it wakes up.'

'Be careful,' said Lucy, flinging her arms round Hannah's neck.

'Go get him, Hannah,' said Ben.

Her brother and sister watched as she picked up the vellypig, both hands around its middle, and heaved it into a comfortable position. The waterfall stopped and Hannah jumped with all her might, wobbling a little as she juggled her load, before disappearing.

'Keep your position open, Mr Water Sprite, please,' said Milli, as they watched Hannah slowly move away from the safety of the hillside.

The Terrosaur's head lay immobile on the grass. Hannah could hear its deep vibrating breaths as she got nearer. Out of the water it looked even more fearsome. Two horns tapered from its scaly green head and a web of spines fanned out from its neck as it breathed in and out. On its back, wings lay tightly folded. Even asleep, it was terrifying. The vellypig was heavy and Hannah knew she couldn't carry it much further. She needed to hold on … just a little more … She struggled forward, trying to concentrate on her direction. Her muscles ached with the strain. She started to veer off course. Hannah leaned the other way trying to correct her position and felt the vellypig lurch … it was going to fall.

WHUMP! The vellypig thudded to the ground but it wasn't close enough. She had to get it nearer. It would only take a minute. Landing beside the vellypig she knelt to lift it onto her lap. That's when she heard it – a great sniff, then a gravely scraping. Hannah saw the Terrosaur's head moving in her direction.

Its eyes sprang open. Staring, eyeball to green eyeball, with the terrifying beast Hannah felt herself go weak. There was an ear-splitting roar. The Terrosaur would reach her in seconds. She had to leave the vellypig – now! The Terrosaur rose up, in a swell of water, and lunged to clear the lake.

'NO-O-O!'

Hannah leapt into the air, straining, stretching, willing herself higher. The Terrosaur's teeth snapped shut centimetres from her shoulder like a massive bear trap. Hannah gasped. Lucy and Milli screamed as they watched from the waterfall. The powerful jaws rushed forward to attack again. Hannah strained hard but the Terrosaur struck.

Wham!

Hannah hit the ground like a spinning ball then stopped spread-eagled in the dirt.

'HANNAH!' Ben and Lucy shot out from under the waterfall towards her crumpled figure without thinking about their own safety. The Terrosaur sniffed the vellypig then scooped it up with the points of its teeth.

'Just get her inside,' said Cordus hooking his arm under Hannah's shoulder. Ben followed his lead whileLucy lifted her feet.

The Terrosaur crunched on the vellypig, cracking its bones like a peanut shell under a shoe.

'Don't look back, just run,' shouted Cordus, hurtling himself towards the waterfall.

'RUN, RUN,' shouted Milli. She watched in horror as the Terrosaur flicked its tail. 'RUUUUN!'

The Terrosaur moved quickly. It snapped at the air less than two metres behind them. They pelted onward. The waterfall was just ahead, the water stilled and hanging. Just one last effort. The Terrosaur lunged again; they dived under the canopy. The water thundered down in heavy waves as they slid along the dust.

'Made it,' panted Ben. But he had spoken too soon. The Terrosaur's nose split the water and a thundering snort blasted the cave.

'Stand back!' the water sprite ordered.

The waterfall instantly began to bubble and hiss. Clouds of steam swirled around them. A roar of pain set the cave walls vibrating and the ground shook under frenzied thumping. The Terrosaur, burned and scalded and bellowing in agony, was retreating to the cool lake.

'Hannah, Hannah!' Ben and Lucy shook Hannah until at last she stirred. There was a lump on her head the size of a tennis ball.

'Diddi eetthe vellyig?' she slurred through a groggy haze.

'Yes, Hannah, rest.'

Milli rubbed the mist from a window in the waterfall. The Terrosaur was slumped at the side of the lake, half in and half out of the water, a heron perched on its head.

'Must be out cold,' said Cordus, 'or that bird wouldn't last long.'

Cordus went off to manage the boat and Gilbert dropped more meat into the bucket of lamp fish and fetched the harnesses. Petina packed sandwiches and some pumpkin pickle in case anyone got hungry.

'You need to rest, Hannah,' said Milli, but Hannah wouldn't be persuaded to stay in the castle. She washed down the air-lilies with a drink of elderberry juice (which was better than water at disguising the bitter taste) and they were ready.

Cordus was waiting in the boat, keeping an eye on the sleeping Terrosaur. Petina gave them the instructions for breathing under water one more time.

'Remember, keep your mouth closed. Breathe in through your nose and out through your ears.'

Hannah and Ben let themselves fall over the sides and held onto the rigging while Gilbert handed them each a lamp fish. Cordus changed into his frog form and took his harness in his webbed hand.

'You ready?'

Ben patted the net attached to his belt, feeling glad he would be using it to collect starfish this time.

'Let's go.'

Cordus, Ben and Hannah released their grip and slipped down under the smooth surface of the lake. The water was cold and cloudy but at least they knew the Terrosaur was snoozing up above and they wouldn't be meeting him near the cave this time.

Down in the shadowy depths leaves floated past their eyes like silent messengers from the turbulent battle that had taken place the day before and the light from the lamp fish shone through many watery graveyards where the remains of grizzly suppers lay in splintered piles or caught in weeds. Hannah and Ben could see Cordus making his way ahead and followed quickly. There was no time to lose. The Terrosaur could be out for the rest of the day or just for an hour. They swam deeper still, pulling against the water with their hands. It took longer than they remembered to reach the cave but when she saw it Hannah tugged excitedly on Ben's sleeve. Cordus was there, beckoning them inside.

The light from the lamp fish fell on a recess on one wall. There it was. The casket containing Puddlelake's key sat surrounded by water snails. Hannah's eyes lit up. She reached forward and lifted it down. Inside shone the gold curve of Puddlelake's key, with an emerald as large as a gooseberry.

'The sixth key must be here too. It must be,' Hannah, mouthed to Ben. Their feet stirred up the sand and everywhere, coloured starfish crawled and glowed – yellow, orange, red, blue. Hannah picked up a red one and pointed to it. She turned it over. Five spiny arms wafted in the water but there was no sign of the sixth key. Hannah shook her head.

She picked up another one, turned it over. Nothing. The third didn't have the key, nor the fourth, and now she didn't know if the starfish she had in her hand was the starfish she'd first looked at or not. The cave was full of starfish, heaped up one on top of the other, and all on the move. Hannah pointed to the net in Ben's belt and started filling it. When the net was bulging and they were sure they had uncovered every red starfish in the cave, they were ready to go.

Quilla Vanepike was standing on the bank waiting when they surfaced. She watched as they pulled in the net.

'Did you get the keys?' she roared across the lake.

Hannah stood up in the boat while Cordus and Ben hauled the starfish aboard. 'We've got Puddlelake's key,' Hannah shouted back.

'Have you found the sixth key?'

'Not yet, but we've brought the red starfish up so we can check every one.'

Ben and Lucy were already reaching into the net and turning over the large starfish to see if they concealed the key, and throwing those with no sign back into the lake.

'Let me know the instant you find it,' the Chancellor commanded and strode off with Vida Vilenewt in her wake.

When every red starfish in the net had been turned over and Hannah threw the last one, glowing and pulsing, back into the lake they sat looking at each other.

'We'd better tell her,' said Ben. Cordus and Petina took the oars and rowed towards the waterfall.

Chancellor Vanepike was looking out of the window down onto the Terrosaur, still sleeping soundly, when they entered the parlour.

'Good news, I hope,' she said, spinning round to look at her guests.

'Here's the casket with Puddlelake's key,' said Hannah triumphantly as she laid it on the table. 'And here's what we found in the red starfish.'

Quilla Vanepike took the folded handkerchief from Hannah's hand.

'Is this it?' she snorted, peeling back the last corner of the handkerchief . 'Is this your idea of a joke?

'WHERE IS IT?' she screamed at the top of her voice as her gaze scanned the handful of snail shells again.

'The sixth key isn't there,' said Hannah.

Chapter 16

The Midnight Raid

Quilla Vanepike paced up and down the parlour, dragging Sweetpea behind her, her fists closed in rage, and insisted that the sixth key must be there. She'd demanded that the orange starfish be collected and searched too because orange is like red 'if you squint your eyes' but relented when Hannah repeated that Cosmick Smallpiece, the Star Map Maker, had said quite clearly that Mars was known as the red planet not the orange planet. Hannah also had difficulty in persuading her that Puddlelake's key should be kept in the vault with the others in Pickletullum. She only agreed when Hannah promised to go on looking for the sixth key and, if it was found, to tell her before the other Chancellors were informed. As they left Puddlelake the Terrosaur was still snoring soundly.

The next day, in Merryberrys, they met to exchange news with Landel, Hunnik and Hornet. Landel told them about the rumour that was spreading about Herbert Rootvine.

'He's definitely disappeared and everyone's saying he's gone because he stole the Precious Fires.'

'They say he wants to make gold and that he was never really interested in them for their healing powers,' continued Hornet.

'It's the talk of the village,' said Hunnik.

'But that can't be true,' protested Hannah. 'Thelma would have known if he was up to no good.'

It was Hornet, making his way back to the table with the drinks, who saw Ben's backpack moving – on its own.

'Hey, what's going on?' he shouted. Everyone turned to see the backpack bobbing though the air and heading towards the door.

'Stop it, ' shouted Ben. 'Someone's stealing our flute.'

Tables and chairs began falling out of the way in front of the escaping backpack and before Ben and Landel could get to their feet it had disappeared out into the street.

'After it,' called Landel, charging outside and knocking Rudor Bizar sideways as he stuck his neck out trying to see what was going on.

Down the street the backpack bounced along in mid-air. Ben, Landel and Hornet chased after it, yelling. The lunchtime revellers followed on behind Hannah, slopping ale and shedding sandwiches shouting at it to stop. The small children charged ahead, whooping and cheering, demanding the backpack come back. It seemed to be slowing down. Hornet threw a stone. The backpack swung round, as if to face them, then galloped forward with new resolve, crashing straight into a water barrel outside the baker's which toppled right over. The water gushed to the dusty earth in retching gulps and the backpack flew like a missile into the ferns beyond.

Everyone looked to where the backpack landed so the wet footprints which began appearing near the water barrel went unnoticed. Gathering speed they headed towards the end of the street.

'Look!' said Hannah, eventually seeing the damp patches in the earth that led all the way to the scarab post where a scarab was taking off. There didn't seem to be anybody on board but it was too far to see clearly. It headed off into the woods. The backpack seemed intact. The flute was still inside with their money, their Fly-by powder, the scroll and the map. It seemed they had come face to face with an invisible raider ... or almost, and they already knew who had given the order to steal it.

'What I don't understand,' said Lucy, flicking back her hair and adjusting her glasses, 'is why anyone would want the flute? It's not as if it's made of gold or anything special and it just plays one song.'

'It is the song that was played to start each meeting of the Council of Alter-Idem when Zamada was alive,' said Hannah.

'Perhaps they think that if the song is never played the Magical Crown won't work ... or something like that,' suggested Hunnik.

'Maybe,' replied Lucy. 'In any case, it looks like Hironymus Grossus and Vasril Odo are in this together. I knew it.'

'And they could only know about the flute if they'd seen it in the Vision Ball,' said Hannah.

'If they've got the Vision Ball then they've probably got the Scales of Balance and Judgement, the airlilies *and* their own key. They might even have the Precious Fires,' said Landel.

'Exactly,' said Hannah.

'We'll need proof,' said Hornet in a tone that suggested he thought getting proof would be impossible.

'And I know how we can get it,' said Hannah. 'We could still sneak into the Council Chambers and look for the stolen things. At the very least we might find Gorgonz City's key. It might be the only way we'll get it. Hironymus Grossus won't give it to us willingly, will he? And if we find the key and take it he won't be able say it's gone because that would mean admitting to the Council he was lying when he told them it was stolen.'

Ben and Lucy's jaws dropped. They had hoped Hannah had given up this wild idea.

'Hannah, we're not doing anything else that's dangerous.' Ben tried to sound firm.

'You don't have to come,' said Hannah, leaning against the scarab post.

'So, if something goes wrong we just leave you, do we?' said Ben.

'Hannah might be right,' said Lucy. 'It might be the only way.'

'Not you too,' moaned Ben. 'I thought you agreed with me?'

'Changed my mind,' said Lucy.

Everyone, except Ben, thought looking around the Council Chambers after dark was a great idea. He threw in every objection he could think of as they sat discussing ways of getting in without being seen and ways of getting out. If they got caught no one knew what would happen. They might just 'disappear' mysteriously like the imps and no one might ever discover what had happened to them. They might get trapped in a secret passageway, or locked up in a room that no one ever went into. Goodness knows there were enough of those in the Council Chambers.

'We'll go tonight,' said Hannah.

That evening, Hannah and Lucy couldn't sleep. After watching some television with Grandma Fred and Ben they went to bed early but were'nt able to settle. On the floor, set out in a pile, were the things they were going to take; the empty backpack, a torch and some bogbean leaves. At half past eleven they heard someone run a tap and close the bathroom door. They thought it must be Grandma because she always took her teeth out last thing at night.

At quarter to twelve, Hannah and Lucy were up and dressed and tiptoeing towards the kitchen door. The clock on the kitchen wall seemed to be ticking unusually loudly.

'We'll be back long before Grandma and Ben get up,' Hannah whispered.

The light from the torch flashed up the garden as they made their way silently through the gate and onto the path by the edge of the wood. A cool breeze fanned the leaves on the trees and an owl hooted deeper in the wood. The moonlight cast strange shadows on the ground and when a bird flew out of a bush onto their path, Hannah and Lucy just managed to stifle nervous yelps.

'Come on, the chestnut tree is just up here,' said Hannah, getting a grip of herself. They waited by the tree for Landel to appear, listening to the leaves rustling in the night air. From down the path they had just come they heard another noise; a twig snapping. Someone or something was coming their way.

'Hurry up, Landel,' Lucy whispered into the night. The noise was getting closer. They edged their way behind the chestnut tree and leaned rigidly against its rough bark, hardly daring to breathe. On the ground, from behind the tree, they suddenly saw a long shadow appear.

'Hannah? Lucy?'

It was Ben's voice.

'What are you doing here? I thought you weren't coming?' Hannah leaped forward and shone the torch in his face.

'I couldn't let you go on your own, could I? You might get hurt,' said Ben, raising an arm and squinting in the glare of the light.

'We can manage perfectly well without you, thank you,' said Lucy from the shadows.

'Well, if you're coming, just don't get in the way.'

'As if I'll get in the way! Girls are useless on their own, everybody knows that except you two, apparently.'

A 'zing' sounded and a hole appeared between the roots in its usual place.

'Sorry I'm late,' said Landel breathlessly, 'I had to sneak past Horace.'

In the Portway scarabs sat at the entrances, two and three deep, dozing sleepily or else munching at their feeding troughs. They could see Horace hovering at Sombrono's tunnel but his back was turned towards them and he was talking to Grinnard.

They edged through the Portway, keeping close to the wall, towards the burroway for Gorgonz City. Horace still hadn't seen them although Grinnard had, but he didn't let on. He kept on nodding at Horace who was talking about Herbert Rootvine.

'They say he was after gold all the time,' Horace was saying. 'They say the imps are in on it too – that they'll get a share of all the gold he makes. Disgraceful business. But I knew all along of course …'

Noiselessly they jumped down beside the scarabs and crept into the darkness. Landel pulled a lump of sugar from his pocket and held it under the first scarab's nose. It teetered forward a few paces, antennae twitching, and eagerly followed the sugar lump out of sight. Hannah, Ben and Lucy followed and once they'd boarded, the scarab soared down the tunnel.

'Neat trick with the sugar lump,' said Ben getting comfy.

'Works every time,' said Landel smiling.

Gorgonz City was in darkness. The moon lay hidden behind a bank of thick cloud which blotted out most of its light. The rocky city loomed like a sleeping black beast against the rolling night sky. The normal entrance into the Council Chambers was locked and sealed and Landel led them behind the jutting rocks.

'We'll try the kitchens first,' he said. 'Round here.'

Through a fissure in the rock, a long way from the front of the building, they entered a sheltered yard.

'This is where the deliveries are made. See, there,' said Landel quietly, pointing to a molehill of flour on the ground where a sack had split. 'Don't get any on your shoes.' Landel shone his glowing wand at the flour and they all stepped over it. A stack of empty crates rose up in one corner and vegetable peelings lay beside two overflowing refuse bins. A rat darted from behind the bins, ran to the wall and disappeared down a drain.

'There are two ways in,' said Landel. 'Follow the rat or go in through the window – rats always know how to get into a place.'

There was no doubt that going down the drain was not the option they preferred. They looked at the window, ajar on the latch.

'My cousin works in the kitchens,' said Landel. 'They bake bread first thing in the morning every day. It's always so hot in the summer they leave the windows open at night to cool the place down.'

They got inside just as the night watchman appeared in the yard. Through the window they could see the outline of a truncheon as thick as a baseball bat in his hand.

'Here, ratty, ratty. Here, ratty, ratty.'

Hannah kept the torch off until they were sure it couldn't be seen through the window and in the darkness they felt their way across the kitchen, along the edge of a long wooden table, and past a mop which looked eerily like a tall, thin elfin with shaggy hair standing in the corner. To their surprise the kitchen door was open, the key still in the other side, as though someone had come in to check the place and left, forgetting to lock it. The kitchen led out to a hall. They had no idea what part of the Council Chambers they were in but reckoned they must be quite far from the Crystal Room.

'This way,' whispered Hannah, shining the torch along the hall. Ben, Lucy and Landel followed, creeping along one at a time after the torchlight as it bounced along the stone floor. The first room was up ahead.

'*Shush*, be quiet,' said Hannah as Ben's trainers creaked.

'I *am* being quiet,'

Hannah tried the door but it stayed stubbornly shut.

'It's locked,' she said.

They moved on. The further they walked the darker the corridor became. And the deeper they ventured into the heart of the Council Chambers, the more they jumped at every small noise. Their very breathing now seemed too loud, and even blinking disturbed the air.

A noise made Hannah drop the torch. Ben ran into her back, Lucy stepped on Ben's toe and Landel fell on top of them all.

'What was that?' Hannah hissed.

'Dunno.'

'Shussh!'

'Quiet!'

On her knees in the middle of the corridor Hannah heard the noise again. But this time it sounded barely a few centimetres from her ear.

'Ben! What are you doing?' she rasped, groping to recover the torch. She found it and shone it in his face.

'I'm just unwrapping a toffee,' he said, squinting and holding up the crinkly paper.

'For goodness' sake!' said Hannah, getting to her feet. 'You can't go five minutes without eating!'

Ben quickly stuffed the toffee into his mouth.

They shuffled towards the next door, Hannah and Lucy still muttering at Ben under their breaths, and tried the handle.

'It's moving,' said Hannah quietly, the toffee instantly forgotten.

The huge door shuddered open. Light from Hannah's torch danced up the walls and shimmered on a polished oil lamp.

'It's a reading room,' Hannah whispered, peering round, but once they were inside it became clear it was more than just a reading room.

Two sides were completely lined with books but some were unmistakably scorched. Blackened steps led up to a narrow galley which ran around the higher reaches of the room. A large twisting candelabra stood on the floor with great blobs of solidified wax hanging from it.

'No wonder they have fires in these places,' whispered Ben. 'All those candles. It would only take one to fall and the whole place would go "whoosh".'

Landel lit three of the candles with his wand.

Rows of red leather *Record of Business* books, all exactly like the one Hannah had seen Vasril Odo writing in, stretched along one shelf.

'The records of Council business,' said Hannah, peering along the shelf and reading the dates on the spines. 'The books covering the years of Zamada's reign are missing – just like it said in the library. Funny how none of these other records were burned though.' The remaining pristine volumes sat neatly in a long row stretching back through centuries, looking as if nothing more dangerous than a duster had swept over them in decades.

But there was no sign of the stolen items or anything that looked remotely like a curved gold key.

Ben opened a wooden box lying on the table and Lucy shone her torch into two glass cabinets. Clean parchment sprang from the box. Inkwells and sharpened quills danced into view through the glass cabinet windows but they found nothing important to their search. Hornet extinguished the candles. With a last flick of her torch to make sure nothing was out of place Hannah closed the door behind her. They crept towards the next room. It was unlocked.

Landel lit a candle. Dark shapes and glinting metal loomed into view.

'A Hall of Honours,' he said, peering closely at a silver cup.

'Look at all those awards on the wall,' said Lucy, her eyes now accustomed to the light. Landel held up the candle and read the plaque below the first award.

'To Peregrine Grossus for Excellence in Archery.'

It was the last thing they expected, a relative of Hironymus Grossus winning an award.

'I don't believe it,' said Hannah.

'There's another,' said Lucy. 'To Ernest Grossus for Excellence in Everything.' The award shields stretched right around the room.

'These awards have all been given for outstanding endeavour,' said Landel, taking in the scene. 'And mostly awarded to goblins by the look of it.'

'What do you expect when the Chancellor of Gorgonz City is a goblin?' said Ben.

'I don't think it's favouritism,' said Landel. 'The Council wouldn't allow it.'

'You're not going to say they're cleverer, are you?' said Lucy, writing her name in the dust then rubbing it out again.

'No,' said Landel. 'They're definitely not any cleverer.'

'What then?' asked Ben.

'Goblins are very focused,' said Landel. 'They concentrate on their goal. They don't care about anything else.'

'Witch Magrew says an extreme of anything is always a bad thing,' said Lucy.

'That might be true, but it means they usually get what they want, doesn't it?' said Landel.

When they were satisfied the room had nothing for them they moved on.

They had been lucky so far: no sign of any guards and no alarm bells ringing. The next door was locked but Hannah shone the torch through the keyhole.

'A key's been left in the lock,' she said quietly 'That's strange. There must be another door into this room.'

Ben checked the coast was still clear.

'Give me your hanky,' said Landel. Ben pulled a crumpled hanky from his pocket, removed two toffee wrappers which were stuck to it, and handed it over. Landel eased the hanky a good way under the door then prodded his wand in the keyhole. They heard the key fall out of the lock and onto the floor with a muffled thud. Landel slowly pulled the white square back under the door – the key lay upon it.

Ben clapped his friend on the back.

'You've done that before, haven't you?'

When the heavy door laboured open Hannah flashed the torch around the room settling its beam on a long table in the middle of the room. Around it, eighteen chairs stood silently as if guarding what lay on top.

In the centre of the table, on a red velvet cloth, was a set of gold scales, one side weighed down with a large blue orb and three gold urns. Soctratown's emblem flashed in the torchlight.

'It's the Scales of Balance and Judgement and the Vision Ball,' gasped Lucy.

'And the air-lilies,' said Ben a bit too loudly.

'Shush' said Hannah.

'So, Hironymus Grossus and Vasril Odo *are* behind the raids after all,' said Landel quietly.

'I told you hey were,' said Lucy.

Hannah flicked the torchlight around the room for anything resembling jars of still blue flame.

'There's no sign of the Precious Fires,' she said softly, noticing at the same time another door at the far end of the room which had been left slightly ajar.

'They might be in there.' Hannah led the way and the others followed. She pushed the door open and stepped inside. But it wasn't jars of Precious Fire they saw in the room …. At the far end, in a large four-poster bed, Vasril Odo lay wheezing into the night. On a little table by his bed sat the remains of his supper, a crust of bread, some cheese and a glass of milk.

Hannah jumped. The torch fell from her hand and clattered to the floor where it came to rest shining up at a painting of an old woman on the wall.

Vasril Odo sat bolt upright.

'Who … who's there?' he stuttered, rubbing his eyes.

Hannah grabbed the torch and they fled before he gathered his wits. For a second it seemed he hadn't seen them in the dark – then came a yell.

'Guards! Guards!'

The yell bounced loudly off the walls and through the silent Chambers. Then came the alarm – the deafening wail of a banshee shrieked through the night.

'Run' shouted Hannah as they took off and flew through the second door. They darted down the corridor, tripping on each other's heels as they went. Within seconds the thundering of heavy boots could be heard from the depths of the Chambers. They sprinted along the corridor, hearts hammering wildly, back towards the kitchen. But the sound of clattering boots was coming from that direction too. They skidded to a halt.

'We're cut off! Quick, down here,' gasped Hannah, dashing down another corridor.

'They're along there somewhere,' Vasril Odo's dampened voice came from some way off. Guards' muffled cries were everywhere.

'Faster!' Hannah shouted, and they galloped to the end of the corridor and swung blindly into another, not sure where they were headed. Speeding past a sofa and a stone fountain spouting water, Hannah remembered the cellar door under the sofa near the Crystal Room.

'Landel, do you know where the Crystal Room is from here?' she puffed.

'I think it must be in this direction somewhere,' Landel spluttered, holding onto his side.

'Down here.' On their left came the noise of boots clattering up stairs. They turned to see the dark shape of guards' heads appearing. Hannah, Ben and Landel shot off along one corridor and Lucy darted down another.

Zooming around another corner they arrived at the Crystal Room. Hannah, Ben and Landel skidded to a halt in front of the bronze statue of the elder tree. The sound of stamping feet came echoing from both directions.

'We're trapped,' wailed Hannah. 'Where's Lucy?'

She backed against the tree. They waited, listening to the sound of boots hurrying towards them. Hannah felt a strange sensation, as if something was melting over her shoulder. She looked down and saw her foot was only half visible; it was sticking out from the bottom of the tree. Hannah grabbed Ben and Landel and pulled them backwards.

'Stay still,' she whispered. 'The tree is hiding us.'

The guards crashed into the hallway in front of the Crystal Room and stood facing those coming from the other direction.

'Where have they gone?' one of them growled.

'They must be here.' Two guards clattered down the escalator while another two heaved open the gold doors of the Crystal Room, all reappearing in minutes

'Not in there,' snarled one.

'Not downstairs,' grunted another.

Some way off there was a dreadful commotion and a clash of swords. An angry cry of pain was followed by piercing scream. Lucy!

'We've got one,' a guard shouted in the distance.

The guards outside the Crystal Room ran off back down the corridor. Hannah, Ben and Landel waited, silently, tightly huddled against each other inside the elder tree until the shouts and march of feet faded.

'We can't leave without Lucy,' cried Hannah.

'We need to get out of here and tell Dolfi and Zanting Barbelly what we've seen. Hannah, it's the only way to get Lucy back,' said Ben.

'Ben's right, Hannah, if we give ourselves up now, no one will know we're here or that Hironymus Grossus is behind the raids. We must tell Dolfi and Chancellor Barbelly.'

The three of them made their way along the corridor to the red sofa.

'There's a cellar door under here,' said Hannah, still shaking. 'I saw it when the mouse ran over Vasril Odo's foot.'

'Let's hope it doesn't lead back into his bedroom,' said Ben. It didn't. It led down to a maze of tunnels, used to keep staff out of sight when they were stoking fires in the winter or serving lunches or running errands.

Landel sniffed the air. 'I smell bread,' he said, although Hannah and Ben couldn't smell anything but the musty dampness of stone.

'This way.' Landel led them through the maze, back to the kitchens. The scarab was still waiting and on their way back through the Underground Burroway the full horror of leaving without Lucy began to sink in. For the second time, coming to this strange land didn't seem such a good idea. Hannah buried her face in her hands, sobbing at the thought of Lucy's screams.

'What's happening to her? Where have they taken her? What are we going to tell Grandma?'

Ben stared fearfully at Hannah, but said nothing.

Chapter 17

The White Ptarmigan

Hannah and Ben crept back into Grandma Fred's house, and slipped upstairs to bed. Hannah felt awful – worse than she had ever felt in her life – and lay awake, tossing and turning, watching the stars twinkling through the space where the bedroom curtains didn't quite meet.

How could she have been so stupid? How could she have thought sneaking around in the dead of night was a good idea? What had happened to Lucy? How could she have left her there? She couldn't sleep for worrying, imagining Lucy lying on a stone floor with only a thin, ragged sheet to keep her warm. Guiltily, she pulled the fleecy blankets close up under her chin.

But Ben was right, she consoled herself. If they had tried to rescue Lucy they would all have been captured. It was best to tell Dolfi and Chancellor Barbelly and let the Council of Alter-Idem deal with Hironymus Grossus and Vasril Odo now.

The hands on the bedroom clock ticked slowly round.

What *were* they going to tell Grandma? Hannah got up and stuffed some clothes under the bedcovers on Lucy's bed just in case Grandma poked her head round the door in the morning. At last, she fell into an uneasy sleep.

'Boiled eggs for breakfast, Ben? said Grandma, filling the kettle with water.

'Just toast will be fine, thanks, Grandma.'

'What do you think Hannah and Lucy will want?'

Ben had to think of something – fast.

'I'd leave theirs, Grandma, I think they lay awake talking till really late last night. They were still sound asleep when I passed their door. I knocked but there was no reply.'

168

'Right oh, then. I'll just make toast for us.' Gertrude mewed at Grandma's feet. 'And I'd better not forgot you, Gertie, eh?'

Gertrude sat and stared at Ben while Grandma poured some milk in her saucer. She had seen Ben and Hannah come home. They had whizzed straight past her and the church warden's cat at the bottom of the garden in their hurry to get inside. Gertrude knew Lucy was not upstairs and mewed at Ben.

'You'll have to wait until Lucy's up if you're wanting fussed,' said Grandma, looking down at her.

'You'll have a long wait,' Ben mumbled.

'What have you planned for today?' asked Grandma as she finished buttering the toast and set it down on the table. It was another gloriously warm day.

'If the weather holds it will be perfect for the Summer Fête on Saturday,' she said before Ben had answered.

'We haven't decided,' said Ben, munching on his second piece of toast. Lucy might be in a dungeon somewhere in Gorgonz City but you couldn't plan a rescue on an empty stomach.

'You can come with me if you like, I'm going over to Farmer Digwell's to discuss the judging of the miniature gardens.'

'No thanks, Grandma. I think I'll just read my book today until Hannah and Lucy are up.'

Grandma finished her toast and washed the dishes; she was always busy doing something. Ben noticed she had on one of her nicest summer dresses to visit Farmer Digwell and was taking him *two* pots of her home-made marmalade. She looked in the mirror and fiddled with her hair.

'Now if you do decide to go out today make sure you're home for tea, won't you dear?'

'Yes, Grandma.'

And she was gone. It was half past ten. A few minutes later Hannah appeared, bleary eyed and still in her nightgown.

'Was that Grandma? Has she gone?'

'Yes, luckily for you.' Ben was still blaming Hannah for going into the Council Chambers in the first place.

'What do you mean "luckily for me"? What did you tell her about Lucy?'

'Nothing. She doesn't realise she's not here. I told her you were both sleeping.'

'Good. Well, at least that's something. We've got until teatime to get Lucy back.' Hannah slumped down into the chair and let her head fall onto her arms on the table.

'You better get yourself ready. I told Landel to meet us at eleven o'clock,' said Ben.

Hannah got washed in super-fast time, brushed her teeth for one minute instead of two, gulped down several bogbean leaves with some milk and ate the jam sandwich Ben handed her on their way to the chestnut tree.

Landel was there to meet them with Hunnik and Hornet. Landel had told them about Lucy being captured.

'We should go straight to the Town Hall,' said Hornet as they all walked towards the Portway.

'Dolfi and Chancellor Barbelly will make sure she's released,' said Landel reassuringly.

Getting past Horace was always difficult and today of all days they wished they could avoid him but he flitted over just as they were settling on the scarab.

'Quite a little party today,' he said, looking round at them all. 'Having a picnic, are we?'

'We're in a hurry, Horace,' said Landel, sounding bored.

'Folk are always in a hurry, in too much of a hurry to notice the obvious. Off to discuss Herbert Rootvine's disappearance then?'

'That's old news Horace. How's your own little problem? Outlanders still around are they?' said Landel.

'I've got that little problem, as you call it, *well* under control, I … ' but Horace didn't get a chance to say any more because Hornet had been babbling in the scarab's ear and without warning, it moved off sharply and took flight.

'Any sign of the sixth key?' Horace shouted to the scarab's back.

There was no reply.

'Devilweed stew!' he bawled, flinging his flag to the ground and jumping up and down on it as the scarab disappeared from view.

Once in Pickletullum, Hunnik led the way to the Town Hall, where Dolfi and Chancellor Barbelly spent much of their time, and pressed through the heavy glass doors etched with the outline of the White Ptarmigan.

'We're here to see Dolfi Greenlees. Tell him the Peeps need to see him urgentl.' The elfin at the reception desk flew down the corridor, straight to his wide arched door, and knocked. She beckoned them to follow and closed the door behind them.

'Lucy's been captured,' Hannah blurted out the second the door was closed.

'Let's start at the beginning …' said Dolfi, pulling on his waistcoat, and he sat down while Hannah told him the full story.

'We only escaped because the tree statue hid us …' finished Hannah, hardly able to believe that was what had happened.

'The full grown elder is our most magical tree,' said Dolfi. 'It will give refuge to the kind hearted but will cast out those who are self-seeking or who harbour ill will. I expect that's why you were able to hide in it.'

'We can't let Grossus get away with this,' said Landel.

'We could go in and rescue her,' suggested Hornet.

In Chancellor Barbelly's office they repeated their story.

'Are you sure it was Hironymus Grossus who captured Lucy?' he asked.

'Vasril Odo gave the order,' said Hannah.

'This is most serious, most serious.' The Chancellor strode up and down the office with his hands clasped behind his back. 'We'll call an emergency meeting of the Council and make Grossus hand her over. Yes, yes, that's what we'll do.'

'I hope it's that simple,' said Dolfi faintly.

Messengers were dispatched to summon the other Chancellors to a meeting that very afternoon. Chancellor Hironymus Grossus protested that he had something else organised that he couldn't rearrange but Zanting Barbelly told him they would go ahead without him if necessary. They hoped the bluff would work.

At midsun and two, there was no sign of Vasril Odo or Hironymus Grossus as Hannah and Ben followed Dolfi into the Crystal Room in the Council Chambers. Sunlight was streaming in through the high windows and dancing through the crystals hanging from the ceiling. Hannah and Ben went to wait on the glass chairs behind Chancellor Barbelly as they had the last time.

Jacobus Mors and Grinnard were the first to arrive and entered the Crystal Room in a dignified silence.

'We meet again,' said Jacobus Mors, nodding sombrely toward Hannah and Ben. His eyes fell on Lucy's empty chair but he did not refer to it.

Chancellor Astra Manda and Clarendon Sisco were next to arrive. They floated into the room as if walking on a cushion of air and Astra Manda bowed in turn to everyone present.

'Such a beautiful day,' she said airily as she took her seat.

'Such a bounteous life,' said Clarendon Sisco, smiling vacantly.

Hannah and Ben managed a half smile back.

'I feel sick with worry,' Hannah whispered to Ben who was busy tucking the backpack under his seat and looping one of straps around his leg just in case there was any funny business during the meeting.

A noisy rustling and clomping issued from the hall and the great gold doors both opened abruptly to allow Chancellor Quilla Vanepike and Vida Vilenewt to stride inside.

'Greetings to you all,' Quilla Vanepike boomed, gesturing with her hand as if she were wafting away a cloud of insects. 'This won't take long will it, Barbelly? I have an appointment with my manicurist and I don't want to be late.'

She sat down, keeping her back very straight, and stared directly at Zanting Barbelly, waiting for an answer.

'I hope not, Chancellor Vanepike,' he said cheerfully. 'We're just waiting for Chancellor Grossus … and Under-secretary Odo.'

'What if they don't come?' Hannah askedBen in a hushed voice.

'What's keeping him? Don't tell me he's with his beauty therapist?' sneered Chancellor Vanepike.

Ben sniggered although no one else did.

'They'll be here shortly, I'm sure,' said Zanting Barbelly.

Dolfi leaned over and muttered in Chancellor Barbelly's ear. 'This won't be easy. We can't let Chancellor Grossus turn this to his advantage.'

Chancellor Barbelly coughed and turned his eyes abruptly towards the gold doors. Standing in the doorway, with his feet spread wide apart and looking defiantly around the room, was Hironymus Grossus. Vasril Odo slipped in behind him and took his seat by the door; Hannah thought he looked more like an earwig than ever.

Hironymus Grossus kept standing, as if to make them all notice how unafraid he was of them or what they thought.

'Come in, Chancellor Grossus. We have been waiting for you,' said Chancellor Barbelly.

Hironymus Grossus did not move and let his gaze fall on them, one by one. When he had everyone's attention he took two heavy steps towards his seat but remained standing

'An emergency meeting of the Council of Alter-Idem is indeed required today. I, Hironymus Grossus, Chancellor of Gorgonz City, host to this very Council, have some important news, news that will be of interest to us all.' Everyone sat in rapt concentration, wondering what he was going to say next.

'My dear Hironymus, if I could just ask you to wait until I have …' began Chancellor Barbelly.

'Wait!?' bellowed Grossus. 'When I have news about the raiders? Those despicable curs who have plundered and stolen our most prized possessions and caused such fear and trouble in our lands of late. Wait? No! I shall *not* wait.' He placed both hands on his belt and spread his elbows to make himself look as large and wide as possible, then carried on.

'Last night the Council chambers were broken into …'

Gasps erupted around the room. Hannah's and Ben's jaw dropped in surprise.

'We believe the raiders were snooping around looking for our records of business and items of value to steal. Their plan was foiled, however, when they stumbled across Vasril Odo in his bedchamber who raised the alarm. They were caught in the act, Chancellors, caught carrying out their evil plan to steal from our people – we, who have welcomed them with open hearts. It was the Peeps, ladies and gentlemen.'

Further gasps, of disbelief this time, burst from the Chancellors and their seconds.

'The Peeps are the raiders!' Grossus thundered. 'Who knows how long they have been plundering our villages!'

'That's not true,' shouted Hannah, jumping up.

'That's a lie,' shouted Ben.

'We have the evidence,' Grossus barked, drowning them out. He turned to the assembled Chancellors and triumphantly announced. 'We caught the youngest and she is in the dungeons!'

Everyone started talking and asking questions at once.

'My word! My word!' stammered Chancellor Barbelly. He looked at Hannah who had tears in her eyes.

'It's not true; He's the one behind all the raids,' she said.

The atmosphere was charged with anger and confusion. Amid the noise and fury no one knew quite what to say or do next.

'But it was him,' shouted Hannah, pointing to the gloating Chancellor. 'It's him and Vasril Odo. We saw the Vision Ball, the Scales of Balance and Judgement and the air-lilies. They have them.'

'You mean YOU have them,' stormed Hironymus Grossus. 'And to think we let you enter our villages freely. And no wonder you were so keen to look for the sixth key – you want it for yourselves. You plan to steal it once you find it!'

'No, no, that's not true,' pleaded Hannah, looking from Chancellor to Chancellor.

'Enough! Enough!' demanded Chancellor Barbelly. 'Quieten down everybody.'

Dolfi patted Hannah on the knee and Zanting Barbelly stood up and raised his hands and appealed for quiet once again. Even the normally unflustered Astra Manda looked concerned by what she'd heard.

'The Council cannot act on unsubstantiated claims by *any* party,' announced Chancellor Barbelly once the noise had died down.

'I suggest that Lucy is released from the dungeons and we have a full hearing so that the facts on both sides can be established.'

'It is a fact that they broke into the Council Chambers and were caught sneaking around in the middle of the night. What more proof do you want?' sneered Grossus.

'A court of law must consider all the evidence, Hironymus, you know that. Now I suggest you release the girl.'

'I will do no such thing! It is my duty to take whatever action I consider necessary to protect Gorgonz City!' Grossus's bulging eyes were bulging even more than usual and his blubbery lips were pressed hard against his yellow tusk-like tooth.

'It is in no one's interests to hold the girl. I say, release her.' Chancellor Barbelly stood his ground. Beads of sweat were springing up on his forehead. Hannah, looking into his big round face, saw a trickle make its way to his chin and hang there, quivering

Hironymus Grossus fell quiet for a moment then, narrowing his eyes, he spoke fiercely. 'I will release her if the Peeps leave immediately and never return to our lands and this whole absurd idea of finding the sixth key is dropped.'

It was now clear to Hannah and Ben what Hironymus Grossus wanted and at that moment they would have gladly agreed to leave and forget all about the sixth key if Lucy was returned unharmed, even if it meant being branded thieves and liars. Lucy was all that mattered. They looked up hopefully but Chancellor Barbelly did not look back at them. He took several deep breaths before speaking.

'This Council abides by the Harmony Rules and we must allow the Peeps their say. Very well, Chancellor Grossus, if you won't release the girl I propose that a hearing be set for two days time. Take a vote, Under-secretary, please.'

Everyone called 'Yae' to the vote except Hironymus Grossus and the date for the hearing was set for Saturday.

Hannah and Ben waited on the red sofas outside the Crystal Room until Dolfi was ready to leave. They would never be able to hide Lucy's disappearance from Grandma Fred for two days. Hannah sat fretting and worrying and twiddling with the backpack. All the Chancellors had left except Grinnard who was still talking to Zanting Barbelly. Goodness knows what *he* believed. He had seen them on their way to Gorgonz City and probably thought they were the raiders too. Hannah raised her eyes wearily and was glancing at the inscription above the great gold doors when something clicked in her mind. 'Didn't Mr Sonorus in Socratown say the song the flute played was called 'An Upright Life?'

'I think so.'

'I need the flute,' said Hannah, fumbling with the ties on the backpack.

'What for?'

'Look at the inscription above the door,' Hannah took the flute and put it to her lips while Ben read the inscription: An Upright Life Free From Wickedness.

Hannah blew. She was sure something would happen when she finished.

'Nothing happened.' Hannah hung her head.

'What did you expect to happen?' Ben asked.

'I don't know,' she replied miserably '… something. It has the same words, doesn't it?'

'Yes, but …' Ben realised it wasn't wise to say anymore. There had been enough disappointments for one day.

They didn't feel like going home straight away. Hannah needed to clear her mind and they had to think of something to tell Grandma. In Pickletullum, Dolfi left them in Ma Molly's with Landel, Hunnik and Hornet who were as sorry as Ben and Hannah that Lucy was not with them.

'What if she's injured?' said Hannah.

'Stop worrying, Hannah. Worrying's no good. There's nothing we can do until the hearing. She'll be all right,' said Ben.

'But we don't know that for sure,' Hannah cried, pacing up and down, thinking this the worst day of her life. As she swung past for the tenth time, Hunnik grabbed her by the arm.

'Let's go for a walk,' Hunnik suggested and Hannah was glad of something to do. As they walked around the village, the townsfolk waved and said hello.

'Everyone's being so friendly. What will they say when they know Hironymus Grossus is accusing us of being the raiders and Lucy is in the dungeons?'

'At least we know where Lucy is,' said Hunnik. 'No one knows where Herbert Rootvine and the imps are.'

What had happened to them? Had they really taken the Precious Fires to make gold for themselves? Hannah thought of Thelma. Maybe she had some news? They headed for the Apothecary at the other end of the village.

Thelma was pouring some crushed weevils into a bag when they entered. 'Two kippa, please,' she said to Mrs Chelsea, the baker, who was being served.

Mrs Chelsea paid and said hello to Hunnik and Hannah as she left. Jasper screeched overhead.

'Not now, Jasper, I've got an 'eadache.' Thelma pulled her black hat down further over her ears.

Hannah and Hunnik smiled nervously – maybe this was not a good time.

'It's good t' see yeh both,' said Thelma. 'Everyone else that comes in 'ere wants to know if Dr Rootvine really did take the Precious Fires. I knows 'e didn't do it but where is 'e? An'where're the imps? Perhaps 'e's gone to find 'em. Then sometimes, I catch meself thinkin' maybe 'e did do it.'

'I'm sure he didn't,' said Hunnik.

'Whatever has happened to him I bet Hironymus Grossus has something to do with it. We thought we had proof … but now …' Hannah looked tearful again. Thelma looked mystified.

'They broke into the Council Chambers last night. Lucy was captured and now Hironymus Grossus is saying they are the raiders,' Hunnik explained in a low voice.

'Oooh! Mean old wart-face … that's awful,' said Thelma.

Too late Hannah realised that everyone in Pickletullum would know the whole story before the afternoon was out.

As they left the Apothecary, Hannah, still turning everything over in her mind, felt Hunnik nudge her arm.

'Hannah, look … there.'

In the sky above the woods, Hannah saw a tiny speck. Slowly, it got bigger and bigger as it headed in their direction. It was a bird, just an ordinary bird, but then Hannah realised there *was* something different about it. Instead of being drab and dark in colour it was pure white.

The bird soared effortlessly in the clear blue sky, all the while making its way towards them. It must have been flying quickly because it was suddenly above them, circling, gliding and … watching them. In a graceful sweep it spread its great white wings and came to rest on the roof of the bookbinder's shop. The scarab waiting at the post below shifted uneasily.

'It's the White Ptarmigan!' said Hunnik, marvelling as the bird preened itself. Hannah looked at its feathered feet. It *was* a White Ptarmigan. Could this be the late, great Zamada?

The White Ptarmigan flapped its wings at full stretch again as if to make sure they were paying attention then bent its long neck down and pecked at the ageing sign.

'You don't think its trying to tell us something, do you?' Hunnik asked doubtfully, but before Hannah could answer the White Ptarmigan sang out its sharp, clear call, pecked the sign once more, and took to the air again. It circled the bookbinder's twice then flew off towards the woods without looking back.

Hannah and Hunnik stared at each other.

'No harm in looking inside, I suppose,' said Hannah, taking a few steps towards the bookbinders.

Inside it was noisy and smelly. A printing machine, working flat out, was making deafening clacking noises and there was a horrible smell of glue in the air; Hannah and Hunnik wrinkled their noses.

'What can I do for you?' A bald man in round glasses shouted above the din. He had a pencil tucked behind one ear.

What could they say? They didn't want anything printed and they didn't know what they were looking for.

'I wonder if we can talk to you for a moment?' said Hannah, trying to make herself heard. 'Can't stop a print run,' shouted the man, then added, 'It'll be finished in a few minutes – have a seat while you're waiting.' He left them while he attended to his pots of glue on the stove.

Several elfin, a goblin and a sprite sat at desks, lovingly pasting colourful bindings onto the books before them. They worked quickly, tucking and folding covers around corners, sticking inside pages and painting intricate borders around the edges. If it wasn't for the smell and the noise it looked like it might have been enjoyable work. The printing press finally stopped and the man came over and introduced himself.

'Mr Hornkettle,' he said, holding out his hand.

'Hannah Bootle,' said Hannah 'and this is my friend, Hunnik.'

'Pleased to meet you,' he said. 'Bootle. Now that's an interesting name. Any relation to Demus Bootle, the inventor of the bootjack?' Noting the blank expression on Hannah's face he continued, 'You know, the device shaped like the letter V for pulling off boots?'

'I'm afraid not,' said Hannah, shaking her head.

'Never mind, never mind. Bootmaker to the great and the good in his day. They say there was not a witching family worth their broomstick that didn't have their boots made by Demus Bootle. No relation then. Well, what can I do for you?'

'Er … we're not quite sure,' said Hannah, feeling herself going pink.

'Can you tell us what kinds of books you print?' said Hunnik, saying the first thing that came into her head.

Mr Hornkettle looked at them suspiciously. 'Well, all sorts really, we turn no work away. What are you looking for?'

Hannah remembered Jacobus Mors telling them about the difficulties not telling the truth could get you into and decided it was best to be honest.

'Mr Hornkettle, to tell the truth, we don't know what it is we are looking for. We think there might be something important we need to know here in your shop, a clue even, something that might tell us something about, er … something that might even lead us to the whereabouts of the lost sixth key.'

Mr Hornkettle's face fell into an expression of shocked surprise as he looked around his shop. (The goblin, two desks away, promptly looked under his seat.)

'Well, if my shop is hiding any of that sort of information I don't know it,' he said, scratching his bald head, 'nor where it might be. All the books printed here leave the shop and go to those who have ordered them. Except those that have gone wrong that is.'

'What do you mean "those that have gone wrong?"' asked Hannah.

'Sometimes the bindings don't stick properly or we might have a little … er, accident, with the inks. It doesn't happen often though and when it does, we reprint the book. The customer always gets his order in mint condition.'

An exciting thought came to Hannah. 'Mr Hornkettle, did Zamada, the last Supreme Parlator, ever have anything printed here?' she asked.

'Oh, that would be in my great-grandfather's time,' said Mr Hornkettle. 'I couldn't tell you without looking back through the old order books.'

'Would it be too much trouble to look?' asked Hannah.

Mr Hornkettle replied that it wouldn't and led them upstairs to the office where a grey- haired old woman was bent over a desk in front of a big ledger, writing entries in red ink. They could see she was adding up the right hand column and was about to write in the total when they interrupted her.

'Bother, I'll have to count it up all over again,' she said and as she spoke the total floated out of the top of her head in a smoky trail.

'Is the total eighteen cala and three kippa?' Hannah asked catching sight of it before if faded completely.

'That's it, that's it. How did you know that?' said the old woman in astonishment.

'Ehh, just a guess,' said Hannah.

The old woman quickly wrote it down.

'This is Great Aunt Ebina, my grandfather's sister. Her mother and father had this shop when Zamada was alive. She'll be able to help you.'

Once they explained what they wanted Great Aunt Ebina went to a door and opened it. In the next room a couple of armchairs and a wide bookshelf sat among dozens and dozens of boxes. They were everywhere. They were piled up on the floor, piled up on the table and piled up on the sideboard. Most of the boxes were open and filled to the brim with books. It seemed that every order book and ledger book that had ever been written in to record orders or payments was stored in this room. It would take them years to look through them all. There was even a book on top of the very large birdcage which stood in the corner. In it, a bird was sitting on a perch, fast asleep and dreaming, making chugging noises, chain-saw noies, whistling and twirling noises, and when he started making rat-atat-atat noises his foot jerked in rhythm as if he was waltzing around a room. His beautiful long curling tail feathers tumbled out of the open door and cascaded to the floor.

'This is my secretary,' announced Great Aunt Ebina. 'GAN-DERRRRR.' The bird woke with a start, shook its magnificent plumage, and hopped out of the cage. It hopped from box to box until it reached them and perched shakily on the edge of the one nearest them.

'Hello.'

'Hello,' Hannah and Hunnik replied together. It didn't seem surprising that the bird could speak and when Great Aunt Ebina started to talk to it that didn't seem surprising either.

'Gander, these people are looking for any order or receipt that was made out for Zamada, the last Supreme Parlator. Can you have a look for us please.'

'"Gander, these people are looking for any order or receipt that was made out for Zamada, the last Supreme Parlator. Can you have a look for us please." Certainly,' Gander replied.

'He can't help himself,' saidGreat Aunt Ebina.

'He can't help himself,' the bird echoed. 'I am a secretary bird after all, got to repeat everything to make sure I'm remembering it accurately … Actually, I'm a lyre bird but you can't have a secretary who's a liar can you?' Gander turned and looked into space. He started making whirring noises like a camera rewinding its film and his eyes blinked so fast that they seemed to flutter. He stood motionless for a few minutes then, when the clicking and whirring stopped, he opened his eyes.

'Three documents,' he said and hopped around the boxes until he reached one by the fireplace. He grabbed the edges of the box between his claws and flapped strenuously. Both Gander and the box rose into the air, moved one metre to the right, then collapsed down in a heap. Gander fluttered back to the box below the one he had just lifted and plunged his head deep into its books and papers. He reappeared with two books and swooped over, flicking the pages of one with its beak, then settled down beside them.

'There,' he said, indicating an entry. 'The Supreme Parlator ordered a bound copy of her Private Personal Journal.'

Hannah and Hunnik looked at the entry. The ink had faded and the page was yellowed but the order was unmistakable. The Supreme Parlator had ordered the pages of her personal journal to be bound into a book.

'And there is the payment.' The secretary bird pointed to an entry in the second book. 'This ledger book records the exact sum the Supreme Parlator paid for the work.'

Something dawned on Hannah.

'Unfortunately this doesn't help us any, does it?' She frowned at Hunnik. 'Zamada got her journal bound, collected it and paid for it. If the journal was kept anywhere it would most likely have been in the library or in the Council Chambers but we've looked in the library and there was a fire in the Council Chambers not long after she died.'

'There was a fire all right,' said Great Aunt Ebina. 'Shocking. All the Council minutes and important papers of her reign were destroyed.'

'"There was a fire all right. Shocking. All the Council minutes and important papers of her reign were destroyed." Sounds like someone was trying to get rid of them,' chirped the secretary bird.

'It does, doesn't it, but who?' said Hannah 'It was too long ago to be anyone in the Council now.'

The secretary bird fluttered over to an armchair and from there hopped up onto the top of the bookshelf where more ledgers and books lay stacked one on top of the other. He grabbed one in his beak and glided back to their side.

'The third document,' he said, holding it up for Hannah.

Hannah wiped a thick layer of dust off the cover. This didn't look like an order book or a ledger book. Hannah lifted the book to her face and blew. Great Aunt Ebina coughed and spluttered as the dust swirled in the air. The secretary bird coughed and spluttered in exactly the same way. Hannah saw some words float from Great Aunt Ebina's head. "I wish that bird wouldn't copy everything I say and do." The words slowly faded into nothing.

'Jumping Juniper!' said Hunnik.

Where the dust had been blown away the word 'Private' was clearly visible. Hannah opened the book and there on the first page, written in green ink, were the words:

PRIVATE PERSONAL JOURNAL
OF
ZAMADA, SUPREME PARLATOR OF ALDORIS.

'This is Zamada's personal journal,' she exclaimed. 'But why is it here of all places?'

They looked again at the order and ledger books.

'Zamada seems to have ordered the pages to be bound and paid for the work on the same day,' said Hunnik, looking carefully at the dates.

'But see there,' said the secretary bird. 'Although it was paid for, there's no date to say when it was collected.'

'Looks like she died before she collected it,' said Great Aunt Ebina.

'Looks like she died before she collected it,' said the secretary bird.

'Perhaps she never intended to collect it,' said Hannah, wondering aloud. 'Maybe she knew it wouldn't be safe in Gorgonz City.'

'The White Ptarmigan must have wanted us to find it,' said Hunnik.

'I wonder what it's going to tell us,' said Hannah, turning the next page as if it might explode.

Chapter 18

The Windoless

Later that afternoon, back in Ma Molly's Muffin House, Hannah sat staring at Zamada's journal which was perched on her knee. Ben, Landel, Hunnik and Hornet crowded round to hear what was inside while Hannah kept her voice low. Luckily, a crowd were playing Wingtang noisily outside and their cheers were carrying in through the open windows. Hannah took another deep breath and spoke Zamada's words in a soft whisper.

I suspect that the fever sweeping the villages is not a fever of the air but a poison. I have instructed an acorn and nasturtium antidote to be made and distributed to all the villages. We are too late to save many dear souls but the antidote may work for some. There is only one person capable of poisoning our kind on such a large scale. It is with great sorrow that I conclude he has turned his great talents to evil purposes. Why he has done so, I do not know.

'The villages were poisoned?' said Hunnik. 'Everyone was poisoned?'
'Who was it?' asked Ben incredulously.
Details of the how the fever had spread quickly and accounts of the villagers' suffering followed … but there was more.
'Go on, Hannah,' urged Landel. Hannah looked back down at the journal and continued reading.

Today I was out walking in the woods with my friends Jessel Magrew, Felone Melandra and Ossinda Odessa, and was telling them of my fears when we were surprised by a dark figure lurking amongst the shadows. It was none other than Fectus Core. He seemed agitated and angry and questioned me about the antidote I had ordered but I made no reference to my suspicions about the poison or of him doing the poisoning.

'Fectus Core!' cried Ben.

But then he pulled out his wand and started shouting I was standing in his way, that I wasn't going to stop him taking his rightful place. If it wasn't for dear Felone flinging herself upon him and biting his leg I would have been killed. Instead, his deadly spell bounced off the Magical Crown of Keys and rebounded on him, shooting him into an old elder tree. It thrashed its branches for hours afterwards as he tried to free himself, until at last it drooped with exhaustion. He is deranged and very dangerous but he is trapped, hopefully till the end of his days, however long that might be.

Their faces were pale. No one spoke.

'Fectus Core,' said Ben spitting out the words as if saying them softly might bring him back. 'Poisoning the villages so he could be ruler of Aldoris.'

'He is … dead now, isn't he?' said Hunnik sounding scared. None of them had considered that he might still be alive.

Hannah suddenly felt faint and clammy. She forced herself to speak the terrible questions that had sprung into her mind.

'What if he survived being trapped in the tree and is now free? And what if he not only caused the first fever but also caused the second – the fever that recently struck Pickletullum?'

The possibility was too awful to contemplate. How could they deal with someone so vile he would kill those who didn't want what he wanted? Someone so cruel he would poison children and leave them to die in agony? No-one answered.

'He can't be alive,' said Hornet finally. 'Not after all this time. And even if he is, there's only one of him and there's hundreds of us.' He kicked in the air at an imaginary Fectus Core and karate-chopped an imaginary neck lying stretched out on the table.

'Lucy! We've got to get Lucy out of the dungeons,' exclaimed Hannah.

'But Hannah, there's going to be a hearing. We'll get her back then,' said Ben.

'We can't wait until Saturday. It's far too dangerous now. Don't you see? What if Hironymus Grossus won't release her. What if Fectus Core is alive. We've got to get her now.'

'But Grandma is expecting us home in half an hour. You're not thinking straight, Hannah.'

'Yes I am. Hunnik and I are going to see Witch Magrew.'

Hannah snapped shut Zamada's journal and stuffed it in the backpack.

'And what am I supposed to tell Grandma?' Ben wailed as Hannah strode towards the door pulling Hunnik by the arm.

'Tell her anything. Tell her Lucy and I have gone to the cinema.'

'To see what?' said Ben, utterly exasperated.

'To see … *Dungeons and Dragons*,' Hannah marched on. 'I hope there are no dragons,' she added to Hunnik once they were out of the door.

Hunnik and Hannah flew through the woods to Witch Magrew's house using Fly-by powder as there was no scarab at the resting post. The entire journey Hannah scoured the way ahead for an old drooping elder.

It wasn't until they were standing in front of number seven Winterbottom Lane that Hunnik found out why they had come.

'I want to borrow Witch Magrew's Windoless,' Hannah confided as she knocked on the door.

Witch Magrew shouted 'Who is it, Rosa?' as Rosa opened the door.

'Quack, quack.'

'Oh, the Peep girl, how splendid. Ask her in, Rosa.'

On the wall facing them the Windoless was still showing the same dull view of the forest outside. Witch Magrew's face lit up when she saw them. Today her hair was pumpkin orange.

'Come in, come in. Make yourselves comfortable. Squawking ducks retreated from the sofa to make room for the guests. Witch Magrew pulled a hanky from her pocket and flicked it at the drifting feathers, but there were too many to make much difference. Hunnik and Hannah settled quickly and comfy she leaned forward and peered down from her floating pink armchair.

'Where's Lucy today?' Witch Magrew asked, leaning forward and peering down from her pink armchair.

'That's why we're here, Witch Magrew. We're having a bit of trouble,' said Hannah.

'Not with Lucy, I hope?'

Hannah explained about their efforts to find the sixth key, about their raid on the Council Chambers, and about Lucy being captured.

'Oh, that poor child,' she exclaimed, which did not make Hannah feel any better. 'And how can I help?'

Hannah came straight to the point.

'The last time we were here you said the Windoless let you see inside if you were outside and outside if you were inside,' she said.

'That is correct,' said Witch Magrew.

'I would like to borrow it, please. I think it will help me find Lucy.'

Witch Magrew frowned and told Hannah how reckless she thought her plan was but Hannah could not be persuaded to wait.

'Very well, Hannah. I can see you've made up your mind. You may have it on one condition.'

'What's that?'

'Well, it *is* very valuable and you know I wouldn't want it to get lost or damaged.' Hannah nodded.

'If I let you have it you must leave something of yours until you return it.'

Hannah considered what she had in the backpack. She couldn't offer the flute because Witch Magrew had once owned that, and she wouldn't want the Fly-by powder because she already had a flying armchair. Hannah doubted Witch Magrew would have any use for the scroll, or the map, or a few cala, or Zamada's journal, and besides, she hadn't finished reading it herself. What could she leave?

'What about your shoes?' suggested Witch Magrew. 'You can take the Windoless if you leave me your shoes.' Witch Magrew had wanted to try them ever since their first visit.

'They might not be the right size,' said Hannah looking down.

'That won't matter,' said Witch Magrew, tipping her wand in Hannah's direction. 'I can make them bigger.' The laces of Hannah's trainers undid themselves, and the shoes wriggled from her feet and bobbed up through the air towards Witch Magrew, whose big pink slippers were already off and hanging in mid-air.

'You can have mine,' she said, and the big pink slippers attached themselves to Hannah's feet and shrank to fit her.

The Windoless unhinged itself from the wall and settled in Hannah's arms.

'Now take good care of it,' said Witch Magrew. 'It was a present from my mother you know.'

'Yes, I remember,' said Hannah, clasping it to her tightly. Witch Magrew looked at them both and sighed.

'I don't suppose you have time to hear about the Youth Witchery Dance Troupe today have you?'

''Fraid not,' said Hannah, casting her eyes down guiltily to the photograph of Zamada, Witch Magrew's mother, Ossinda Odessa and Felone Melandra, whose slightly pointed teeth did look perfect for biting. 'But next time. I promise.'

Hunnik and Hannah set off for Pickletullum again. The rushing air seemed to whip the words right out of their mouths but it was just as well really because Hannah's mind was too busy to talk. She hadn't got a proper plan but the thought of Lucy alone and frightened in a cold dungeon firmed her resolve. She *had* to find her.

In the Portway, Landel and Hornet distracted Horace so that Hannah and Hunnik could slip into Gorgonz City's burroway without being seen. They hitched a lift on the next passing scarab and disembarked, unnoticed, outside the Council Chambers in Gorgonz City. The kitchens still seemed the best place to get in but when they arrived the window was closed.

'What about through the drains,' suggested Hunnik.

'There's got to be a better way,' said Hannah, grimacing at the thought of meeting a rat nose-to-nose.

'Why don't you look in the Windoless then while I think,' suggested Hunnik.

Hannah held the Windoless in front of her. On its surface, shapes started to appear. They were indistinct at first and grey; then the images slowly came into focus. The inside of the kitchens appeared; the mop was still propped up in the corner by the door and a kitchen boy was standing at the table chopping carrots.

'I can see inside the kitchens,' saidHannah. Hunnik was still trying to think.

Hannah aimed the Windoless in another direction and the corridor outside the kitchens came into view.

'Any sign of Lucy?'

'No, not yet,' saidHannah pointingthe Windoless at the ground and moving it around. A picture of the cellars that meandered under the chambers appeared. Hannah tilted the screen, following the path, until she saw a pair of feet.

'I've got something,' she said, watching a pair of thick leather boots stomp along the corridor. She guessed they belonged to a guard. He seemed to be carrying something but whenever she tried to get a closer look, the image went fuzzy. She followed him until he came to a door, unlocked it and went in. The image faded. Hannah showed the image to Hunnik who thought they were too far away for the picture to be clear but they could still see his outline laying a dish on a table. Then they saw her, no more than a blur on the screen, but Hannah was sure it was Lucy. She seemed to be crouched in a corner, sobbing into her arms. The guard left. Lucy slowly rose and made her way to the table; she seemed to be dragging one leg behind her; she started to eat the food on the plate with her hands. Hannah watched, transfixed and horrified at the same time, unable to pull her eyes away.

'We've got to get her out of there. 'Hannah's voice was trembling. 'There must be a way in.'

Hunnik clapped a hand to her head.

'Why didn't I think of it before. The chimneys. See …' She pointed at the Windoless. In the background, behind Lucy, was a fireplace.

'I don't get it,' said Hannah.

'You will,' said Hunnik. 'Come on. We need to get closer.'

They moved along behind the Council Chambers, Hannah watching the uneven ground beneath her feet while Hunnik watched the rooftops. Not that there was anything much to see. From the outside everything looked like solid rock. They scrambled over bare stones and scratchy gorse until Hunnik stopped at a likely place.

'There are several chimneys up there now,' said Hunnik, and Hannah just had to take her word for it because she couldn't see anything that looked like a chimney.

'Ready?' asked Hunnik.

Hannah saw the familiar yellow and blue stars hurtling towards her and felt her bones rattle and her skin squeeze tight but this didn't feel like the other times she'd been made large or small.

'There!' Hunnik's voice seemed strangely high.

'What have you done to us?' squeaked Hannah.

'We're so small now,' said Hunnik, 'we can fly down the chimneys and not be noticed.'

Hunnik sprinkled Hannah with Fly-by powder then soared up into the air with the backpack. Hannah followed with the Windoless. They swooped down the first chimney trying to keep away from the thick black soot that clung to the sides. Down they plummeted, straight towards the hearth below, then shot out into Vasril Odo's bedchamber. They landed on his bed, sending a gust of soot into the air. There was no one was around.

'This isn't where we want to be,' said Hannah, seeing once more the portrait of Vasril Odo's mother on the wall. Only, in the daylight, something about her seemed oddly familiar.

'We'll just have to try all the chimneys around here,' said Hunnik, 'unless you have a better idea?'

'Ossinda Odessa!' exclaimed Hannah.

'What?' said Hunnik.

'The portrait,' said Hannah, 'the nameplate says "Ossinda Odessa". She's Vasril Odo's mother!'

'So?' said Hunnik, scrutinising the portrait but shaking her head and wondering what was so important about Vasril Odo's mother.

'She was a friend of Zamada's,' said Hannah hurriedly.

'Was she?' said Hunnik.

'Witch Magrew's photograph! She's in the photograph.' There wasn't time to go into it now. 'Let's go. I'll explain later,' said Hannah.

They flew back up the chimney, which was harder with the down-draught working against them like a tide, and down the next chimney, through damp, gritty air, and found themselves in a cold basement. Once again Lucy wasn't there. Instead, through the gloom, something was glinting in the moonlight. Shiny armoured breast plates lay piled up on the floor and hundreds of shields stood stacked against the wall. Spiked balls hung from the ceiling and long-handled axes skulked in the dark corners as if trying to hide from the shaft of light that was coming in from the skylight.

'What's all this?' said Hannah.

'Could have been here for hundreds of years.'

'But then everything would be rusty. Everything in here is new.' Hannah landed on a crate beside a piece of folded paper. She picked it up.

'It's a bill,' she gasped 'from Demus Bootle, thirteenth generation bootmaker, for five hundred pairs of combat boots.' Their eyes travelled over to three crates on the other side of the room where a studded boot was poking from a splintered corner. 'It's got last week's date on it.' Army supplies – someone was preparing for a battle. The more they found out the worse things seemed.

'Let's get out of here,' said Hannah, trying to sound calm. 'We've got to get Lucy.'

The next chimney was blocked halfway down with soot and grime.

'This is revolting,' Hannah coughed and blinked soot from her eyes. 'We can't get through.'

'Try the Windoless again,' urged Hunnik. 'We must be near now.'

Hannah rubbed the filthy dust from the Windoless and waited till the image sharpened. 'No, NO!'

'What's happening?' Hunnik stared at the screen. In the Windoless Lucy was backing into a corner, screaming and hiding her face. A hand was rising ready to strike her. A metal blade flashed.

'Quick! We have to save her!'

Hannah raced to the next chimney, praying it was the right one. Like bullets from a gun they shot down the chimney and out into the dungeon, unnoticed in a gust of soot. Lucy was screaming and wrestling wildly with her attacker. Hannah fumbled in the backpack, felt the flute, grabbed it and flew at the face.

'Arrgghh.' The attacker's hand flew to his eye. He fell to one knee and a knife dropped to the floor.

On the mantle Hunnik noticed a hammer. She heaved at the handle while the attacker groped on the floor for the knife. He struggled to his feet. Hunnik strained and pushed and shoved. The hammer fell hitting him on the head. The attacker raged in pain and dropped the knife again - but only for a moment. He snatched it up and staggered towards Lucy. Hannah hurled herself forward and sank her teeth into the very tender tip of his nose. The blade gleamed. Hannah heard a sickening slash as it sliced down.

She fell to the floor in despair. Then something fell on her, something soft and the colour of gold. Heavy footfalls crossed the floor and the door slammed.

'Hannah, Hannah, are you here?' called Lucy.

Hunnik flicked her wand, uttered her growing spell, and they stood before Lucy at full height.

'Lucy!' Hannah rushed forwards and hugged her hard. Something felt horribly wrong against her cheek. Lucy's beautiful long hair, once so lustrous and shiny, was gone, and what remained looked more like the stuffing from an old chair.

'I thought I was going to die,' sobbed Lucy. 'How did you find me.'

'I swapped my trainers for the Windoless,' said Hannah, looking down at Witch Magrew's soot-stained pink slippers. Lucy managed a sobbing laugh.

'What do they want your hair for?' asked Hannah, smoothing it flat. Lucy shrugged.

Hunnik was staring into the Windoless. Once more the picture was clearing and before long they had their answer. In the very next dungeon, steam was swirling above two caldrons and a voice suddenly boomed.

'Got the hair, Grunt? Good. Now add some to the potion.'

Licking up the sides of the bubbling cauldrons, they saw familiar magenta flames. The Precious Fires! A hand was adding strands of Lucy's golden hair.

'Dr Rootvine!' gasped Hannah.

'Anything happening?' the voice in the Windoless growled.

'N-n-not yet,' stammered Dr Rootvine, and a second later a whip cracked through the air. Dr Rootvine yelled out, and they saw his book, *Alchemy Through The Ages*, fall to the floor.

Hannah moved the Windoless around the room and saw Eeny and Meeny, exhausted and frightened, stirring the second cauldron. Miney was cowering over a table.

'They are being forced to try and make gold,' gasped Hannah. 'Look … The jars of Precious Fires are on the wall.'

They could see the four remaining jars of the still, blue flame sitting on a shelf. From somewhere in the Windoless they heard a door opening.

The voice spoke again. 'What is it, Odo?'

Who was that? Hironymus Grossus? The tone was strange and crackly through the Windoless and Hannah couldn't see who was speaking. She shook the Windoless and moved it around trying to get the best picture. In the open doorway Vasril Odo stood stammering, greasy head bent in servitude.

'The Co-council of Alter-Idem are de-m-manding a hearing on Saturday. We will be e-e-expected to show the Lucy girl. She is to be questioned.'

The gravelly voice replied, 'The Council of Alter-Idem are powerless to demand anything now. They'll never see the girl again.' They heard a whip lash across the table, and the imps whimpering in the background.

'GET ON WITH YOUR WORK,' the voice roared.

The Windoless cleared. A hand reach towards the casket on the table and opened it. Inside, a gold key glowed. Cruel laugher filled the dungeon.

'Without this there will be no Supreme Parlator ever again.'

Which key was it?

'Why don't they run? The door is open. Run! Run!' Lucy shouted at the Windoless, but Dr Rootvine and the imps couldn't hear her.

'They seem to be stuck somehow,' said Hannah, tilting the Windoless towards their feet. Thick, smooth, ropes bound their ankles so they could barely hobble without falling over. She followed the rope along the floor. It led to some sort of net up on the wall. Hannah angled the Windoless to get a better view. In the middle of the net, the fourth imp, Mo, was bound and hanging motionless.

'We've got to get out of here!' Hannah's hands started to shake and her voice trembled as she tore her eyes away from the Windoless, not wanting to see any more.

Hunnik made them all small again and just before they escaped back up the chimney the way they had come, they heard:

'Those infernal, interfering Peeps. If it wasn't for them I'd have control by now … but soon … very soon. Nothing can stop me now. Is everything ready, Odo? A hearing … Pahh! Let's see them try and stop us. We've got all their precious toys now. The Vision Ball, The Scales of Balance and Judgement, the air-lilies and the Precious Fires; riches and soon … gold! Their powers are mine. ALL MINE.'

Chapter 19

The Sixth Key

Grandma was asleep by the fire when Hannah and Lucy returned. They left a note for her saying they had enjoyed the cinema and had gone to bed. Still pale and shaken, they crept into Ben's room.

'It was just awful,' sobbed Lucy, collapsing onto the bed. Ben stared at her shorn hair, relieved that she was safe at least. He listened carefully as they told the whole story.

'What are we going to do now?' Ben asked.

'The hearing's tomorrow. We'll go back and tell Dolfi, Chancellor Barbelly and the Council what we saw, give them Zamada's journal, then leave,' said Hannah firmly.

'Leave?' said Ben in a mocking voice. 'What about finding the sixth key and all that? Don't tell me you're giving up.'

Hannah blinked hard. 'OK, you were right. It *is* too dangerous. Maybe we should have given up earlier – but at least we did what we could. We can't do anymore now and besides, we've run out of time. There's only tomorrow left; we go home on Sunday.'

Ben looked at Hannah with smug satisfaction. 'I've been telling you for ages it was too dangerous but would you listen?'

Hannah looked down at Witch Magrew's blackened slippers.

'I just didn't want to let them down,' she said. 'We did say we'd try and find the sixth key for them.'

'Well, we *have* tried,' said Ben. 'But like Milli says, they're no worse off now than when we started …'

'Apart from Grossus and Vasril Odo planning to take over,' said Lucy.

'But that's not *our* fault,' said Ben. 'There's nothing more *we* can do.'

'I suppose not.' Lucy reluctantly agreed.

Hannah sighed. 'I guess we'll just have to leave them to sort it out themselves. It'll be a relief really to leave it to the Council of Alter-Idem to decide what to do.'

'Poor Dr Rootvine and the imps …' Lucy stopped, remembering Mo. 'We need to tell them everything as soon as possible before anything else bad happens.'

*

It wasn't until the second cup of tea at breakfast that Grandma noticed anything different about Lucy's hair. Hannah had tried to trim all the ragged edges straight; it was now so short it was up at her ears.

'I like it,' said Ben.

'Let's hope your mum likes it,' said Grandma Fred. 'Whatever will she say? I don't know what possessed you to cut it, Hannah. I hope she doesn't think I gave you permission.'

'I wanted it cut,' lied Lucy. 'I asked her to do it.'

'Your beautiful hair,' lamented Grandma, as she cracked the breakfast eggs.

'Is everything ready for the Village Fête today, Grandma?' asked Ben, tactfully changing the subject. This was exactly the right thing to do.

'Everything's done. Starts today at ten o'clock, the judging's at two and the prizes will be awarded at four. Mr Goodstanley will be judging the chutneys, jams and vegetables. He's the head chef at the Ritz, you know. It was such a coup that he agreed to come. Mrs Perriwinkle on the committee was so jealous that I'd managed to persuade him to do the judging for us that she's hardly spoken to me since. Wouldn't it be marvellous if … no, I mustn't get my hopes up.' Grandma Fred calmed herself, wiped her hands on her apron and pushed the bacon around the frying pan. Gertrude jumped up onto Lucy's lap and sat staring at her short hair.

'Are you coming today?' Grandma asked distractedly.

Hannah, Ben and Lucy exchanged glances.

'Yes, we'll come,' said Hannah. 'Should be fun.'

'There will be lots to do,' said Grandma, setting their plates down. 'It would be nice if you could be there for the prize-giving.'

'We'll be there, Grandma,' said Hannah.

After breakfast they helped Grandma collect her best herb specimens for the show and put the most attractive labels on her marmalade, jams and chutneys. Everything seemed almost normal. Grandma Fred laid her exhibits carefully in her basket and set her hat straight in the mirror.

'See you later then,' she said on her way out, leaving the coast clear for the last journey to Pickletullum.

Landel met them as arranged and they set off briskly towards the Portway. The five burroways lay before them, busier than usual, but Horace, for once, was nowhere to be seen. The Sound Modulator hummed its usual low hum as they stood on the platform looking round. When they left they wouldn't be seeing this place again. Standing right next to the Sound Modulator as they had on that first day, its purr seemed almost comforting. Hannah looked up at its handsome face.

'Won't be seeing this any more,' she said, patting its metal frame and wiping her hand across the thick dust. A nobbled surface swept under Hannah's fingers. Hannah wiped again … letters appeared … as she rubbed, words formed. Hannah stared at the inscription that had appeared: An Upright Life Free From Wickedness.

'Ben, quick, give me the flute.'

'What is it?'

Hannah blew into the Unitune. The first notes of the song lifted into the air and the tune played more vigorously than it had ever done before.

With a heavy clunk the face of the Sound Modulator sprang open.

'Of course – it's making sense now. The map!' cried Hannah. 'Read the bit about the stars.'

Ben unrolled it and started to read:

IF THE KEY IS WHAT YOU'RE AFTER
THEN LOOK INTO THE STARS
FIND THEM WHERE THEY COME AND GO
CHOOSE ONE THAT GLOWS LIKE MARS

'Don't you see?' said Hannah 'this could be it.' She was already sprinkling Fly-by powder over herself.

'Up here,' she said, rising and pointing to the clock face, then, opening the glass front as wide as it would go Hannah looked again at the wonderful revolving mechanism. From up here she got a much better view of the twelve, jewelled stones, the moving moons and the floating pointing finger.

'This is where people come and go – the Portway,' she said, her face flushing. 'And look at this clock face of the planets. There are two red suns. Cosmick Smallpiece told us stars are really suns didn't he?' They had to agree he had. Hannah started to tug on the red stone at the top of the clock face but nothing happened.

'Then one of these two suns …' she said, now pulling hard on the large red stone at the bottom 'could be …'

Hannah shoved and pushed the stone. She could feel it move. Another yank and it came free. In her hand lay a glowing, curved gold key. Fixed to the top was a ruby the size of a fat Victoria plum.

'The sixth key!' said Landel, amazed.

'We've found the sixth key!' said Lucy floating up to see it.

'Read the last verse of the scroll, Ben,' urged Hannah. He tore his eyes away from the sixth key:

Gold is what he's after
Power and glory his heart's desires
When all else fails, be careful
Guard the Precious Fires.

'The poem is warning us. Hironymus Grossus is planning to take over. It's so obvious now. We can't let him do it,' said Hannah. It added up all right; the disregard for the Council of Alter-Idem, the stockpiling of combat uniforms; forcing the imps and Dr Rootvine to try and make gold using the Precious Fires. He had to be stopped.

'What should we do?' asked Landel.

Time to think, that's what they needed. What they didn't need was Horace making his way towards them.

'What have we here?' he said slyly, looking from face to face for clues. Hannah slid the sixth key behind her back. Ben took it from her and slipped it into the backpack.

Lucy grabbed the flute and started twirling it around her fingers, smiling engagingly at Horace.

'Taken to playing musical instruments now, have we?' he said, watching and hovering.

Unnoticed by Horace, Landel quietly clicked shut the glass face with a twitch of his wand and shot a fresh layer of dust over everything.

'Just the flute,' said Lucy sweetly.

'Play any good tunes, does it? Horace persisted.

'Just one, but it does it very well,' said Ben.

'I hope you've not been interfering with the Sound Modulator,' said Horace, looking up at the face but not noticing the gaping hole where the sixth key had been. The Sound Modulator continued to hum efficiently.

'It's very dusty, Horace,' said Landel, spreading the dust even more thickly over the inscription. Horace looked over the dirty, dull exterior.

'Yes, about time it was cleaned I suppose.'

To their horror, Horace reached inside his uniform, extracted his wand and pointed it at the Sound Modulator.

'*Dustus departus.*' Instantly, the dust disappeared. The Sound Modulator gleamed. The hole where the ruby had been seemed even larger than it had before. It was only a matter of seconds before Horace noticed it. Hannah leapt forward, turned Horace around and hooked her arm in his.

'We have to go now, Horace,' she said, trying to sound calm and taking a few steps away from the Sound Modulator so that he had to follow. 'What do you think of Lucy's hair?'

Lucy danced in front of Horace flicking and patting her shorn hair.

'I … Well …' he mumbled and looked down at his feet, embarrassed. 'Very nice,' he said quickly, then just as quickly flew off spluttering something about late passengers.

'That got rid of him,' said Hannah.

'But what are we going to do now?' asked Landel nervously.

The sixth key, missing since the last Supreme Parlator had died, was safe and sound in the backpack but the sight of it was still burning in Hannah's mind.

'We've got to return the sixth key to the Council of Alter-Idem and stop Hironymus Grossus. All we need is Gorgonz City's key and the Magical Crown of Keys can be reassembled. The villages will listen to a new Supreme Parlator. They'd know then what to do next.'

'But you're not thinking of ...' said Ben.

'If everyone in Aldoris turned up at Gorgonz City, Hironymus Grossus would be forced to hand over the key and let Dr Rootvine and the imps go.'

'But, but you're not ... Hannah, we're not ...' but Hannah was already issuing orders.

'Lucy, you go to Pickletullum and tell Dolfi and Chancellor Barbelly. Landel, you go to Socratown and speak to Astra Manda. Ben, you go to Sombrono and tell Jacobus Mors and Grinnard; and I'll go to Puddlelake. We should catch the Chancellors before they set off for the hearing. We'll all meet in Gorgonz City in two hours' time.'

As Lucy dragged Ben along the platform towards Sombrono he was still calling 'Hannah, we can't ... Hannah, this is madness!' But Hannah was talking to Landel.

'Landel, I need to go back to Grandma's for something. Can you come with me? We won't be long.'

They ran to the end of the chestnut tree tunnel and arrived, puffing and panting, at the bottom of Grandma's garden. The top of Mrs Whitehead's head, hovering just above the fence, popped up in full view when she heard Hannah coming.

'Hello, Hannah. Grandma off to the Summer Fête already?'

'Yes, she's already gone Mrs Whitehead.'

Mrs Whitehead nodded. 'I hope she wins a prize today. Mrs Perriwinkle won't be pleased though, if she does. We'll be seeing you there later, I expect.'

'Yes, see you later,' said Hannah breathlessly. She let herself into the house while Landel waited, scanned the shelves of herbs and powders for what she wanted and came back to Landel with her pockets bulging.

Back in the Portway, Landel left for Socratown and Hannah, avoiding Horace's suspicious stare, rushed over to join Cordus when she saw him boarding a scarab for Puddlelake. She told him all about rescuing Lucy, finding the sixth key and the plan to meet in Gorgonz City, but as the journey ended she wondered uneasily about facing the tasks ahead.

Quilla Vanepike was surprisingly easy to persuade and was positively jubilant at the thought of marching into Gorgonz City to challenge Chancellor Grossus.

'Always thought he was up to no good,' she said, peering at Hannah through narrowed eyes. 'And you say you've seen Gorgonz City's key. Ha! So, he's been lying to the Council of Alter-Idem. Time we got rid of him.'

Vida Vilenewt's thin mouth creased into a gloating smile and the gardope slobbered on the carpet.

Hannah knew from the way the Chancellor was swanning around the parlour with her head held high that she was imagining the Magical Crown of Keys on her own head and thinking her finest hour was nigh.

Cordus came back into the room with the news that he had sent out the decree ordering the citizens of Puddlelake to report to the foot of the castle on the hour.

'But what about the Terrosaur?' asked Hannah.

'Didn't you hear?' said Chancellor Vanepike distractedly. 'It's gone.'

'Gone?'

'When it came to after eating the vellypig it was so groggy it staggered around, crashing into everything. I watched it from up here. It bent to take a drink from the pool at the foot of the waterfall ... and fell in.'

'Fell in?' Hannah repeated. 'Where is it now?'

'Gone. I told you. That pool is miles deep. Nothing ever returns once it's been caught in the down current.' She was quite unconcerned. 'With any luck it's gone forever. Now, back to business ... I must go and get changed.'

Hannah was left in the parlour with Cordus while they waited for the Chancellor.

'We'll march overland,' said Cordus, standing by the window, looking out over the hills. 'Gorgonz City is not far from here. We'd be the first village to be taken over if there was an invasion. In a way it's a shame the Terrosaur's gone. I doubt whether Hironymus Grossus would have risked his life invading Puddlelake if it was still here.'

When Quilla Vanepike appeared she was wearing robes of crimson and crushed grape silk lavishly hung with pearls and crystals and covered with gold embroidery. Pearls and gold braid were woven in her hair and golden slippers adorned her feet. Even the gardope was dressed up with a crimson ribbon round its neck.

'We are ready,' she said grandly, picking up her wand which had a bunch of purple crystal grapes hanging from the end. 'What a momentous day! This day will be recorded as the finest our lands have ever seen ... since the last Supreme Parlator died, at any rate. And just think ... all my subjects will be there to see me.'

She was getting quite carried away and spent the entire journey, as they sat back in the richly upholstered carriage, telling Hannah and Cordus about her own wonderful qualities.

'I'm so *caring* – I let Sweetpea sit down in my presence when his legs get wobbly from standing; I'm so *considerate* – I let Petina cook every day of the week and do all the cleaning because she is *so good* at it; I'm so *level-headed* – I never get mad at people if shouting at them will do instead.'

The talavan in which they were travelling flew silently overground, the ornate carriage pulled gently by four winged griffins. The people of Puddlelake followed behind good naturedly and cheerfully, as if they were all going on some jolly adventure – some even carried picnic hampers – but all that changed when they arrived in Gorgonz City.

In Pickletullum, Dolfi and Chancellor Barbelly greeted Lucy with shocked surprise.

'Oh my dear girl,' panted Zanting Barbelly when she told them the story. 'I feel quite faint. My head is reeling.' Chancellor Barbelly held onto the chair as if his legs had just gone weak.

'Thank goodness you are safe,' said Milli.

'If I understand you correctly Lucy, not only is Hironymus Grossus guilty of stealing, corruption, intimidation and lying to the Council of Alter-Idem but he and Vasril Odo are guilty of, if Hannah's fears are confirmed, planning to terrorise and rule by force,' said Dolfi. Chancellor Barbelly was strutting around the office, turning this way and that, ankle wings flapping. Every few seconds he rose into the air exclaiming 'Dear me! Dear me!'

The entire village of Pickletullum turned up in the street when the word got round. Many were prepared to 'take prisoners if necessary' as one old timer said, brandishing an old-fashioned wand that was bent and chipped with no lustre left on its surface.

'Still plenty of fight left,' he said, accidentally sending a fireball up into the sky which landed behind the bookbinder's and set the dried grass alight. Hunnik and Hornet rushed over with buckets of water and doused the flames. Wisps of smoke remained, curling into the air and over the rooftops.

Chancellor Barbelly and Dolfi Greenlees, dressed in their ceremonial robes, set off on the backs of two brightly coloured scarabs and led the procession out of Pickletullum the children lining the streets cheering at the sight of the long ribbons of reedweed and cowslip trailing behind them. A canopy of fireflies flew above the procession like a glowing gold cloak and two scarlet and yellow trumpet birds, magnificent plumage specially inked for the occasion, escorted them on their way. Milli and Lucy followed next and every fit and able elfin, wands in hand, flew behind on every available beetle. The fittest flew themselves and took Fly-by powder to use when they got tired.

Had they known what they would see in Gorgonz City some might not have volunteered to go.

In Sombrono, Jacobus Mors already knew that something was happening. His jackdaws had reported seeing large crowds gathering in Puddlelake. He was also concerned to hear that an unusual number of guards had been seen on the streets in Gorgonz City that very morning, so he wasn't surprised by what Ben had to tell him.

'I always knew there was a chance he might do something like this,' he said, turning from Ben to look up at the portrait of his great-grandmother, Felone

Malandra.

'He'll have to be stopped,' he said, echoing Zamada's very words all those years before.

In the centre of the village Grinnard tolled the bell which was only sounded on holidays, days of celebration and when important announcements were made. The darkness stirred in every doorway and every window as brownies poured into the square like curious moles to hear the news.

'We must not let Hironymus Grossus get away with this,' Jacobus Mors told the crowd 'He must be held accountable for his actions. We must show him he cannot break the Harmony Rules and terrorise imp, fairy or Peep. The sixth key has been found and a new Supreme Parlator may be chosen this very day … but only if we let our voices be heard. We cannot allow Chancellor Grossus to remain in office and impose his will upon the rest of us. Those who want to take this opportunity to restore the Magical Crown of Keys and have it choose a new Parlator, come with us. We must stand united with our fellows or Grossus will succeed.'

The crowd roared approval and the roof plugs were pulled. They hung swaying slowly as the congregation flew skyward and gathered in the clearing above.

A dark cloud emerged from the trees beyond and a faint hum grew as it was carried on the breeze. The noise became a growling as the dark cloud drew nearer. The swarm of ants descended, dropping all around the clearing like large black raindrops.

Ben watched a wave of growing spells transform the ants into flying machines the size of land eagles. The brownies climbed aboard and darted here and there, intent and alert, exchanging words and passing on information. Astride the ants' sleek, glossy backs, the dull, slow brownies had become a fast, organised, focused platoon. Jacobus Mors, Grinnard and Ben set off in the lead on the largest of the soldier ants. The rest, with antennae twitching and jaws clacking, followed in formation, none knowing what was waiting.

In Socratown, Landel went to the Major Hall where a full debate was in progress. When Landel interrupted proceedings to tell Chancellor Astra Manda and Clarendon Sisco the news every floating cushion turned to listen. Landel tried to keep his voice quiet but as he bent to whisper, his words boomed across the hall as though he was speaking through a loudspeaker with the volume turned up.

'THE SIXTH KEY HAS BEEN FOUND AND HIRONYMUS GROSSUS HAS THE SCALES OF BALANCE AND JUDGEMENT!'

The hall exploded with excited gibbering. Cushions zoomed around the room; some shot forward so sharply their riders fell off backwards, arms and legs still folded. Others held on tightly, looking most undignified, as their cushions zigzagged, stalled or collapsed like punctured balloons.

'What *should* we do? The very *thought* of change makes me feel ill.'

'You *are* looking rather green.'

Of *course* the Magical Crown of Keys should be restored.'

'Help!'

'Couldn't we just *ignore* him?'

'Oh, what *are* we going to do?'

As usual, no one could agree. Not even about how to get the Scales of Balance and Judgement back.

'Even if we ask nicely Grossus might say no!'

Landel was wondering if order would ever be restored when the beautiful sound of harp music filled the Major Hall and drowned everyone out. Landel turned to see a harp plucking its own strings with a look of perfect calm on its face. Its small wings lay folded along its back. The Harpolite's flowing rhapsody was immediately soothing. Landel felt like closing his eyes, lying back on a soft, plump pillow and thinking fluffy thoughts.

When everyone was quiet the music faded and the Chancellor stood up to speak.

'Peace, peace my friends. Let not our hearts be vexed. This is good news and bad news but our mission is clear. We must claim back our Scales of Balance and Judgement. Once they are returned all other decisions will come to us. Let us assume our neighbour, Chancellor Grossus, will be open to persuasion. To this end I suggest we all visit Gorgonz City and show ourselves. With one voice we can ask for what is ours to be returned.' While the suggestion was discussed, conferred and eventually agreed, the Harpolite combed its long white hair.

'Should we take some soothing sounds?' asked Mr Sonorus coming forward from the crowd.

'I think that would be an excellent idea,' said the Chancellor. 'Some calming music might be just right if things get tense.'

Three Harpolites sat at the head of a white carriage in the courtyard. Landel was invited to join Astra Manda, Clarendon Sisco, several elders and Mr Sonorus, who had at his feet a huge glass jar filled with bubbles and silver quavers and crotchets bumping into each other and a most peculiar trumpeting contraption which Landel assumed was for sending the calming sounds out to a wider audience.

With a galloping zithering on the Harpolite's strings the magnificent white carriage rose into the air, sailed out past the oak trees into the woodland, followed by most of the residents of Socratown, and made its way towards Gorgonz City. From the carriage's window a cloud of bubbles trailed like a fine mist, releasing the sounds of brooks tinkling, butterflies sighing and chocolate melting, for the villagers to walk through. Landel had a feeling they might need more than a few soothing sounds when they got there.

No one knew how, but Hironymus Grossus had been tipped off. It was bad enough that he was expecting them, but the sight that greeted them was as chilling as it was unexpected. Hundreds of villagers from Pickletullum, Puddlelake, Sombrono and Socratown lined the stony embankment around Gorgonz City, from the entrance to the Underground Burroway up to the granite-fronted mountains that looked down onto the rocky city. In the heat of the day they sat unprotected and without weapons, armed only with the knowledge of right and wrong and their wands.

Before them, guarding the city, was an army of goblins, all wearing armour and new studded boots, all jeering and rattling their shields, all astride screeching barging Outlanders clacking their terrifying jaws.

'Those shields will be charmed to deflect spells no doubt,' Dolfi said to Ben and Landel as he took in the scene. Hannah, Lucy and Milli, stricken and pale, stood nearby.

On a large rock, in full view of everyone, Hironymus Grossus sat astride a huge stag beetle. The animal reached for a stone pillar and its steel-sharp mandibles crushed the pillar as if it was a breadstick. The message was clear: nothing would stand in his way.

It was hard to tell who shot the first blast. Spells began zapping and zinging backwards and forwards like demented fireworks and crazy Catherine Wheels, going off in all directions at once, bouncing from shield to stone wall and back again.

'Take cover,' Dolfi ordered and made Hannah, Ben, Landel and Lucy run into the Underground Burroway. The tail of a spell whizzed past their heads and hit a firefly which fell to the ground as stiff as a piece of wood, with its wings stuck together.

Curses and hexes flew overhead; sprites collapsed as their legs went rigid; brownies screamed as their hair went on fire; elfin shouted as their arms moved of their own accord and started to lash out at their friends and their children; kelpies turned into toads through fright and jumped to avoid being trampled underfoot in the chaos. Midas Plank, the bank manager, was spun around upside down in mid-air by a whipper hex, kippa and cala falling from his pockets onto the goblins below. He was sucked off into the distance still shouting 'Put me down! Put me down!'

Everywhere, burrroway scarabs started buckling under their riders, as the goblins threw disabling spells in one great wave. The next wave of spells stuck everyone's wings together to stop them from flying and Sombrono's ants fell to the ground. Counter curses bounced off the goblins' shields doing them no harm at all. The goblins were too well protected and too well prepared. They knew exactly what to do and when to do it.

The villagers tried whatever they could to hit back. Some kelpies from Puddlelake turned into herons and used their long beaks to pull the goblins' shields away and jab at the armoured scarabs but there were too few successes. Even when a spell hit, too few goblins fell to make much difference. The itching charm the brownies used had some success in breaking the goblins' concentration but Landel reckoned that they itched so much normally that it was only when the spell was double strength that it was having much effect. Dolfi and Milli threw freeze charms and shouted to everyone to do the same … but they mostly rebounded off the shields and froze those who sent them.

'We've got to do something.' Hannah watched the scene of utter confusion and desperation before them. Hironymus Grossus and his small group on the stag beetles took to the air. She saw him point to each of the Chancellors as if giving orders for their capture.

'I can't bear to look,' said Lucy, ducking as a stray triple hex whizzed into the burroway.

'There must be something we can do,' said Ben.

Hannah remembered – what she had in her pocket.

'Can you multiply this, Landel?' she asked, holding out Grandma Fred's pepper pot, and when Landel touched it with his wand the pot trebled in size and multiplied by four.

Hannah handed them out and threw some Fly-by powder over herself.

'I thought there might be trouble. I know it's not much but maybe we can give Dolfi and the others some time.' Hannah launched herself out of the burroway and flew over the first of the goblins, sprinkling the pepper as she went. The others followed in a wide sweep behind her. The first Outlanders sneezed violently, shooting their riders straight off their backs and into the rock face, knocking them unconscious. Some goblins sneezed and dropped their shields; some fell off their mounts. Their helmets were flying off too. Dolfi and Milli took advantage of what was happening.

'Freezing charm, NOW!' Dolfi shouted. Bolts of cracking light sped from Pickletullums' wands and hit the first lot of sneezing goblins. They all stopped in mid-sneeze, mid-fall and mid-attack as if they were playing 'statues' at a birthday party.

'Well done, Dolfi,' spluttered Chancellor Barbelly, wiggling his wand, which was the wrong way up. 'Well done everyone.' Those at the front rushed forward and grabbed the enchanted shields.

'Bombs away … WATCH OUT, HANNAH!' Ben shouted. A spell missed her head and split open the rock behind her.

Lucy and Landel too sprinkled the pepper, dodging spells and spiked balls as they went. More and more of the goblins sneezed and continued sneezing.

On the ground Dolfi organised each village into groups and Milli ushered the Chancellors into the Underground Burroway out of Grossus's way. The odds were slowly evening up. The more shields they collected from the frozen goblins the more they advanced, pushing Hironymus Grossus and his group back into the bleak landscape.

'DISARM THEM' Grossus thundered angrily above the noise of clashing shields and whizzing spells. 'DISARM THEM! KILL THEM IF NECESSARY!'

More goblins swooped, swinging spiked balls and kicking anything in range from the backs of the Outlanders. The brownies from Sombrono and sprites from Socratown scattered. Those that could not fly dived for cover.

'*Frezka Icelandis!*' shouted Dolfi again, and another wave of spells shot towards the goblins. Not even the best could hold on, wave an iron ball and throw a spell at the same time. Down the goblins clattered, crashing into the sleeping ants and scarabs already on the ground, thumping rigid and motionless in the dirt.

'*Artemistus Dreamora,*' called Cordus from the ranks of Puddlelake, and a mist descended over the goblins sending them into a blissful daze. Sombrono and Pickletullum blasted them with more of the freeze charm. Cordus had realised from Hannah's example that they needed to disarm the goblins to have a chance of hitting them with a charm that would render them harmless.

The pepper sprinkling continued until all the remaining goblins were caught in uncontrolled fits of sneezing – except, that is, the group on the stag beetles who kept their distance and watched from the highest rocks.

Hannah, Ben Lucy and Landel regrouped beyond the fighting hordes and took a rest high above the city beside a rise of flat stones. The landscape looked strangely familiar to Hannah.

'This is where the dungeons are,' she said, realising they were sitting beside a chimney. 'Dr Rootvine and the imps are down there.'

'Hironymus Grossus is over there with every guard in the place,' said Lucy. 'They'll be on their own.'

'We could rescue them now.'

In the heat of the moment it was agreed, and before Ben had time to think, they were travelling down the sooty chimney and hovering at the fire grate, where the day before Lucy herself had been standing. The dungeon was empty and everything was quiet. But as they started towards the door a piercing scream ripped through the silence.

Chapter 20

The Magical Crown of Keys

The cry was coming from the next dungeon. Someone was terrified or in pain, or both.

'What are we thinking of?' Ben was having second thoughts. 'Not that I don't want to help. But all of a sudden this doesn't seem such a good idea.'

'We can't just leave them,' said Hannah. 'Dr Rootvine and the imps are in there, we saw them in the Windoless when we rescued Lucy.'

'But the Council of Alter-Idem will make sure they're released,' said Ben, trying to sound reasonable. 'C'mon. Let's go back. They'll be all right.'

'You wouldn't want to wait another moment if it was you,' said Lucy.

'This is mad,' Ben was still muttering outside the next dungeon when they heard something else; something that made them stop dead. An voice rang out. It wasn't Dr Rootvine or the imps, they were sure of that. There was someone else in the dungeon with them.

The handle on the door ahead turned abruptly.

'Quick, up here,' called Landel, and they flew up to the cold, stone ceiling and waited.

A shadow fell on the wall opposite, then a burly figure passed below them in the corridor.

'It's the guard who cut off my hair,' Lucy whispered as he hurried off down the dimly lit passageway.

The sounds of potions bubbling and plopping, cackling fires and tearful snivelling seeped through the open door. They edged nearer, drawn by the glow from inside and the fear of what they might see. Unable to stop themselves, they peered around the door frame ... Dr Rootvine, bedraggled and pale, stood hunched over the cauldron before him, stirring it as though in a trance. Eeni and Meeni were standing on chairs, looking ready to fall down from exhaustion. Dr Rootvine had sprouted an untidy white beard and the imps were wearing the same woolly jumpers they had been wearing when they were last seen in the Apothecary.

Hannah's eyes shifted to the table where Miney was still chopping Lucy's hair and the casket containing Gorgonz City's key lay. Out of the corner of her eye Hannah caught a movement just as there was a crack like wood snapping. A dark-cloaked figure stepped out from the shadows.

'Get on with it! Work harder!' the figure bellowed. A whip lashed the air again. 'You must find the elixir that makes gold from metal today! I will have it. TODAY, YOU HEAR!'

On the wall behind the cowering figures sat the four glass jars each with the still, blue flame, frozen in time, inside.

'Now that I have the Precious Fires *no one* will stop me. My potions will become a hundred times stronger and my *poison* ... there will be no stopping my *precious* poisons, my clouding, clogging, *choking* poisons. Nothing will stand in my way now. No feeble antidote, no interfering Peeps. The Precious Fires will make me invincible. There will be no escape. KNEEL, you scurvy wretches! KNEEL, before your King!'

The air cracked again. Dr Rootvine and the imps immediately obeyed and knelt down at his feet.

'Fectus Core, the greatest Potion Maker the world has ever known, *will* become King – King of Aldoris then King of *ALL* Fairies!'

At the sight of them trembling before him, Fectus Core laughed cruelly.

'He's *a-alive*,' stuttered Lucy.

'NO!' Hannah gave an anguished cry. Fectus Core was the Potion Maker the scroll had been warning them about. Even though it had told them in black and white Hannah hadn't wanted to believe it. Ben and Landel were too scared to speak.

The hooded figure turned. The mean, black eyes, sunk in the yellowing grey face, noticed the door was open. He strode towards it with his arm outstretched. Hannah, Ben, Lucy and Landel darted inside.

The door slammed, echoing around the dungeon. In the corner of the dungeon which had been hidden from view by the door, was the net they had seen in the Windoless – only it wasn't a net. It was a web, and settled in the middle of it, covered in thick black hair, was a spider the size of a well-fed pig. Its eight legs took turns to paw the air. Beside it, hanging from a single glistening thread, bound tight and barely breathing, was Mo.

Ben, Lucy and Landel reeled back.

Hannah felt the blood drain from her head. A feeling of sickness swept over her and the spider began to blur. She fell to the floor.

'Hannah, Hannah,' said Ben, shaking her shoulders as she lay crumpled at their feet.

Hannah moaned.

'It's not real. Tell me it's not real. It can't be,' Hannah forced her eyes open to look again hoping that she'd imagined it, but the spider was still there, monstrously huge from where she lay.

'What are we going to do? Hannah speak to me!' Ben shook her again but Hannah couldn't reply. Stupefied by the sight of the spider, she sat rigidly on the floor, breathing fast. Sweat began to trickle down her face.

'Should we let Dr Rootvine and the imps know we're here?' Landel asked nervously. 'How are we going to get out of this?'

Ben stayed with Hannah, who was making soft whinnying noises, while Landel and Lucy moved towards Dr Rootvine and the imps and tried not to startle them.

'Dr Rootvine, it's us, Landel and Lucy,' said Landel, hovering by his ear. 'We're here with Ben and Hannah. We're going to try and create a diversion. Be ready to run when your chains unlock.'

Dr Rootvine stopped stirring his cauldron for a moment and the whip lashed again, barely missing his head.

'No Slacking!'

The imps whimpered and added more ingredients to the cauldrons. They didn't look up when they heard Lucy's voice.

The cocooned Mo, wriggling with the very last of his strength, tried one last time to break free from the web. The thread snapped. Mo fell and rolled across the floor towards Ben and Hannah. Hannah stared ahead, rigid and unblinking, focused on something miles away. Mo's watery brown eyes stared straight into hers.

'Help me. *Please*.'

The spider shot down from its web and scuttled towards them. Ben would have screamed if his mouth hadn't been so completely dry. The spider arched its fangs. Terror filled every corner of Hannah's heart but forgotten words sprang unbidden into her mind. *Audentes fortuna javat*. Fortune favours the bold. Hannah grabbed at her pocket … the other package she'd brought from Grandma Fred's.

The spider, jaws clicking, hovered above them. It started pulling the cocooned Mo back towards itself. Its drooling mouthparts gaped, the poisonous fangs glistened. It was about to strike. Fear rose choking to Hannah's throat.

She launched herself at the spider, threw the package with all her might and watched it disappear down the spider's gullet.

It only took a few seconds for the deadly nightshade to take effect. The spider let go of Mo and shot back to the safety of its web. Ben, Lucy and Landel, eyes still wide with horror, undid Mo's bindings.

As the gripping bellyache took hold the spider's legs began to twitch, its fangs began to quiver, it shrieked horribly and its eyes swivelled in all directions at once. Fectus Core wheeled round, throwing Dr Rootvine's book, *Alchemy Through The Ages*, into a corner.

'What's wrong, Septimus?' he growled.

A wretched gurgling was coming from the spider's throat and its whole body shook with spasms. Fectus Core was standing before the convulsing creature trying to comprehend what was wrong. Hannah was quick to see their chance.

'Make us full size, Landel,' she shouted. 'Do it NOW.'

Landel did as Hannah said, casting the spell wide to cover Ben and Lucy too. '*Ad maximus totalis!*'

Hannah felt the rushing air pull her face and a second later she was standing with Ben and Lucy, at full height, behind the dark hooded figure of Fectus Core. He turned sharply. His grey face convulsed with fury at the sight of them.

'*PUSH!*' screamedHannah.

They gave an almighty heave. Fectus Core crashed on top of the spider and the sticky web collapsed around him. His legs kicked and his arms flailed but the web drew tighter and tighter. The spider screeched and twitched hideously and Fectus Core yelled and wrestled.

Landel flicked his wand again. '*Locktari operandum*,' he commanded.

The leg locks holdingDr Rootvine and the imps sprang open.

'Run, Run!' Hannah lifted the four jars of Precious Fire and jammed them in the backpack. She grabbed the casket, dropped it in the backpack and reached for the wand that still lay on the table. The wand began to quiver. Something was making it move. Hannah spun around. Fectus Core's arm was stretched through the web, pulling the wand to him. Harriet snatched it up.

'Go, go, go!' shouted Ben, holdingthe door open as Lucy and Landel bolted through it helping Dr Rootvine and the imps as best they could.

The wand in Hannah's hand began vibrating firecely; she struggled to hold on.

'You won't win,' sneared Fectus Core. 'You're just a stupid girl!' The wand shuddered; it was starting to get hot. Hannah dropped the backpack to free both hands.

'Hannah! Leave it! Leave it!' screeched Ben.

'Prepare to die, Peep.'

Every muscle in Hannah's arms and shoulders ached, her hands were burning, her legs were trembling.

'Drop it Hannah!. Drop it!'

'No!'

Hannah swung the wand wildly, shouting 'Suo Loco' and a flash leaped from the wand and struck the stone ceiling. A terrible crashing and shrieking sounded all around them and a cloud of dust swooped up from the floor.

The pull from the wand vanished and there was a moment of silence.

'Lets get out of here!' Ben grabbed the backpack and Hannah's arm and made for the door.

They ran along the dark passageway and around a corner, then another, up a flight of stone stairs, past flickering wall torches, along another corridor, every so often looking behind and listening through the sound of their own feet for anyone following. But there were no other sounds. They hurtled along until they reached the end of the corridor beyond the Crystal Room where, panting, they finally came to a stop. Dr Rootvine and the imps lay collapsed on a red sofa, unable to run any further.

The corridor was thick with villagers. Hannah and Ben sqeezed through the crowd toward Lucy andLandel.The whole place was buzzing. The great gold doors of the Crystal Room were open and those who could not fit inside spilled out and crammed the passageways in every direction.

'What took you so long?' asked Lucy.

'Don't ask,' said Ben. In Hannah's hand the wand was still and cool. It had stopped vibrating and the heat had gone.

'Them goblins won't be going anywhere in a hurry,' they heard the coppersmith say as they passed.

'Would serve them right if a hoard of vipners came along and sharpened their claws on 'em while they're lying there,' his companion replied.

The fighting seemed to be over.

They eased towards the gold doors. Above the commotion they could hear Chancellor Barbelly shouting 'Order! Order!' and heard a 'Whump!' as he banged the table with the padded hammer.

The crowd parted to let them through. The Crystal Room was packed with as many villagers as it could hold. Those who could find no room to stand, hovered around the walls, like living tapestries. All the Chancellors and their seconds were seated around the table except Hironymus Grossus and Grunt who were bound tightly to chairs and floating high above the heads of the crowd for their own safety. Vasril Odo floated beside them in a third chair looking very shame-faced.

'It is a matter of great concern to this Council and the peoples of this land that three of the members of the Council of Alter-Idem have chosen to work against its principles, its other members and betrayed the people of Aldoris.'

A braying howl erupted from the crowd. Hironymus Grossus hardly blinked but Vasril Odo's knees could be heard knocking together.

'The accused will stand trial and if found guilty will be sent to the Castille de Strop for reconfiguration.'

'The Castille de Strop.' The words echoed down every corridor until it became a faint murmur.

'That doesn't sound like a retirement home,' Ben murmered to Landel.

Chancellor Barbelly saw them standing in the doorway.

'Come in, my dear friends,' he called, more soberly than usual. They eased their way through until they stood pressed against the edge of the table.

'Chancellors,' began Hannah. The room fell silent except for the sound of Vasril Odo's knees knocking.

'At the end of the corridor Dr Herbert Rootvine and the four imps, Eeni, Meeni, Miney and Mo, are resting on a sofa. They were being held captive by the cruel sorcerer Fectus Core.' The Crystal Room filled with sharp gasps of disbelief from the crowd.

'Fectus Core is alive!' The strangled cry ran through the chambers.

'He was behind the goblin rebellion today. Hironymus Grossus and Vasril Odo are merely his eager servants, willing to do his bidding.'

'No! It can't be true,' burst out Quilla Vanepike who had, up until this news, been looking as smug as a cat with a bath full of cream. 'Grossus is to blame,' she declared, making it clear just being reconfigured was not what she called justice.

'Continue, Hannah,' urged Chancellor Barbelly.

'Fectus Core has been keeping Dr Rootvine and the imps captive in a dungeon below the Chambers here. He has been forcing them to try making gold using the Precious Fires. He is the reason so many died of the fever in Zamada's time. He poisoned them all to show how powerful he was when no one would follow him. And he was planning to do the same again, only we made a Cleansing Potion. That is when he stole the Precious Fires. With them he would not fail again. There would be no antidote; no Cleansing Potion would work next time. But he wanted gold too. He is still in the dungeons trapped in his spider's web.'

Hannah looked down at the wand whch she had placed on the table.

'And this is his wand,' she said, pushing it forward. The crowd behind Hannah tried to back away despite the wand looking dull and flat as if it had no spark left in it at all.

'Guards! Go down to the dungeons and seize Fectus Core. Immobilise him. Be careful, he will still be dangerous,' said Chancellor Barbelly, and the guards marched heavily down the corridor, the crowd parting to make way for them.

Lucy noticed the wand on the table begin to vibrate but before she could say anything a burst of white smoke erupted from it and it turned into a snake. A large black 'V' ran down its neck. It rose hissing and baring its fangs, flicked onto the floor and writhed under the table.

The crowd staggered back, yelling. Hannah quickly bent down to see where it had gone but it had already disappeared.

'Nothing surprises me,' declared Chancellor Vanepike when several of the villagers expressed disbelief that it could disappear into thin air.

'It's a sorcerer's trick. Those guards will need to have their wits about them. I take it they *have* wits, Barbelly?'

Chancellor Barbelly looked worried, as if wondering the same thing.

Ben opened the backpack and handed Hannah the casket.

'And what is in the casket, Hannah?' Dolfi asked when the panic subsided.

'It's Gorgonz City's key,' she said, lifting it out to show everyone. The large sapphire seemed an even more intense blue in the light and the gold gleamed as if it had been polished for hours. She laid it on the table.

'I took the liberty,' began Chancellor Barbelly, 'of bringing with me the village keys we have had in the vault in Pickletullum for safekeeping.' In full view of everyone he unwrapped what looked like a short velvet scarf. In each pocket lay one of the keys. He removed them all carefully and set them in a row.

This was the moment Hannah had been waiting for. This was what they had come to do – to return the sixth key to the villages. The Magical Crown of Keys was about to be reassembled and a new Supreme Parlator chosen. The atmosphere was charged.

Quilla Vanepike fidgeted in her seat; Jacobus Mors straightened up, looking sober and alert; Astra Manda breathed deeply and leaned forward to listen carefully; Hironymus Grossus, still floating above the crowd, humphed and denounced the proceedings.

'*Sugar fancy*! This is a mistake. A disaster for us all.' Dolfi poked the chair and sent it spinning around in a circle. When it stopped Hironymus Grossus was too dizzy to speak.

The trumpet birds, standing on long spindly legs, plumage dazzling, blew a fanfare at the top end of the Crystal Room.

'Do you have the sixth key, Hannah?' asked Chancellor Barbelly. Hannah nodded and reached into the backpack. Everyone gasped.

All eyes fell on Hannah's hand. Poking from her grasp, glowing brightly as though on fire, was the ruby on the end of the lost sixth key. A deafening cheer exploded and spilled out into the corridors. She handed the key to Chancellor Barbelly who held it up for all to see. Quilla Vanepike sat bolt upright, fixing her eyes upon it.

'You wonderful girl,' she cried. 'I knew we could depend on you. When I'm Supreme Parl ehehe ... I mean, when the new Supreme Parlator is chosen I'm sure you will be rewarded.' A look of discomfort flitted across her face. 'What are you all looking at? Get on with it, Barbelly.' Vida Vilenewt flapped her wings impatiently.

Dolfi handed a yellow parchment to Chancellor Barbelly who unrolled it and gave it a little shake. Dust and a tiny dead fly puffed into the air and fell to the table. Chancellor Barbelly thrust out his chest and spoke in a voice filled with pride.

'Let us rejoice this day as we bring together these six keys so that our people may once again live in peace and kinship. Once assembled, the Magical Crown of Keys will choose a new Supreme Parlator to walk among us once more and guide us as the late great Zamada did six hundred moons ago. Let us not waste another minute. The time has come.'

Blinking hard, the Chancellor peered at the old curly writing on the parchment, then, filling his lungs once more, he began the age old tradition.

'In the name of justice and harmony for the peoples of Aldoris, I hereby enact the Assembling Ceremony in accordance with the Consecrated Act of Fairy Fair Law and Order 1367.'

With fumbling fingers Chancellor Barbelly lifted the first two keys and chanted '*Incantatus honestus spiritus.*' He then recited Sombrono's motto, '*Vivimus veritas* – let us live with truth', and linked the blue sapphire key with Pickletullum's emerald key, saying '*Ab sit in via dia* – let there be no envy or ill will.' A chime rang out from two of the silver crystals in the ceiling and the two linked keys seemed to fuse together. The silver crystals glowed brightly.

The hair on the back of Hannah's neck started to prickle.

Socratown's ruby key was lifted next and carefully slid into place.

'*Ae quo animo* – with an even mind,' said Chancellor Barbelly, reading from the parchment. Another silver crystal rang out – a single clear note and that crystal lit up too. The three keys locked tight. You could hear a pin dropping, thought Hannah. Everyone in the room stared as if mesmerised by the scene unfolding before them.

Chancellor Barbelly picked up the fourth key.

'*Ad extremum* – to the extreme,' he announced gravely. Gorgonz City's sapphire key slid into place and melded with the others and as it did so another note sounded. Four of the silver crystals were now ablaze and singing in harmony.

The fifth key – Puddlelake's emerald – was slotted into place as Chancellor Barbelly chanted their motto, '*Respice finem* – look to the end.'

The Crown sat resting in full view, almost completed. Five keys were now in place, teeth locked, jewels upright and vibrant. The crystals in the ceiling above were singing melodiously. The crowds in the corridors strained forward to catch a glimpse inside, and the great gold doors thudded flat against the wall.

Chancellor Barbelly picked up the sixth key and held it high. Hannah couldn't take her eyes off the magnificent ruby, blazing deep with mystery and magic. The Chancellor circled it above his head then manoeuvred it into place.

'*Integer vitae scelerisque purus* – an upright life free from wickedness,' he announced with great solemnity.

The six silver crystals above trilled together then started to play the flute's tune When the song finished the crystals hit a single note and started to shake violently, throwing out bright light in every direction. The Chancellors stood back, fearing they might fall. The Magical Crown of Keys, now completed and with jewels glowing, rose up into the air and turned slowly. Shafts of sparkling colour shot across the room and out of the gold doors.

'Oooohh!'

'Aahh!'

'Isn't it wonderful!'

The Crown hovered in front of Chancellor Barbelly then in front of Dolfi. It passed around the table, revolving all the while. It seemed to be looking for something ... or somebody.

'I wonder who it will choose?' whispered Ben. Hannah shrugged.

Quilla Vanepike smoothed her robes and tweaked the pearls and braids in her hair so they lay just right, an expression of expectation on her face. Zanting Barbelly, still standing at his full height and looking very pink and rosy, held onto the table to stop himself fluttering into the air. Dolfi bounced up and down on the balls of his feet. Jacobus Mors furrowed his brow and pulled his cloak tighter. Grinnard kept clearing his throat. Astra Manda sat serenely with her hands clasped before her. Clarendon Sisco's eyes darted from face to face as if he didn't know where to look.

The next second all eyes returned to the Magical Crown of Keys as it suddenly rushed to the ceiling where its jewels glowed even more brightly. Without any warning, it swooped down and dropped itself on Hannah's head.

The silver crystals fell silent.

The Magical Crown of Keys had chosen Hannah to be the new Supreme Parlator.

'There must be some mistake,' said Hannah, propping up the Crown, her words almost drowned out by the noise of rapturous cheering.

'Haw, Haw, Haw,' guffawed Hironymus Grossus from up in the air. 'Well, you got what you deserved. A Peep for the new Supreme Parlator. She wouldn't know the difference between Fly-by powder and powdered toad …'

'Shut up, Grossus,' Dolfi hissed and snapped his fingers. A row of clothes pegs clamped themselves to Grossus's lips and a hard poke from Dolfi's wand sent the chair twirling vigorously again.

An urgent clamouring of feet was growing outside the gold doors.

'Let us through, let us through.' The guards suddenly appeared, breathless. 'He's gone,' they said, wheezing over the table.

'Gone?' repeated Zanting Barbelly.

'There's nothing there but the cauldrons. He's disappeared.'

'What about the spider?' Hannah felt surprisingly calm in the face of this bad news.

'No sign … Your Supremeness.' The guards bowed and fell to their knees when they saw the Magical Crown of Keys on Hannah's head.

'So, he's escaped …' said Hannah, her voice firm and clear. 'We must be ready if he ever returns.'

Everyone in the corridors knelt down – young and old, every villager. Everyone in the Crystal Room bowed their heads – except Quilla Vanepike.

'There's been some mistake, surely!' she pleaded. 'You heard her. She said so herself.'

'A mistake,' echoed Vida Vilenewt.

Hannah looked round at the sea of faces. All eyes were on her, waiting for her to speak, waiting for her to respond. What should she say? What should she do? Had the Crown made a mistake? Hunnik, Landel and Hornet were smiling from the crowd, willing her to stay. What should she do? What did she really want?

When she asked what would be best for Aldoris *and* for herself she knew the answer.

'We have learned much from each other,' she said at last, 'and we can continue to learn, but Chancellor Grossus is right. We are but visitors to your wonderful land and while we would like to return, we cannot stay. You need someone who can be with you at all times, one of your own people.'

'Listen to the girl, she knows the truth,' urged Quilla Vanepike, straining her neck until the veins stood out.

'Very well, Hannah … we understand … if you are sure,' said Chancellor Barbelly, smiling kindly.

'I am,' replied Hannah. She lifted the Crown from her head and placed it in the middle of the table directly under the six silver crystals. The crystals burst into light and sound once more and the Magical Crown of Keys rose into the air. It rotated once, making the air around it glow, then swooped as it had before.

Quilla Vanepike closed her eyes, clasping her fingers as if in prayer and stood proud and erect waiting for the crown to descend.

The crowd erupted once more in joyous cheering.

'Three cheers for the new Supreme Parlator,' Dolfi shouted.

'Hip hip, hooray! Hip hip, hooray! Hip hip, hooray!'

Everyone present bent on one knee to honour their new Supreme Parlator. Hannah, Ben and Lucy knelt too.

With one voice the room echoed to the name 'Supreme Parlator.'

'Noooooooooooooo!' Quilla Vanepike stamped her foot on the floor and stormed out of the great gold doors, leaving the new Supreme Parlator, Astra Manda, nodding sympathetically, the Magical Crown of Keys sitting perfectly on her head.

Chapter 21

Grandma's Prize

For services rendered to the community, the new Supreme Parlator granted Hannah, Ben and Lucy special citizenship of Aldoris which would allow them to visit every year. They were also granted Other Sight so they could see citizens without having to keep a supply of bogbean leaves with them all the time. Much to Ben's relief the spell wasn't painful and much to Hannah's relief it didn't involve spiders. Best of all, they were given a special present, their own wand which was disguised as an everyday Peep object – their own wooden spoon. It could do three spells: the *Suo Loco* spell for opening up and closing the entrance to the Underground Burroway and the *Ad Minima* and *Ad Maxima* spells to make themselves small enough to enter the burroway and then return to their normal height. This was all made possible by the new Supreme Parlator's special dispensation powers which allowed her to make an exception to Section 108 of the Consecrated Act of Fairy Fair Law and Order 1367 sub-clause (iv) which states that no magic should pass into the hands of Peeps.

Hannah, Ben and Lucy were sad to leave, but glad too. They had had enough excitement they thought, to last them at least until next year. On the scarab back to Pickletullum with Dolfi and Milli sitting beside them, Ben was looking thoughtful.

'We've still got three kippa to spend,' he said. 'That'll buy loads of hawthorn muffins.'

'I'd like to buy some fairy cakes,' said Lucy.

'And I'd like to buy something from the Apothecary,' said Hannah. 'We should let Thelma know that Dr Rootvine and the imps have been found.'

'Yes, we should let her know,' agreed Milli.

Ben and Lucy met Hannah, Dolfi and Milli in the Apothecary once they had made their purchases.

As they entered, the usual deafening cawing greeted them but this time a sleek, black raven was perched on Thelma's shoulder instead of the little yellow canary.

'The spell's worn off at last then,' said Ben, striding towards the counter. Jasper greedily gobbled crumbs of hawthorn muffin from Ben's open palm.

'Yes, about time too,' said Thelma, stroking Jasper's smooth black throat. 'Never found out 'oo it was tho'.'

'It seems some things are destined to remain a mystery forever,' said Dolfi, with what Hannah thought looked a faintly guilty smile.

'Yes, it's a pity we'll never knows 'ow the sixth key got lost in the firs' place an' 'ow it ended up in the sound modulator,' said Thelma. 'I'd like ter 'ave known that.'

'We all would,' said Dolfi 'but it may stay a mystery.' Jasper poked his head inside Ben's pocket looking for another hawthorn muffin.

'But I think I know what happened,' said Hannah quietly and everyone's eyes swivelled in her direction. Hannah felt herself blush.

'Ossinda Odessa,' said Hannah, but everyone still looked blank.

'Ossinda Odessa was Vasril Odo's mother and she was a friend of Zamada's. I think she could have been on Fectus Core's side all the time.'

'Oow!' squealed Ben as Jasper pecked his thumb, but Thelma, Dolfi, Milli and Lucy were too busy listening to Hannah to pay him any attention.

'If she was on his side, it would explain a lot ...' said Hannah continuing, 'like how Fectus Core knew where Zamada and her friends would be when he attacked them in the woods. They might all have been killed if Felone Melandra hadn't bitten his leg.'

'Possibly,' said Dolfi, tugging his waistcoat straight.

'And she would have been there when Zamada died. She could have taken the sixth key knowing another Supreme Parlator couldn't be appointed without it, and waited, hoping Fectus Core would get free.'

'I suppose she *could* easily have hidden it in the Sound Modulator,' said Dolfi, now scratching his ear.

'And set fire to the council records,' said Milli.

'But why?' asked Ben, sucking his sore thumb. 'After all, she died before Fectus Core managed to escape.'

Hannah shrugged. 'Don't know. Perhaps Fectus Core promised she'd be rich. She probably spent years trying to free him.'

'So she left the map to Vasril Odo, telling him where the key was, thinking her son would be rich instead,' said Lucy.

'Seems so,' said Hannah.

'Odo and Grossus were perfect accomplices for Fectus Core when he did eventually get free. Both greedy and ambitious,' said Dolfi, nodding as it all made sense.

'So you just need to prove the map belonged to Ossinda Odessa to have your answer,' said Thelma, holding up a jar of fingerprint fungus. 'Shouldn't be too difficult.'

Hannah smiled at Dolfi then turned to Thelma. 'Before we go, Thelma, I'd like to buy something.' She looked carefully once more at the strange ingredients for potions, draughts, elixirs, spells, charms, vapours and transfigurations that lined the walls.

Below the drawers marked terrapin tonsils and mongoose entrails, amongst a tray of ready made enchantment mixes, Hannah spotted what she was looking for.

'I'll take two feckles of that powder please, Thelma,' she said. Thelma weighed it out, scooped it into a little white muslin bag and set it on the counter. Hannah paid Thelma with her last kippa.

'What's that for?' asked Ben. 'It's no good if you can't eat it.'

'Do you ever think of anything other than your stomach?' askedHannah.

'Not often,' said Ben, stuffing the last of his last hawthorn muffin into his mouth.

'It's for Grandma,' Hannah explained.

After saying their goodbyes to Thelma and Jasper they boarded the scarab. The large elytra descended and they banked round the ferns along the flight-path they now knew so well and flew into the Underground Burroway for the last time this summer. Whizzing past the fireflies, Hannah reached into the backpack and pulled out the Windoless and the sooty pink slippers.

'Can you give these back to Witch Magrew for me?' she asked.

'Of course we can,' said Milli, taking the slippers and the Windoless. Images of tall grasses, shady trees and a family of woodpeckers flitted across the Windoless's surface.

'Tell her thanks and tell her she can keep my trainers. They were my old ones anyway.

'And you better have this ....' It was Zamada's journal. Dolfi took it and ran a hand over the cover.

'I wonder what other thoughts are waiting for us in here?'

'We haven't read it all yet,' said Ben. 'There hasn't been time.'

'Well, next year perhaps,' said Dolfi.

The Portway was getting nearer and Hannah still had unanswered questions. 'Do you think Fectus Core will come back?' she asked. 'And where has he gone?'

'Unfortunately there are places he can go,' said Dolfi. 'There are still dark wizards and witches around, mostly in places far from here, but he will find safe refuge, of that I have no doubt.'

'But what if he comes back?' persisted Lucy.

'In that case, we'll just have to be ready, as a Supreme Parlator I knew, once said,' Dolfi winked at Hannah. 'Working together we will be prepared. You see, Lucy, our problem has been that with no Supreme Parlator to guide us, each village's best characteristic became their worst. Pickletullum, for example, became too concerned with being fair and helpful to everyone else and in doing so we became passive and didn't look after our own needs; Sombrono, always a people to hold to truth and honesty, became only able to see the harshness and bleakness in life. They stopped seeing the lighter possibilities; Socratown, always striving for a balanced view, always trying to see both sides of an argument, ended up in frozen indecision, never being able to move forward; Puddlelake's belief in themselves and in life's possibilities became an obsession with what they would get out of any situation. They became manipulative and unable to see the bigger picture; and Gorgonz City's ability to focus and be single-minded turned into total selfishness, ruthlessness and a power for destroying all others.'

The scarab rose up suddenly to avoid a family of moles crossing the burroway and just as suddenly their stomachs jolted back into their laps.

'Working together, our strengths complement and balance each other. Working apart they threaten our existence,' said Milli. 'The new Supreme Parlator will keep us right.'

'We will be able to work together to deal with Fectus Core if he ever returns. And he didn't get these,' Dolfi held up one of the four jars of Precious Fire Hannah had placed in his lap. 'Without these he's much less dangerous.'

'We've had such a great time …' said Lucy, smiling and pushing her glasses into place, 'apart from my hair.'

Everyone laughed.

The scarab slowed and came to rest in the Portway and they disembarked. Horace immediately buzzed over.

'Leaving us so soon?' he asked, hovering.

'Yes, but we'll be coming back next year,' said Ben. Strangely though, Horace didn't seem to think this was good news and left in a hurry to stop two scarabs at the Socratown burroway fighting over a sinewy root.

At the foot of the chestnut tree they said goodbye.

'Well, take care,' said Dolfi finally, shaking their hands. 'Things will seem awfully quiet around here without you.'

'See you next year,' said Milli before performing the growing spell.

Dolfi and Milli waited until Hannah, Ben and Lucy had walked out of sight then, with a little zing like an arrow being fired from a bow, the entrance to the Underground Burroway closed.

*

The Summer Fête was in full swing when they rushed past the Cottage by the Church and up the street. Ben headed straight for Mrs Best's comic stand and Lucy went to the pet section where Gertrude was sitting on a satin cushion, looking newly washed and fluffy.

'In time for the prize-giving, I see,' said Mrs Whitehead as they all stood at the edge of the crowd a little later, watching Mr Goodstanley open another of the prize-winning envelopes. They waved to Grandma Fred across the marquee. She was standing with Farmer Digwell who had one of his pigs on a string.

'And the Gold Ribbon winner in the Preserve Section for her hazelnut and redcurrant jam is ...'

Mrs Perriwinkle held her handbag tightly and glowered across at Grandma Fred.

'Mrs Freda Bootle, of the Cottage by the Church.'

Hannah and Lucy cheered loudly and clapped their hands and Ben whistled much to Grandma's embarrassment. Mrs Perriwinkle sniffed and walked off with her Pekinese yapping at her heels.

'And there's a special prize this year,' Mr Goodstanley continued, opening the last envelope. 'For the Most Bounteous Harvest – and these certainly are the biggest, most glorious parsnips and carrots this show has ever seen – goes to ... Mrs Freda Bootle, of the Cottage by the Church.'

Grandma Fred looked startled.

'There must be some mistake,' she was heard to say. 'They weren't very good this year.' The crowd erupted in laughter and applause as Mr Goodstanley held up one of the enormous carrots, tucked it under his arm and wrestled an equally enormous parsnip under the other. The roots of both reached down to the ground.

'You will have to tell me your secret,' whispered Farmer Digwell into Grandma's blushing ear.

Hannah jammed the small bag of Kwik Gro Powder deep in her pocket.

*

Sunday arrived too quickly. The holiday with Grandma was over and Hannah, Ben and Lucy sat waiting in the kitchen for Mum to arrive to take them home. Grandma still couldn't understand how her puny carrots and parsnips had sprouted so much while waiting to be judged. Ben suggested it was a delayed growth spurt brought on by the afternoon sun, but Grandma looked sceptical. Gertrude sniffed the vegetables suspiciously, noticing the bites that had been taken out of the carrots overnight as they lay outside the back door.

A car horn blasted. Hannah, Ben and Lucy ran out of the cottage. Mum stared, open-mouthed, first at Lucy's shorn hair and then at the strange sight that caught her eye through the church gates. Running between the gravestones she was sure she had seen a rat the size of an Alsatian. Gertrude and the Church Warden's cat sat crouching high in a tree, looking terrified.

'Had a nice time?' Mum called through the open car window.

'It's been magic,' said Hannah, running towards her, laughing. 'Just magic, from start to finish.'